The Question of Her Existence

James Quigley

 This is a work of fiction. Names, characters, businesses, places, events, locales, and incidents are either the products of the author's imagination or used in a fictitious manner. Any resemblance to actual persons, living or dead, or actual events is purely coincidental.

Chapter 1 Life Now

Life can unfold in a hundred different directions. Paths cross every single day—some only for a moment, others that can leave an impact for a lifetime. If I could go back and warn myself about what was coming, I would. About the journey I was nowhere near prepared for. About the truths that were better left buried.

It's 2009. I'm fifty years old now, divorce looming like a storm cloud, and I'm haunted by the kind of thoughts that always arrive too late—regrets, missed chances, moments I should've grabbed with both hands. But one regret rises above all the others, heavy as a ten-ton weight pressing down on my chest. Man, I'd love to see that girl again.

What I didn't realise then was how far that single thought would take me. How it would rip me out of the life I knew and pull me into a labyrinth of shadows. How it would consume my sleep, my sanity, and every piece of the man I thought I was. That simple, desperate wish would become an obsession—one that would cost me far more than I ever expected to pay. Because beneath it all burned a single, merciless question, the question of her existence. Had it all been real?

That summer. Those months that felt like the best of my life. And *Her*. Looking back to where it all began in 1979, I wonder how I ever missed the signs—how the truth had been staring me in the face the whole time. Ahead of me waited a darkness I couldn't fathom, a path littered with the pieces of a truth I wasn't sure I wanted to find. But before I could face any of it, I had to go back—back to the very beginning, back to the one place I still understood… My own version of that summer.

Jonny stood on the porch of his two-story ranch house, the fading Kentucky sunlight catching the glass of Clyde May's

whiskey in his hand. The yard stretched out in wild, open country, no fences, no neighbours close enough to hear the silence he'd grown used to.
This place was supposed to be a haven. A family home. Instead, it had become a shell of a life that had stopped fitting him. His favourite baseball cap, faded from years of sun and sweat, sat backwards on his head. A vivid farmer's tan, etched onto his skin by the relentless sun, glowed in the evening light a testament to countless hours spent outdoors.

Scattered throughout the yard, artful wood sculptures were carved into the trunks of the trees, each reflecting Jonny's craftsmanship and love of nature. His favourite was a family of owls. He remembered long afternoons spent playing with his daughter amongst those trees, her laughter echoing through the branches. Those memories felt like a lifetime ago… but they weren't as distant as the memories of *Her*. The memories of 1979.

A soft rumble rolled up the driveway, pulling Jonny from his thoughts. He didn't need to look. His recently divorced ex-wife Amanda, pulled up in her black Chevrolet had a sound he'd grown to associate with tension. The engine cut off, followed by the slam of a door. Her dog, Trueman hit the ground first, tail wagging with reckless joy as he bounded into the yard.

"I'm here for my things" Amanda called, her voice clipped.

It didn't take Amanda long to begin her barrage of snide remarks. Her eyes immediately landed on the glass in his hand, as if he were some habitual drunk. Every expression, every movement, became a critique, a calculated jab meant to undermine him. The tilt of his head, the way he shifted in place, even the quietness of his sighs seemed to invite her scrutiny. Her presence filled the room, sharp and cutting, as though she could pick apart every detail of him. For a moment, Jonny felt the weight of all nineteen years of their marriage compressed into this single, unbearable instant. Then Charley, their daughter, stepped forward, her calm presence a small anchor against the storm threatening to overwhelm them both.

"Can we play nice, just for today… please?" Charley interjected, her voice soft but firm.

His mind was somewhere else entirely. As soon as Amanda was gone, he was free. Free to search for *her.* Someone who he thought about often, a few times a year maybe. But since the divorce he had found himself thinking about her more and more.

"Tell that to your dad, Charley. He's been slinging me remarks all evening since we got here."

"You just got here…" Jonny said defensively.

"SEE! There he goes again!" Amanda exclaimed, throwing her hands up in the air.

Amanda moved from room to room with cool efficiency—lifting boxes she'd packed weeks ago, checking drawers, gathering small pieces of herself from the life they'd shared.

While Amanda collected her things, he tried to conjure *her* face – a girl who seemingly vanished into smoke – desperate to bring her image into sharp focus. Thirty years was a long time. He had been in love, truly, deeply in love, and he wondered where she was now, how life had treated her. So many questions, so much curiosity.

"You okay, Dad? You seem distracted." Charley asked, her voice laced with concern.
Jonny sighed. "I'm better than I have been in years, Charley. There's something I need to do."

"What do you mean?" she asked.

“Something I should have done a long time ago,” he said quietly, his eyes distant.

He met her confused look. She could see a seriousness she had rarely seen in him. “I’m going to find someone, Charley. I don’t think I ever loved your mom,—not truly. I’m in control of my own destiny now. I chose *her*. I need to go and find her.”

Charley stayed silent, her chest tight, trying to make sense of his words. The room felt heavy with unspoken truths, and for the first time, she saw the depth of the path her father had decided to take.

“I don’t understand,” She enquired.

"It was a long time ago," Jonny said, a wistful smile playing on his lips. "Thirty years. Back in sweet home Alabama. I was fresh out of college, twenty, your age. Heading back to stay with your great-uncle Larry. Cutting and fixing trees were what he was good at, and I was wanting to become an arborist in his footsteps. I packed a bag, said goodbye to your grandma and grandpa here in Kentucky, and headed back to my home town, Cedar Bluff, so he could teach me everything he knew. It was hot that year, one of the hottest summers I remember. I wasn't just excited to be working with Uncle Larry; I was excited for the parties, on the pontoons in Weiss Lake. It was a hell of a party town back in the seventies. But I was not expecting meeting someone like *her*."

"Who was she?" Charley asked, noticing the sheer impact she had left on her father. Even after all these years later.

Jonny paused, his eyes filled with a distant longing. "Her name… was Jess."

Chapter 2 Homecoming

1979

It was June 6th. The wind ran its fingers through Jonny's hair as he sped across Alabama highway 68, on his motorbike, the long bridge stretching out before him like a ribbon of memory. Beneath him, Weiss Lake shimmered under the late afternoon sun, its waters catching the light like liquid silver. The air smelled of pine and summer and something else—something electric. For Jonny, this bridge had always been more than concrete and metal. It was the gateway home.

Cedar Bluff was just ahead, nestled like a secret between the trees and the lake's edge. He hadn't seen it in five years—not since his parents uprooted their lives and moved to Kentucky. But now, at twenty, Jonny was back. Wild, free, and brimming with a sense that this summer would be the one to change everything. As he drove through the quiet streets of the small town, the sights felt like old friends, —all exactly as he'd left them. Familiarity stirred excitement in his chest.

He pulled off the road, tyres rolling gently to a stop over the grass outside his aunt and uncle's house. The house stood just as he remembered it, weathered but warm, its porch a stage for many summer memories. He grabbed his duffel bag and made his way up the front steps. Jonny stretched his stiff muscles, the residue of the four-and-a-half-hour journey still clinging to him. As he ascended the porch steps, his aunt Glenda emerged from the doorway, her arms outstretched in a welcoming embrace.

"Ahh, Jonny! It's so good to see you!" she exclaimed, her voice brimming with genuine affection.
"Hey, Aunt Glenda!" Jonny responded, a smile lighting up his face.

She enveloped him in a warm hug. Glenda and Larry had never been blessed with children of their own, so Jonny's visits held a special significance. They delighted in making his stays memorable, especially Glenda, who poured her nurturing spirit into ensuring his comfort and happiness.
"Larry! Larry, come out here! Your handsome nephew's here!" she called out, her voice carrying into the depths of the house.
"Handsome? Now, I know you're not talking about the same nephew I'm thinking of," Larry muttered, a playful scepticism wrinkling his brow.
Larry stepped outside, a figure sculpted by the sun and toil. He was a compact man, his frame sturdy despite his height, clad in practical dungarees that spoke of long days spent amidst the whispering leaves and a black Stetson shielded his eyes from the lingering sun.

A moment of silent appraisal passed between them, a gaze locked that might have seemed charged to an outsider.
"JONNY!" Larry boomed. Jonny laughed, a warm, hearty sound, as they embraced. "Uncle Larry!"

"Get yourself settled, boy. I'm glad you're with us for the summer. You wanna know everything there is to know about being an arborist? Rule number one: your chainsaw's your best friend. I know just the place to pick one out. And you'll never guess what Glenda's been cooking up all day for ya," Larry said, a mischievous glint in his eye.

"No way!" Jonny exclaimed, his anticipation palpable.
"Beef brisket!!!" Jonny and Glenda chorused together. Jonny's favourite meal, no one made beef brisket quite like Glenda did.

Glenda took Jonny's bags, insisting—almost fussing—that he shouldn't lift a finger while he was with them. She and Larry were the definition of over-hospitable, their home always warm with the kind of easy banter that two people deeply in love could share. Their playful teasing filled the space around them, soft jabs wrapped in affection, the sort of warm noise that made a house feel lived in.

For Jonny, being back in Cedar Bluff brought a quiet, unexpected happiness. He hadn't realised how much he missed it until he was standing there again, letting the familiarity settle into him. It felt good to be home. Larry was just as thrilled, maybe even more so. Having his nephew back home brought a spark of warmth and excitement to him, the kind only family could stir. He'd always cared for Jonny like he was his own, and the fact that Jonny wanted to follow in his footsteps as an arborist made him prouder than he ever said aloud. A shared sense of excitement hung in the air, an unspoken premonition that this summer held something extraordinary, something big about to unfold.

Later that evening, Jonny headed down to the 360 Bar and Grill, the most vibrant spot in Cedar Bluff. It was a place where the atmosphere was both wild and welcoming, where people came to drink, laugh, and forget their troubles. As Jonny walked in, three men were gathered by the bar, their laughter echoing through the room. One of them turned, his eyes widening in disbelief.
"Shit... I don't believe it," Bronko breathed.
The others turned to follow his gaze.
"Jonny!!" Pete yelled, his voice cracking with excitement.
"HE'S BACK IN TOWN!" Dave roared, his face splitting into a grin.

Without hesitation, the three of them surged forward, engulfing Jonny in a bear hug. His old childhood friends, their excitement was infectious, the feeling of the gang being complete once more filled the air. Bronko, a towering African American, radiated confidence, his charisma undeniable. He was the one with the connections, the ideas, and a voice that could persuade anyone. He sported black bell bottoms and a dark denim vest, sleeves ripped to show off toned arms, a red bandanna tied jauntily around his head, his small afro neatly groomed. Pete, the smallest of the trio, compensated with boundless energy and a razor-sharp wit, perpetually accompanied by the aroma of a joint. His feathered hairstyle and thick moustache were distinctly retro, framed by round, orange-tinted glasses. He wore a brownish-orange turtleneck and jeans, his thick Southern accent adding to his unique charm. Dave, the tallest of the group, exuded a gentle strength. His long blonde hair and leather jacket gave off a soft-core biker vibe, but beneath the intimidating exterior lay a kind soul, the voice of reason within the group.

"You're home, man!!" Bronko exclaimed, slapping Jonny on the back.
"I thought I was just hallucinating for a minute, man," Pete said, his eyes wide. "Like, I thought the dope had caught up to me."
"You better lay off that crap before it turns you into a zombie, Petey!" Jonny retorted, a playful jab in his voice.
"He's already a zombie, look at that moustache," Dave quipped. "Ain't nobody alive wants something like that on their face."
"Yeah, I said the same thing to your mom last night, Dave," Pete shot back with a mischievous grin
Their laughter erupted, filling the bar, louder than any other sound.
Dave didn't waste a second hooking Jonny up with what he knew he loved—a Clyde May's over ice, the same drink Jonny had always ordered. He still remembered. Dave had stayed close with Big Rick, the bar's owner, so every pour came with a grin and a little extra generosity. The playful teasing flowed just as easily as the whiskey, with Bronko itching to spill the news about Dave's new girlfriend, Laurie—the one who apparently didn't like him spending too much time with his friends. Pete chimed in too, effortlessly tossing out quick, funny remarks that had all of them laughing. And though Dave joined in with the banter, Jonny caught the slight stiffness in his smile, the quiet hint that maybe he didn't find the jokes quite as funny as he let on.

"Hell, I can't believe Laurie's letting you out so late today, Dave," Pete teased. "Isn't it bedtime already?"
"Damn it, Pete, can it already!" Dave retorted, a playful annoyance in his voice.

"Me and Bronko's still grieving, it's a sensitive time, man," Pete added, pretending to feel sad
"I gotta meet her, man. How long has this been going on?" Jonny asked, curiosity piqued.
Pete followed behind as they looked for a table, talking outwardly.
"Ashes to ashes," Pete said dramatically.
"Almost a year now, she's the real deal, man," Dave said, his voice filled with genuine affection.
"Dust to dust," Pete continued, playing along.
"She's gorgeous, really grounding, she's good for me," Dave said, a soft smile gracing his lips.
"And so we remember Dave for what he was," Pete said, his voice laced with mock solemnity.
"A complete asshole, hahaha!" Bronko finished, erupting in laughter.

The table erupted in boisterous teasing and loud, shameless jokes, the kind that rolled over each other in waves. Bronko, as always, planted himself squarely at the centre of the chaos, thriving on every laugh and eager to top whatever had been said last. Pete and Dave fired back with their own quick jabs, each one earning another round of loud groans or belly laughs. They mocked each other in turn, nothing off-limits, everything delivered with the easy warmth of men who'd grown up side by side. And beneath all the noise and banter, one thing was unmistakable—they were genuinely, fiercely glad to have Jonny back where he belonged.

"You're just jealous, man, you could never get a girl like Laurie," Dave retorted, a playful challenge in his voice.

"Hey, man, I can get any girl I like, I can hook you up with anyone! The ladies love Bronko, hahaha!"
"Not when you roll with the Night Hounds, Bronko" Dave said half serious
For a brief millisecond, the table went quiet at the mention of the Night Hounds, a notorious biker gang from across the lake in Antioch. Jonny had grown up hearing stories about them, and the thought of Bronko mixing with that kind of danger sent a shiver through him. One thing was certain—the Night Hounds were trouble, and their creeping connections in Cedar Bluff were bad news.
But the tension didn't last long. The laughter and teasing soon returned, louder than before, and they even raised their glasses in a raucous toast to Jonny, celebrating his return. Everyone around the table was genuinely glad he was back, the warmth and excitement in the room impossible to ignore. It felt like the start of a summer they would never forget, a summer of mischief, friendship, and long-awaited reunions that promised to linger in their memories long after the days were gone. It felt as if no time had passed at all. They had met way back in elementary school and were now drinking together in the town bar. A bond forged in childhood, an unbreakable connection between four friends, a love that ran deeper than anything else.

"BRONKO!" a voice called out.
"Yo, Stu! How's it going, man?" Bronko replied, turning to greet the newcomer. "Come meet one of my brothers, man. Jonny, Stu… Stu, Jonny."
"Hey, man," Stu said, extending a hand.

Bronko had friends everywhere, and Stu—tall, lean, with that unmistakable '70s vibe of long hair, flared jeans, and a worn denim jacket—fit right in with the rowdy energy at the table. He jumped straight into the jokes, matching Bronko's banter effortlessly, and Bronko made sure to tell him just how glad he was that Jonny was back.

Stu didn't waste a second before dropping some news that made the group practically vibrate with excitement: a bonfire party down at Lake Weiss that very night. It was the perfect way to celebrate Jonny's return. Pete's eyes lit up as he asked about girls and drugs, and when Stu confirmed both, he almost leapt from his seat. Dave, however, was tethered by the curfew of his girlfriend Laurie, having promised her only one drink before coming home—a promise she was already none too pleased about—so the party was out for him.

Stu looked to Jonny for his answer. Jonny shrugged casually. "My aunt Glenda's cooking her beef brisket, but I'll head down after." At the mention of Glenda's legendary brisket, the table erupted again in cheers and laughter; everyone knew it was the best in town. Plans were quickly made, the air crackling with energy, and Bronko raised his glass high, a wide grin on his face, toasting to the start of a summer none of them would ever forget.

"TO SUMMER!" They cheered, clinking their drinks together, a symphony of camaraderie and anticipation filled the air, a summer that promised unforgettable moments, though none of them had any idea of the challenges, surprises, and secrets that awaited ahead. This night marked the first of many, the quiet beginning of a seemingly innocent summer, but beneath its surface lay a tangled web secrets. A mystery that wouldn't come until far into the future, pulling them all into a story far more complex and dangerous than they could yet comprehend.

Chapter 3 The Face Behind the flame

As the darkness settled over the horizon, Jonny finished the last bite of his beef brisket — tender, smoky, and just as good, if not better, than he remembered. The promise of the night, the reunion with his friends, and the thrill of summer's arrival mingled within him, a potent cocktail of excitement and anticipation.

"Alright, boy," Larry said, pushing back his chair with a creak. "Have fun with your friends. We'll start work at six-thirty tomorrow morning."

Glenda gave him a shocked look, halfway between disbelief and protest. Before she could scold him, Larry broke into an amused smirk.

"I'm only kidding," he chuckled. "Go on, enjoy yourself this weekend. We'll start Monday."

Jonny laughed. "It won't be a late one, Uncle Larry. I'm keen to get going."

Jonny wheeled his bike out into the dimming evening. The night air had cooled. He kicked the engine to life, the low growl of the motor echoing off the quiet road as he rode toward the lake. He followed the distant glow of a campfire that pulsed like a beacon across the dark water. When he arrived, the party was already in full swing — the whole beach alive with people his age. The stereo in the back of someone's jeep blared "Slow Ride" by Foghat, the gritty guitar riff cutting through the laughter and shouts. Groups clustered in loose circles along the sand, bottles in hand, conversations overlapping in the humid air. Jonny didn't recognize anyone immediately, but the atmosphere was good. Strangers nodded as he passed, offering friendly half-smiles or the raise of an eyebrow that said you belong here. The pontoon out on the lake was crowded with people dancing in bikinis and swim trunks, silhouettes moving against the shimmer of the firelight. A drunken stranger, spotting Jonny's empty hand, called out, "Hey man, where's your drink? No matter — I got you!"

He tossed Jonny a can of beer.

"Thanks, man!" Jonny cracked it open, the hiss of carbonation almost lost under the music. The first sip was cold and crisp.

Bronko spotted Jonny across the crowd almost immediately, weaving through the throng of people with effortless confidence. When he reached him, he clapped Jonny on the shoulder and guided him toward Pete and Stu. Pete sat there, eyes red and glassy, clearly stoned already, as if the night had already taken hold. Stu, by contrast, stood tall in the sand, easy-going but alert, taking in the scene with a relaxed grin.

Stu grinned. "How you doing, Jonny? How was the beef stew?"

Jonny laughed. "Good, bro — brisket!" He corrected.

Pete burst out laughing. "Stu wants to know about the stew!"

Even Jonny couldn't help but chuckle. Only Pete could find his own jokes that funny.

"Alright, let's get drunk!" Bronko shouted.

"I'll grab more beers!" Stu yelled.

"Yeah! Beef Stu's getting the beers!" Pete cackled.

And they did drink — bottle after bottle, laughter spilling into the night air. Soon Bronko stood in the centre of the crowd, downing a full beer to a chorus of "DRINK! DRINK!

DRINK!" The crowd roared when he finished, and Bronko basked in their cheers like a rock star.

When *"Free Bird"* came on, the four of them threw their arms around each other, voices rising in half-sung, half-yelled lyrics. The song had been out six years — one year before Jonny moved to Kentucky — and it hit like nostalgia reborn. It was their anthem, a memory of being young together. If only Dave were here, Jonny thought. It wasn't the same without him. Time blurred. The early hours crept in unnoticed. The joint went around in slow, lazy circles.

Stu swayed on the spot, finishing the last of his beer, and then froze with a dismayed look. "We're out," he announced, his voice tinged with disbelief.

Pete threw his arms in the air and shouted overdramatically, "It's a crime!"

But Bronko, as always, had a plan. He led them down to a small wooden rowboat pulled up near the water's edge. They would row out to one of the pontoons nearby, calling in a favour from the guys who knew Bronko and who, thanks to him, had more than enough supplies to keep the party going. Jonny and Stu took the oars, muscles straining with the effort, while Bronko leaned at the front, arms spread wide, pretending to be a pirate captain commanding the waves. Pete slouched at the back, too stoned to do much beyond mumble and laugh.

When they reached the pontoon, Bronko's reputation preceded him. The guys there grinned instantly and tossed a crate of beer into the boat, knowing Bronko had already supplied them—and probably the whole beach—with pot. Laughter erupted, the boat rocking lightly as the crate thudded into the bottom. It felt like everybody loved Bronko, the self-appointed king of the night, orchestrating chaos and fun with effortless charm. The boys rowed back triumphant. The night rolled on — one of the best Jonny could remember. But the energy began to fade. The alcohol caught up with them; people drifted away in pairs or small groups.

Pete stretched. "Hey, Bronko, think you can get us some more pot?"

"Ain't nothing Bronko can't do, brother! I'll be back soon!" Bronko left, leaving the three of them at their spot. "I'm gonna head closer to the bonfire. My girl's around there somewhere." Stu said. Pete grinned. "Didn't know you had a girlfriend, Beef Stu."

"Come meet her." Stu said.

Jonny and Pete followed him over to the roaring campfire, where another group sat laughing.

"Stu!" a voice called from near the shore.

Sally was perched on a fallen log, petite, with long blonde hair and a blue collared top. Her jeans were ripped at the knees, and she radiated easy confidence.

"Hey, baby," Stu said, kissing her.

"Come sit!" she said, waving them over.

Pete blinked. "Sally Strooker? I didn't know you were Stu's girlfriend!... Mind you I didn't really know Stu till a couple hours ago" He remembered. Sally laughed. "Got any pot?"

"Smoked it all," Pete said. "Bronko's getting more."

"Groovy. Who's your friend?" she asked, nodding to Jonny.

"This is Jonny — Our estranged brother. Back in town after five years."

They joined the circle. Jonny slouched against the log, half-empty beer dangling from his hand. He fished for his cigarettes, finding only one left in the packet. Using his mouth to pull it out, he searched his pockets for a lighter, then remembered Bronko still had it.

“Shit.”

“Need a light?” The voice came from just above him, perched on the log. An arm extended down, a flame flickering in the dark.

He looked up — and time slowed.

His eyes landed on her for the first time. She had a pretty face with features that drew attention without trying to. Her skin was fair, lightly dusted with freckles across her nose and cheeks, the kind that became more noticeable when she smiled. Her eyes were a clear, steady blue-grey, framed by long lashes that gave them quiet intensity. Her brows were naturally, arched just enough to lend her expressions quiet strength. Her hair fell loose, just below her shoulders, a warm brown that caught the campfire light in subtle shades, always looking a bit windswept no matter how she styled it. There was a naturalness to her, no heavy makeup, just the quiet confidence of someone who did not need it. Her lips curving easily into half smiles that never quite gave away what she was thinking. She carried herself in a way that blended warmth with restraint. Shoulders drawn in slightly if savouring her own quiet. Even when still, there was something alive about her, a sense of unspoken thoughts just behind her calm expression. He was immediately drawn to her with affection, by one mere glance.

Jonny took the lighter, their fingers brushing. “Thanks.”

“Keep it,” she said softly. “You look like you need it more than me.”

"What about you?" He asked

"I don't smoke."

He grinned. "Why'd ya have a lighter for?"

"You never know when you'll need one," she replied. "Or who you'll meet who does." She joked

Jonny looked down. The lighter was engraved with *Michigan 1977.*

"You from Michigan?"

"Originally."

"Long way to come for a party."

She smiled faintly. "I heard the parties in Cedar Bluff were legendary. I had to see for myself." She continued the humorous sarcasm

He liked her already. "Jonny Phillips."

"Jess Judy."

"So what really brings you here, Jess?"

"I'm staying with Sally for the summer — first time in Alabama. I'm studying to be a nurse."

Jonny nodded. "You live here?" She asked.

"Used to," he said. "My folks moved to Kentucky when I was in high school. I'm back to study — learning the arborist trade from my uncle."

"No way" Jess said surprised at the coincidence. She raised her bottle. "A summer of studying in Cedar Bluff."

"And drinking," he added.

"Cheers to that."

She took a sip, wrinkling her nose. "Not much of a beer drinker. I prefer Clyde May's."

Jonny grinned. "No way. You're a whiskey woman?"

"Guilty as charged."

He laughed. She intrigued him — grounded yet playful, reserved but not shy. He was there at the party with all his friends, but all he wanted to do was spend time with her. He picked up a vibe that she was interested in him too, it felt like an unspoken mutual feeling. She slid down the log sitting next to him on the sand. They sat side by side as someone began strumming a guitar across the fire, the familiar tune of Elvis's *"Can't Help Falling in Love."*

The song quieted the chatter, and one by one, people joined in the chorus. Everyone but Jonny and Jess. They just listened — the fire crackling, smoke twisting up into the dark sky. Silently, his mind wired with her enticing presence. He couldn't help but wonder if she was thinking the same. But she must have sat next to him for a reason, he thought. There was so much he wanted to get to know about her, but knew not to rush. That would hopefully come in time. But right now, they sat in silence listening to the music.

When the song ended, Pete raised his glass. "Did I hear you two talking about Clyde May's? There's a guy down by the 360 Bar selling bottles."

Jonny stood. "I could use one."

Pete, Jonny, and Jess pushed their way through the crowd, the warm hum of conversation and music folding around them like a blanket of noise. “I can’t wait for Bronko to get back with our pot” Pete said, his grin crooked as ever.

Jonny shook his head, fearing judgement from Jess if he partook in any drugs.

Pete smirked. “Don’t be a bitch in front of the lady, Jonny. I’m sure she don’t mind… Who are you, by the way?”

Jess laughed lightly. “Jess.”

“She’s a friend of Sally’s,” Jonny added.

“I’m with you,” Pete said, offering a mock bow. “Sorry, I’ll be more gentlemanly and stop talkin’ ‘bout drugs.”

Jess waved him off. “You’re fine. I’ll take a puff on that pot.”

Pete slapped his knee. “I like you! When Bronko gets back, I’ll roll a big long one—we can have more fun with it.”

Jess smiled slyly. “Do you say that to all the ladies?”

Jonny laughed, genuinely this time. He liked her humour; it was easy, unforced. Just like his.

“Just the special ones,” Pete replied with a wink.

It wasn’t long before they each had a glass of Clyde May’s whiskey in hand. The golden liquor glimmered under the bonfire’s light.

Jonny raised his glass. “Now this is what I’m talking about.”

Jess nodded. “So much better.”

"Yo, Jonny! Pete!" Bronko came jogging up, a brown paper bag in hand. "I wondered where you got to. I got your stuff."

He handed Pete the bag, and the earthy scent of weed escaped as Pete peeked inside. Bronko didn't seem to notice her; he simply turned, shoulders broad, and started back through the sand. Jonny noticed the slight distance—Bronko's lack of interest, or maybe he just hadn't registered Jess was part of their group. Either way, they regrouped with everyone else near the bonfire, the joint already being rolled and lit.

The sweet smoke drifted between them as they passed it around. Jess sat beside Sally—the person she seemed most at ease with—but not before giving Jonny a fleeting glance, one that silently invited him to sit beside her. He did, without hesitation.

What had started as a group of strangers—or at best, passing acquaintances—now felt almost like old friends. They laughed, traded jokes, and told half-remembered stories while taking turns with the joint. Jess was quieter, an observer more than a participant. Jonny chalked it up to her only really knowing Sally. Still, she laughed when the group's teasing grew bawdy, and her eyes seemed to dance when the conversation hit the right notes.

Bronko, as usual, took centre stage. His easy charisma drew attention like moths to a flame. But as the crowd thinned, the energy of the night began to soften, people leaving in small groups until only a few clusters of friends remained by the fire. Jonny wanted the night to last longer—not just because the vibes were high, but because of Jess. There was something unspoken between them, fragile and electric.

Then came the sound—low, mechanical, and growing louder. The ground itself seemed to tremble. The roar of motorcycles tore through the night. Three bikes emerged from the parking lot, their headlights sweeping across the sand. Conversations died instantly. The once-playful crowd froze, the crackling of the fire suddenly too loud.

"Oh shit, old salty" Bronko muttered.

Stu's face went pale. "That's the goddamn Night Hounds."

Jonny frowned. "What are they doing in Cedar Bluff?"

"Why are they here, Stu?" Sally asked, her voice trembling slightly.

"I don't know, baby," Stu said. "Stay back."

Sally moved closer to him, gripping his arm. Jess's expression tightened, but her calm was impressive—too calm, almost rehearsed. Jonny noticed that about her already: she could hide what she felt.

"They don't usually leave Antioch," Pete said under his breath.

Bronko hissed, "Hide the joint, Pete—HIDE THE JOINT!"

Confused but obedient, Pete buried the smouldering stub into the sand.

Three men climbed off their bikes. They were older, dressed in black leather, faces hardened by sun and age. The one in front—the leader—was built like a tank. His arms were thick and roped with muscle, his beard streaked black with grey, his gut hanging slightly over his belt. His voice, when he spoke, carried a coarse Southern drawl.

"Well now," he said, sweeping his gaze over the tense faces around the fire. "Looks like you folks are havin' a hell of a party. We not get an invite?"

No one answered. A few of the men—Jonny, Stu, and Pete among them—stepped forward instinctively, shoulders squared. Jonny noticed Bronko hang back, his expression uneasy. There was something else in that look, something more than the fear of three of the Night Hounds presence. Jonny spoke first. "What are you boys doing out here on the other side of the lake? This ain't Antioch—you're in Cedar Bluff territory now."

The leader smirked. "Didn't realise I was on a curfew. It's a free country, ain't it?"

Stu raised a hand. "We don't want no trouble. So why don't you just get back on your bikes and leave us to have our fun? Ain't nothing here of interest to you."

Pete muttered, "You tell 'em, Beef Stu."

The biker turned to Pete, sneering. "Aren't you a cute little thing. I didn't realise this was a children's party." He stepped closer, looming.

"Hey!" Jonny snapped, stepping between them. "He didn't do nothin'. Why don't you just back up, okay?"

Jonny didn't flinch under the man's stare. The others stayed firm beside him.

"You look high as a kite there, friend," the biker said. "Wanna tell me where you got your stash?"

Pete swallowed. "A friend."

"And what friend would that be?"

Stu cut in. "What difference does it make?"

Jonny said, steady and cold, "I think it's about time you boys got back on your bikes and headed home."

A few voices from the background joined him.
"Yeah, you ain't welcome round here!"
"Beat it, assholes!"

The leader eyed them all, recognising he was outnumbered. His jaw flexed. Then he gave a small nod. "Let's get outta here, boys."

The three men climbed back onto their bikes. Engines roared, sand kicked up, and soon they were gone—swallowed by the dark beyond the parking lot. Jonny, Pete, and Stu turned back to the group.

Sally rushed forward. "I don't like you confronting them like that, baby. They're dangerous."

Pete exhaled, shaking his head with nervous laughter. "I thought he was gonna slap the shit outta me. My asshole was flappin' like a fish outta water."

Bronko's tone was serious now. "Sally's right. They ain't the kind you wanna mess with. If they come back around, we walk the other way. Dig?"

Jess leaned toward Jonny. "You good?"

He nodded. "Thought he was about to start a brawl."

"So did I." She paused. "Who are they?"

"A biker gang called the Night Hounds," Jonny said quietly. "Shady people. Grew up hearing horror stories about 'em round the campfire. They usually terrorise Antioch. Theres a hell of a lot more of them than there was here tonight. Lord knows why they came this far over the lake."

Stu stretched, his voice tired. "Alright, I think it's about time we hit the hay."

"Good idea," Pete said. "Anybody for ice cream when we finally wake up?"

With a shared nodding in agreement, the plan for tomorrow solidified. It wasn't just their group leaving now. The bikers' appearance had killed the mood entirely. The beach, once alive with laughter and music, felt emptied—like something sacred had been broken.

Jonny glanced toward Jess as she started to walk away with Sally. Coincidentally, she turned at the same time, meeting his eyes over her shoulder.

"See you around," Jonny said.

She smiled faintly. "See you around."

The party had finally thinned, the last of the music fading against the gentle lap of the lake. Jonny caught up to Bronko as the scattered crowd drifted away.

"Bronko, hey—Bronko, wait up," Jonny called, jogging to match his pace.

Bronko glanced back, already guessing what Jonny wanted.

"What happened back there?" Jonny asked, eyes narrowing.

"The damn Night Hounds crashed the party, that's what happened, Jonny," Bronko replied, voice low and tight.

Jonny shook his head. "Cut the crap. I might have been gone five years, but I can still see right through you, brother. They were after the pot. Please don't tell me you got it from them?"

Bronko licked his lips, staring down the path, thinking carefully. "The Night Hounds have been poking around Cedar Bluff. They're making their move. It shouldn't be anything to worry about. They just want to know who's selling the gear. It's those cats who should be worried about the Night Hounds."

"That's it?"

"That's it, man. Go get some sleep. Sun'll be up soon."

Bronko walked on, leaving Jonny with a nagging sense there was more beneath the surface. Still, his mind settled enough to roll his bike back to Uncle Larry's. The moment he hit the bed, sleep claimed him utterly, dragging him into an afternoon-long oblivion.

Chapter 4 The Pull of *Her*

When he awoke, the lingering buzz of last night's laughter still hummed through him. The first thought that crept in: how damn good it felt to be back home in Cedar Bluff. He dressed quickly and made his way downstairs, where he was immediately met with Glenda and Larry's teasing remarks, the familiar, playful banter wrapping around him like a warm, friendly blanket. Glenda fussed over him, offering to make pancakes, but Jonny only smiled politely—he remembered he was meeting his friends, and all he could think about was her. A woman he knew so little about, yet the pull she exerted on him was undeniable, tugging at every thought and stirring a restlessness he couldn't ignore. Outside, two friendly beeps from a car horn drew Jonny's attention. The summer heat pressed through the window, and he spotted a battered, rusty red Ford F-100 waiting. "Jonny! You in there?" Pete called. Jonny stepped outside. Pete poked his head out of the truck window, grinning broadly.

"You're alive, haha! Get on in and we'll grab some food," Pete said, waving him over.

Jonny smirked. "Didn't recognise you all sober there, Pete, haha."

Pete leaned back with mock seriousness. "Don't get used to it. Bronko's got an endless supply—I have no idea where he gets it from."

They drove through town, the streets warm and shimmering under the afternoon sun. On the sidewalk, a familiar figure appeared.

"Is that Dave?" Pete exclaimed, squinting ahead.

Jonny looked back. Dave walked hand in hand with his girlfriend, Laurie. Her dress caught the sunlight softly, a fabric of fine weave, somewhere between faded blush and dusty mauve. It hugged her waist before falling into a modest, flowing skirt below her knees. A sharp collar framed her neck, lending poise to her posture, while long sleeves ended neatly at her wrists with single, precise buttons. Her hair cascaded in golden waves, each strand feathered and catching the light. Her stance radiated an air of quiet superiority, and Jonny felt it instantly—she wanted Dave to herself.

Pete pulled to the curb. "DAVE!" he shouted.

Caught in the moment, Dave's expression flickered between surprise and unease. "Uh… hey guys," he said, hesitantly.

Pete leaned out, grinning. "This must be Laurie."

Laurie looked down her nose. "Who are these men, David?"

"These are my friends," Dave said quickly, anxious to smooth things over.

Jonny immediately sensed Laurie's subtle judgment. She had drawn a line between them and her, and she didn't want Dave to step across it.

"You guys wanna hang out?" Pete asked.

Dave glanced at Laurie. He wanted to go, but he could tell she didn't approve.

"We're getting food and shakes," Laurie said firmly, taking the decision out of his hands.

"No way! So are we. Get in—I'll drive us to the diner. Beef Stu and his girlfriend are meeting us there," Pete said with a grin.

Laurie hesitated, clearly unhappy, but she had no choice. Dave wanted her to integrate with his friends, even if she didn't want to.

"Who the hell's Beef Stu?" Dave asked under his breath.

Jonny opened the passenger side door and gestured Laurie in. She hesitated, scanning the truck interior with a faintly disapproving frown. Dave and Jonny climbed in the back. Pete pulled back onto the road, and Jonny thought of Jess from last night, hoping she would show again.

"No Bronko?" Dave asked.

"No idea," Jonny replied, shrugging.

Jonny knew Laurie would never approve of Bronko. He also saw that she was trying to change Dave, to pull him away from his friends. That wasn't right. Dave needed to see it for himself. He had fallen for Laurie hard. Jonny would try to make her feel at ease as best as he could. Laurie's gaze flicked toward Pete, who gave her a reassuring smile. She returned a tight, forced grin and looked ahead, her discomfort obvious.

The diner appeared, tucked among the trees at the edge of town, overlooking a stretch of Weiss Lake. Dave opened the door for Laurie, who gave him a sharp, unimpressed look. They slid into a booth. The waitress approached, chewing gum and radiating disinterest.

The waitress, whose name badge read Caryn, took their orders. Soon after, she returned with a towering strawberry milkshake, whipped cream piled high, chocolate drizzled across the top. Jonny didn't order one—too sweet—but didn't comment, instead letting his eyes scan the entrance. Sure enough, Stu and Sally arrived hand in hand, Jonny looked with hope, and sure enough Jess followed.

"There they are!" Stu called.

"What's up, Beef Stu!" Pete shouted.

"Stu Baskin? Why are you calling him Beef Stu?" Dave asked.

Jess, quieter than the rest, slid into the booth beside Jonny. Their eyes met, and the familiar scent of her followed him like a trail of warmth.

"Hey again," Jonny said softly. "How's the head after last night?" He asked.

"I don't get hangovers" Jess said as an impressive smile broke out on Jonny's face.

"This sounds like a challenge. At the next party, we've just gotta keep the drinks coming." He said playfully.

"If you're paying for them," she teased back.

He laughed, impressed and amused. Her quick wit, as it often did, had bested his. He liked that about her. Her personality ever intriguing, the more he spoke to her. The food arrived, plates steaming, syrup dripping. The group ate, laughed, and exchanged stories. Jess and Jonny drifted into their own little bubble, quiet but playful, while Laurie barely spoke, giving Dave disapproving glances from time to time. The group was lively, easily the noisiest table in the diner. Humour threaded through every exchange, playful jabs and friendly banter bouncing back and forth, creating a warm, electric energy that made it clear—they were a great bunch, bound together by mischief, camaraderie, and the sheer joy of being in each other's company.

Laurie wasn't hiding her frustration; she didn't want to be there. Jonny and Jess were able to sit back and observe this making them laugh even harder. Stu flicked a cherry off his milkshake at Pete—it hit his chest, whipped cream exploding. Laurie squealed, brushing it off. Dave laughed awkwardly. Pete retaliated, and soon a full-blown whipped cream fight erupted, Jonny and Jess joining in gleefully.

"HEY! YOU KIDS, STOP THAT!" the waitress shouted.

Laurie jumped up and grabbed Dave, pulling him away from the chaos—she didn't approve and didn't want to be associated with the group. The two of them left, walking briskly in the opposite direction, while the rest bolted down the street, whipped cream dripping from their fingers and laughing wildly. Jonny noticed a clump of whipped cream in Jess's hair.

"You've got a little something there," he said, brushing it away with his finger and wiped a dab on her nose.

"No, you didn't," she scoffed in mock outrage. Jonny laughed.

"Jonny! That you, boy?" Larry's voice boomed across the street, his hand shading his eyes as he leaned against his truck, a wide grin splitting his weathered face.

"Hey, Uncle Larry!" Jonny called back, waving as he started across the street.

"Hey, Uncle Larry!" Pete and Stu joined in.

Larry let out a sudden, unexpected laugh "Whichever one of you is my nephew, why don't you get on over here and pick your chainsaw for when the store opens tomorrow?" Jonny crossed the sun-dappled road, the rest of the group following behind. Pete shouted from behind, full of energy, "Pick the best one, Jonny boy!" Jonny pressed his hands against the cool glass of the store window, Larry leaning beside him. Their eyes immediately rose to the top shelf, where the largest, most impressive chainsaw gleamed under the light. Chrome and steel caught the sun, reflecting it in sharp, bright flashes.

“Ah, she’s a beauty,” Larry said, nodding appreciatively. “The Stihl Contra, sixteen inches. You might have to lower your expectations, son, but that’s every arborist’s dream right there.”

Jonny’s gaze dropped to the price tag: five hundred dollars. A flicker of disappointment passed across his face. He knew he’d have to start small, but the sight of the chainsaw also lit a spark of ambition—something to work toward, a goal to chase. Larry noticed immediately.

“I’ll tell you what,” Larry said, clapping Jonny on the shoulder. “Give it some thought. We’ll come back tomorrow. I was just down here picking up some gas for the truck. I’ll let you get back to your friends. Catch you later.”

“Bye, Uncle Larry!” Pete called enthusiastically, waving.

Larry climbed into his truck and started the engine, the rumble fading as he drove off down the street. Sally threw out the idea of heading down to Buffington’s Island, and it was met with immediate enthusiasm. Laughter and teasing punctuated their agreement, each person eager for the chance to dive into the water, soak up the sun, and enjoy the carefree chaos that seemed to follow them wherever they went.

The group set off down the sunlit street, their laughter and conversation spilling into the warm afternoon air. Buffington’s Island stretched quietly just west of Cedar Bluff, a narrow ribbon of land where the lake lapped gently against sandy banks. It was the perfect spot for an afternoon of peace, whether you wanted to wade into the cool depths for a swim or sit quietly with a rod in your hand. The sun bore down relentlessly, warming their shoulders and turning the skin a shade of pink from the walk down. They weren’t alone—other families and anglers dotted the distant shore—but Buffington's Island was wide enough to offer a sense of solitude, a space that felt entirely their own.

Their chosen spot lay at the water's edge, Stu's fishing line sliced through the air, the spool singing with a sharp, steady whirr before the bait landed with a soft plunk that sent ripples across the mirrored surface.

Stu grinned, proud of his cast, as he watched the tip of his rod tremble. Jonny and Pete cast their lines into the glassy lake while Jess and Sally stretched out on the grass, letting the sun warm their skin. Suddenly, his rod jerked violently. He planted his feet in the sand, bracing against the pull, the line dancing over the lake as a strong fish fought beneath the surface. The tension was electric—Stu and Pete could barely believe it, certain he wouldn't land the creature. The reel screamed, water splashing against his bare arms and shoulders as he coaxed it closer, muscles straining with every motion. Through it all, Jonny loved the way Jess's eyes were on him, quietly watching, and it gave him a small, steady surge of pride.

With careful, practiced movements, Jonny finally lifted the fish from the water, sunlight catching its wet scales as it gleamed like molten gold. The group erupted in cheers, stunned that he had actually caught it. Jonny's chest swelled with pride, a grin tugging at his lips as he felt the weight of the achievement settle in. Around him, Stu and Pete clapped him on the back, laughing and cheering, their excitement genuine, and Jess gave him a quiet, approving smile. One that spoke of more than proudness for catching his fish.

The afternoon was just as carefree as the party the night before. Lake Weiss shimmered under a blazing Alabama sun. Jonny lay sprawled on a faded towel, sunglasses slipping slightly down his nose, the coarse grass tickling his arms and the warm breeze ruffling his hair. Somewhere nearby, Stu had propped the old cassette stereo against a tree, and the opening chords of *Sweet Home Alabama* drifted into the air. Jonny tilted his head, letting the music wash over him.

"I love this one" Jonny exclaimed, with a glint in his eye. "Me too!" Jess said. Yet another favourite thing in common together. Stu chuckled and cranked the volume, the warm, scratchy chords of *Sweet Home Alabama* filling the air. The music seemed to lift everyone's spirits, and without thinking, they all began singing along.

Their voices rang out across the lake, loud and unpolished, but it didn't matter. The heat of the afternoon, the shimmer of the water, and the shared joy of the moment wrapped around them like a blanket. For a few minutes, it felt like nothing else in the world existed but the sun, the lake, the music, and the people he liked being around the most. When the last notes faded, they all laughed and cheered, finishing the song together with wide smiles and a shared sense of joy.

Stu stood at the edge where the shallow water lapped over the sand, suddenly grabbed Sally by the waist and gave her a playful push. She shrieked, stumbled, and splashed into the water with a laugh, sending droplets sparkling across the sunlit lake. Stu jumped in after her, laughing, and Pete cheered from the bank, daring Jonny to follow. With a grin he couldn't resist, Jonny ran forward and cannonballed into the cool water, the shock of it perfect against the heat of the afternoon. Jess sat on the bank with her legs dipped in the water, smiled and shook her head, that small, knowing smile that Jonny found himself watching more than he should. When Jess finally eased herself into the shallow water beside him, Jonny swam closer almost without thinking. Their shoulders brushed once, then again, and that familiar, electric tug returned—the kind of spark that made his stomach twist pleasantly, a warmth that had nothing to do with the sun.

Jonny couldn't stop sneaking glances at Jess, noticing the way her hair clung damply to her neck, how droplets ran down her shoulders, and the way her laughter sounded softer, almost intimate, when it was just for him. The water caught the sunlight, turning her hair to flickers of gold with every movement, and he felt a quiet thrill just being near her.

Eventually, the group drifted back toward the shore until they collapsed onto their towels, hair and skin still glistening with water. The sun had baked them warm again, drying the last chill from the lake. Stu and Sally sat close, teasing each other quietly, while Jonny and Jess lay side by side, the heat drying their skin and the cassette stereo still playing softly in the background. The classic rock music filled the air. Jonny let himself relax, letting the moment soak in—the sun on his face, the water glinting across the lake, Jess's quiet smile beside him, the sound of their friends laughing—and thought that if this was what life in Cedar Bluff felt like, he could move back here forever.

"So, this is where you kittens are hiding, huh?" a voice boomed.

Heads turned. Bronko, a figure as familiar and welcome as the sun itself, was making his way across the grass towards them, a brown paper bag clutched in his hand. His grin, wide and infectious, promised good times and easy laughter.

The group surged forward. Bronko, ever the showman, revelled in the attention. He loved the feeling of excitement his presence sparked in others. It was a drug, and he was addicted. Bronko was the undeniable life of the group, a human spark plug. While Jonny was genuinely glad to see him, he couldn't help but notice Jess receding slightly, retreating into her shell. She was always less social in groups, more comfortable in one-on-one. But the security of the group had its own appeal. It diffused the pressure to fill awkward silences, the sheer volume of activity a convenient shield.

"What's in the bag, Bronko!?" Sally wondered, her eyes dancing with anticipation.

Bronko chuckled, a low rumble in his chest. "You already know, Sally, haha. Did you guys think I'd come empty-handed? Weed, my guys!"

"ALRIGHT!" Pete roared, throwing his hands up in the air.

They settled into a loose circle, an unspoken ritual unfolding. All eyes were on Bronko as he expertly rolled the joint, his fingers moving with practiced ease. He lit the end, the sweet, pungent aroma filling the air, and took the first toke. His grin widened as he exhaled a plume of smoke, feeling the weight of expectation, the unspoken need for his approval.

"That's some good shit," he declared, his voice a low purr of satisfaction.

"Alright! Pass it over, man!" Pete said, practically bouncing with eagerness.

The joint made its way around the group, each person taking a slow draw before handing it along. Sally recounted the chaos at the diner, filling Bronko in on the day's events and the food fight that had everyone laughing. Bronko found the story hilarious, shaking his head in mock disapproval at their antics. Pete mentioned that even Dave had shown up—along with his girlfriend, Laurie. Bronko raised an eyebrow, curious but masking it with playful laughter. The group's irritation with Laurie was impossible to miss. Every forced smile, every hesitant laugh from Dave made it painfully clear that he wasn't allowed to be himself in her presence. She hovered like a shadow over him, controlling his every move.

Bronko clicked his tongue, his gaze drifting towards the lake, his expression unreadable. "We've gotta rescue our Dave. This calls for an urgent mission. This evening, I've got the location of an exclusive poker game, invite only. I'm getting you all on the list, but before we do that, we go to this Laurie's house and rescue our fallen comrade."

"Poker? Where's this?" Stu asked, his eyes lighting up.

"A friend of mine, he wanted to keep it quiet, but quiet ain't Bronko's thing, dig?" Bronko said, puffing out his chest. "Goes by the name Bullfrog, lives north of Cedar Bluff on 68."

"Isn't that near Antioch?" Sally asked, frowning. Bronko shrugged.

"Who is this guy Bullfrog?" Jonny pressed, a seed of unease planting itself in his mind.

"He ain't nobody," Bronko dismissed.

"Ain't nobody like one of the Night Hounds?" Jonny persisted, his voice hardening.

Sally's eyes widened in alarm. "I'm not going nowhere near them Night Hound kind."

"Relax, relax," Bronko soothed, holding up his hands. "He ain't nothing to worry about."

"But he is a Night Hound?" Jonny challenged, refusing to let it go.

"He's got connections, sure, so what? We all got connections. Look, it's a small party. Beers, poker, and weed."

"Weed! Count me in!" Pete declared, his reservations vanishing at the mention of his favourite pastime.

While the conversation flowed around him, Jonny looked over at Jess, a question forming in his mind. "You're a poker player?"

"Yep!" Jess confirmed, her eyes sparkling with confidence. "I hope you've got deep pockets, Jonny."

Jonny grinned, accepting the challenge. "Sounds like fighting' talk."

They smiled at each other. It seemed the group was interested. The stakes had been raised, and the game was on!

Chapter 5 Comrade Down, Brain Cells Missing

Night had fallen, draping the street in a cloak of quiet. The only sounds were the low murmur of voices, the strained grunts of exertion, and the occasional hushed whisper cutting through the stillness.

“Slow down, slow down!” Stu hissed, his breath coming in ragged gasps.

“Don’t steer it into the curb!” Pete grunted, his muscles straining with the effort.

“I got it, I got it,” Sally replied, her voice tight with concentration as she wrestled with the steering wheel.

The gang was pushing Pete’s beat-up truck up the slight incline of the street. The truck’s engine was off and Sally steered. Stu and Pete, their faces flushed with effort, pushed from the front, while Jonny added his strength from behind. Jess, perched in the truck bed, watched with a mixture of amusement and concern.

“Alright, stop here, stop here!” Pete finally gasped, his legs threatening to buckle.

Sally yanked the handbrake and the truck settled, still, at the side of the road. The three men stumbled away from the vehicle, their chests heaving as they tried to catch their breath and shake off the ache in their muscles. Meanwhile, Bronko was nowhere to be seen. A rustling in the bushes revealed his position, close by. He stood behind a thick hedge, a pair of binoculars pressed to his eyes, scanning the house on the other side of the street. He probably didn’t need the binoculars; he could likely see just fine without them. But they added to the effect, a prop in the elaborate act Bronko was playing.

“Would have been really grateful for the help, Bronko,” Stu said, his voice dripping with sarcasm, though he kept it low to avoid attracting attention while catching his breath.

“Shh! I’m casing the joint,” Bronko hissed, lowering the binoculars slightly. “I’ve come up with a plan.”

“I just need a minute before we do anything else,” Pete groaned, leaning heavily against the side of the truck, his face pale in the dim light.

“Alright, Bronko, what’s the plan?” Jonny asked, impatience creeping into his voice.

“All the lights are out. The happiness hoover has got our man going to bed at nine PM.” Bronko declared, his voice a dramatic whisper.

Jonny played along with Bronko’s act. “Good lord, the situation is worse than we thought, captain.”

“We’re really going to have to pull out all the stops here, troops,” Bronko continued, his tone overdramatic.

“What’s your plan of attack?” Jonny pressed, eager to get this over with.

“We’re going to have to enter the enemy’s territory,” Bronko announced, his voice dropping to a conspiratorial whisper.

“You’re going in!?” Sally exclaimed, her eyes widening in alarm.

"I'm afraid so, Sally…" Bronko replied, his voice filled with mock solemnity. "But it's a risk we need to take. For our fallen soldier."

There was something undeniably fun about overdramatising the situation, Jonny had to admit. "The window's on the latch in the yard. That's our entry point," Bronko explained, pointing across the street. "Pete, you're clumsy as shit, so we need you to stay outside and make sure our cover isn't blown."

"Yes, captain," Pete replied, saluting with mock seriousness.

"My man Jonny, you come in with me. We need him to be awake and the enemy to be asleep."

"How are you gonna do that!?" Stu asked, his brow furrowed in confusion.

"I don't know, pinch his toe or something!" Bronko retorted, waving his hand dismissively. "Jonny, we grab him and get him out of this hostage situation. I'm anticipating a struggle; poor man doesn't even know he's in a hostage situation. Stu… you grab his clothes."

The over-the-top dramatics finally got to Jonny, a snort of laughter escaping his lips. He quickly stifled it, trying to maintain a semblance of seriousness. They darted across the road, their footsteps a quick, hushed rhythm on the asphalt, and scrambled over the low hedge bordering Laurie's parents' yard. The garden was a typical suburban affair – neatly trimmed bushes, a couple of plastic gnomes lurking in the shadows, and a meticulously manicured lawn stretching towards the darkened house. The rescue mission, as they had put it, had truly begun.

The four men huddled around the window, a knot of tension and anticipation. Bronko stretched his arm inside, his fingers fumbling for the latch. He strained, his muscles taut, but managed to reach it, the click of the mechanism echoing in the stillness. Jonny and Stu, their faces etched with concentration, held the window steady, preventing it from slamming shut. Slowly, cautiously, they widened the opening, a gentle wave of warm air escaping from within. Bronko ducked under the window frame, momentarily resting on the ledge, his silhouette a dark shape against the faint light filtering from the house. He adjusted the latch, securing it so Jonny and Stu could release their grip. With a final glance back, he climbed inside, disappearing into the silent darkness. The house was eerily quiet, the air thick with a sense of undisturbed slumber. Bronko raised a finger to his lips, signalling for silence, and beckoned them inside with a subtle wave of his hand.

Pete, his eyes wide with a mixture of excitement and trepidation, stood back, allowing them to climb through the window, he tripped on a garden gnome. There was a soft thud, followed by the distinct sound of ceramic shattering, as it fell into the other.
"Oh shit!" He whispered.
The others froze, their heads snapping back towards the sound. Frustration and annoyance flashed across their faces.

Bronko, his senses on high alert, tilted his head towards the ceiling, listening intently. He couldn't detect any movement, no telltale creaks or rustles. They were in the clear… for now. They crept through the hallway, and peered up the staircase, a dark, looming presence in the dim light.

"After you, Bronko," Stu whispered, his voice tight with nervous anticipation.
With deliberate caution, they ascended the stairs, each step a calculated risk. The faint hum of electric fans, emanating from the rooms upstairs, provided a welcome shield of noise, masking their movements. The first room was Laurie's parents' bedroom. Jonny, his curiosity piqued, peered inside, his eyes adjusting to the darkness. Both were fast asleep, lost in their own private worlds. Her dad lay closest to him, an

older, overweight man clad in a white vest top, his face glistening with sweat in the warm air. Her mum faced away from him; her form shrouded in shadow. Suddenly, Laurie's father let out an almighty snore, a sound that resembled the grinding gears of a failing motor vehicle. His lips trilled with each exhale, a bizarre and comical symphony of sleep.

Stu, unable to resist, poked his head around the corner, his face breaking into an amused smirk as he tried to decipher the unearthly noise. He and Jonny exchanged glances, their eyes widening in shared amusement, before quickly looking away, struggling to contain their laughter. Sniggering like a pair of schoolgirls in the shadows, they fought to maintain their composure. Bronko shook his head, finding Jonny and Stu's silent laughter even funnier than the snoring itself.
Jonny moved to the next room, the door once again ajar, inviting them in. Bronko and Stu followed close behind. Laurie and Dave were in bed, both seemingly asleep. Dave's feet, however, stretched out beyond the confines of the bedding, dangling precariously off the edge of the bed. Two pillows were wedged between them, a clear indication of Laurie's territorial claim.

"Can you believe this shit?" Bronko muttered, his voice laced with disbelief.

Jonny shook his head, a mixture of amusement and mild incredulity on his face. "Alright, Stu, grab his clothes."

Stu nodded and snuck over slowly and quietly to a rickety straw chair nestled in the corner of the room, his movements as silent as a whisper. Bronko scanned the hallway his gaze landed on a cabinet, upon which sat a plant pot containing a snake plant, the topsoil concealed beneath a layer of small, black pebbles. A lightbulb flicked on in his head. He carefully plucked a single pebble from the pot and turned back towards the doorway, a mischievous glint in his eyes.

“Psst, Dave,” Bronko whispered.

He flicked his wrist, sending the pebble arcing through the darkness. His aim, hampered by the lack of light, was slightly off. The pebble struck Laurie on the side of the cheek. She stirred, her eyes fluttering open, and rubbed her face, startled by the unexpected impact. Bronko and Jonny quickly ducked out of sight, concealing themselves on either side of the doorway. Stu, who now clutched Dave’s clothes in his hands, could only cower behind the small, thin electric fan, his eyes wide with panic. He was barely concealed, and he fully expected Laurie to spot him at any moment.

“David! Was that you?” Laurie mumbled.

Dave stirred beside her, still half-asleep. “Huh?”

“You just hit me in your sleep!” Laurie complained, rubbing her cheek.

“Sorry,” Dave mumbled, already drifting back to sleep.

Bronko and Jonny exchanged glances, struggling to suppress their laughter. The whole situation was absurd, a chaotic mix of slapstick and suspense. Laurie rolled over and almost instantly fell back asleep, a slight rattle in her breathing confirming her return to slumber. Dave, however, was now awake, and the pebble incident had triggered a different kind of urge. He itched his crotch, he needed the bathroom.
He lumbered out of bed, moving with the slow, deliberate steps of a zombie. His eyes were half-shut, his senses dulled by sleep. He shuffled past Jonny and Bronko, oblivious to their presence, and stumbled into the bathroom opposite the bedroom. Stu, still clutching the clothes, stood frozen in place, wondering how on earth they hadn’t been caught yet. The flush of the toilet confirmed that Dave was about to re-enter the landing.

The door creaked open, and Dave emerged from the bathroom, slightly more alert than before. His eyes focused on Bronko and Jonny, who stood blocking his path. A confused expression spread across his face. Before he had a chance to speak, to question their presence, Bronko acted.

"NOW!" He hissed the command, his voice low but filled with an undeniable urgency. Bronko and Jonny sprang into action, grabbing Dave before he could react. Bronko clapped a hand over Dave's mouth, stifling any protests. Dave shook his head, his eyes wide with confusion and alarm, but he was helpless against their combined strength. Jonny grabbed his legs, and together they lifted him off the ground. Stu, finally snapping out of his stupor, bolted after them, clutching the clothes like a lifeline.
Bronko released his hand from Dave's mouth, freeing him to speak, as they struggled to carry him down the hallway. Dave, realising that he was in the hands of his friends, his initial panic subsided, replaced by a growing sense of bewilderment and concern. He spoke quietly, his voice a desperate plea. "Put me down! Bronko! Jonny! What are you doing! Stop! Put me down!"

They carried him towards the stairs, Dave's desperate pleas echoing softly in the silent house. As they turned the corner at the bottom of the staircase, Dave's head collided with the stair rail, a sharp thud punctuating the air. "Aggh!"

"Sorry, Dave, it's for your own good, man," Jonny whispered, his voice filled with mock sympathy.

They stumbled through the hallway, their arms aching with the strain, and made it to the window. Pete, who had been watching from outside, was in disbelief that they had actually pulled it off. He bounced on the spot, his excitement barely contained.

Pete rushed forward, helping them to manoeuvre Dave through the window. One by one, they clambered out into far less stifled night air. They carried Dave across the front yard and across the road to the truck, their movements a chaotic dance in the darkness. Sally and Jess, who had been watching from the truck, burst into laughter.

"I can't believe you guys did it!" Sally exclaimed, her voice filled with amusement.

"Did anyone else wake up?" Jess asked, her eyes sparkling with disbelief.

"Nope! Mission success, boys, haha!" Stu declared, throwing his arms up in the air in a gesture of triumph.

"Put me down!" Dave demanded, his voice now laced with a hint of anger.

They gently lowered him to the ground. He stood there, swaying slightly, clad only in his underwear, his expression a mixture of confusion and indignation. "What the hell are you guys doing!?"

Bronko stepped forward. A mischievous smile still sat firmly on his face "Rescuing you, man!"

"I don't need rescuing!" Dave protested, his voice rising in frustration.

"It's summer, and you're in bed at nine o'clock! You needed rescuing," Jonny retorted with a grin.

"I can't believe you broke into my girlfriend's house!" Dave exclaimed, his voice incredulous.

"Relax, she'll never know you're gone!" Bronko reassured him.

"Bronko's got us into a poker game tonight… It'll be like old times. Come on, man, you used to love poker!" Pete chimed in, trying to entice him.

"Laurie says it's bad for me. Gambling is a sin, and I'll lose all my money," Dave countered, his voice laced with a hint of guilt.

Bronko squeezed Dave's shoulder, his expression softening. "I miss you, brother. Things haven't been the same since Laurie came into the picture…"

"Don't start this again…" Dave interrupted, his voice weary.

"Just wait, hear me out," Bronko pleaded. "I'm glad you found someone. I really am. You deserve happiness. I just… I feel like my best friend is slipping away through my fingers."

A silence fell over the group, the weight of Bronko's words hanging heavy in the air. Bronko was always the entertainer, the life of the party, but right now, he was speaking from his heart. Dave and Bronko had always been the closest of the group, their bond as solid as a rock.

"You're still allowed to be you," Bronko continued, his voice filled with emotion. "You still have your friends. You can still have all that and Laurie. I just wish sometimes you'd come and hang with us. Me, Pete, Jonny's back in town, only for three months. You're brothers. You're my guy, my wingman. You're like another part of me, brother. I don't want to lose that because of a chick."

Dave nodded slowly, his eyes filled with emotion. He knew Bronko was right. He had been neglecting his friends, allowing Laurie's influence to isolate him from the people who had been there for him long before she came along.

"One night…" Dave conceded, his voice barely above a whisper. "And not a word of this to Laurie."

"Not a word," Bronko promised, his eyes gleaming with triumph.

Stu handed Dave his clothes, and he quickly slipped into them under the dim glow of the streetlights. They piled into the truck, a chaotic jumble of limbs and laughter. The engine roared to life, shattering the silence of the night, and they drove off into the darkness, their destination unknown, their spirits high.

Chapter 6 A Hand Full of Hearts

Bullfrog's home was a sprawling ranch house with a weathered facade, perched on a rise overlooking the inky expanse of the lake. The air was thick with cigarette smoke, a hazy cloud filtering the soft glow of the nightlights. A cool breeze rustled through the trees. They'd gathered out back, beneath a pagoda draped in strings of delicate nightlights.

The table, a sturdy oak affair scarred with years of use, dominated the space. Empty beer bottles ringed its perimeter. Amidst the clutter of discarded butts and overflowing ashtrays sat a faded deck of cards and a haphazard pile of poker chips, their colours muted by the dim light. The table was generously sized, but the group was large enough that elbows still bumped and overlapped.

Bullfrog, their host, was a formidable presence. He was a tall, powerfully built man, his physique hinting at a life lived on the edge. Even in the dim light, his bald head gleamed, reflecting the soft glow of the nightlights. He perpetually donned a pair of black shades, obscuring his eyes and adding to his aura of mystery. A supple leather jacket, worn but impeccably maintained, draped over his broad shoulders, and a neatly trimmed goatee framed his mouth, lending him an air of understated menace. He exuded an aura of quiet authority, a man who was used to being in control.

Bullfrog leaned forward, his gaze fixed on Bronko. "So, Bronko," he rumbled, his voice a gravelly baritone that commanded attention, "you think you and your crew can beat me at poker, eh?" He pushed his black shades onto his head, revealing eyes that were sharp and piercing, capable of both charm and intimidation.

Bronko grinned, unfazed by Bullfrog's intensity. "This man *is* unbeatable," he declared, his voice laced with playful exaggeration. "Bullfrog the money stealer!"
Dave, emboldened by the beer and the camaraderie, chimed in. "Until tonight! Bullfrog, I think it's great and all you're hosting for us, but you are about to be *destroyed*."
Bullfrog chuckled, a low, rumbling sound that vibrated in his chest. "We'll see about that, boy! The only thing that's gonna be destroyed is your pride... and your wallet!"
Pete, eager to contribute, started to speak. "Only thing that's gonna be destroyed is—"
Jonny cut him off with a playful threat. "Pete, I swear, man, if you're about to make another 'mom joke,' I'll throw you in the lake."
Dave laughed, slapping the table. "Haha! I want him to finish, just to see Jonny throw him in the lake!"

The table erupted in laughter, the tension momentarily dissipating. Bronko, his eyes crinkling at the corners, took a moment to observe Dave. He was genuinely pleased to see his friend relaxed and carefree, unburdened by Laurie's restrictions. His friend was back. For tonight at the very least.
Sally, ever the pragmatist, rolled her eyes. "Are you boys gonna put your rulers away and deal, or what?!"
"Alright! Let's do this," Jonny said, his voice laced with anticipation.
"I'll deal. Pass me them cards, Bullfrog," Stu offered, reaching for the deck.
Bullfrog slid the cards across the table, his expression unreadable. "You know what would go down just nicely right now…" he drawled, "A joint."
"I got some! I have a bag full!" Pete exclaimed. His enthusiasm outweighing his common sense.

Bronko's expression darkened, his eyes narrowing almost imperceptibly. He seemed to disapprove of Pete's eagerness, as if he knew that revealing the presence of drugs could attract unwanted attention. Pete, however, was too naive to understand the nuances of the situation, too eager to impress to think before speaking. He pulled out the small brown bag of marijuana and tossed it onto the table.

Jonny and Jess, ever the astute observers, exchanged a quick glance. They both sensed a shift in the atmosphere, a subtle tension radiating from Bronko. It wasn't Pete's offer of the joint itself, but something about the way Bronko reacted, a silent warning that Pete seemed oblivious to, that made them uneasy. They could tell that Bronko didn't want Pete to reveal where he'd gotten the weed, and that Bullfrog was someone you didn't want to lie to.

As Pete began to roll a joint, Bullfrog spoke, his voice suddenly steely. "Where'd you get that from, Pete?"
Bronko quickly interjected, attempting to defuse the situation. "I bet he doesn't even know. He'll take pot from anyone selling it, right, Pete?"
Pete, finally catching on to the tension in the air, stammered, "Uh, yeah... shady fella from Antioch. Can't think of his name."
Bullfrog clearly didn't believe him, but before he could press the issue, Stu chimed in, eager to get the game started. "Alright, let's go! Enough chatter!"

The game settled into a comfortable rhythm, a blend of friendly competition and easy banter. Laughter echoed through the pagoda as fortunes rose and fell with each hand. Stu, fuelled by a steady stream of beer, played with reckless abandon, often bluffing his way to victory with a boisterous shout and a devil-may-care grin. Dave, emboldened by his newfound freedom, played aggressively, relishing the thrill of the gamble and the camaraderie of his friends. Even Pete, despite his earlier faux pas, managed to win a few small pots, his face beaming with pride as he raked in the chips. Between hands, Jonny found himself drawn to Jess, their eyes meeting across the table in shared amusement. There was a comfortable ease between them, a silent understanding that transcended words. He enjoyed watching her, the way she subtly observed the other players, her mind always working, calculating the odds.

As the night deepened, the stakes climbed higher, and the air crackled with anticipation. Piles of cash and colourful stacks of chips, now significantly larger than before, dominated the centre of the table, reflecting the fortunes won and lost. The once-casual game transformed into a battle of wits and wills, fortunes hanging in the balance with every card dealt. Bronko, his brow furrowed in concentration, played with a quiet intensity, his eyes scanning the faces of his opponents. Stu, fuelled by bravado and egged on by Sally's enthusiastic cheers, rode a rollercoaster of wins and losses, his emotions as volatile as the cards he held. The pagoda became a world unto itself.

Eventually Stu nervously patted his pockets, a visible tremor in his hands as he counted his remaining bills. "Man, you guys are going to take me for everything I have," he lamented, his voice laced with a mixture of resignation and forced humour.

Bullfrog's gaze drifted to Stu's dwindling pile of chips, amusement flickering in his eyes as Jonny took the deck and dealt the next hand. The players tossed in their bets. Something in the spread made Bullfrog sit straighter, confidence sharpening his features.

Then Stu shoved in everything he had left, a reckless push that made Pete wince as the pot swelled. Before Bullfrog could lean into the moment, Jess moved with calm precision, sliding a fresh stack of chips into the centre. The sharp clatter echoed through the wooden beams, freezing the table.

Her raise shifted the entire atmosphere—sudden, bold, and completely unexpected. For a breath, no one moved. Jess had just changed the course of the game, and every player felt the tension coil tighter around them.

"Well, little lady thinks she's onto something here," Bullfrog chuckled, his eyes narrowing as he studied Jess's face.

Bronko, leaning back in his chair, whistled softly. "That was hella bold, alright. Fifty." He tossed in his chips, his expression a mixture of curiosity and amusement.

Dave followed suit, his eyes gleaming with excitement. "Fifty!"

Bullfrog, intrigued by Jess's audacity, reluctantly threw in his share. Jonny, his gaze locked on Jess, sensed something unusual. Her poker face was a mask of serene confidence, unreadable, yet somehow… unsettling. Deciding not to gamble on a hunch, he folded his cards, followed by Pete. The pot was the highest it had been all night, a tempting mountain of cash and chips in the centre of the table.

Jonny turned over the next card, and a ripple of energy passed through the table. Bullfrog settled deeper into his seat, confidence radiating from him—whatever he held, he believed this hand was his. But Jess met every shift in momentum with an unnerving calm, her chips sliding forward without hesitation. The pot swelled dangerously, swallowing bill after bill, tension tightening the air with each raise.

Even Bronko, usually unfazed, began to shift uneasily, glancing from Jess to the growing mountain of money. Her expression stayed unreadable—steady, quiet, almost serene—as if she were playing a game only she understood. One by one the others folded beneath the pressure, unwilling to follow her into such deep waters.

Jonny revealed the final card. Bullfrog sat back, certain he had the winning hand—certain enough that a slow, self-satisfied smile crept across his face. Yet Jess still didn't look shaken. She simply pushed in the last of her cash, leaving herself with nothing behind. A move that could've been brilliance… or ruin. No one at the table could tell which.

Bullfrog, his brow furrowed in thought, knew he had to test her. "Raise to one hundred." He threw in his chips, the sound echoing through the suddenly silent pagoda.

Jess knew the truth: her pockets were practically empty. She had barely ten bucks to her name outside of what was on the table. But none of them needed to know that. With a practiced air of nonchalance, she gathered her chips, adding them to the pot with a decisive push. Each chip was a carefully constructed lie, a piece of the facade she was building to mask her precarious situation. She was all in, not just with the chips in front of her, but with every ounce of her courage and cunning. A collective gasp swept around the table. Dave, shaking his head in disbelief, threw his cards away. "Nope, I'll have nothing left."

Bullfrog, his eyes locked on Jess's unwavering gaze, said, "Well, aren't you a determined lady."

"I'd just give me your money now," Jess replied, her voice cool and steady.

Jess didn't break eye contact, her expression unwavering. Dave, his eyes darting between Jess and Bullfrog, said, "She aint playing."

Bullfrog, his face a mask of frustration and grudging respect, threw his straight flush face down onto the table. With a slow, deliberate motion, Jess laid her cards down.

"WHAT!" Bronko roared, his voice echoing through the pagoda.

"SHE DIDN'T HAVE NOTHING!" Pete shouted, his eyes wide with disbelief.

The table erupted in chaos. Everyone was in complete shock. Bullfrog's eyes widened, his jaw dropping in stunned silence. She had completely bluffed him! It was a hell of a gamble, but it had paid off in spectacular fashion. Jess calmly dragged her winnings closer, her eyes catching Jonny's across the table.

Jonny, a slow smile spreading across his face, murmured, "You dark horse!"

Bullfrog, shaking his head in disbelief, said, "I ain't never been bluffed so bad by a woman before! I'm too impressed to even feel angry about it!"

Jess giggled, a light, musical sound that danced through the smoky air, somehow cutting through the tension that had been building for hours. It was a sound that spoke of intelligence, courage, and a hint of mischief, a combination that both intrigued and captivated Jonny. He didn't just admire her giggle; he admired the woman behind it, the one who had just pulled off the most audacious bluff he'd ever witnessed.

The final round had been a masterclass in psychological warfare. The air in the pagoda had grown thick and heavy, charged with unspoken tension. Every rustle of cards, every clink of chips, every drawn breath seemed amplified. Dave pushed away from the table first, admitting defeat with a sigh. The others began to fall out soon after, each laughing off their losses as their stacks shrank. Bullfrog lingered the longest, weighing the pot against the sting of Jess and Jonny's rising momentum, before finally leaning back with a resigned grunt. He decided to quit while he still had a few dollars left, tapping the table in surrender. That left only Jonny and Jess, the last two standing.

"I told you my crew were good; didn't I tell you?" Bronko crowed, nudging Bullfrog playfully.

"You sure did," Bullfrog admitted, his eyes narrowing as he watched Pete. Pete, oblivious to the intense scrutiny, was practically vibrating with excitement, thoroughly enjoying the spectacle of the final showdown. Bullfrog's gaze, however, held a different quality – a simmering intensity that didn't quite match the jovial atmosphere. He didn't seem particularly interested in the poker game itself, as if the outcome was irrelevant to him. It was almost as if he'd already gotten what he came for, and the rest was just a show.

It all came down to this—Jonny and Jess, the final two. The others gathered close, the table humming with anticipation as the last hand loomed like a storm waiting to break. Friendly banter flickered around the edges, but underneath it lay a charged silence; everyone knew this was the one that mattered.

Jonny set the big blind, steady and unflinching. Jess slid in the small. She checked her cards with that unreadable calm she wore like armour, then matched his bet without a word. The gesture alone was enough to thicken the air. The first three cards were laid down: King of Spades, Queen of Hearts, and Ten of Diamonds.

"Oh, here we go!" Bronko exclaimed, his eyes glued to the board, knowing some big hands were already possible.

Jonny checked his cards, his heart quickening slightly. After a moment of deliberation, threw in a twenty-dollar chip. A collective murmur of anticipation rippled through the onlookers.

"Twenty, huh? I raise it to fifty," Jess declared, throwing in her chips with a decisive flourish.

The outburst was even louder this time, a wave of sound that washed over the table. Pete sat forward so fast that his chair shot back from under him, clattering against the wooden floor.

Jonny, despite himself, felt a surge of admiration. Jess's audacity was both unnerving and incredibly attractive.

"Fifty it is," Jonny replied, meeting her gaze with a steady intensity.

The next card was placed down: the King of Clubs. Over Jonny's shoulder, Bronko caught a glimpse of his cards. He had the King of Diamonds and Queen of Clubs. A strong full house – Kings over Queens.

"Why don't we raise the stakes… One hundred fifty," Jonny announced, pushing a stack of chips into the pot.

The table erupted in excitement once again, a cacophony of gasps and murmurs.

"You are two fearless sons of bitches!" Bullfrog declared, his eyes wide with admiration.

The stakes were higher than they had ever been before. The bets were bigger, the tension thicker, and the poker faces on both Jess and Jonny were utterly unreadable.

"Two hundred!" Jess countered, throwing in another stack of chips.

"This is too crazy!" Sally exclaimed.

Jonny raised an eyebrow, a hint of amusement playing on his lips. He knew his hand was good, damn good. But Jess… she had bluffed Bullfrog out of a small fortune earlier in the night. He wasn't going to make the same mistake. The final card was drawn: the Nine of Spades.

"This is it!" Dave exclaimed, his voice tight with anticipation.

"You ain't bluffing your way into my pocket," Jonny declared, his eyes locked on Jess's.

"We'll see about that," Jess retorted, a hint of a smile playing on her lips.

"I ain't never seen a poker game so intense," Stu muttered, wiping the sweat from his brow.

"All in," Jess announced, pushing all her remaining money onto the table.

Jonny's mind raced. Was she trying to scare him? Was this another elaborate act? It wasn't going to work. He met her gaze, his expression unwavering, and pushed all his chips into the pot, creating a towering mountain of cash and plastic.

"Here we go! Show us your cards!" Sally exclaimed, her voice trembling with excitement.

Jonny revealed his hand "Full house," he announced, his voice confident.

Bronko whistled, shaking his head in admiration. "Damn! That's gonna be hard to beat!"

Bullfrog leaned forward, his eyes narrowed. "The thing with bluffing, little lady… people learn you ain't telling the truth."

"The thing about bluffing… I never make the same mistake twice," Jess retorted, her eyes glinting with triumph.

She revealed her hand: Jack of Spades and Eight of Spades. A moment of stunned silence hung in the air as everyone at the table tried to process the information.

"Holy shit!" Bullfrog exclaimed, breaking the silence.

"She's got a straight!" Bronko shouted, his voice filled with disbelief.

Jonny's face dropped. He had been so sure she was bluffing! He had convinced himself that he could read her, that he had seen through her act. But he had been wrong. Terribly wrong. She had played him perfectly, leading him into a trap with her cunning and her unwavering confidence. Not this time, she had the winning hand, taking home ALL of the winnings. He thought he had her sussed, but he really couldn't read her at all and it was enticing.

"Jess, you won!" Sally cheered, jumping to her feet.

Jonny, despite his disappointment, couldn't help but be impressed. "That was some good playing," he said, extending his hand to Jess.

"There you go," Bullfrog said, sliding her winnings across the table. "Just a little under six hundred bucks."

"You want me to help you carry it, haha?" Pete offered, his eyes gleaming with avarice.

"It's all good, Pete. I have deep pockets." Jess replied, patting her pockets with a wink.

A short while later, they strolled down the quiet, moonlit street, all heading in roughly the same direction.

"Man, I wish I could have put more cash down," Pete lamented, his voice slurring slightly. "Only thing is, I gotta buy wood for the shop. It's going up, worse than gas at the minute. I ain't got anything to carve with."

Dave and Bronko walked close together, a comfortable silence settling between them.

"I'm glad you came, my brother," Bronko said softly, breaking the silence.

"Me too… Thanks for kidnapping me, man," Dave replied, a hint of amusement in his voice.

"Love you, man," Bronko said, his voice thick with emotion.

"I love you," Dave echoed, squeezing Bronko's shoulder.

Bronko knew a night like this might not come again any time soon. It was back to Laurie's control tomorrow. Dave could tell Bronko was fighting back his emotions, a silent testament to the depth of their bond. Jess and Jonny walked ahead, slightly apart from the rest of the group. Jess held a green poker chip, a souvenir from her winning game.

"That was impressive," Jonny said, breaking the comfortable silence.

"My heart was pounding inside," Jess confessed, a hint of vulnerability in her voice.

Jonny chuckled, shaking his head in disbelief. "How'd you learn to play like that?"

"Poker's easy once you learn the rules," Jess replied, shrugging nonchalantly. "I'm just good at knowing people, making it easy to play you all."

"Is that so?" Jonny teased, raising an eyebrow.

"You're an observer, like me," Jess explained, her eyes sparkling with amusement. "Wasn't hard to clock them. Bullfrog, man's got luck, but he's honest. If he was going big, he had something. Pete's not so lucky, he's too easy to read. Dave was going big no matter what, he's got no restrictions tonight. Bronko and Stu couldn't bluff well, and they tried too hard."

"And what about me?" Jonny asked, a hint of challenge in his voice.

"You were a bit harder," Jess admitted, her gaze locking with his. "I couldn't read you as well as the others. But I could tell you were studying the others, too."

"And what about outside the poker?" Jonny pressed, his curiosity piqued.

"You're a good man, Jonny," Jess said softly, a hint of warmth in her voice. "Fun. I can see why the boys are happy to have you back in town."

He liked having her to himself, away from the prying eyes of the group. The others were close enough, but they hung back, engaged in their own conversations, giving Jess and Jonny the space to connect. He could tell Jess appreciated it, too. It was the most she'd spoken all night, the most animated he had seen her.

"How old are you, by the way?" Jonny asked, his curiosity getting the better of him.

"Eighteen," Jess replied. "You?"

"Twenty," Jonny answered.

"Do you miss your parents, being out in Alabama." Jonny asked, his voice gentle.

"I do really miss my mom," Jess admitted, her voice softening. "My dad… isn't around anymore."

"I'm sorry," Jonny said, his voice filled with genuine sympathy.

"Vietnam," Jess replied, her voice slightly croaky.

Jonny could tell this was a difficult topic for Jess, and as much as he wanted to know more, he didn't want to make her uncomfortable.

"That… is shit," Jonny said softly, searching her eyes.

"Yeah…" Jess replied, forcing a smile. "So, what do your parents do?"

"Dad's a lawyer, Mom has a small cake shop back in Kentucky," Jonny explained, his voice matter-of-fact.

"And you didn't want to be a lawyer like your dad?" Jess asked, her curiosity piqued.

"My dad can be an asshole, looks down at a lot of people. Uncle Larry and Aunt Glenda included," Jonny explained, his voice laced with resentment. "I don't like what that job does to people. Nah, I want to be outside, using my hands, you know?"

"Yeah, you don't seem like the suit-and-tie kinda guy," Jess said, smiling. "I like it, wild and free."

"Jess! We're this way!" Sally called out, her voice echoing through the night.

Jess looked back, realising they had walked past their turning. A subtle hint of disappointment flickered across Jonny's face as they prepared to part ways. He wasn't sure when he'd see her again. His work with Larry was going to start tomorrow, so it wouldn't be for a few days. But that was the motto back then – anything could happen at any time. Part of being young and free was living in the moment, day by day.

"I guess I'll see you around," Jonny said, his voice tinged with regret.

"Yeah, see you around, Jonny," Jess replied, her eyes meeting his for a brief, intense moment.

She turned and walked away with Sally and Stu, her laughter echoing in the night air. Jonny watched her go, careful not to let his interest be too obvious to Pete and Dave. So much intrigued him about her – he knew the basics, but felt there was so much more to discover.

Chapter 7 Summers First Cut

Jonny woke to the comforting aroma of pancakes. A quick shower washed away the last vestiges of sleep, and he pulled on his jeans and an old top, a sense of anticipation bubbling inside him. Today was the day he'd finally start learning the trade he'd always dreamed of.

He made his way downstairs, the scent of maple syrup growing stronger with each step. The kitchen was bathed in the warm glow of the morning sun, and his Aunt Glenda was already at the stove, flipping pancakes and humming a quiet tune. His Uncle Larry sat at the table, a steaming mug of coffee at his elbow, engrossed in the morning paper. He was excited. He had always wanted to learn this trade. Today, that dream was finally becoming a reality.

"Morning, honey," Glenda chirped, her voice warm and welcoming. "Hope you like pancakes! I went down to the store early to pick up a mix just for ya!"

"Auntie Glenda, you really didn't have to," Jonny protested, a hint of genuine gratitude in his voice.

"It's your first day at work, let me make a fuss," Glenda insisted, waving away his protest with a playful flick of her wrist.

Larry, who was already halfway through his breakfast, chuckled knowingly. "Wasn't the only person making a fuss of you this morning, boy. Have a look on the porch."

Curiosity, a potent and irresistible force, tugged at Jonny. He screwed up his face in confusion, a question mark etched on his brow, and walked out onto the porch. The sun, already a scorching presence in the sky, beat down on the weathered wooden planks. And there, on the old wooden table, gleaming in the morning light, he saw it. The very chainsaw he'd been admiring in the store, the one on the top shelf, the one he knew was far beyond his current budget. He was even more confused now, his mind racing, trying to decipher the mystery. Who had the money, the generosity, and the inclination to treat him so lavishly? He was close with Bronko, Pete, and Dave, sure, but this didn't feel like something they would do. Too extravagant, too thoughtful. His eyes landed on a note, tucked beneath the chainsaw's handle. He unfolded the crisp paper. The message was brief, written in a bold, confident hand: "Had to put my winnings to good use. Good luck on your first day. J." An uncontrollable smile stretched across his face. They'd just met, and yet she'd spent a significant portion of her winnings on him. A warmth spread through his chest, a happy feeling that settled deep in his bones, a feeling so profound that he knew, in that moment, nothing could get him down.

He walked back inside, the smile still plastered across his face, radiating an almost palpable joy.

"I don't know who 'J' is, but they must be rolling in it," Larry said with a laugh, shaking his head in mock envy. "You lucky man."

"That's so nice of him!" Glenda exclaimed, correcting Larry with a gentle nudge.

"It's a her, actually," Jonny said, his smile widening, a mischievous glint in his eyes. He knew exactly how Larry and Glenda would react to this revelation. Glenda's head snapped up, her eyes widening in surprise, while Larry dropped his newspaper with a dramatic flourish, his gaze locking onto Jonny's with undisguised intrigue. The same question hung in the air between them.

"A girl!?" Glenda echoed, her voice laced with a mixture of surprise and excitement.

Jonny felt a blush creep up his neck, a giddy smile playing on his lips. He felt slightly embarrassed, almost like a little schoolboy caught with a secret crush. "Just a friend I met over the weekend," he mumbled, trying to downplay the significance of the gesture.

Larry teased him with that easy, unfiltered humour he was known for, and Glenda quickly joined in with her own light-hearted jabs. Their playful ribbing only deepened Jonny's embarrassment, though he knew it came from a place of fondness. After a moment, Larry finally took pity on him; he picked up his Stetson from the chair and settled it on his head. "I'll see you later, darlin'," he said, leaning in to kiss Glenda on the cheek.

"Bye, honey, and don't work your nephew too hard!" Glenda called after them as they headed towards the door.

Larry winked at Jonny, a mischievous glint in his eyes. "Not as hard as 'J' does, haha!"

Glenda shook her head in amusement, a fond smile playing on her lips. Larry and Jonny walked down the porch steps towards Larry's faded green truck.

"Alright, my boy," Larry said, clapping Jonny on the shoulder. "We've got some crown cleaning to do down by the bridge into town. You drive."

Larry tossed him the keys, and they made their way to the trees they were ready to work on. They looked up, assessing each branch, formulating their plan. It quickly became apparent that Jonny possessed a natural aptitude for the work. He moved with a fluid grace, scaling the trees with surprising agility, his cuts precise and efficient. It was as if he'd been doing this his whole life, despite never having used a chainsaw professionally before. Larry watched, initially offering a few pointers, but soon fell silent in impressed amusement. A sense of pride swelled in Larry's chest as he observed his nephew thriving in this new environment, finding a purpose and a passion he hadn't known he possessed.

As the hours passed, the heat intensified, the air thick with humidity. Soon, both Jonny and Larry, now shirtless, worked side by side, the rhythmic roar of the chainsaws echoing through the air. Jonny felt a sense of exhilaration he hadn't experienced in years. The physical exertion, the satisfaction of shaping the trees, the bond with his uncle. Larry, too, seemed to be enjoying himself immensely. He'd always been a solitary worker, but having Jonny by his side, sharing the load and the laughter, brought a renewed sense of purpose to his work.

Mid-afternoon arrived, bringing with it a lull in the relentless heat and a shared sense of accomplishment. It was time for a break. They found a comfortable perch amongst the sturdy branches of one of the larger oaks, its thick foliage offering a welcome respite from the sun's harsh glare. They uncapped their water bottles, the cool liquid a welcome balm to their parched throats, and leaned back against the rough bark of the tree, their feet dangling freely in the air.

"Good work, boy," Larry said, breaking the silence, a note of genuine pride in his voice. "We nearly finished a whole two-day job in one."

The peaceful atmosphere was shattered by the sudden roar of engines. The air erupted with the cacophonous sounds of no less than seven motorbikes, speeding across the bridge and heading into town, their chrome gleaming menacingly in the sunlight. Larry's face, previously relaxed and jovial, instantly hardened.

"That's all we need in this town," he muttered, his voice laced with disapproval. "Damned Night Hounds. Been seeing more and more of them in Cedar Bluff lately."

"So I hear," Jonny replied, his gaze following the departing bikes. "Been hearing more and more about 'em ever since I got here."

"You don't go messing around with them, boy," Larry warned, his voice stern. "They aren't the kind to be involved with. I've heard the stories from over in Antioch. Promise me you won't have anything to do with them. When you see one of their hogs, you make sure you walk the other way."

Jonny noticed the genuine fear in Larry's eyes as he spoke about the Night Hounds. This was the largest group of them he had seen since arriving in Cedar Bluff. A troubling thought crossed his mind: Bronko. Was he involved? Bronko had always craved excitement and a sense of belonging, but Jonny knew that the Night Hounds would chew him up and spit him out without a second thought. They carefully climbed down from the tree, their earlier light-hearted mood now replaced by a sense of unease. They surveyed the pile of wood on the ground, a reminder of the work that still needed to be done.

"So, you gonna tell me who this 'J' is?" Larry asked, his earlier concern replaced by a mischievous curiosity. He raised an eyebrow and a big grin spread across his face, a clear indication that he wasn't going to let the subject drop.

"I told you, she's just a friend," Jonny insisted, trying to sound nonchalant. "Met her through a friend of a friend. We had a poker night last night, and she kicked my ass… kicked all of our asses, actually."

"A woman? Damn, son, women like that you either wanna run a mile or never let her go," Larry declared, his eyes twinkling with amusement.

"I think she felt bad; she took a lot from us, haha," Jonny said, trying to downplay the significance of the gift.

"Trust me, son, a woman you just met doesn't just buy you a five-hundred-dollar chainsaw just because she feels bad," Larry countered, his voice filled with worldly wisdom. "She buys you a five-hundred-dollar chainsaw because she likes what she sees."

"You think?" Jonny asked, his brow furrowing in thought.

Jonny's mind, which had been focused on the task at hand, suddenly drifted back to Jess. This was the first time he had consciously thought about her today, and the mere thought sent a familiar flutter through his chest, a feeling he couldn't quite define, but one he knew he wanted to explore further.

Jonny and Larry loaded the last of the leftover logs into the truck. The haul wasn't much, but it would mean something to Pete, whose little wood shop sat in town, squeezed between a barbershop and an old laundrette. He carved whatever he could—bowls, toys, signs, little ornaments—and with money always tight, Jonny and Larry offered to bring him their leftover wood whenever they could. He dropped Larry at home and made his way into town. When he arrived, they carried the logs around the back, Pete let out a laugh as he picked up a chunk of cedar, shaking his head. He started teasing them about the poker game the night before, joking about how Jess had cleaned them all out without breaking a sweat. Then, with a sidelong look that told Jonny he'd been thinking about it for a while, Pete added that she and Jonny seemed to have something—some kind of spark, a bit of chemistry he couldn't miss. The comment hit Jonny harder than he expected; it stirred up the truth he'd been quietly avoiding, the pull toward her that felt stronger every time he thought about her.

The more he thought about her, the more he found himself missing her company, the easy banter, the shared laughter. With others seeming to think she was "into" him, he couldn't help but wonder if there was some truth to it, or if they were simply planting a seed that would inevitably lead to disappointment. Once the wood had been unloaded at the back of Pete's shop, Jonny drove away, back towards Glenda and Larry's, but the thought of Jess still lingered in his mind, a persistent and alluring presence. Instead of continuing straight at the next junction, he impulsively turned left, driving towards Sally's house. A wave of apprehension washed over him as he parked the truck, a sense of unease about whether Jess or Sally would find his sudden appearance strange or inappropriate. He reluctantly got out of the vehicle, steeling himself for a potentially awkward encounter. He walked to the front door and knocked, fighting the urge to turn around and drive away immediately. The door swung open, revealing Sally's kind and welcoming face.

"Jonny! What are you doing here?" Sally asked, her brow furrowing slightly in surprise.

Jonny could sense Sally's confusion, as he asked for Jess. The unspoken questions swirling in her mind. Jess appeared behind Sally, her face lighting up with a smile that looked genuinely happy to see him.

"Hey," Jonny said, his voice softening.

Sally left them to it, disappearing back into the house. Jonny could almost feel the weight of the many questions swirling in Sally's head, the unspoken curiosity about the nature of his visit. They walked down to the sidewalk together, putting some distance between themselves and the house.

"I just… I just wanted to say thank you…" Jonny stammered, the words tumbling out in a rush. "The chainsaw, you really didn't have to."

"I wanted to," Jess replied, her eyes sparkling with sincerity. "I saw the look in your eye when you saw it."

"But that was your money," Jonny protested, still feeling a sense of guilt.

"Money comes and goes," Jess said, shrugging her shoulders dismissively. "Sally and I are getting a job at the grill over the bridge, so it's not like I won't have any."

"Thank you," Jonny said, his voice filled with genuine gratitude.

They grinned at each other, a comfortable silence settling between them, a silent acknowledgment of the connection that was forming between them.

"I'm glad you liked it," Jess said, breaking the silence. "Larry keeping you busy for the rest of the week?"

"Oh yeah!" Jonny exclaimed. "Tree removing tomorrow, cleaning up the trees down near the lake Wednesday."

"Going to the party on Saturday? Tall Oaks," Jess asked, her eyes searching his.

"Uh, yeah… sure," Jonny stammered, caught off guard by the invitation.

"Awesome, let your friends know," Jess said, her smile widening. "Seems to be a small crew of us now, haha."

"I will do…" Jonny replied, feeling a surge of excitement at the prospect of seeing Jess again.

"Good. See you Saturday," Jess said, her eyes locking with Jonny's for a brief but intense moment, before she walked back into the house.

Each day that followed fell into a comfortable rhythm, a blend of hard work, shared laughter, and the quiet satisfaction of a job well done. Jonny quickly proved himself to be a natural, but as Jonny's confidence and competence grew, so too did his thoughts of Jess. She had become a constant presence in his mind, a persistent and alluring distraction that seemed to intensify with each passing day. He found himself replaying their brief encounters, analysing her words and gestures, searching for hidden meanings and subtle signs of reciprocation. He wondered about her, about her life, her dreams, her past. The more he tried to focus on the task at hand, the more Jess seemed to consume his thoughts.

Jonny and Larry laboured beneath the relentless sun, their shoulders glowing a fiery red under the intensity of the heat. Both were shirtless, a familiar sight by now, their tanned skin glistening with sweat as they moved with practiced ease among the branches. Chainsaws snarled and whined. As Jonny paused for a moment, wiping the sweat from his brow, his gaze drifted towards the grassy bank below. He squinted, his eyes struggling to adjust to the glare, and recognised three familiar figures walking towards them.

"Hey Jonny!" Sally's voice carried up to him, her cheerful tone cutting through the din of the chainsaws.

"Looking good up there, dude!" Stu added, his words laced with playful admiration.

Larry, who had been mid-saw, stopped abruptly, his brow furrowing in curiosity. Jonny, his heart suddenly pounding a little faster, recognised Sally, Stu... and Jess.

"What's up, guys!" Jonny called back.

"Friends of yours?" Larry asked, his eyes narrowing slightly as he assessed the approaching trio.

They both made their way safely down to the ground, the chainsaws silenced and secured.

"Well, if it ain't the lady that puts the 'Bluff' into Cedar Bluff!" Jonny exclaimed, a wide grin spreading across his face.

Jess immediately erupted into laughter, her head thrown forward, her eyes sparkling with amusement.

"What are you guys doing here?" Jonny asked, his gaze locking onto Jess's.

"We all had the day off," Sally explained, her smile wide and welcoming. "Thought we'd come keep you company… Jess's idea, actually."

A wave of warmth washed over Jonny, a feeling of pure, unadulterated joy. The fact that she had remembered where he was working, that she had suggested spending their day off with him, filled him with a sense of elation.

"Well, seeing you working so hard in the sun, I thought I'd be nice and share my Clyde May's with you!" Jess announced, a mischievous glint in her eyes. She held up a brand-new bottle of whiskey, the amber liquid glinting in the sunlight.

"Aren't you one big ball of generosity," Jonny teased, his heart swelling with affection.

"I'll send the bill in the post," Jess retorted, her smile playful and inviting.

"Will you two stop flirting already and crack that bottle open," Stu interjected, his voice laced with mock exasperation. He spread his towels on the grass, a clear indication that he intended to settle in for a while, and the others followed suit.

Sally greeted Larry with the easy warmth of someone who'd grown up around him, and the old man's face lit up in that familiar, weathered smile. Jess eased the cork from the bottle with practiced fingers, and passed the bottle around the group.

Jonny took the bottle next. The whiskey was strong and smoky, settling deep and warm in his chest, smoothing out the edges of the day. When he passed it to Jess, she tipped it back with quiet confidence, and the shared look between them said she felt the same burn, the same warmth. She handed the bottle to Larry next, the same way she would to any of the others, her hand steady, her smile easy. And Larry accepted it just as naturally, sliding into their circle without a hint of awkwardness. The group shifted to make room for him, their laughter softening, their banter widening to include him as though he was part of the group. They called him Uncle Larry the way you'd call a friend by a nickname, nothing forced, nothing obligatory—just an easy welcome. In that small moment, he wasn't the older guy dropping in on a bunch of kids; he was one of them, folded seamlessly into the warmth of their little gathering. He took a generous swig, his eyes closing in satisfaction. Larry then turned his gaze towards Jess, a knowing look on his face, his mind piecing together the puzzle. He pointed at her with a curious expression, the unspoken question hanging in the air.

"J," he confirmed, his voice laced with amusement. "Jess," she clarified.

"Well, it's good to meet you, Jess," Larry said, his tone warm and sincere. "You made my nephew a happy man with that chainsaw."

Jess gave Jonny a warm smile. The afternoon unfolded in a languid haze of sunshine, laughter, and whiskey. They basked in the warmth, their faces tilted upwards, soaking in the golden rays, their voices rising and falling in a comfortable rhythm of easy conversation. The bottle of Clyde May's circulated freely.

Meanwhile, high above them, Jonny and Larry continued their work, their figures silhouetted against the bright sky. The roar of their chainsaws provided a constant, almost hypnotic soundtrack to the scene below, a counterpoint to the laughter and chatter of their companions. Jonny, fuelled by the whiskey and the presence of Jess, moved with a renewed energy, he glanced down occasionally; catching glimpses of her.

The afternoon continued, a tapestry woven with threads of easy conversation, playful banter, laughter and the shared warmth of friendship. As the sun began to dip below the horizon, casting long shadows across the landscape, a sense of contentment settled over the group. The whiskey had loosened their inhibitions, and they all felt a little tipsy, a little silly, and thoroughly content. Larry, never one to overindulge, was feeling the effects nonetheless. He pushed himself up from the grass, swaying slightly, his balance a little less steady than usual.

"Alright, boy, let's get this wood in the back of the truck and over to Pete," Larry announced, his words slightly slurred. "You best drive. I can't even see straight."

"Oh shit, I can't even see straight, too," Jonny replied.

Jess shook her head, laughing, clearly more sober than the rest. "I'll drive," she offered, her voice steady and clear. "You boys can't handle your whiskey."

"I'm impressed," Larry said, his eyes widening in admiration. "I ain't never seen a woman handle her whiskey so well."

"And poker! There ain't nothing she can't do!" Stu added, shaking his head in mock disbelief.

"Sally, Stu, jump in the back, you can grab a ride!" Larry called out.

Everyone pitched in, tossing the heavy chunks of wood into the back of the truck, the rhythmic thud of timber against metal echoing through the stillness of the evening. Jess, surprisingly steady despite the afternoon's revelry, slid behind the wheel, with Stu and Sally perched precariously on top of the wood pile in the back.

As the days bled into one another, Jonny's routine was filled with hard work. Each swing of the axe, each pull of the chainsaw cord, was accompanied by an unspoken hope that Jess would suddenly appear with Stu and Sally. But the days passed without a sign. The more he thought about her, the more he realised how much he longed to see her again. He was left to wonder whether she ever thought of him as he thought of her.

Chapter 8 A Growing Presence

Friday night crawled by. Jonny found himself thinking, "One more night to go," the anticipation building with each passing minute. One more night before he could see her again, at the party up at Tall Oaks. Away from the lake, nestled deep within the woods, it was a quiet spot overlooking Antioch, with a breathtaking view of Lake Weiss. Darkness had fallen, and he watched the television aimlessly, his mind preoccupied with a question that tugged at his heart: Why was seeing Jess more enjoyable than the very reason he'd returned to Alabama, his friends, his work alongside Uncle Larry?

Suddenly, the shrill screech of tyres shattered the peaceful evening, followed by the raucous blare of a truck horn.

"JONNY! YO, JONNY, GET OUT HERE!" Bronko's booming voice echoed through the night.

He cautiously peered out the window, his curiosity piqued.

"Do you think he heard us? Shout him again," Pete's voice called out.

"YO, JONNY, HURRY UP!" Bronko bellowed once more.

Jonny grabbed his worn brown leather jacket, and walked out onto the porch, a mixture of confusion and amusement etched on his face.

"What the hell's going on!?" he demanded, his voice laced with a hint of exasperation.

"You're needed, man! We all are! We've got a fallen comrade!" Pete declared, his tone a mix of urgency and concern.

"More like a damn liberation! Laurie's broken up with Dave! His hearts broken, we need to fix it!" Bronko exclaimed, filled with a theatrical flair.

Without hesitation, Jonny hopped into the back of the truck. Pete lurched forward, tyres spitting as they sped away into the night.

Barely fifteen minutes later, they found themselves crammed into a booth at the local bar, the air thick with the smell of stale beer and desperation. Dave sat across from them, his face a mask of misery, tears streaming down his cheeks as he let out an uncontrollable sob. The others exchanged uneasy glances, unsure of how to console him.

"I just can't see a way forward without her," Dave choked out, his voice thick with emotion. He blew his nose into a soaked tissue, the sound muffled and pathetic. "My life is over."

"Hell, he's a broken man… I ain't never seen anything like it," Pete said, his voice filled with a mixture of pity and disbelief.

Bronko backslapped Pete on the arm, a disapproving tut escaping his lips. "That ain't helping. I know this is hard for you to see now, my man, but you will be okay. Life will go forward without her."

"It's gonna hurt until it stops, brother," Jonny added, his voice soft and empathetic.

"I miss her so much," Dave wailed, his voice cracking with grief.

"Why'd she break up with you anyway?" Pete asked, his curiosity overcoming his tact.

"She said she's grown feelings for Mike Stevens," Dave mumbled, his voice barely audible.

"Ginger Mike from the year above us? Ginger Julie's brother?" Jonny asked, his eyebrows shooting up in surprise.

"Well, shit, I'm beating him up," Pete declared.

"Pete, you couldn't beat up a damn slowworm," Bronko scoffed, rolling his eyes.

"She said if she stays with me, she'll end up bored out of her brains living in Cedar Bluff her whole life with my roadkill friends," Dave revealed, his voice filled with pain.

"Man, let me tell you something!" Bronko began, his voice rising with passion. "You're a way, way better person than she could ever be! One hundred times better. All she did was look down her nose at people and boss you about, what you're doing, who you're seeing. She was controlling you, my brother"

"Do you guys really think I'll be okay?" Dave asked, his voice filled with doubt.

Jonny let Bronko take the lead, knowing they were close and that Bronko's words would carry more weight. "Hell yeah, man. Just think what you can do now, there's a party up at Tall Oaks tomorrow, Big Rick is taking his karaoke, fun, beers, and us three. Just like the poker night last weekend. Remember how much fun you had? With no restrictions," Bronko declared, his voice filled with enthusiasm.

"That was pretty fun," Dave admitted, a flicker of a smile gracing his lips.

"I ain't gonna leave your side, bro. I'll help you through this, anything you need. I got you," Bronko reassured, his voice filled with genuine care. "What you need right now… Is fun!" Bronko declared, his eyes twinkling with mischief.

Talk of the evening drifted naturally into plans, and Pete—always the one chasing a bit of harmless adventure—brightened at the idea of the drive-in showing that night. A film was playing out by the highway, and if they cut through the woods, he said, they could slip in without paying. The suggestion earned a burst of laughter from Bronko, who clapped him on the back as if it were the best idea he'd heard all week. Dave mentioned that Amityville Horror was on the schedule. And while the group tossed possibilities back and forth, Bronko stepped away already plotting something, telling them to meet him outside with a conspiratorial grin that promised trouble.

Wondering what he was up to, Pete, Dave, and Jonny walked outside, waiting on the sidewalk, having no idea what Bronko had in store. About five minutes later, he snuck out of the bar with his arms full of beer bottles, his eyes darting around nervously.

"GO, GO, QUICK!!" Bronko hissed urgently.

"What the! Did you steal those!?" Jonny asked, his eyes widening in disbelief.

"Yeah, man, quick, we gotta get out of here before Big Rick catches me!" Bronko exclaimed, his voice filled with a mixture of excitement and panic.

They laughed at Bronko's audacity and ran off, making their way through the dark woods, drinking beers as they stumbled through the undergrowth. The distant sound of the movie's soundtrack guided their way. They climbed the fence, the cold metal biting into their skin, and snuck into the drive-in area, ducking between the parked cars, their loud whispers a futile attempt to maintain some semblance of quiet. They settled down between two vehicles, the flickering screen casting eerie shadows on their faces.

A few rows in front, he noticed Stu's truck, the familiar vehicle instantly recognisable. Stu's head popped over the top of the cab, silhouetted against the flickering screen.

"That's Beef Stu's truck!" Pete exclaimed, his eyes widening in surprise.

Jonny's gaze instinctively searched the truck, his heart skipping a beat as his thoughts immediately turned to Jess, wondering if *she* was there too. They snuck over to the truck, Bronko banging his hands on the sides, making Sally and Stu jump in surprise. Jonny walked over, and lo and behold, Jess was also sitting in the truck with them, her eyes immediately locking with his, as if they had both been searching for each other.

"Hey again, getting used to bumping into you around town," Jonny said, his voice a mixture of amusement and anticipation.

"It's becoming a habit," Jess replied, her eyes twinkling with mischief.

They filled Sally, Stu, and Jess in on what had happened with Dave, though Dave himself seemed content enough now, buoyed by his friends' efforts to lift his spirits and the mischief they'd just gotten away with sneaking in. The others welcomed the two of them without hesitation, they all crammed into the back of the truck, the space becoming increasingly tight. Jonny and Jess's arms were pressed tightly together, a subtle electricity passing between them. He took a sip of his stolen beer.

"Are you gonna share or keep it all for yourself?" Jess teased, her eyes twinkling with playful challenge.

Jonny offered her the bottle, a nervous flutter in his stomach.

Their fingers brushed as she took it from him, a fleeting moment of contact that sent a jolt of electricity through his veins. He watched, captivated, as she took a sip. The movie itself had become more of a backdrop to the real entertainment: their own antics. Sharing stolen beers, trading wisecracks, and generally making the most of their illicit drive-in adventure. Dave, though still clearly hurting, managed a few genuine smiles, spurred on by Bronko's relentless teasing and Pete's over-the-top reactions to the film's jump scares. Jonny and Jess, their arms still pressed together in the cramped space, exchanged knowing glances. However, their boisterous fun wasn't going unnoticed. A chorus of irritated shushes emanated from the surrounding cars, punctuated by the occasional glare over a lowered window. Undeterred, Bronko simply raised his voice, offering a mock apology before launching into a loud, off-key rendition of the film's theme music, earning a fresh wave of complaints and a few grudging chuckles.

Sally and Pete eagerly jumped down from the truck bed, with a mission, more popcorn! Their footsteps muffled by the soft grass, and made their way towards the brightly lit kiosk near the entrance, leaving behind the comforting darkness of their makeshift viewing area. As they approached the kiosk, a beat-up van screeched to a halt beside them, its presence immediately unsettling. The side door slid open with a jarring, aggressive motion, revealing three imposing figures who could only be described as bikers, their leather-clad bodies and menacing expressions leaving no doubt as to their affiliation: the infamous Night Hounds.

"What the—!" Pete began, his words cut short by the sudden eruption of violence.

Before he could react, one of the bikers lunged forward, punching Pete hard in the face with a sickening thud. Pete let out a pained "ooft," his body reeling from the impact. Sally screamed, her voice piercing the night air, a desperate cry for help that seemed to hang unanswered in the vast expanse of the drive-in. The person inside the kiosk, a young attendant caught completely off guard, recoiled in fear, unsure of what to do in the face of such blatant aggression. The three bikers, their movements swift and coordinated, grabbed Pete, their hands like vices, and dragged him towards the van. With a final shove, they forced him inside, the side door slamming shut with a resounding clang that echoed through the night. The van roared to life, its engine spitting and sputtering as it accelerated away, the tyres spinning wildly and kicking up a cloud of dust and gravel. Sally, her heart pounding in her chest, stood frozen for a moment, the image of Pete's terrified face seared into her memory. With a surge of adrenaline, she turned and ran back towards the group, her footsteps pounding against the soft earth, her breath coming in ragged gasps as she desperately sought the safety and comfort of her friends.

"HELP! HELP!" Sally's voice pierced the night, a raw, desperate cry that cut through the laughter and murmur of the drive-in, sending a chill down everyone's spine.

Stu, his face etched with concern, immediately jumped down from the truck bed, his arms outstretched to console her. "What is it!?" he asked, his voice filled with urgency.

"Where's Pete?" Jonny demanded, his eyes scanning the crowd, a knot of dread tightening in his stomach.

"THEY TOOK HIM... THEY..." Sally stammered, her words fragmented by sobs, her body trembling uncontrollably.

"Shit," Bronko muttered, his face paling, the playful glint in his eyes replaced by a hardened resolve.

Jonny and Dave, their faces now masks of grim determination, jumped down from the back of the truck, their movements swift and purposeful. Sally took a shaky breath, her chest heaving, her eyes wide with terror. "I think it was the Night

Hounds," she whispered, the name hanging in the air like a curse.

"What the hell do the Night Hounds want with Pete!? He ain't never hurt a fly," Dave exclaimed, his voice filled with disbelief and anger.

"That don't matter right now," Jonny said, his voice cutting through the rising tension. "Stu, throw me your keys, we need to find him!"

Without hesitation, Stu tossed Jonny the keys, the small metal object glinting in the dim light. They all piled into the truck, the air thick with a mixture of fear and adrenaline. Jonny slammed the key into the ignition, the engine roaring to life, shattering the relative peace of the drive-in. With a screech of tyres, they sped away, leaving behind the flickering screen and the unsuspecting crowd, their mission clear: to find Pete.

They drove through the night, the headlights cutting through the darkness as they desperately searched for the van that had snatched Pete away. Frustration gnawed at Jonny, a growing sense of dread consuming him as he imagined what Pete was enduring.

Inside what appeared to be an abandoned barn, hay scattered haphazardly across the dirt floor, Pete sat hunched beneath a single, harsh lightbulb, his face already marred by a trickle of blood seeping from his nose. Four hulking figures, their faces grim and unyielding, stood guard, their presence a silent threat. The heavy wooden door creaked open, and Bullfrog strode in, his eyes glinting with a cold, predatory intensity.

"Bullfrog!? I thought we were friends… What'd I ever do to you!?" Pete gasped, his mouth filling with the coppery taste of blood.

"Who brings the pot through Cedar Bluff?" Bullfrog demanded, getting right down to business.

"What!?" Pete stammered, his mind struggling to comprehend the sudden shift in their relationship.

"I'm not a patient man, Pete. Why don't you just go easy on yourself and tell me," Bullfrog said, his eyes narrowing, his patience wearing thin.

"That ain't a Night Hound problem… It ain't in Antioch," Pete retorted, his voice defiant despite the pain.

Bullfrog's response was immediate and brutal, his fist connecting with Pete's face once more, the impact sending a searing jolt of pain through his body. "Cedar Bluff is our turf now. Where are you getting the drugs from?"

Pete found himself caught between a rock and a hard place, his loyalty to his friends pitted against the very real threat to his life. Bronko had always provided him with marijuana, a steady supply that he never had to pay for, a gesture of friendship that now carried a deadly price. Bullfrog clenched his fist and Pete braced himself for another crushing blow, his body tensing in anticipation.

Meanwhile, Jonny, consumed by worry and guilt, pulled the truck over to the side of the road, the sudden stop sending a jolt through the vehicle. They all piled out, the cool night air offering little comfort to their frayed nerves. Jonny paced back and forth, his mind racing, his frustration mounting with each passing second. He felt responsible for Pete, knowing that his friend's easy-going nature and unwavering loyalty made him an easy target to the Night Hounds.

Jess approached Jonny, seemingly the only presence that had the ability to calm him. "Surely, if it's the Night Hounds, they'd have taken him to Antioch, right?" Jess suggested, clinging to a sliver of hope.

The others nodded, she had a point. Jess and Jonny stepped away from the others, their voices dropping to a hushed whisper.

"I've got a bad feeling..." Jess began, her eyes locking onto Jonny's. "Bullfrog... He was questioning Pete at the poker night about the drugs. What if... What if they have him?"

Jonny's gaze snapped towards Bronko, his eyes narrowing with suspicion. He walked past Jess, his movements purposeful and intimidating, and confronted Bronko, his voice low and dangerous.

"Tell me about Bullfrog," Jonny demanded, his gaze unwavering. "Is he one of the Night Hounds?".

"How's this going to help us find Pete?" Bronko deflected, his unease growing.

"IS HE A NIGHT HOUND!?" Jonny roared, his patience snapping, his frustration boiling over.

Bronko knew he couldn't evade the truth any longer, the weight of his deception pressing down on him. "Yeah... Shit, yeah, he's a big player in their army," he admitted. Jonny's frustration with Bronko grew to a new level, after playing down who Bullfrog was on their poker night.

A flicker of recognition crossed Bronko's face, a memory surfacing from the depths of his mind. It wasn't long before they had located the abandoned barn, its dilapidated structure a stark contrast to the surrounding fields. Sally and Jess stayed by the car, their faces etched with worry as they watched Jonny, Stu, Dave, and Bronko disappear into the darkness.

Inside the barn, Pete was a bloody and bruised mess, his body trembling with pain and fear.

"Why don't you just tell me where you get the drugs from, Pete?" Bullfrog pressed, his voice menacingly calm. "Who are you covering for? Give me a name, and this can all be over... Is it Bronko... Your friend? Is that why you're not talking?"

The heavy wooden door was kicked open with explosive force, sending one of Bullfrog's henchmen sprawling to the floor. Jonny, Dave, and Stu strode into the barn, their faces hardened with determination, their bodies tense and ready for a fight.

"Yo, Bullfrog," Jonny said, his voice ringing with defiance, "you wanna hit someone... come hit me!"

The barn erupted into chaos as Jonny's challenge hung in the air, Bullfrog's eyes narrowing on Jonny with a guttural roar, Bullfrog lunged forward, his massive frame a force to be reckoned with, and Jonny met him head-on, in a brutal exchange of blows. Bullfrog's strength was undeniable, each punch carrying the weight of a sledgehammer, but Jonny was quick and agile, dodging and weaving, landing precise strikes that chipped away at Bullfrog's defences. Meanwhile, Stu and Dave found themselves locked in a fierce struggle with the other Night Hounds, a whirlwind of fists and fury as they fought to protect their friend.

Above the fray, Bronko scrambled onto the lower section of the barn's roof, his trusty slingshot in hand, and began firing a barrage of stones, peppering the Night Hounds with painful projectiles, disrupting their attacks and providing much-needed support to his friends below. Hearing the commotion from the roadside, Jess's instincts kicked into high gear. Grabbing a crowbar from the back of the truck, its cold steel reassuring in her grip, she told Sally to stay put, her voice firm and resolute, before disappearing into the darkness, determined to even the odds.

Back inside the barn, Jonny, battered but unbowed, finally managed to gain the upper hand, landing a series of rapid blows that sent Bullfrog crashing to the ground. He quickly untied Pete, helping him to his feet, and together they stumbled towards the exit, desperate to escape the confines of the barn. As they emerged into the night, Bullfrog, fuelled by rage and humiliation, staggered to his feet and gave chase, his eyes burning with vengeance. But just as he was about to catch them, Jess emerged from the shadows, a figure of righteous fury, and swung the crowbar with all her might, connecting with Bullfrog's groin in a sickening thud. He crumpled to the ground, gasping in agony, and before he could recover, Jess delivered a final, decisive blow to his face, the crowbar connecting with a resounding crack. Bullfrog's eyes rolled back in his head, and he slumped into unconsciousness, defeated and humiliated. A stunned silence fell over the group, broken only by Pete's ragged breathing. Jonny, Stu, and Dave stared at Jess in awe, their faces a mixture of shock and admiration. She stood there, crowbar in hand.

"Get him out of here!" Jess commanded, her voice sharp and urgent, snapping them back to reality.

The remaining Night Hounds were groggily stirring, attempting to regain their footing, their eyes filled with a mixture of pain and fury. Jess, her movements swift, slammed the barn door shut and wedged the crowbar between the locking mechanism, effectively barricading their pursuers inside.

Bronko, his face a mask of relief, ran into the scene, his arms outstretched to help Pete. Together, they guided him towards the back of the truck, mindful of his injuries. Jonny jumped into the driver's seat, his hands gripping the steering wheel tightly, and with a surge of power, they sped away into the night, leaving the chaos and violence behind them, seeking refuge in the familiar safety of Bronko's trailer back in Cedar Bluff.

Pete sat on the edge of the truck bed, his body swaying slightly, his face pale and drawn. Sally gently held a makeshift ice pack to his bruised head, while he tilted his head back in an attempt to stem the flow of blood from his nose.

"I'll be fine!" Pete insisted, his voice slurred.

"Pete, you're concussed!" Sally countered, her voice laced with worry.

"What did he want?" Bronko asked, his voice tight with anxiety, his eyes filled with guilt.

"To know where the drugs came from… Don't worry, Bronko, I didn't sell you out," Pete replied, his voice filled with loyalty, his words a silent promise.

Bronko's face remained etched with worry, the realisation that his involvement with the Night Hounds was now impacting his friends weighing heavily on his conscience. Jonny and Jess, their faces illuminated by the truck's taillights, hung back from the others, their eyes locking in a silent acknowledgment of the night's events.

"Thanks for saving our asses back there," Jonny said, his voice filled with gratitude, his eyes reflecting the flickering lights.

"I'm just glad we found him," Jess replied, her voice soft but sincere, her gaze fixed on Pete's battered form.

"That was on you, too… Thank you, Jess," Jonny said, his voice filled with admiration, his eyes conveying a depth of emotion he couldn't quite express.

"You can thank me tomorrow at the Tall Oaks party... Clyde May's on you," Jess said, a playful smile gracing her lips, breaking the tension that had gripped them.

"Deal," Jonny replied, his voice filled with amusement, his eyes sparkling with anticipation.

"Alright, we're gonna shoot off before them Night Hounds circle back around," Stu announced, his voice filled with urgency, his eyes scanning the darkness.

"You coming, Jess?" Sally asked.

Jess nodded, her gaze lingering on Jonny for a moment before turning away. "See you tomorrow," she said.

As Stu, Sally, and Jess disappeared into the darkness, their taillights fading into the distance, Dave approached Jonny, his face thoughtful, his eyes filled with curiosity.

"You and her seem to be close," Dave observed, his voice casual but probing.

"What are you talking about?" Jonny deflected, his cheeks flushing slightly, his heart skipping a beat.

"Chatting on your own away from everyone else... Do you like her?" Dave pressed, his voice gentle but persistent.

Jonny knew he could be honest around Dave, one of his oldest friends, a confidant he trusted implicitly, a man whose feet were firmly planted on the ground. "Yeah... I think I do," he admitted, his eyes fixed on the ground.

"Well, you know what you need to do, brother," Dave said, clapping Jonny on the back, his voice filled with encouragement. "She'll keep you on your toes."

It was nice for Jonny to hear that from Dave, a subtle nudge of encouragement that affirmed his feelings and eased his anxieties. The next day seemed to fly by, a blur of anticipation and nervous energy. Pete, still recovering from his ordeal, stayed behind to rest, leaving Jonny, Jess, Dave, Bronko, Stu, and Sally to head to the Tall Oaks party. They spent the evening together, enjoying the lively atmosphere and their ever-wild sense of friendship, but Jonny found himself increasingly distracted. He was desperate for some alone time with Jess, his heart pounding with a mixture of excitement and trepidation. The party was in full swing, the sounds of laughter and music filling the air. Big Rick's karaoke machine was a focal point, with people belting out their favourite tunes, some with impressive talent and others with hilarious enthusiasm. The air was thick with the smell of barbecue and beer, and the bonfire crackled merrily. Despite the atmosphere, Jonny couldn't shake his nervousness. He wanted to finally express the feelings that had been building between them, but he was paralysed by uncertainty, unsure of what to say or how to make the moment perfect.

The music hammered from the nearby stage, each bass note a thrum against their chests. Jonny, perched on one of the mismatched wooden chairs scattered near the edge of the crowd, found his thoughts snagging, a restless current pulling him between Jess and a distant concern for Pete. Across the way, Bronko held court, his booming laughter a familiar landmark in the chaotic landscape of the party. He was a perpetual motion machine, drawing people in with his infectious energy and easy charm.

"Jonny! Jonny!" Jess's voice, a warm thread through the din, snagged his attention. "You okay? You're quiet tonight."

"I'm fine," he said, perhaps a little too quickly. "Ready for your first hangover?" He said, forcing a smile.

A slow smile spread across her face. "Bring it on."

The drinks arrived in a flurry of clinking bottles and boisterous laughter, and the party truly ignited. Jonny and Jess found themselves caught up in the infectious energy, trading playful banter and daring each other to increasingly ridiculous feats. It started with a simple challenge: who could chug their beer the fastest? A brief moment of hesitation, a shared glance, and then a silent agreement. They raised their bottles in a mock salute; their eyes locked in fierce competition. As the last drops disappeared, a thunderous roar erupted from the crowd. "CHUG! CHUG! CHUG!" The chant echoed through the air, fuelled by the sheer absurdity of the moment.

Emboldened by the attention, Jonny and Jess escalated their competition, transforming the party into a personal battle of boozing prowess. They started taking turns ordering increasingly potent concoctions, each trying to outdo the other in their ability to down the foul-tasting mixtures without flinching. Then, they moved on to a game of "shot for shot," downing shot after shot of whatever liquor was closest at hand, their faces flushed and their laughter growing louder with each round.

With each challenge, the crowd's fascination grew. The karaoke singers were all but forgotten as the spotlight shifted to Jonny and Jess, their infectious energy drawing everyone in. Cheers and jeers followed their every move, the air thick with anticipation. Bets were placed, sides were chosen, and the party became a battleground of good-natured rivalry. It was clear that something special was brewing between them, a spark of attraction that was amplified by the competitive spirit and the shared laughter. The night was young, and the crowd was eager to see what Jonny and Jess would do next, their impromptu contest transforming the Tall Oaks party into a night to remember.

"Feeling beat yet?" Jonny asked, a playful smirk tugging at his lips.

Jess tossed her hair back, a spark of defiance in her eyes. "I'm just getting started."

With Bronko ensuring Dave's spirits remained high, and Sally and Stu lost in their own cozy world, Jonny and Jess found themselves almost adrift in their own bubble, a pocket of near-privacy within the bustling group. Then, the opening chords of "Sweet Home Alabama" ripped through the air, the resonant strings instantly igniting a wave of recognition and cheers from the crowd. It was an anthem, a guaranteed crowd-pleaser.

Bronko, seized by the infectious energy, surged forward, grabbing Jonny's arm. "Come on, man! This is your song!"

Jonny recoiled, a flicker of panic in his eyes. "What!? No… No, no, no."

"Get up there, bro!" Bronko insisted, his grin unwavering.

Sally mirrored Bronko's actions, seizing Jess's hand and dragging her towards the stage. "Come on, Jess!"

"NO!" Jess protested, digging her heels in.

"Everybody loves you two tonight!" Sally declared, her voice ringing with mischievous glee.

Before they could mount a proper escape, Jonny and Jess found themselves unceremoniously hoisted onto the makeshift stage – little more than a raised wooden platform nestled amongst the trees – the roar of the crowd a wall of sound that effectively sealed their fate. They exchanged a wide-eyed glance, each mirroring the other's mixture of fear and bewildered amusement. The forest, usually a place of quiet solitude, now vibrated with the chaotic energy of the party.

The initial moments on stage were a blur of awkwardness. Jonny gripped the microphone stand as if it were a lifeline, while Jess stood frozen beside him, her eyes wide with a mixture of panic and disbelief. "Sweet Home Alabama" seemed to mock their discomfort, the cheerful melody a stark contrast to the knot of anxiety in their stomachs. Hesitantly, Jonny began to sing the first verse, his voice thin and reedy, barely audible above the enthusiastic, if slightly off-key, chorus of the crowd that surged around the base of the small stage. Jess, after a moment of frozen hesitation, picked up the second line, her voice initially trembling and uncertain, but gradually gaining strength as she found the rhythm of the song. The crowd, sensing their initial reluctance, roared with encouragement, their cheers and applause washing over them like a wave. Bit by bit, something shifted. As they traded lines in the verses, a shared grin flickered between them. Then came the chorus, and their voices joined together, finding a surprising harmony. With each passing line, their voices grew stronger, their confidence encouraged by the energy of the crowd. Jonny began to move, his stiff posture loosening as he found himself caught up in the infectious beat. Jess, emboldened by his newfound enthusiasm, started to dance, her initial awkwardness melting away as she connected with the music and the energy of the crowd. By the time the chorus rolled around again, they were singing at the top of their lungs, their voices blending together in a surprisingly harmonious duet. The crowd responded in kind, their cheers reaching a fever pitch as Jonny and Jess, now completely lost in the moment, gave it their all. The forest around them echoing with the joyous sounds of music and celebration. By the final chords, Jonny and Jess were transformed, their initial nervousness replaced by a triumphant exhilaration. They stood side-by-side, breathless and beaming, as the crowd erupted in a deafening ovation, a testament to their unexpected and utterly captivating performance.

The cheers and backslaps of their friends enveloped them as they rejoined the crowd, their friends engulfing them, a boisterous wave of congratulations washing over them, their voices a joyous cacophony of praise and playful ribbing after their unexpected performance on stage.

"Yo, you guys rocked it!" Bronko boomed, slapping Jonny on the back.

"I didn't know you had that in you, man," Dave added, a surprised grin on his face.

"Neither did I!" Jonny admitted, still buzzing from the adrenaline.

"That was so scary!" Jess exclaimed, still shaking.

"You were both amazing!" Sally gushed.

"Felt like I was at a damn rock concert!" Stu declared. "I wish Pete could have seen you both." A shadow crossed his face at the mention of their absent friend.

Bronko, ever the provider, stepped forward. "Big Rick liked you two so much he gave me this to give to you!" He presented them with a small bottle of Clyde Mays whiskey. "Gonna help him set up the fireworks now."

Bronko grinned and headed off, leaving them to navigate the now-calming crowd. The energy of the performance began to dissipate, the party resuming its previous rhythm. Jonny looked at Jess, both still slightly dazed by what had just transpired.

"Whiskey?" Jonny offered, holding up the bottle.

Jess pressed her hand to her chest. "I think I need a minute sat down… But yes, to the whiskey."

They navigated their way through the throng of revellers to the quieter outer edge of the party, finding a secluded spot by the dark, looming forest. Settling onto the cool earth, they passed the bottle back and forth, each taking a slow, contemplative sip.

"That was pretty wild," Jonny said, breaking the comfortable silence.

"Never done anything like that before," Jess admitted. "I hate all eyes on me."

"I kinda noticed that about you," Jonny said, a thoughtful expression on his face.

"Oh yeah?" Jess challenged, raising an eyebrow.

"Yeah, when the group gets big, you go quieter. I figured it's because of the observing. Studying everyone else."

Jess faintly nodded, a flicker of surprise in her eyes, as if he'd glimpsed a hidden part of her. "Well, don't you just have me all figured out."

"Haha, I'm trying… But you're a hard girl to read. It's like you got this whole heart-on-your-sleeve thing… but I don't know, there also seems like a side you don't want anyone to see, what you're thinking, what you're feeling… Like a coin. Two sides"

"I'm impressed." Jess took another sip of the whiskey; her gaze fixed on the dark woods. "You, on the other hand…" Jess paused, her eyes meeting his. "I can read you like a book. You're a good man, Jonny. Loyal. I'm glad I met you."

Unintentionally their eyes locked, an undeniable chemistry sparking between them that neither could ignore. Unable to look away. The soaring guitar solo from "More Than a Feeling" by Boston suddenly filled the air, seeming to amplify the emotions swirling between them. Seizing the moment,

Jonny leaned in slowly, his gaze never leaving hers. Knowing this moment would change the summer, for the better or for the worst. Jess mirrored his movement, her eyes reflecting a mixture of anticipation and desire. Their lips met, a soft, tentative pressure that sent an electric current through Jonny's entire being. The first firework exploded in the sky behind them, painting the forest in a fleeting burst of vibrant colour.

Breaking the kiss, they gazed at each other, the intimacy palpable.

"You've no idea how long I've been wanting to do that," Jonny confessed, his voice husky.

Jess's lips curved into a playful smile. "Then don't stop."

They kissed again, this time with more passion, their hands finding each other as the fireworks illuminated the night sky. Lost in their own private world, they were oblivious to the spectacle behind them. Sally, noticing their embrace, poked Stu on the shoulder and nodded in their direction. A knowing smile spread across Stu's face. Bronko and Dave looked back, donning the same expression as Sally and Stu.

"About time," Stu murmured, a hint of satisfaction in his voice.

Jonny and Jess, oblivious to their friends' knowing glances, smiled at each other, their eyes shining with a newfound excitement.

"You wanna ditch these guys tomorrow and spend the day… just us?" Jonny asked, his voice laced with hope.

Jess's smile widened. "Sounds perfect."

Chapter 9 Beneath a sky of new stars

The rhythmic click-click of a lighter lid echoed in the stillness, the sound a nervous counterpoint to the already sweltering morning. Jess leaned against the rough bark of a tree, her mind seemingly miles away as her thumb repeatedly flicked the lighter open and shut, a tiny flame dancing momentarily before being extinguished. The air hung heavy with the promise of another scorching day. The rumble of an engine broke the silence as Jonny pulled up beside her on his vintage 1974 Harley Sportster. He was clad in his familiar brown leather jacket, the soft leather moulded to his form, worn jeans, and a simple black t-shirt peeking from beneath the jacket's open front. A genuine smile bloomed on Jess's face as he cut the engine.

"Morning!" Jonny greeted, his voice warm and genuine.

Jess pushed herself off the tree, closing the distance between them and leaning in to kiss him, a kiss that was both passionate and lingering.

"I could get used to mornings like this," Jonny murmured against her lips, his voice slightly husky.

"I get you all to myself today," Jess replied, her words a promise and a shared desire.

Jonny felt a surge of contentment wash over him, knowing she felt the same way. A whole day, free from the usual interruptions of their friends, a chance to truly connect. Yet, beneath the excitement, a tremor of nervousness flickered. What if it became awkward? What if she changed her mind? What if there were uncomfortable silences? He desperately wanted this day to work, to be special, to live up to the anticipation that had been building.

"Another lighter?" Jonny asked, noticing the familiar object in her hand, trying to sound casual.

"Had to get me a souvenir from Cedar Bluff!" Jess quipped, a playful glint in her eyes.

Jonny smiled, relieved by her light-heartedness. "You ever ridden on one of these before?" he asked, nodding towards his bike.

"Once," Jess replied, a hint of mischief in her voice.

"You know to hold on to me tight, then?" Jonny teased, raising an eyebrow.

"I wasn't on the back," she said with a wink, her gaze locking with his, sending a shiver of anticipation down his spine.

Jess giggled, the sound light and carefree, as she swung her leg over the back of the bike, settling in behind him. With a twist of the throttle, they roared to life, speeding away together. No helmets, just the wind whipping through their hair and a shared sense of freedom. Jess instinctively wrapped her arms tightly around Jonny's waist, holding on for dear life. Both had not felt this kind of unadulterated happiness in a long time. They sped down the dirt track towards the lake, a secluded spot they had prearranged, a sanctuary where they knew they wouldn't be disturbed, a place where they could finally be alone.

The Harley rumbled to a stop, the engine's vibrations fading into the stillness of the secluded area. Jonny killed the engine, and the sudden silence was almost deafening, broken only by the gentle lapping of water against the shore and the distant chirping of unseen birds.

The small, sandy beach was tucked away, almost hidden by the dense wall of trees that lined the water's edge. Towering pines, their needles a vibrant green against the clear blue sky, stood shoulder-to-shoulder with bare-branched hardwoods. The trees cast long, dappled shadows across the sand, creating a mosaic of light and shade that danced with the gentle breeze.

Jonny swung his leg over the bike and hopped off, the leather of his jacket creaking softly. He reached back to help Jess dismount, his hand lingering on hers for a moment longer than necessary. Jess slid off the back of the bike, her jeans brushing against his.

Jonny leaned the Harley onto its kickstand, the metallic clink echoing in the quiet air. He pulled off his leather jacket, draping it over the handlebars. Jess, meanwhile, wandered closer to the water's edge, kicking off her boots and digging her toes into the cool sand. She took a deep breath, her eyes closed, her face tilted towards the sun, as if soaking up its warmth and energy.

The scene was simple, almost unremarkable, yet it held a certain magic, a sense of possibility and promise. It was a place where they could escape the noise and distractions of the outside world, a place where they could finally be alone, together, and get to know each other without the interference of anyone else.

The day unfolded like a lazy summer dream. Before even thinking about the water, Jonny retrieved the half-empty bottle of Clyde May's whiskey they'd won at the party the night before from his saddlebag. They sat on the edge of the towel, taking turns sipping the liquor, the warmth spreading through their veins, easing any lingering tension.

With a shared glance and a silent understanding, they decided it was time to brave the water. The lake, surprisingly cool at first, quickly became refreshing under the blazing sun. Their laughter echoed across the water as they splashed each other, their playful banter a mix of sarcasm and genuine affection.

A challenge was issued. A race to the old wooden pontoon anchored a short distance from the shore. Jonny, confident in his athletic ability, took an early lead, but Jess, fuelled by determination and a competitive spirit, quickly gained ground. With a final burst of energy, she surged ahead, reaching the pontoon just a fraction of a second before him.

She perched on the edge of the pontoon, breathless but triumphant, her wet hair plastered to her face. Jonny grumbled good-naturedly, hauling himself onto the pontoon beside her.

Jonny, breathless from the race, grinned at her, genuinely impressed. "How'd you learn to swim like that?!" he asked, still slightly winded.

Jess, perched on the edge of the pontoon, tossed her head back, sending droplets of water flying. "I was just determined to beat you, haha," she said, her eyes sparkling with playful triumph.

Jonny chuckled, shaking his head. "I'm starting to realise 'determined' is your middle name," he teased, the admiration clear in his voice.

"When I set my mind on something, I do it!" she declared, her tone light-hearted and confident, as if stating a simple fact of life.

"How's the hangover today?" he asked, a mischievous glint in his eyes.

Jess wrinkled her nose playfully. "Non-existent, nice try though," she said playfully. A smile tugged at the corner of his lips. He reached out, his hand finding hers, his fingers lacing through hers easily. He looked at her, a comfortable warmth settling between them, and then he leaned in and kissed her. It was a sweet, easy kiss, a comfortable expression of their connection, a simple enjoyment of the moment. The world around them was still there, the sun on their skin, the gentle lapping of the water, but for that moment, it was just them, connected and content.

The swim back was more leisurely. They floated on their backs, side-by-side, gazing up at the endless blue sky, the sun warming their skin. The silence wasn't awkward, but comfortable, filled with a sense of shared contentment.

Back on shore, they spread out a large, worn towel on the sand, letting the sun dry their skin. Jonny leaned back against the trunk of a sturdy pine tree, its rough bark providing a surprisingly comfortable support. Jess nestled beside him, resting her head in his lap.

There were moments of intense eye contact, unspoken emotions flickering between them. Jonny gently stroked Jess's hair, his fingers tracing the delicate curve of her cheek. She closed her eyes, savouring the feeling of his touch, a sense of safety and comfort washing over her.

"So how come you're not studying in Michigan?" Jonny asked, watching Jess's face. He saw a subtle shift in her expression when he mentioned her home state.

"Honestly, I've been itching to get out of Michigan for years," she said, her voice just a little too casual. "Ever since Dad and Nam..."

Jonny saw her jaw tighten, a subtle clenching that betrayed the pain she was trying to suppress. He knew that mentioning her father was like poking a bruise, so he quickly changed the subject. "I hear you. What does your mom do?"

Jess sighed, a weary sound that seemed to carry the weight of the world. "Her best. Years haven't been kind to her since Dad. Wrong kind of boyfriends, you know. She works in the local grocery store when she can. We're close, I just can't help but feel sad for her."

The sadness clung to her voice like a shadow, and Jonny wondered what it was like to carry that kind of responsibility, that kind of sadness for someone else. He reached out and gently touched her hand, offering a silent gesture of support. "Any brothers or sisters?"

"Nope. Just me," She said quietly.

"Snap," Jonny stated.

Jess raised an eyebrow, "So no hotshot lawyer following in your dad's footsteps?"

Jonny gave a short, humourless laugh. "Nope, man I can tell he's real pissed about that, ha!"

"Families, eh?" Jess said, shaking her head.

"I'm not so sure my parents wanted kids," he admitted, the words tumbling out before he could stop them. "My mother ain't in the slightest bit maternal. She has a better relationship with the bottle than she ever did me."

Jess's eyes softened with sympathy. "I'm sorry."

Jonny shrugged, trying to dismiss the pain with a casual gesture. "It's all good. She's been clean a few years now. But I know her. I'm just waiting for the next relapse."

Cedar Bluff felt like a world away from all that, a refuge from the tangled mess of their families. Maybe that was the point.

They'd both found something here, a connection that transcended their troubled pasts.

"Did your dad buy you your bike?" Jess asked, her gaze drifting towards the gleaming machine.

Jonny snorted. "Hell no. He wouldn't do anything like that. That, I've been building that since I was ten years old. Fixed it up, got the parts from scraps. That's my own doing."

Jess's eyes widened with admiration. "I'm impressed, Jonny Phillips."

He grinned, feeling a surge of pride. "So how you liking Alabama?"

"I like it," Jess continued, her voice softer now. "I could stay here forever, in Cedar Bluff. Hidden away from the rest of the world."

"She's 'Ally Bamy' converted," Jonny teased, grinning.

"Just call me Miss Ally," Jess laughed.

"Just imagine," Jonny said, his voice taking on a dreamy quality. "over the lake there, a nice ranch house. A porch, sitting out there on summer evenings, and a big fireplace for the winter. Me cutting and fixing trees, you a nurse..." He stopped, suddenly self-conscious, realising he was getting carried away. "Sorry, I'm getting carried away."

Jess smiled, her eyes fixed on the distant horizon. "A balcony from the bedroom," she murmured, "a place for us to sit and look at the stars at night together."

She was building the dream with him, piece by piece, and Jonny felt a thrill of excitement course through him.

"Sipping Clyde May's at night and hot coffee in the morning," Jess continued, her voice laced with longing. "I want that, Jonny."

Jonny looked into her eyes, and for a moment, he believed it could be real. "So do I," he said.

They kissed passionately, a comfortable familiarity quickly escalating into something more. Clothes became an afterthought, discarded with playful urgency. The sun-warmed sand became their bed, the gentle breeze a soft caress against their skin. This was new territory for both of them, a first exploration of physical intimacy together. There was a tenderness in their touch, a shared vulnerability as they navigated this new landscape. Laughter mingled with soft sighs, the sounds of their passion echoing softly in the secluded cove. They moved together, bodies entwined, lost in the moment, their connection deepening with each touch, each kiss. Afterward, exhaustion and contentment washed over them. They lay tangled in each other's arms, the rhythm of their breathing slowing, the warmth of their bodies melding together. Soon, sleep claimed them, a peaceful slumber embraced by the tranquillity of the lake.

Jonny awoke sometime later; the sun having shifted in the sky. He stretched, his muscles aching pleasantly, a smile playing on his lips as he remembered the passion of the afternoon. He reached out for Jess, his fingers brushing against the cool sand. She was gone. A pang of disappointment shot through him, quickly followed by a sense of understanding. Jess was independent, unpredictable. He wasn't entirely surprised she'd slipped away. He sat up, running a hand through his tousled hair, a wry smile twisting his lips.

Then, a rustling in the trees caught his attention. He turned to see Jess emerging from the shadows, a brown paper bag clutched in her hands. Relief washed over him, quickly followed by a surge of affection. She hadn't left him.

Jess came bounding back, her cheeks flushed from the walk, a mix of guilt and excitement shining in her eyes. "You're awake! Shit, I was hoping to be back before. So I could surprise you."

Jonny, propped up on one elbow, watched her approach, a lazy smile tugging at the corner of his mouth as the sun dipped lower in the sky, painting the surrounding trees in hues of amber and gold. "Surprise me?"

Jess, a little breathless but radiating energy, held up the brown paper bag like a triumphant offering. The scent of chocolate and graham crackers wafted from within. "I walked back into town, figured you'd be hungry when you woke up. I wanted to set it all out ready for you."

Jonny felt a surge of affection, a warmth that spread through his chest and made him want to hold her close. He held his arm out, an unspoken invitation, and she readily nestled in beside him, her warmth a comforting presence against his side. He really had found a good one, he thought, a quiet contentment settling over him. A treasure. She was one in a million and she was all his.

Jess, close beside him, tilted her head, her eyes bright with playful anticipation. "S'mores?"

Jonny's grin widened, crinkling the corners of his eyes. "Hell yeah."

Jess smiled, a radiant expression that lit up her entire face, clearly pleased that she had anticipated his cravings. Together they made a campfire. Jess flicked open her trusty lighter, the small flame flaring to life with a soft whoosh, casting flickering shadows on their faces.

The afternoon sun burned gently over the lake, its light rippling across the water as Jonny and Jess sat beside the fire, marshmallows turning golden on their sticks. The day had been theirs alone—easy, lively, and full of laughter. They'd spent hours talking, trading stories, teasing one another, and sharing thoughts that drifted between playful and personal. Until today, Jess had been something of a mystery to him—a bright, intriguing presence he couldn't quite pin down. But after a day of conversation and quiet fun, he felt he finally understood her more deeply. She was quick-witted, sincere, and carried a warmth that drew him in without effort. Watching her now, the glow of the fire lighting her face as she grinned at him over the flames, Jonny realised he knew her better than he'd hoped.

"What do you think your friends will say about us?" she asked, her voice carrying a light, playful curiosity.

Jonny smiled, leaning back on his elbows. "I think they'll be happy for us. Bronko will probably give me some shit, but you know what he's like—nothing serious."

Jess laughed softly. "I fully expect it from him. Bring it on."

Jonny grinned, watching the way the firelight caught in her hair. "What do you make of them—Miss Observer?"

She tilted her head, pretending to study the flames while she gathered her thoughts. "I like them," she said finally. "You can tell you're all close. Bronko loves being right in the middle of everything, soaking up the attention. Pete's… sweet. There's not a bad bone in him, though he's a little slow."

Jonny chuckled, nodding in agreement.

"Dave," Jess went on, "he seems the most sensible. Wouldn't surprise me if he ends up sheriff of Cedar Bluff in thirty years' time."

"You reckon?" Jonny asked, laughter in his voice.

"I'm putting money on it," she said with a grin.

"We'll see in thirty years' time," Jonny replied.

Jess smiled. "When we're living in our house over the lake."

"Exactly," he said, matching her grin. The image of that life—simple, sun-warmed, and quiet—floated between them for a moment, neither willing to break it.

That night, the sun had slipped below the horizon, leaving a warm, humid darkness over Cedar Bluff. The town seemed to glow under the soft yellow streetlights as Jonny rode his bike into town, Jess perched behind him, her hands resting lightly on his waist. He pulled up outside the bar, the low hum of music and chatter spilling out from the open doors. Jess swung herself off the bike, landing gracefully on the pavement.

From a cluster of crowded tables outside, Bronko had one foot propped on a bench, laughing loudly with his friends. A rucksack rested against his side, the telltale sign he'd been dealing again. Bronko's gaze swept over the scene, pausing when he saw Jess lean forward to kiss Jonny, who was still perched on the bike. With a wolf whistle, Bronko sauntered over, his grin as wide as the night itself.

"Well, well, well… Look who's showed up after disappearing all day," he said, his hands gesturing theatrically.

Jonny nodded. "Hey man."

"Where have you cats been hiding?" Bronko asked, raising an eyebrow in mock suspicion.

"Just down at the lake," Jonny replied, his lips twitching as Bronko's humorous grin broke across his face, making both Jonny and Jess laugh.

“Down at the lake, huh?” Bronko said, raising both eyebrows. “Getting all wet down there, haha!”

“Ha, get out of here, Bronko,” Jonny chuckled.

Bronko leaned in slightly, his tone teasing. “Pete and Dave are inside. I’m sure they’d LOVE to hear about what went on down at the lake… You joining us, or is it a table for two?” He winked, eyes twinkling.

Jonny glanced back at Jess, who shrugged with a grin, happy enough to follow. Together, they stepped inside, finding Pete and Dave already seated. Pete’s face still bore cuts and bruises. Bronko emerged from the shadows with a theatrical flourish, announcing Jonny’s arrival as though presenting a long-lost hero. Dave greeted him with an easy smile, and Pete—never one to miss a beat—asked where he’d been all day. Jonny hesitated just long enough for Pete and Dave to exchange a pair of wide-eyed, knowing looks. The realisation hit them instantly, amusement sparking between them. Pete clapped him on the shoulder, laughing as he teased Jonny about there being a woman in their little gang now. Jess laughed along with them. Bronko only added to the mock drama, declaring it was time to say their final goodbyes to their boy, as if Jonny had been stolen away forever.

“We need a funeral… We need to mourn,” Dave added, and all five of them laughed at the absurdity of it.

Jess rolled her eyes but smiled, unbothered by the playful teasing. “He’s not going anywhere, boys. First round’s on me—let’s call it a peace offering,” she said with a wink.

Pete grinned. “I like this one!”

Jess shrugged, placing the money on the table. “Well really, it’s on you all… couldn’t afford it without kicking your asses in poker.”

"Oh, she's sassy!" Dave laughed.

"She's gonna keep you on your toes, Jonny boy!" Bronko added, giving Jonny a knowing grin.

Jess handed over the money for the drinks, mentioning that Big Rick would never serve her, and Bronko immediately snatched up the cash, striding off toward the bar with the confidence of someone who knew exactly how to handle it. Jonny's attention shifted to Pete, whose face still carried the fading bruises from the night before. Pete brushed it off with a laugh, though the memory of Bullfrog and lingered heavily between them. He admitted how close things had come, how grateful he was that they'd stepped in, and how the encounter had shaken him enough to avoid smoking since. The mention of the Night Hounds brought a shadow over the table—a quiet acknowledgement of the danger that still lurked nearby—just as the bar's music surged louder, drowning most conversations under its pulse.

Jonny, Jess, Pete, Dave, and Bronko settled into their table, sharing food and drinks as the evening wore on. Bottles were passed around with easy familiarity, laughter rising over the hum of the bar. They joked, teased, and talked about this and that, the conversation flowing effortlessly, sometimes loud, sometimes quiet, but always filled with the kind of energy that comes from close friends.

The laughter and chatter at their table were suddenly shattered as the doors of the bar slammed open. The Night Hounds stormed in like a pack of wolves, their presence terrifying. Bottles flew and tables toppled as they moved through the room, striking anyone bigger than them with sharp, punishing blows, marking their territory with brazen authority. Shouts and screams filled the air as patrons scrambled for cover, ducking under tables and bolting for the exits. Jonny's eyes went immediately to the one calling the shots—the same imposing figure who had led the chaos at the party on his first night back in Cedar Bluff. Instinctively, his mind went straight to Jess, a protective surge tightening in his chest. He strode through the bar with a terrifying confidence, scanning the crowd as if daring anyone to stand against him, and the room fell into a tense, fearful hush.

Bronko's eyes went wide. "Oh shit… Old Salty," he whispered under his breath.

The leader's voice boomed across the bar, sharp and commanding. "EVERYBODY GET ON THE DAMN FLOOR!! THIS IS NIGHT HOUND TERRITORY NOW… CEDAR BLUFF IS OUR TOWN!"

Pete's face went pale. "Screw this, we gotta get out of here!" There were simply too many of them to fight, and the sheer chaos of the gang made it clear any resistance would be suicide.

Jonny's heart pounded, adrenaline surging. "Get to the back door and run!!" His mind instinctively went to Jess, every instinct screaming to protect her above all else.

Jonny didn't hesitate. His first instinct was to get everyone to safety. He dashed toward the back door, weaving through the chaos of the bar, and called over his shoulder, "Follow me!" Jess, Dave, and Pete didn't need any more encouragement—they sprinted after him, dodging flying chairs and ducking under swinging fists. The crowd screamed and scattered as the Night Hounds wreaked havoc, but Jonny kept his focus on guiding his friends to the exit.

Bullfrog entered the bar, his face still sporting fresh cuts and bruises from the barn. He zeroed in on Bronko, who was trying to find a way out. With a sudden, brutal move, Bullfrog grabbed Bronko by the shirt and slammed him against the wall with a thud, pinning him fast. Bronko struggled, caught in the grip of the larger man, as the chaos of the bar roared around them.

"Hey, Earl! That's them!" Bullfrog barked, pointing toward the group.

"BOYS, GET 'EM!" Earl roared, his voice slicing through the chaos like a blade.

Earl strode over to Bronko, eyes cold and calculating. "Bronko… I think it's time we had a little chat," he said, every word deliberate, carrying the weight of authority and menace.

Bronko froze in place, his usual bravado draining from him. He had always thrived on being involved in everything Cedar Bluff had to offer, weaving himself into every corner of town life, always knowing what was going on. But now, standing face-to-face with the Night Hounds, with their snarling presence and violent intent, he felt a strange and unwelcome vulnerability. The usual thrill of being "in the know" vanished, replaced by a knot of fear twisting in his stomach. He realised he had bitten off far more than he could chew this time. This was no ordinary bar brawl or local skirmish—this was a test he was not ready for, and Bronko could feel the walls closing in, his usual sense of control slipping through his fingers like sand.

They burst into the street, Jonny hoisting Jess onto the back of his bike, the throttle growling beneath them, while Pete and Dave sprinted just a few steps behind. The street had been transformed into a tense battlefield. Rows of sleek black vans and gleaming motorcycles lined the curb, evidence of just how many Night Hounds had poured into Cedar Bluff tonight. Their numbers seemed endless, the vehicles forming a menacing wall along the thoroughfare. Pedestrians and partygoers scrambled in every direction, darting between cars, pressing themselves into shadowed doorways, or throwing themselves flat against brick walls, desperate to avoid the chaos erupting around them. The low rumble of engines mixed with distant shouts and the crash of overturned objects. Every movement felt charged with danger. Jonny's pulse raced, his instincts razor-sharp, locked on a single priority: protect Jess, and get them all out of this alive.

Bullfrog burst out of the bar, eyes blazing as he shouted, "GET EM!"

"Get out of here! We'll split! GO!" Jonny shouted, slamming the throttle on his bike. Jess clung tightly to his back, her grip firm as the engine roared to life beneath them.

Pete and Dave darted toward Pete's truck, weaving through the chaos as Bullfrog and a swarm of Night Hounds moved toward the black van parked across the street. Jonny leaned forward, cutting through the pandemonium as they sped into the night.

They shoved Bronko down between two hulking Night Hounds, the men's heat and slow, sullen breathing crowding him in. Earl crossed the shattered carpet of glass with the calm of a man who knew he owned the room and dropped into a chair facing him, the circle of the bar now ringed with leather and hard faces—no regulars left, only Night Hounds.

"What the hell is going on, Earl?" Bronko's voice came out tight, too quick, the tremor in it betraying the sweat at his temples.

"Cedar Bluff's about to learn the Night Hounds are in charge around here now. Just like Antioch," Earl said, each word cold and measured, his eyes boring into Bronko as if weighing him for punishment.

"Look—I been doing what you asked. I been selling your pot. I haven't told anyone where it came from," Bronko stammered, palms slick, the lie sounding thinner the more he repeated it.

"That's the thing, Bronko…" Earl leaned forward, voice slow and dangerous. "Our drugs are going missing. Money ain't adding up. Someone's been stealing from us. We know it ain't our guys over in Antioch, and the only two people that's been selling in Cedar Bluff is you and Big Rick."

Bronko's heart thudded violently against his chest, each beat echoing like a drum in his skull. He had been handing out weed to his friends—little freebies, gestures to be liked, a way to stay at the centre of every party, to maintain his web of connections. But looking at the cold line of Earl's mouth, he knew the truth would be his undoing. If Earl discovered what he'd been doing, the fallout would be far worse than anything Bronko could imagine.

"It ain't me, I swear," Bronko blurted, the promise raw and pleading.

"See, Big Rick is out back saying the same… Bullfrog's out there hunting down your friends right now." Earl's voice flattened into something that felt like a sentence. "One of you will talk, and if you don't, I hurt your friends. They'll be sleeping at the bottom of Weiss Lake."

Fear tightened in Bronko's throat until he could hardly swallow. The image—friends gone, water swallowing their lifeless, beaten bodies—was immediate and sickening. He'd never meant for this to go so far.

"Please, please don't touch my friends… I'll find out. I'll find out where your weed's gone, I promise. Just please don't touch them." His words tumbled out in a rush, bargaining and pleading braided together.

Bronko understood that this desperate plea was the only bargaining chip left in his hands, even if it had only dug him into an even deeper, more precarious hole. If he could just talk his way out of it now, it would buy him a sliver of time—a fleeting window to manoeuvre, to dig through the mess he'd created, to try and find some way to patch the chaos he'd caused. But deep down, he knew it was only temporary, a fragile reprieve that could shatter at any moment. The weight of the situation pressed down on him; sooner or later, the game would run out, and when it did, the trouble would come fast, brutal, and unstoppable. For the first time in his life, Bronko felt cornered, trapped, unable to see any clear path forward, and the fear of what was coming gnawed at him with every heartbeat.

Jonny tore through the main street, Jess clinging tightly to his back, her arms locked around his chest, letting go meant death itself. Behind them, Bullfrog's black Volkswagen van came charging out of the chaos, its headlights cutting through the dark like the eyes of a beast. The guttural growl of its engine echoed off the walls of Cedar Bluff's narrow streets, growing louder with every swerve and turn. Jonny's heart pounded so hard he could feel it in his throat, each thud a desperate reminder that this wasn't just a chase—it was survival.

They darted between cars and scattered townsfolk, the wind whipping through their clothes as the night blurred into streaks of yellow lamplight and shadow. Jess could hear the distant barks of the Night Hounds closing in on their bikes somewhere behind. Jonny's hands were white-knuckled on the handlebars, his breath sharp, his body tense but alive with adrenaline. The engine screamed as he twisted the throttle harder, pushing the bike to its limits, sparks flying when they skimmed the curb of a corner too fast.

They shot out of town and onto the back dirt roads, the tyres skidding across the loose gravel. The night grew darker here—only the pale light of the moon and the relentless glare of the van's headlights guiding them. Dust billowed behind them, clouds that seemed to swallow the bike whole. The roar of the van drew closer again, the sound bouncing through the trees that lined the winding road. Jess dared a glance back—Bullfrog's face was visible through the windshield, a twisted mix of fury and glee, his van jerking wildly as it tore over potholes and stones.

"Hold on!" Jonny shouted over the deafening wind. His voice was raw, desperate.

Jess's arms tightened around him, her heart hammering against his back. The road narrowed, twisting through a tangle of forest. The van barrelled after them, its high beams flickering over the trees like searchlights. Bullfrog's driving was manic, swerving around logs and rocks, determined not to lose them. Jonny leaned into a sharp bend, gravel spraying behind, but the van was still there, relentless, chewing up the distance between them. Every second stretched into eternity—each turn, each bounce, each moment where the bike felt like it might give out under them.

Jonny could feel the vibration of the road shaking through his bones, the air tearing past his face. He knew one wrong move would end it. Jess pressed her face into his back, every bump jolting through her as she held on.

The forest around them became a blur of motion and noise—their world narrowed to the sound of the bike's engine, the crash of branches, the howl of tyres, and the roar of Bullfrog's pursuit.

Then, in a desperate move, Jonny veered off the main path, turning sharply onto an overgrown dirt trail that cut through the trees. The van followed, crashing through the brush, but it was slower now, struggling against the rough terrain. Jonny pushed harder, weaving through the woods, ducking low branches, his body moving with the rhythm of the bike. For a fleeting moment, it seemed they might have a chance. The growl of the van began to fade behind them, swallowed by the roar of the forest.

But the reprieve was short-lived. As Jonny rounded a bend too sharply, the bike's front tire clipped the edge of a jagged rock half-buried in the dirt. The world lurched violently—the sound of metal scraping stone split the night, followed by a sickening crash. The bike twisted out from under them, and both Jonny and Jess were thrown into the air like rag dolls. They hit the ground hard, the impact cracking through the silence that followed.

Jonny's head struck the earth with a dull thud, his vision exploding into white light before fading to black. Jess tumbled beside him; the breath ripped from her lungs as she landed face-first in the dirt. The bike skidded a few more feet before collapsing in a heap, its engine still sputtering weakly before dying out.

For a long, terrible moment, the forest was silent except for the soft ticking of the cooling engine. Blood trickled from the side of Jonny's head, running down his temple and into the soil beneath him. His chest barely rose and fell. Jess lay still beside him, a dark stream of blood pouring from her nose, her hand just inches from his. Neither moved. The night that had been alive with noise and chaos now hung still and heavy, with a darkness that followed.

Chapter 10 Under the Radar

Jonny woke to a blur of white light and the faint rhythmic beep of a monitor beside him. The world came back to him in fragments — the sterile smell of disinfectant, the low hum of machines, and the weight of a dull, throbbing ache pressing behind his eyes. A bandage circled his head, tight and unfamiliar, and when he tried to move, pain pulsed through his skull like an echo. He blinked hard, trying to piece together where he was, how long it had been. The last thing he remembered was the forest — the screech of tyres, the crash, Jess's scream swallowed by darkness.

Turning his head slightly, he saw her. Jess sat slumped in a chair beside his bed, fast asleep, her arms folded loosely across her chest. A small plaster crossed the side of her eyebrow, a faint bruise colouring the skin beneath it. Strands of hair fell across her face, and even in sleep she looked exhausted, the kind of tired that came from days of worry. For a long moment, Jonny just watched her breathe, relief washing through the haze of confusion. He didn't know how long he'd been out, but seeing her there — alive, whole — was enough to quiet every other question in his mind.

Jonny stirred, his voice hoarse and dry. "Jess," he whispered.

Her eyes blinked open, dazed for only a moment before widening with recognition. She shot to her feet and hurried to his bedside, grasping his hand as though she were afraid he'd slip away again. "You're awake! Nurse—NURSE!" she cried, her voice cracking with equal parts relief and disbelief. A radiant smile spread across her face — one that told him she'd been waiting far too long for this moment.

A nurse entered moments later, her kind expression softened by the practiced calm of someone used to seeing chaos.

“Morning, Jonny,” she said warmly. *Morning?* Jonny thought hazily. He must have been out all night.

“How are you feeling?” the nurse asked, stepping closer to check the monitors beside him.

Jonny gave a weak half-smile. “Like I was in a bike accident.”

She chuckled lightly. “You remember the accident — that’s good. Let’s see how clear your head is, alright? I just need to ask a few questions.”

He nodded faintly, the motion tugging against the tight bandage wrapped around his head.

“What year is it?”

“1979.”

“Who’s the president?”

“Jimmy Carter.”

“And what state are we in?”

“Alabama,” he replied, his voice steadier now.

“Very good,” the nurse said with a satisfied nod. “Doesn’t sound like there’s any memory loss. You had a nasty gash to the head, though.”

Jonny’s brow furrowed. “How long have I been out?”

“It’s been four days since the accident,” she said gently.

The words hit him like a jolt. *Four days.* He couldn’t believe it — time had slipped away from him completely.

"You're a lucky guy," the nurse added, glancing at Jess with a smile. "Your girlfriend's been right here beside you the whole time."

It was the first time anyone had called Jess his girlfriend, and the word made him smile without even meaning to. It just felt right. A light, steady warmth spread through him, easing some of the ache in his head. He looked over at Jess, still holding his hand, her head tilted slightly as she watched him with tired eyes and a soft smile. The thought that she'd stayed by his side all this time filled him with quiet gratitude. He gave her hand a gentle squeeze and smiled, feeling lucky in a way that went deeper than words.

"Yeah," he murmured. "I am lucky."

The door creaked open, and Glenda rushed in, her face lighting up with relief. Larry followed close behind. "Oh, Jonny!" Glenda exclaimed, bending over to embrace him carefully, mindful of the bandages.

Larry's voice softened as he stepped closer. "Good to see you awake, boy."

The nurse gave them all a reassuring smile before slipping out of the room, leaving the family to their moment of reunion.

Glenda stayed close to him, hovering with that familiar, gentle fussing that made Jonny feel both nurtured and slightly self-conscious. She straightened his blankets, brushed stray hairs from his forehead, and adjusted the pillows under his head, her movements deliberate and careful, as if every little action could somehow chase away the pain he felt. Larry leaned against the wall a few feet away, arms crossed, a quiet, grounding presence that spoke volumes without a word.

Jonny's mind drifted briefly to his own parents, the absence of care and attention that had always lingered in the background of his life. Their distance didn't sting as sharply now — he had come to expect it — but it left a hollow echo, a reminder that he and his parents were not close. Sitting there, surrounded by Glenda's warmth and Larry's steady reassurance, Jonny felt a profound contrast. This was a kind of family he had never truly known, people who showed up when it mattered, who stayed even when it was inconvenient or difficult. And then there was Jess, sitting in the chair beside him, quietly watching and offering the steady presence that made everything feel a little lighter. Cedar Bluff itself, with its familiar streets and slow, comfortable rhythms, seemed infinitely more appealing now, a place where life could be simple but meaningful. A life with Glenda and Larry, who had taken him in and cared for him as if he were their own, combined with the growing connection he shared with Jess. He wanted a future here, one where he belonged. The thought of returning to Kentucky in September felt hard to think about.

As evening came, Glenda and Larry said their goodbyes. Glenda gave Jonny one last gentle hug, fussing briefly over his blanket, while Larry offered a firm, encouraging nod. Jonny watched them leave, a quiet warmth settling in him at their care. The room felt calmer now, the two of them alone, and he turned to Jess with a small, contented smile. Jonny shifted slightly in the hospital bed, glad for the privacy now that Glenda and Larry had left for the evening. Finally, he could talk about everything without worrying them.

"What's been happening while I've been out?" he asked, his voice still hoarse, but steady.

Jess squeezed his hand gently, her thumb brushing across the back of it. "The Night Hounds have taken over Cedar Bluff. They're everywhere you look. They've taken the bar from Big Rick. Bronko seems to have cut a deal with them, keeping us, Dave, and Pete out of harm's way."

Jonny frowned, the weight of her words settling in. "What the hell are you caught up in, Bronko?"

She shook her head slightly. "He won't say. He's keeping a real low profile. That's what we need to do."

Jonny nodded, pressing a quick, grateful kiss to the back of her hand. "I'm glad you're okay."

Jess gave him a small, reassuring smile. "You too. We'll get you home in a couple of days."

Jonny's recovery came faster than anyone expected, though it didn't come easy. The first day out of bed felt like learning to move all over again — every muscle stiff, every movement echoing the dull ache that lingered behind his eyes. But he was determined, pushing a little harder with each day that passed. The nurses called him stubborn in that half-joking way they used for patients who refused to stay still. The doctors said he was lucky — lucky to have survived at all — and deep down, he knew it was true. Jess was there through it all, her presence a steady comfort. When she wasn't working long hours at the restaurant with Sally, she was in that chair by his bed. Sometimes they'd talk for hours, and other times they just sat together in silence, the kind of silence that felt full rather than empty. Having her there made the days blur together in a gentler way, each one a little less painful than the last.

Three days later, the doctor finally cleared him to leave. The morning sunlight spilled through the window as Jess helped him gather his things, the crisp air outside hitting him like a reminder that he was still here, still breathing. Walking out of the hospital doors, the brightness of the world felt almost too real — colours sharper, sounds louder, life itself somehow magnified. Jess carried his jacket over her arm, smiling up at him in that soft way that made everything else fade for a moment. Outside, Larry was waiting beside his truck, leaning against the door with that patient, steady posture of his. He gave Jonny a quiet nod and a proud smile before helping him into the passenger seat. The drive back to the house was calm and familiar, the kind of ride where words weren't needed — just the sound of the road beneath them and the quiet comfort of being homeward bound.

When they pulled up outside the house, Glenda, Pete, and Dave were already waiting on the front path, their faces breaking into smiles the moment they saw the car. The late afternoon light caught the porch rail, throwing a soft glow across the scene that made the place feel warmer than Jonny remembered.

He climbed out slowly, his movements still stiff from the hospital stay. Larry shut the door behind him, slinging Jonny's duffel bag over his shoulder. Before Jonny could say a word, Glenda rushed over and wrapped him in a hug that spoke louder than anything else could.

"Oh, Jonny," she said, her voice breaking with relief. "I'm so glad you're home. Your favourite, beef briskets on the stove."

Jonny smiled, returning the embrace gently. "Thanks, Aunt Glenda."

Dave was next, giving him a clap on the shoulder. "Welcome home, brother."

Then Pete stepped forward, grinning wide. "Come here, you big, indestructible bastard."

Jonny laughed, wincing only slightly as Pete pulled him into one of those heavy-handed hugs that nearly knocked the wind out of him. For a moment, everything felt the way it used to. Jonny noticed an emptiness without Bronko. It didn't feel quite right without his lively presence.

Dave nodded toward the yard. "We did our best. Tried to fix your bike up good."

Jonny turned, and there it was — his motorcycle, resting on the grass like some loyal old friend waiting for his return. The chrome caught the sun, the frame patched up in places, and though it was clear the repairs were rough, it was the thought behind them that hit hardest.

"You fixed my bike?" he asked, stunned.

"Dave did most of the work," Pete said with a grin.

Jonny shook his head, smiling. "Thanks, both of you. Really."

Dave gave a small shrug, doing his best to downplay the emotion hanging in the air before he and Pete waved their goodbyes and headed down the drive. The rest of the group wandered toward the house in the afternoon light. Larry scooped up Jonny's bag and carried it toward the porch with a quiet sense of duty.

Glenda, meanwhile, slipped her arm through Jess's, the two women hanging back as they walked.

"Thank you for taking care of our nephew," she said. "You can stay here whenever you like — you don't even need to ask. You're always welcome."

Jess's expression softened. "That's very kind of you, Glenda. Thank you."

As they stepped toward the porch together, the scent of slow-cooked brisket drifted from the open window, and for the first time since the accident, Jonny felt the weight lift just enough for him to breathe freely again. The house, with all its familiar creaks and warmth, finally felt like home.

That evening, Jess stayed at the house. What was meant to be a quiet dinner turned into one of those easy, laughter-filled nights that seemed to stretch time in the best way. Glenda fussed over everyone, piling extra helpings onto plates, while Larry kept the table alive with his quick-witted humour — those dry one-liners that landed perfectly between bites and even had Jess nearly choking on her drink. She fit right in, trading playful remarks with Larry, matching him beat for beat until Glenda needed to wipe away tears of laughter. Jonny sat back for a while, just watching, taking it all in — the warmth, the light bouncing off familiar faces, the sound of laughter filling the house again. It felt like something he hadn't known he'd missed until that moment — the feeling of belonging, of home.

The next morning, Jonny and Jess decided to make pancakes for Glenda and Larry as a small thank-you for all the care they'd shown. The kitchen quickly became a scene of chaos and laughter. Jonny, trying his best, kept getting the measurements wrong, pouring too much milk or flipping the pancakes too early, while Jess barked gentle instructions, half-exasperated, half-amused. At one point, Jonny couldn't resist and flicked a glob of pancake mix right onto Jess's nose, making her squeal and grab for the spatula. They both doubled over laughing, flour dusting the countertop and their clothes. Just then, Glenda walked in, eyebrows raised in surprise at the slightly chaotic but unmistakably heartfelt breakfast spread. She blinked at the pancakes stacked haphazardly on plates, then smiled, shaking her head at the pair. "What are you kids doing?" she asked, her voice warm and curious.

Jonny glanced at the counter and then back at her, a grin tugging at the corners of his mouth. "Pancakes, Aunt Glenda. It's about time someone made them for you as a treat for a change."

"They smell good!" Glenda said, stepping closer, her eyes lighting up at the smell of the cooking batter.

Jess pointed the wooden spoon at him, laughing. "Jonny, you left the gas on!" She hurried over to switch off the burner, still grinning.

Glenda shook her head, a smile tugging at her lips. "What would you do without her, Jonny!"

Jess leaned toward him, the spoon still in hand, her eyes bright with amusement. "I had an accident back home once where the gas was left on! Do better!" she said, her tone teasing but light-hearted.

Jess fit in with Glenda and Larry in a way that made Jonny's chest warm with quiet relief. She was cheerful but easy-going, quick to laugh at Larry's dry wit and sharp humour, and Glenda's gentle fussing seemed to come naturally around her. It was the sort of easy companionship that made Jonny realise just how much of a family he had here, even if it wasn't the one he'd been born into. Larry, in particular, took a liking to her instantly, teasing her with his quick remarks and sly observations, while Jess met each one with a spark of clever retort that had him chuckling more than he expected. She spent a lot of time at the house, sometimes just lounging with Jonny after work, sometimes helping Glenda with errands or keeping Larry on his toes. Her presence became a rhythm in their days, steady and comforting, a reminder of home in a place where safety and warmth weren't always guaranteed.

As Jonny's head healed and the soreness faded, he returned to work with Larry, cutting and fixing trees, hauling limbs and managing equipment with the kind of satisfaction only manual labour could bring. They kept a low profile, aware of the Night Hounds' presence in Cedar Bluff, their shadow stretching over the town like a quiet warning. The parties still happened, raucous and lively, but they carried an edge now, a subtle awareness that someone was always watching, always marking territory. Jonny barely saw Bronko anymore, and Dave was seldom around, their carefree presence of earlier weeks replaced by caution and distance. Instead, Jonny, Jess, Pete, Stu, and Sally formed a tight circle, the bonds of friendship deepening over shared laughter, shared meals, and long afternoons of fun.

Some afternoons, after a particularly exhausting day tackling a stubborn tree or carefully sawing through thick branches, Jess would find Jonny standing stiffly, his shoulders sore from lifting and manoeuvring heavy timber. Without hesitation, she'd kneel behind him and begin massaging his shoulders, gentle and precise, coaxing the tension out of him as he leaned back, grateful, feeling a warmth that had nothing to do with the sun. The quiet intimacy of those moments, shared without words, became another layer to their growing connection, one that Jonny cherished more than he could fully admit.

All the while, the rhythm of the summer carried on. Jess and Sally worked together at the restaurant, flipping burgers, serving meals, and laughing through the chaos of orders during the busy evenings. Jonny, Pete, and Stu made regular appearances, claiming a corner booth, teasing the waitresses, and joining in with light-hearted banter. Before long, the calendar crept forward, and it was August — the heart of summer, when the sun seemed to hang forever in the sky, and life, with all its small comforts, felt unusually full and vibrant.

Over the weeks, Jonny and Jess's relationship blossomed naturally, shifting into something effortless and full of fun. They became each other's closest confidants, sharing jokes that no one else would understand, teasing one another, and laughing until their sides ached. Their connection was easy and complete; there was never a moment of awkward silence, never a question about whether they could be themselves around each other. Trust was at the heart of it — Jonny felt he could reveal the parts of himself he usually kept hidden, and he knew she would accept him fully, just as he accepted her. Their closeness carried into every part of their lives. The sex was fiery and plentiful. At home, by the lake. Together, they found a rhythm in Cedar Bluff that made the world feel smaller, safer, and infinitely more theirs, a space where laughter, honesty, and affection flowed freely, and the bond between them deepened with every shared glance, every whispered joke, and every moment of being completely, wonderfully known.

That weekend, the group found themselves at a party down by Weiss Lake — one of those summer nights that seemed made for music, laughter, and the shimmer of moonlight dancing on the water. Pete had brought his truck down early, parking close to the shore, its doors open wide with a stereo in the back blasting rock and roll into the warm air. Coolers were scattered around the grass, filled with beer bottles clinking in the hands of old friends and new faces. The smell of barbecue smoke hung thick in the air, mingling with the scent of lake water and summer heat. People lounged on the hoods of their cars, some waded knee-deep in the shallows with their jeans rolled up, and others danced barefoot on the dirt and grass, the glow of the bonfire flickering across smiling faces.

Jonny and Jess stayed close through it all — laughing, touching, wrapped in that easy kind of affection that didn't need to prove itself. She leaned into him when they talked, his arm resting comfortably around her waist, her hand finding his when the music slowed. There was a lightness between them, a private warmth that seemed to set them apart from everything else. Stu and Sally were nearby, Sally teasing Jess about how inseparable the two had become, while Pete worked his usual charm. For a moment, it almost felt like how things used to be — before the tension, before the unease that now seemed to linger around every corner of Cedar Bluff.

But even under the laughter and music, there was a shadow no one could ignore. The Night Hounds were there too — leaning against their cars, watching, silent and territorial. They didn't start trouble, but their presence was enough to sour the air, a reminder that Cedar Bluff no longer belonged entirely to its own people. Conversations dipped when they walked past; laughter thinned, eyes turned away. The bonfire's glow felt dimmer somehow, swallowed by something colder lurking just beyond the light. It was strange — a party meant to bring everyone together now had invisible lines drawn across it.

Jonny's gaze wandered across the crowd, half-expecting to see Bronko's loud grin or hear his voice carrying over the music, but there was nothing. The space where he would have been — telling jokes, showing off, lighting up the night with his restless energy — was empty. His absence was loud in its own way, a reminder of how much had changed since that night in the bar. Jonny couldn't shake the feeling that the party, as alive as it was, had lost something — that spark of safety and wildness that once made summers in Cedar Bluff feel endless. Now, there was only the dance of firelight, the hum of guitars, and a quiet undercurrent of unease threading through the night.

Jonny watched Jess and Sally dance by the bonfire, their silhouettes flickering in the firelight. He sat at a rickety picnic table, a beer bottle warming in his hand, his thoughts drifting even as the sight of Jess—laughing, free—kept him steady. Pete and Stu were nearby, heads bent together in conversation and easy jokes, the kind that makes noise feel like comfort.

"Jonny."
Pete's call snapped him back from wherever his mind had wandered.

"Me and Beef Stu are gonna go get more beer, you want one?" Pete asked, already half-turning toward the trucks.

Jonny glanced down at his own bottle, gave it a slight shake — still three quarters full — and shook his head. "I'm good for now."

A new weight settled when someone else took the empty seat: Old Salty. Earl. He had eased into the chair by himself, and the casual confidence of his presence only made the table's atmosphere colder. He looked Jonny over as if committing a face to memory.

"Jonny Phillips." Earl was saying the name aloud, as if confirming it to himself. "Names Earl Jones. Your Bronko's friend, right?"

Jonny didn't bother with false politeness. "Something you want, Earl?"

"Just being friendly, that's what parties are about, right? Socialising." Earl's tone was smooth, practiced; it felt like a test more than a greeting.

Jonny took another sip of beer, unsure how to answer.

"No Bronko tonight." Earl's voice was a statement and an accusation.

"Doesn't look like it," Jonny replied.

Earl shook his head slowly. "I used to see him around all the time. He seems to be getting more and more elusive."

"And what would you want with Bronko?" Jonny asked.

"Just business."

"Yeah well, your business ain't really welcome in Cedar Bluff." Jonny met Earl's eyes, refusing to look away.

Earl leaned forward a fraction. "I'll be honest with you, Jonny, I don't know whether to be pissed or to respect you. I'd have smashed that bottle round your pretty-boy face for that remark. But I'm a man of my word… Promised Bronko I wouldn't touch you or your friends. Now he owes me information and my patience is wearing thin. You tell him from me when you next see him if I don't get answers soon. I'll be going back on my word… First person I'll be going for is that pretty little girl of yours."

The words landed like ice. Before Earl could finish, Jonny's hand shot out across the table; he grabbed Earl's collar in a flash of furious motion.

"Easy, Jonny," Earl warned, voice calm but hard. "Lay one hand on me and my guys will come after you, and there's more of them than there are you."

"Don't you even think about going near her," Jonny spat, then sat back down, scanning the crowd to see if anyone had noticed. Relief flickered when he realised most people were too caught up in their own noise to pay him any mind.

"You beat my man Bullfrog up pretty good," Earl said, regaining his seat. "There's already a lot of my hounds that want after you… Don't give them a reason."

Earl pushed away from the table and walked off into the thicker shadows, leaving Jonny raw and rattled — angry, worried, and confused all at once. What had Bronko dragged them into? And worse: what had Jess been pulled into because of it?

Familiar voices rose nearby as Pete came back toward them, talking with Stu. "Have you heard the new AC/DC track, 'Highway to Hell'? Man, I thought it was awesome. Hey Jonny." The casual pop of conversation cut through the tension awkwardly, as if nothing dangerous had just happened.

"Jonny, are you okay, man?" Stu asked, noticing Jonny's expression at the same moment Jess and Sally returned.

"Jonny?" Jess pressed, perched close, searching his face.

Jonny ran a hand through his hair. "I don't know what the hell Bronko's caught up in. But I just had a friendly chat with Old Salty."

"What!?" Sally exclaimed, dropping her bag to the bench.

"What the hell's that bastard want?" Pete blurted.

"Something about information from Bronko," Jonny said, trying to steady his voice. "He threatened us."

He looked at Jess. "He threatened you."

"Man, what the hell!?" Pete said again, louder, disbelief and anger colliding.

"We have to do something about these Night Hounds," Jonny said, the words coming sharper now.

Sally's face hardened. "Yeah — and it'll be your funeral, Jonny. No way. We need to stay out of this." Her tone left no room for argument. "Stu, I want to go."

Sally and Stu hurried away, the night reclaiming its raucous rhythm as they moved toward the trucks, and Pete lingered a beat before finally following. Jonny watched them go, the party noise rising and falling around him.

Jonny felt a hot, desperate knot tighten in his gut — not just anger, but a fierce, ugly hatred aimed straight at Earl. It wasn't bravado; it was raw, protective fury, the kind that rose up when someone threatened the people you couldn't bear to lose. He wanted to see Earl taken down, to strip the Night Hounds of the easy power they'd bruised Cedar Bluff with, and he wanted it for Jess first of all — to make sure no one ever looked at her the way Earl had just done — and for Pete, Dave, Sally, Stu, for everyone. The idea of standing up to them felt righteous and necessary, but it also tasted like ash.

He knew exactly how stacked the odds were: more of them, better armed, and willing to do things he wasn't. Any move he made now would be playing with fire, and the memory of the van, the makeshift weapons, the way Bullfrog had moved in the bar, warned him that a single mistake would cost more than pride. Still, the thought of doing nothing felt worse, and that conflict — it became a determination to save Cedar Bluff itself. This town meant a lot to him.

A lake house sat in the kind of quiet that only deep woods could hold — a small, weathered structure half-swallowed by nature itself. It was hidden behind a curtain of pine and tall reeds, the kind that brushed against your legs and whispered in the evening breeze. The old wooden boards were silvered, the windows dimly glowing with light that spilled out onto the dark water below. Crickets hummed, frogs croaked somewhere near the shallows, and beyond it all, the faint echo of engines broke the stillness.

Earl's motorcycle came into view first, its low rumble growing louder until it cut through the trees and rolled into the clearing. A few other bikes were already parked close together. Earl shut off the engine, the silence that followed somehow heavier than the noise had been. He swung his leg off, straightened his jacket, and surveyed the place like he owned it. Every step he took toward the back of the lake house carried purpose — a quiet, deliberate authority that made even the hardest men nearby stand a little straighter.

Rounding the corner, the flicker of firelight from the dock caught his attention. Down there, the air was thick with tension. Big Rick was on his knees; his hands tied tightly behind his back with coarse rope. Blood had dried along his jawline, his lip split open, one eye already swollen shut. He looked broken — a big man reduced to trembling breaths and quiet defiance. Behind him stood Bullfrog, a smirk twisting his face as he toyed with a knife, running the tip along the edge of the rope as if daring Rick to move. Around them, several other

Night Hounds lingered in the shadows, cigarettes glowing red in the dark, their low murmurs fading to silence as Earl approached.

And then there was Bronko. He stood a little apart from the others, sweat dripping on his brow. His usual bravado was gone — replaced by something smaller, shaken. His eyes darted between Earl and Rick, as if trying to find a way out of whatever hell he'd walked into. Earl's boots thudded against the dock as he approached, the boards creaking under his weight. He came to a stop behind Rick, looking down at him with a calmness that was somehow more menacing than anger.

"Bronko, where've you been hiding lately?" Earl asked, the question clipped and dangerous.

Bullfrog answered for him, voice rough as gravel. "Found him outside of town, boss. Trying to talk his way out of all this. Then told me it wasn't him, who's been eating into our supply. I figured if that was the case, it must have been Big Rick."

Earl's eyes narrowed. "Is that so? You wouldn't be lying to us now would Bronko?"

Bronko's guilt had weight to it; he kept his gaze lowered, avoiding Rick's face because he knew the man was innocent and because looking up felt like daring fate. He didn't want to be hurt, didn't want to make things worse, and it showed in the tremor of his voice. "Yeah," he said, small and shaken. Big Rick tried to answer through the gag, muffled words collapsing into a helpless shake of the head.

"Well, Rick… looks like we're gonna need to make an example out of you," Earl said, calm and final as a judge's sentence.

From the back of his jeans Earl drew a pistol and set it on the splintered table. The metallic clack was obscene in the quiet;

Bronko and Rick's hearts hammered as if they might burst their chests.

"Shit, Earl, do we have to do this?" Bronko asked, panic thin in his voice.

"Yes, we do," Earl replied, eyes locked on Bronko without a flicker.

"You don't have to shoot him, man," Bronko said, pleading.

"Oh, I ain't gonna shoot him," Earl said with a laugh that didn't touch his eyes. For a breath it seemed like a reprieve—then Earl's hand pushed the pistol forward. "You are."

The gun landed in Bronko's shaking hands like a verdict. His face went pale. "No, no way. I ain't a killer," he protested, voice cracking.

Earl's eyes had a coldness behind them. "You wanted to roll with the big dogs, Bronko. You're backing out now when the heat is turned up a bit?"

Bronko's voice begged. "Please don't make me do this, man, please!"

"Shoot him and this will all be over," Earl said, the offer of mercy wrapped in menace.

Bronko stood frozen, the gun trembling in his hand, sweat slicking his grip. The air felt thick, every sound drowned beneath the pounding of his heart. Big Rick knelt helpless before him, the Night Hounds watching in silent expectation. Fear crawled through Bronko's chest as Earl's cold stare bore into him. He couldn't breathe, couldn't move — trapped between terror and guilt, knowing that no matter what he chose, there was no way out that didn't end in blood.

Earl's voice was calm, almost bored, as he turned to leave. "Fine. Bullfrog, let's head out — I guess we're going after Jonny and that small guy… Pete, is it? Maybe that'll get Bronko to cooperate." He started down the dock when a deafening gunshot cracked through the still night air. Earl froze mid-step, the echo rolling across the lake. Behind him came the sound of a body collapsing onto the wooden planks. Turning slowly, he saw Bronko standing there, the pistol trembling in his hands, smoke curling from the barrel. Big Rick lay motionless at Bullfrog's feet, blood spreading across the weathered boards, from a bullet hole in his heart. Even Bullfrog looked stunned.

Earl let out a low whistle. "Well, shit. I didn't think you'd have the balls, Bronko." But Bronko wasn't listening — his face had gone pale, eyes wide and unfocused, the weight of what he'd done crashing down all at once.

"Get him in the lake," Earl said coolly.

Bronko's body moved before his mind could catch up. He grabbed Rick's arm — heavy, lifeless — and dragged him across the dock. The sound of the body hitting the water was followed by the quiet splash of bubbles rising to the surface. Bronko doubled over, vomiting into the lake, shaking from head to toe.

Bronko wiped his mouth, anger and horror mixing in his voice. "This what y'all get up to on weekends? Killing people?"

Earl's grin turned sharp. "We didn't kill anyone." He exchanged a glance with Bullfrog, who stepped forward with a grim smile. "You're the one who shot him, Bronko. You dumped his body in the lake. You better hope it stays there."

The words hit harder than any punch. Bronko felt his knees weaken — he'd crossed a line he could never step back from.

The hole he'd dug for himself had finally swallowed him whole.

Chapter 11 Secrets Beneath the Surface

August in Cedar Bluff unfolded with a slow, easy rhythm, the kind of heat that clung to the skin and made the evenings stretch into long, amber-lit nights. Jonny found himself moving with a newfound confidence, his hands steady on the saw and his instincts for cutting and fixing trees sharper than ever. Each day with Larry was a lesson in precision, patience, and sometimes just plain endurance, but he thrived in it. The work gave him purpose, and he liked the satisfaction of a job well done, the quiet camaraderie between him and Larry settling comfortably around him. Bronko had all but disappeared, a shadow that no longer clouded their days, leaving space for real friendships to grow. Sally and Stu had become constants in his life, easy company, always ready to joke, tease, or just sit in quiet companionship. Pete, of course, was always around, the anchor that kept their group feeling whole.

One warm afternoon, Jonny, Stu, and Pete sat in the diner, the familiar hum of conversation and clatter of plates forming a gentle backdrop. Jess and Sally moved effortlessly behind the counter. Pete was ready for his cheese platter, one that Jess insistently recommended. Jonny couldn't help but steal glances at her, a spark of anticipation coursing through him each time their eyes met. He could feel the pull of the day ahead, the plan to escape down to the lake lingering like a promise. Being alone there with Jess was their little refuge, a place where they could forget the watchful eyes of Cedar Bluff and simply exist together, laughing, teasing, skipping stones, and letting the gentle lapping of the water mark the hours. Every glance, every smile, every touch between them carried a quiet thrill, a reminder that even in a summer filled with shadows and uncertainty, there were moments of freedom and happiness to be claimed—and Jonny couldn't wait for the day to stretch before them, to be just theirs.

Eventually, when the time came, Jonny waited on his bike out back. Jess emerged from the diner, her steps quick and eager, a bright smile lighting her face as she made her way toward him. Their lips found each other in a kiss that felt like the perfect punctuation to the anticipation that had been building all morning. The world around them seemed to dissolve as they mounted the bike together, the ride to the lake a familiar rhythm, the wind tugging at their hair and clothes, carrying them away from the small worries of Cedar Bluff. Once they arrived, the lake welcomed them with its familiar, quiet embrace, tucked away behind the trees and tall grasses, a hidden pocket of freedom that belonged to them alone.

In the privacy of the lake's edge, they made love. They came together with a fierce, breathless urgency, hands roaming, mouths finding each other in a way that left no doubt about what they needed. Bodies pressed tight, moving with a deep, undeniable hunger. Time seemed to stretch endlessly as they gave themselves over to the intimacy they had nurtured throughout the summer. As they lay there, basking in the sun and catching their breath, Jonny's eyes flicked toward the far edge of the shore. Something—or someone—was lying there, still and silent. His heart skipped a beat, and a jolt of panic surged through him. Jess followed his gaze, her eyes widening in the same frozen shock. For a moment, neither of them moved, both imagining that they'd been overheard, that some intruder had caught them in their private moment.

"Oh shit, do you think they heard us?" Jess whispered, eyes darting toward the still figure half in the water.

"I don't know," Jonny replied, a nervous laugh escaping him despite the tension. The sight of the motionless person sent a chill down his spine, and he couldn't shake the feeling that something wasn't right.

"Do you think they're asleep?" Jess asked, her voice tight, unsure.

"Drunken pass-out, from the looks of it," Jonny offered, trying to sound confident but failing to hide the unease curling in his stomach.

They hurriedly grabbed their clothes, dressing as quickly as they could while keeping a careful eye on the figure. Every instinct screamed that this wasn't ordinary—something about the stillness, the way the person merged with the shoreline, felt wrong. They crept closer, moving with tense caution, hearts thundering in sync. Jonny looked at Jess, catching the same wide-eyed apprehension mirrored in her expression.

"Hello!?" Jonny called out, voice cracking slightly in the stillness. There was no response.

"Something doesn't seem right," Jess murmured, her hands gripping her shirt.

"Stay behind me," Jonny said, positioning himself protectively in front of her, ready for whatever lay ahead, every nerve alert as the summer air seemed to thicken with silent menace.

It was Big Rick. The skin was pallid and bloated from weeks in the water, darkened patches and small abrasions marking the time he'd spent submerged. His clothes hung in limp, waterlogged folds, and his hair clung damply to his skull. Jonny's stomach twisted as he took in the sight.

Jess stood frozen, her hand gripping his arm for support, but when she saw the bloodied chest and the gunshot wound, she couldn't bear it. She turned sharply, backing onto a thick tree, her head pressed against the rough bark, refusing to look at the grim truth before her. Jonny's own chest tightened with horror, and he could barely breathe as the weight of the discovery pressed down on them both. "SHIT! SHIT! SHIT!" Jess screamed, her voice trembling.

Jonny dropped onto the sand, staring blankly at what lay before them. Disbelief weighed heavy in his chest as the crash of the distant surf filled the silence. He dragged a shaky hand down his face, wiping grit and sweat away, before pushing himself to his feet. His jeans were smeared with damp sand as he rubbed his palms against them, more to ground himself than to clean them.

Without a word, he crossed the few feet to Jess and wrapped his arms around her. She clung to him tightly, trembling against his chest, both of them shaking for different reasons—fear, shock, and the grim reality of what they'd found.

"Sorry… I've just never seen a dead body before," Jess whispered, her voice small, almost swallowed by the wind.

"Me either," Jonny admitted, his tone hollow.

Jess turned to him, eyes wide. "What the hell, Jonny?"

He looked down at the lifeless figure half-buried in the wet sand. "It's Big Rick. He didn't drown either."

Jess knew it too. "He was murdered," She stated.

Jonny's jaw tightened. "This has got Night Hounds all over it. Big Rick never did nothing to no one."

Rage flickered beneath his skin, his hands curling into fists as the name Night Hounds left his lips. The thought of those bastards out here, doing this, made his stomach turn.

"We need to talk to the sheriff," he said, his voice sharp now, cutting through the tension.

Jess shook her head. "I don’t like this, Jonny."

"We’ve got to shut them Night Hounds down."

Her breath came quick, uneven. "Jonny, I want to go."

Jonny softened then, looking at her pale face under the fading light. He reached out, brushing his thumb along her arm in quiet reassurance. "Okay, baby, let’s go." Together, they turned away from the body and the encroaching tide, leaving the grim discovery behind as the waves crept closer, erasing the footprints they left in the sand.

Later, Jonny found himself sitting alone in the sheriff’s office, the faint hum of the fluorescent lights above filling the uncomfortable silence. He spent hours recounting everything that had happened on the beach—the body, the wound, the unmistakable signs pointing to the Night Hounds. Every question from the deputies felt like a drawn-out test of patience, and each time he insisted on who was responsible, they pushed back, citing lack of evidence and reminding him they couldn’t just accuse anyone without proof. Jonny could feel his frustration building like a storm behind his ribs. He knew the department was small, and everyone there was too scared to confront the Night Hounds, too cautious to step out of line. The boredom of waiting, the monotony of repeating the story, and the obvious fear in their eyes made his blood boil. By the time he left, his hands ached from gripping the chair, and his chest felt tight with anger and helplessness, the weight of knowing the killers would walk free pressing down on him like a physical force.

Jonny left the sheriff’s building, the stale smell of coffee and old paperwork still clinging to his clothes as he stepped into the cool evening air. The sun had nearly dipped below the rooftops, throwing long shadows across the quiet street. His boots scuffed the cracked pavement as he walked down the road toward his bike, the tension of the last few hours still coiled in his shoulders.

Jess was already there, standing beside the motorcycle, flicking the lid of her lighter open and shut in that familiar rhythm she always fell into when she was waiting—or thinking. The metallic click echoed softly in the cooling air, oddly comforting to Jonny after the lifeless hum of the sheriff's office. Seeing her there, bathed in the fading light, steadied him more than he'd admit.

"You got out before me," Jonny said, his voice rough from the long day.

"Yeah, how did it go?" Jess asked, lowering the lighter but keeping it in her hand.

"Long and tedious," Jonny muttered, rubbing the back of his neck. "They don't want to do shit against the Night Hounds. What did they say to you?"

"Uh, yeah — the same," Jess said wanting to brush off the whole situation.

Jonny kicked at a small stone near the curb, his jaw tight. "If the sheriff's department isn't going to do anything then I will. I'm coming for Earl. The rest will fall in line. I'm not gonna ask you to get involved, Jess…"

"I'm with you, Jonny," she said softly but firmly, stepping closer. "I know you want to keep me safe. But if there's one person you can count on, it's me. I'll be right by your side. I love you."

It was the first time Jess had ever said "I love you" to him, and the sound of it sent a shiver through Jonny, as if the world had slowed just for that moment. Her words were soft, certain, and full of a warmth that made his chest swell with joy and longing. Looking at her, seeing the trust and devotion in her eyes, he felt a surge of wonder so intense it almost took his breath away. It was as if everything else—the danger, the anger, the fear—had faded, leaving only the two of them suspended in a quiet, perfect intimacy that felt impossibly real and achingly, beautifully in love.

"I love you," Jonny breathed, his voice low and steady, carrying every ounce of certainty and longing he felt. He reached for her, letting his hands trace the curve of her shoulders as he drew her close. He leaned in, and their lips met in a slow, tender kiss.

A truck screeched to a sudden stop behind them, tyres kicking up small clouds of dust and gravel. Jonny and Jess spun around, and Dave's head popped out the window, his expression tense and worried, eyes darting between them and the road ahead.

"Yo Jonny! I need you, brother!" he called urgently, his voice carrying over the quiet hum of the evening.

Without a second thought, Jonny grabbed Jess's hand, and they climbed into the cab, hearts pounding in unison. "What's going on?" Jonny asked, his voice low and cautious, glancing at Dave's worried face. For a moment, he braced himself, half-expecting this urgency to be about the Night Hounds.

Dave's jaw tightened. "It's Bronko," he said.

Dave rushed them back to Bronko's trailer. The air seemed heavier as they stepped out of the truck, the faint smell of stale smoke and rot drifting from the trailer. Dave moved quickly, opening the door and gesturing for them to go in first. Inside, the cramped, dimly lit space smelled sharply of alcohol and chemicals, the flickering light giving the room an uneven, unsettling glow. And then, in the far corner of the room, swaying slightly and almost blending into the darkness, was

Bronko—off his face, barely able to stand, muttering under his breath and completely unaware of their presence until Jonny and Jess were right there.

Jonny's eyes followed Bronko's unsteady movements, taking in the wild look in his bloodshot eyes and the way he swayed as if the floor itself were tilting beneath him. "What's wrong with him?" Jonny asked, his voice tight with concern.

Dave sighed. "He's been getting worse, disappearing for days at a time, coming home in the same clothes, stinking of piss and vomit. Every moment he's awake, he's rooting around for his next fix."

Jonny's stomach sank. "Shit, how did it get this bad?"

Dave shook his head; frustration etched into his features. "He won't listen to me."

Jess stepped closer, her eyes flicking toward Bronko with a mix of worry and determination. "We've got to get him in the shower," she said, her tone calm but firm, as if laying out the first step toward pulling him back from the edge.

Jonny and Dave moved cautiously toward Bronko, but as soon as they tried to get close, he lashed out, swinging his arms and stumbling, letting out a string of incoherent shouts. Every step toward him became a battle; he fought back with surprising strength, thrashing against their grip, and forcing them to adjust constantly to keep him from falling or hurting himself. Jess moved quickly to the shower, twisting the knobs and letting hot water run, the hiss and splash filling the cramped trailer with steam and a faint chemical smell. Manoeuvring Bronko into the small shower stall was a nearly impossible task—his body stiff, erratic, and unpredictable. Every angle required careful coordination, every shove met with resistance, and the three of them worked in tense, awkward unison, balancing desperation with caution as they tried to get him under the water.

"GET OFF ME!" Bronko shouted, thrashing violently as Jonny and Dave tried to hold him steady.

"We're doing this for your own good, brother," Dave said, struggling to maintain a grip on him.

"Shut up, Dave! You're pathetic! Look at you—no job, no home, even Laurie didn't want you!" Bronko spat, his words venomous and unrelenting.

"Don't listen to him, Dave, he doesn't mean it," Jess said quickly, her voice firm as she reached for the shower controls, trying to turn the hissing water just right.

Dave's hands froze for a moment, then he let go, offended and shaken by the cruelty in Bronko's words.

"You're a damn loser, Dave! Someone who has absolutely no personality, someone easily forgotten about. You are weak. You are nothing!" Bronko yelled, pounding his fists lightly on the tiles, his voice cracking with fury and intoxication.

"Bronko, shut the hell up!!" Jonny barked, his own anger flaring.

"You know what? Screw you, Bronko. I've done nothing but try and help you… I don't need this shit," Dave snapped, turning on his heel and storming toward the door.

"Wait, Dave!" Jonny called, but it was too late—the slam of the front door echoed harshly through the trailer.

For a tense moment, only the sound of the shower and Bronko's ragged breathing filled the room. Jess and Jonny exchanged a glance and carefully manoeuvred him under the running water. At first, he jerked and swayed, resisting with every ounce of strength he could muster, but slowly, almost imperceptibly, his struggles began to lessen. His thrashing became weaker, the resistance fading as the water ran over him, hot and relentless, and a strange stillness settled over the cramped, steamy trailer.

Once Bronko's struggles had subsided under the shower, Jonny and Jess exchanged a quick nod and began guiding him toward the bedroom. He offered minimal resistance now, more like a dead weight than a fighting man, his arms and legs loose and heavy as they manoeuvred him through the narrow trailer. His head lolled to the side, and he muttered incoherently under his breath, fragments of words lost in the hum of the shower and the trailer's stillness. Every step required careful coordination to avoid him slipping or collapsing, but with steady hands and quiet determination, they managed to get him inside. Jonny finally eased the door shut behind them and turned the lock, leaving Bronko in the dimly lit room, his mumbles fading into a low, aimless murmur as he slumped against the bed, barely aware of the world around him.

"This is going to be a rough few days, you know that, right?" Jess said quietly, her voice low in the dimly lit trailer, the weight of the moment pressing down on them.

Jonny nodded, his jaw tight, eyes fixed on the floor as if staring down the magnitude of what lay ahead. "I've seen it with my mom," he admitted.

"Me too," Jess replied softly, the memory in her eyes flickering and fading quickly as she tried to stay present.

They sank to the floor together, their backs resting against the closed bedroom door, fingers brushing the cold, worn wood as they held themselves steady. Their hands pressed against the floor, grounding them, sharing the small comfort of physical contact amidst the heavy tension.

"I had no idea things were this bad," Jonny said, voice tight, guilt and helplessness flickering across his face.

Jess noticed immediately, her heart softening at the sight. "It's okay," she said gently, leaning slightly toward him, her tone firm but full of reassurance. "All that matters is that we're here now."

The night stretched endlessly. Jonny and Jess stayed on the floor just outside the bedroom, leaning against the door, listening as Bronko raged inside. His shouts of abuse echoed off the thin walls, sharp and cutting, punctuated by the occasional thud as he banged fists against the door. Every word he spat felt designed to hurt, to push them away, but neither of them moved. They stayed vigilant, trading glances in the dim light, exhaustion gnawing at their limbs and their minds, each moment heavier than the last. The trailer creaked under the strain, the only other sounds the occasional drip of the shower plumbing and the hum of the fridge in the corner. Sleep was impossible; every shout made their hearts jump, their nerves taut like wires ready to snap.

When the first streaks of dawn crept through the grimy windows, Jonny shifted and stretched, grimacing. The coming days promised more of the same—long hours, endless noise, and the unrelenting unpredictability of Bronko's mood. They quickly realised they would need a system. Taking shifts became the only way to survive, each watching the door for an hour or two before collapsing for a brief rest, only to be replaced by the other. Even then, their sleep was fractured and shallow, punctuated by Bronko's occasional screams or the sound of him stumbling across the room, muttering and swearing at anyone—or nothing at all.

Despite the chaos, they found small ways to care for him, sneaking food and water into the bedroom whenever the shouts would fade into quiet muttering. It was awkward and tense, trying to coax the tray toward him while he slouched against the bed, barely acknowledging their presence. Sometimes he would snatch at it aggressively, other times he ignored it entirely, lost in his own haze. But Jonny and Jess persisted, shifting plates and cups gently until he ate or drank enough to keep him from fading completely. The trailer became a battleground of patience, endurance, and quiet acts of care, each moment a small victory in a struggle that stretched endlessly, as exhausting for the caregivers as it was for the man they tried to save.

Through it all, they leaned on each other, exchanging silent glances of understanding, offering brief touches of reassurance when the shouting subsided. It was gruelling, draining work, but they never wavered. Every time Bronko quieted, even for a few seconds, they felt a small flicker of hope—proof that despite the rage, despite the self-destruction, he was still there, still reachable, and still worth every second of the battle.

Days had passed, each one blurring into the next, leaving Jonny and Jess exhausted and drained, their bodies sore from long hours of vigilance and sleepless nights. Yet despite their fatigue, a fragile sense of relief had settled over the trailer—Bronko's fits of aggression had finally eased, his shouting and lashing now replaced by long stretches of quiet muttering and stillness. The tension that had once wrapped the room in a suffocating grip had loosened, and though every moment required care and attention, the absence of chaos allowed Jonny and Jess to breathe, to sit back against the bedroom door with worn muscles and tired minds, sharing the quiet triumph of having made it through another day without incident.

A gentle knock broke the silence.

"Jonny…" Bronko's voice came through the door, soft and uncertain.

"Hey, brother," Jonny said, leaning closer.

"Can I come out? I just want some fresh air."

Jess and Jonny exchanged a wary glance, both bracing themselves for whatever might come next. Jonny turned the handle slowly and opened the door. Bronko stood there blinking against the dim light, his body trembling from withdrawal, sweat plastering his hair to his forehead. He looked smaller somehow—shrunken, frail, a man stripped of everything but regret. Jess stepped forward without hesitation, gently draping her blanket around his shoulders and tucking it close.

"Thank you… Can I go outside?" Bronko asked, his voice fragile, almost childlike.

Jonny nodded. Together they stepped out into the hot, late-August sun. The air was thick and heavy, the heat clinging to their skin, but to Bronko it felt like the first breath of freedom after a long confinement. He stood still for a moment, eyes half closed, taking it all in. It was the first time he'd been outside in days.

"I'm sorry for what we did, man," Jonny said, his voice low but steady. "You know it was for your own good, right?"

Bronko nodded weakly, emotion welling up in his tired eyes. "Thank you both," he murmured. Tears began to slip down his cheeks, his face twisting with guilt and exhaustion. Jonny could see just how broken he was. "I can't remember much, man," Bronko said, his words faltering. "But I'm sorry."

"It's okay," Jonny said gently, moving closer. "It's okay. Just promise me you're gonna stay away from whatever crap you've been taking."

Bronko sniffed, his breath catching as tears streamed freely now. "I'll try, I just… anything to block it out, brother."

His voice cracked, trembling through sobs that seemed to shake his whole body. Jonny's chest tightened, his own eyes burning as he reached out and gripped Bronko's shoulder.

"I don't know what demons you're battling with, man, but I got you," Jonny said, his voice rough with emotion. "You're my brother—for life."

Jess stood nearby, her own eyes glistening. The man before her barely resembled the Bronko she had first met in Cedar Bluff. Now, he was hollowed out—haunted, fragile, and drowning in remorse.

"I just want it to stop, Jonny," Bronko whispered. "I can't take this feeling anymore. I'm a bad person."

"No, you listen to me," Jonny said firmly, his hand tightening on his friend's shoulder. "You're my brother. You always will be. You're gonna beat this."

Bronko nodded faintly, though the shame in his expression lingered. The guilt, the self-hatred for what he'd done—it all pressed down like a weight he couldn't escape. He wanted to tell Jonny the truth, to confess everything, but he couldn't. Not now. Deep down, he knew it would destroy what little was left between them. For now, all he could do was hold onto that blanket, that small spark of comfort, and try to believe that staying clean might be enough to keep his demons at bay.

Chapter 12 The last heat of summer

September was only days away. The long, hazy stretch of summer that had once seemed endless was now folding in on itself, the evenings arriving a little earlier, the air beginning to cool just enough to remind them that change was coming. Jonny was heading home in mid-September, and though it had been a long couple of months, it somehow felt like it had all gone by too fast—like time had slipped through his fingers while he wasn't looking. The end was right around the corner, and both he and Jess knew it. They didn't speak about it much, not because they didn't think about it, but because putting it into words would make it real.

Jonny had taken to the work easily now. He was taking jobs on his own, running the routes and handling the equipment like he'd been doing it for years. Uncle Larry didn't have to hover anymore; Jonny had proven himself more than capable. Each morning he'd wake before sunrise, the air still thick and warm, and head out with a quiet sense of purpose. It gave him something solid to hold onto amid everything that was changing around him. But beneath the surface, under the routine and the long workdays, there lingered that quiet knowing—that once September came, nothing would be the same.

Jonny helped Pete unload wood from the back of the truck, an arrangement they'd kept all summer. After long days cutting and fixing trees, Jonny would bring Pete the spare wood—thick branches, knotted stumps, and odd cuts that would've otherwise gone to waste. Pete had a knack for seeing shapes hidden inside the grain, and over time he'd taught Jonny a thing or two about carving.

Pete wiped his brow, staring off toward the fading light. "Man, I can't believe summer's nearly over, man. I don't want you to go back to Kentucky."

Jonny set down a split log and brushed his hands together, feeling that ache of truth in Pete's words.
"I'm not looking forward to it myself, brother."

"It's been fun," Pete said with a half-smile. "I mean, I know Bronko's had a lot going on, and Dave. But you, me, Jess, Beef Stu, and Sally—the parties, I never want this summer to end."

Jonny nodded, a small grin tugging at the corner of his mouth. "It's had its ups and downs… mostly ups."

Pete let out a rough laugh. "Yeah, I bet something's been 'up' a lot with you, haha. I'm gonna miss you, brother."

The shift in Pete's tone caught Jonny off guard. It was rare to hear him drop the jokes and speak from the heart. For a second, Jonny saw past the humour and the swagger—saw the friend who'd been there through every wild night and long day. He was going to miss this more than he wanted to admit.

"I'm gonna miss you too, Pete," Jonny said quietly. "Ya' know you're a real one, don't you, man? You're always there no matter what, through thick and thin."

Pete clapped him on the shoulder, his grin returning but softer this time. "Same with you, Jonny boy. You make sure you get your ass back here soon."

"I will do, don't you worry about that. I need you to look after Jess for me while I'm gone."

Pete chuckled. "She gon' be the one taking care of me, brother."

Jonny laughed, the sound carrying off into the warm air. After a while, Jonny left Pete to finish stacking the last of the wood and climbed into his truck. The drive back to Uncle Larry's was quiet, the road lined with trees swaying gently in the fading light. When he pulled up, Glenda and Jess were sitting together on the porch, talking softly. Jonny stepped out, brushed the dust from his jeans, and walked up to join them.

Jonny approached with an easy grin, the sun warm on his back as he joined them. Glenda greeted him with her familiar warmth, and after a brief exchange, she waved him and Jess off with a knowing smile. Jess rose from her chair, sliding her sunglasses down just enough to show a teasing smirk before disappearing inside. Moments later she returned, a backpack slung over her shoulder and a shovel in hand. Glenda lifted an eyebrow at the sight of them but simply shook her head, choosing not to ask what they were planning as the two headed out together. Jess and Jonny both laughed as they headed toward the bike. Jess climbed on behind him, wrapping her arms around his waist. With the engine roaring to life, they sped off down the road, Glenda's amused voice fading behind them into the warm afternoon air.

Jonny and Jess rode down the familiar winding path to their favourite overlook above the lake. The late summer sun glinted off the water, and the warm air carried the faint rustle of leaves as autumn crept in. When they reached the edge, Jonny leaned the bike against the worn wooden fence, and they both wandered through the tall grass, scanning the area for a good spot. They moved carefully among the wildflowers and tufts of green, searching for a place that felt right, letting their eyes take in every corner of the overlook as they decided where to settle. "What about here?" Jess asked.

"Here's good! I can see this being our back yard one day," Jonny replied, grinning at the sweep of the lake below.

"One day baby," Jess said, and they kissed before Jonny hefted the shovel and began to dig. The ground gave up the hot, dry earth in clods; dust rose around his boots while the lake murmured quietly behind them. A few feet down, he paused and set the shovel aside. Jess unzipped the backpack and took out a small red tin box, cradling it like something fragile and important.

"Alright, I think that should do it," Jonny said, wiping sweat from his brow.

"I wonder if we'll even remember to do this in thirty years' time?" Jess asked, looking at the neat hole and then out over the water.

Jess sat on the grass, the box in her lap and the backpack beside her. "What did you bring?" she asked, curiosity glinting in her eyes.

Jonny pulled out the first item: the lighter Jess had given him the day they met. He held it out, and she laughed, remembering that first spark of connection. Jess then produced her own offering, a green poker chip from the night she had bluffed and crushed the table, sending everyone else home with their egos in tatters.

Next, Jonny retrieved a folded note, the one Jess had handed him when she bought him his first chainsaw. Even now, reading her words—*Had to put my winnings to good use. Good luck on your first day. J*—made his chest warm as it had all those weeks ago. The final item was a cassette tape, scrawled with the words *Sweet Home Alabama*, their song, the one they had sung together the night they first kissed.

Jonny lowered the lid, and Jess stopped him with a hand on his wrist.
"Wait! I want one more thing to go in there," she said, smiling.

She reached into the backpack and produced the Polaroid camera she'd saved for. She leaned into Jonny, aimed it at them, and he wrapped his arm around her. The instant the picture slid out, Jess waved it in the air. They both laughed—she had missed, and the tree behind them dominated the shot.

"That's terrible!" Jess exclaimed through her laughter.

"Here, let me do it. I've got longer arms," Jonny said, taking the camera. His second shot captured them closer, softer, the moment suspended in the frame. When the photo came out, they held it together, smiling, before Jess carefully placed it in the tin box.

They sealed the lid with a small padlock and buried it, patting the earth down until it was smooth. Jonny leaned back on his heels and looked at her, dust streaked on his hands, expression serious. "Okay… are you ready to sneak into Antioch and take those night hounds down?"

Nerves flickered across Jess's face for a moment, then she nodded, determination settling in her eyes. She reached for his hand, squeezing it tight.

Jonny and Jess carefully made their way through the woods skirting the lake, moving low between the trees and keeping to the shadows where the sunlight filtered through in narrow streaks. Every crack of a twig or rustle of leaves made them flinch, but they pressed on, knowing the risk. They needed daylight for the Polaroid to capture everything clearly, to catch the Night Hounds in the act. The air was warm but tense, each step measured, as they inched closer to Antioch, hearts pounding with both excitement and fear, aware that one wrong move could expose them.

After nearly an hour of weaving through the trees, they finally caught sight of it—a rundown lake house nestled deep within the Antioch woods. The place looked abandoned from a distance, its paint peeling and roof sagging, but the closer they crept, the more signs of life appeared. Rows of marijuana plants grew behind the house, stretching out in uneven patches of green beneath the hot sun. Makeshift drying racks leaned against the porch, and a few oil drums sat nearby, reeking of gasoline and fertilizer.

Jonny and Jess crouched low in the undergrowth, their breaths slow and controlled. From their hidden spot, they could see figures moving around the property—Night Hounds, unmistakable even in daylight, their tattoos and leather cuts glinting faintly in the sun. Jess steadied her Polaroid camera, the faint click and whir of each photo barely audible over the wind rustling through the trees. They stayed that way for hours, snapping pictures of everything: the drug plants, the stash being sorted into bags, the men passing cash and loading crates into the back of an old pickup.

Then, the crunch of tyres broke the stillness. A truck pulled up fast, kicking up a cloud of dust. Bullfrog climbed out and yanked a man from the passenger side—a stranger, bloodied and terrified. Earl followed, calm and deliberate, his face hard as stone. Jonny's stomach twisted as Earl struck the man across the jaw, sending him to his knees. Each blow echoed through the woods, cruel and sharp. Jess flinched with every hit, her fingers trembling around the camera.

Jonny wanted to run out there, to stop it—but he knew they couldn't. This was evidence. Proof. Every photo Jess took now would mean justice later. They watched as Earl barked orders, his men bagging up bundles of weed and handing them off to younger recruits who sped off on their bikes toward town. It was sickening, watching it unfold, but they both understood—this was the moment that would bring the Night Hounds down.

As the sun dipped below the trees and the woods began to darken, Jonny and Jess knew it was time to go. The air grew cooler, and the faint buzz of insects replaced the harsh sounds of the day. They crept back through the trees, careful not to snap a branch or draw attention. Each step away from the lake house felt heavier, the weight of what they'd seen pressing on them. Jess clutched the photos close to her chest, like fragile secrets that could change everything. When they finally reached the edge of the woods, Jonny turned for one last look at the dim glow of the Night Hounds' hideout before taking Jess's hand. Without a word, they walked back toward the bike.

That night, the bar that had once been the pride of the town was almost unrecognisable. The neon beer signs still flickered in the windows, but the laughter and music that once filled the place were long gone. Now it served as the Night Hounds' base—dimly lit, smoke curling in the air, the tables cluttered with bottles, ashtrays, and the sour scent of old liquor. Earl sat in the corner booth that had once belonged to the regulars, his broad frame hunched over piles of cash, counting through dirty bills with slow, deliberate precision. The jukebox hummed faintly in the background, playing an old outlaw tune that gave the place an eerie calm.

A heavy knock echoed through the room, cutting through the quiet. The door creaked open, and Bullfrog stepped inside, the light from outside casting a brief glow across his weathered face. His boots thudded against the wooden floor as he crossed the room, a brown envelope clutched firmly in his hand. When he reached Earl's table, he set it down without a word, the soft, weighty thud of it landing sharp against the silence.

"What's this?" Earl asked.

"You should take a look, boss," Bullfrog said quietly.

Earl set the money aside and tore open the envelope. Inside were a handful of Polaroid photographs. His chest tightened immediately. Each one showed him in the middle of the illegal operations he ran. The images captured every angle, each detail sharp enough to ruin him.

At the bottom of the envelope was a folded piece of paper. He opened it slowly, thumb brushing the edge as he read: "Money's Bend Bridge, midnight tonight. Come alone or the copies go to the police."

Earl looked up at Bullfrog, the weight of the threat settling on his shoulders.

"Who do you think it is?" Bullfrog asked.

"I know exactly who it is," Earl muttered.

Meanwhile, back at Uncle Larry's, the night had deepened. Jess and Jonny paced quietly, nerves taut, as midnight crept closer.

"How are you feeling?" Jonny asked, his voice breaking the silence, soft but steady.

Jess looked up at him, fear and determination mixing in her eyes. She didn't answer, but her gaze spoke volumes. Jonny felt it all without needing words.

"If anything happens to me—"

"Don't say that, Jonny," she interrupted, her hand brushing his arm.

"But if it does… I love you."

"I love you too," she said, voice trembling slightly.

A shadow shifted against the porch light, and Bronko stepped forward from the darkness. He moved with his usual casual gait, but the energy that used to shine in his eyes was gone, dulled by the weeks he had been struggling. He forced a grin onto his face, trying to sound light and joking, but it didn't quite reach him. "This is cute," He said "Am I ruining a moment here"

"Bronko… what are you doing here?" Jonny asked, voice low, wary.

"I was just out for a walk," Bronko said with an easy shrug. "I kind of like the darkness of night. Fewer people around, you dig? Then I saw you two lovebirds on the porch. Figured I'd come say thanks. I owe you both my life."

Jonny's jaw loosened, a half-smile tugging at his lips. "I know you'd do the same for me, brother."

Bronko's eyes darted between them, scanning the tension that neither seemed willing to voice. "What are you two doing out here anyway? Something seems up?"

They didn't answer. Silence stretched tight, taut as a drawn bowstring, confirming what Bronko already suspected.

"What's going down?" he pressed again.

Bronko's gaze shifted to Jess. She shook her head. "Just stay out of this, Bronko," she said softly. "Take care of yourself, okay?"

"You're going after the Night Hounds, aren't you?" Bronko asked, voice low, almost a whisper, but sharp enough to cut through the night.

Jonny's tone was flat, unwavering. "Jess is right, Bronko."

Fear and stubbornness warred across Bronko's face. "Jonny… Earl will eat you up and shit you out. These guys aren't playing."

Jonny's reply was quiet but hard. "Which is exactly why we need them out of Cedar Bluff."

Bronko's hands curled into fists at his sides. "He will kill you! What about Jess? You guys have got a big long future together. Don't let nineteen seventy-nine be a memory for her. For me. For Dave and Pete."

His pacing was restless, the boards of the porch groaning beneath him. He knew they weren't going to change their minds.

"Fine…" he said, finally, the words heavy. "Then I'm coming too."

Jonny pressed a hand to Bronko's chest, stopping him in place. "No. You're not."

"You can't stop me," Bronko muttered stubbornly.

"You're not ready," Jonny said. "You're still building your strength. Besides, showing up and mouthing off won't make our plan work."

A short laugh escaped Bronko, breathy and relieved. Jonny was right, and he knew it.

"We've got to go, brother," Jonny said, nodding toward the bike.

"Be safe," Bronko said. His worry was noticeable.

Jonny swung onto the bike with Jess. Bronko watched them go, knowing the danger — and that this might be the last time he saw them. The engine roared, swallowed by shadows, and they sped toward the meeting place.

A few minutes before midnight, Jonny pulled the bike off the road, hiding it behind a stand of dense trees. The engine quieted, leaving only the subtle rustle of leaves and the tension coiled between them.

“If anything happens to me,” Jonny said, voice low and sharp, “you picture all of it. You hear me? Take it all to the cops.”

Jess cupped his face, her fingers trembling. Words failed her; worry spoke through touch. They kissed, fierce and desperate, before Jonny pulled back, eyes lingering on her for one last heartbeat. Then he walked toward the bridge, boots heavy on the old wooden planks. Jess climbed into position near the meeting point, hidden in shadow, every sense straining. The night waited with bated breath.

The headlights slammed on, stabbing through the darkness. At the far end of the bridge, Earl and his three Night Hounds stood waiting, eyes locked on Jonny. In that instant, there was no doubt—they had seen him.

He froze for a heartbeat, mind sharpening, muscles coiling. The night had tightened its grip, leaving no room for mistake. Every move he made now would count. This was the point of no return.

Jonny's words sliced through the tense atmosphere. "I said to come alone."

Earl smirked, a glint of defiance in his eyes. "I don’t really take orders from anyone, Jonny."

They moved towards the bridge's centre. At the other end, the three Night Hounds stood like silent sentinels. Jonny felt a knot of dread tighten in his stomach; escape seemed impossible.

Earl's voice, laced with a dangerous amusement, broke the silence. "You've got some pretty big balls to call me out, Jonny. So, what is it you want?"

Jonny's gaze hardened. "Those pictures. I have other copies."

Earl chuckled, a low, guttural sound. "Yeah, I bet you do. That girlfriend of yours… Bronko. Your other friends here…" He gestured dismissively.

Jonny's voice remained steady despite the tremor in his heart. "You think I'd make it that obvious, Earl!? No, I have contacts outside of Cedar Bluff, and if anything happens to me or anyone else I care about… they get leaked to the cops."

Even though Jonny was bluffing, a flicker of doubt crossed Earl's face. It seemed he was buying it. His eyes narrowed. "Then I suppose you're here to cut a deal. What is it you want?"

Jonny stood his ground, his voice firm. "Go back over the lake, back to Antioch, and stay the hell away from Cedar Bluff. That's all I ask."

Earl repeated the words with a mocking tone. "All you ask?" A menacing laugh rumbled in his chest. "Cedar Bluff has brought me a lot of business. That's a lot of money I'd be walking away from, and those pictures… they'd still be out there."

Jonny met his gaze, unflinching. "I'm a man of my word. Stay away from Cedar Bluff, and they'll disappear. Money or freedom, Earl?"

Earl fell silent, lost in thought. For a moment, Jonny dared to hope he might actually take the deal. Then, the chilling click of a gun shattered the fragile hope. Bullfrog emerged from the shadows, a cruel grin on his face, a gun pressed against Jess's head. Jonny's heart plummeted.

"Look who I found hiding in the shadows, Earl," Bullfrog sneered.

Earl erupted in laughter. "Holy shit, now haven't the tables just turned?"

Jonny's voice was tight with suppressed rage. "You hurt her, and those photos…"

"Yeah, yeah. You already made that clear," Earl interrupted. "Maybe you'll leak them, maybe not. But she'll still be dead. Is that worth it for you? Me locked away, but your girl dead in the ground?"

Jonny was paralysed by the impossible choice. Instead of answering, he ripped off his jacket and threw it to the ground behind him. The unspoken challenge hung in the air. Earl understood immediately: Jonny wanted a fight.

"You want to fight me, boy?" Earl taunted.

"JONNY NO!" Jess screamed, her voice filled with terror.

Jonny ignored her plea; his eyes locked on Earl. "Man to man, Earl."

"You know only one of us is walking away from this, don't you, Jonny?" Earl sneered.

Jonny readied his fists, his body tense. Earl threw his own leather jacket to the ground. The other Night Hounds surged forward, eager for a fight, but Earl raised a hand, stopping them.

"Stay back, boys," Earl commanded. "If he wants a fair fight, a fair fight is what he'll get."

The challenge accepted, Jonny lunged forward, a raw, animalistic roar escaping his lips. His first punch connected squarely with Earl's jaw, snapping his head back. Earl stumbled but quickly regained his footing, a furious glint igniting in his eyes. He retaliated with a brutal right hook that landed flush against Jonny's temple, sending a jolt of pain through his skull. Jonny staggered, momentarily disoriented, but he refused to fall.

They circled each other, a whirlwind of fists and fury. Each blow demonstrated the animosity that had been building between them all summer. Jonny, fuelled by adrenaline and desperation, fought with a ferocity that surprised even himself. He dodged a wild swing from Earl and countered with a series of rapid jabs to Earl's face, each strike drawing a grunt of pain. Earl, bigger and stronger, relied on brute force, his punches carrying significant weight. He landed a crushing blow to Jonny's ribs, and Jonny gasped for air, a searing pain radiating through his torso. But Jonny stood firm.

Blood began to paint the cold wooden beams of the bridge. A crimson mask formed around Earl's nose and mouth as Jonny relentlessly targeted his face. Earl, in turn, managed to land a vicious uppercut that snapped Jonny's head back, a spray of blood erupting from his lip. The fight was a brutal dance of attrition, neither man gaining a clear advantage. Each punch, each block, each desperate lunge was met with equal force. The sounds of their grunts, the sickening thud of flesh against flesh, and their ragged breaths filled the night air. It was impossible to predict who would emerge victorious from this savage display.

Jess, forced to watch this brutal spectacle, felt her stomach churn with each sickening impact. Bullfrog's gun was a cold, unwavering presence against her temple, a constant reminder of her helplessness. Tears streamed down her face as she watched Jonny, battered and bloodied, continue to fight with a desperate courage. Each blow he took felt like a physical wound to her own body. She wanted to scream, to beg them to stop, but her voice was trapped in her throat, choked by fear and despair. All she could do was watch, her heart breaking with every drop of blood spilled on that desolate bridge.

The fight devolved into a savage, desperate brawl. Jonny and Earl traded blows with reckless abandon, each punch carrying the force of their hatred. Jonny's face was a swollen mess, his eyes barely visible through the slits. Jonny unleashed a furious punch, hearing and feeling Earl's nose crack with a sickening crunch under the force of the blow. Earl screamed, a high-pitched, animalistic sound of agony that echoed across the bridge. They grappled, each trying to gain the upper hand, their bodies slick with sweat and blood. Earl managed to land a series of brutal blows to Jonny's midsection, sending him staggering backward.

Jonny collapsed to the concrete, gasping for air, his body screaming in protest. Earl loomed over him, a triumphant sneer on his bloodied face. He raised his fist, ready to deliver the final blow, but Jonny, fuelled by a surge of adrenaline, lashed out kicking Earl's ankle. A sickening crack echoed through the night air, and Earl howled in agony, clutching his leg. His ankle now broken.

Jonny scrambled to his feet, his body trembling with exhaustion. Earl, hobbled and in immense pain, was now vulnerable. Jonny unleashed a furious barrage of punches, each one landing with brutal force. Earl crumpled to the ground, his body convulsing with each impact. Jonny continued to pummel him, his fists a blur of motion, until Earl lay motionless on the concrete, his face a bloody pulp. Jonny stood over him, panting, his body shaking, his knuckles raw and bleeding. He had pushed Earl to the brink of death.

Earl's voice was a ragged rasp, barely audible. Blood gurgled in his throat as he spat out the words, his eyes burning with a mixture of defiance and desperation. "Finish it…" he choked out, then, with a surge of adrenaline, he screamed, "GO ON JONNY FINISH IT!" The words were a challenge, a taunt, a final act of rebellion against the inevitable.

Suddenly, the distant wail of sirens pierced the night air, growing louder with each passing second. Headlights appeared on the horizon, illuminating the bridge like a stage. A wave of vehicles, police cars and civilian trucks alike, descended upon the scene. What felt like the entire town had mobilized, their faces grim, their eyes filled with a righteous fury. They emerged from their vehicles armed with whatever they could find: baseball bats, pitchforks, shovels, anything that could serve as a weapon. The Sheriff led the charge, the police and townspeople right behind him, including Uncle Larry, Dave, Pete, Stu, and Sally, all standing united, crowding the bridge, their presence a united front against the Night Hounds. The town had come to reclaim their own.

The Sheriff stepped forward, his voice booming across the bridge. "Stand down, Night Hounds!"

Dave, his face flushed with anger, added, "We've had enough of you in our town!"

Stu, brandishing a shovel, chimed in, "Yeah! Now we want you out!"

The Sheriff, without hesitation, moved towards the unmoving Earl. He knelt down, and with practiced efficiency, cuffed Earl's bloodied wrists behind his back. The sight of their leader being arrested seemed to break the Night Hounds' resolve. They exchanged nervous glances, and then, one by one, they began to scarper, melting back into the shadows from whence they came. Even Bullfrog, his face a mask of fury and frustration, couldn't stand against the united front of the town. He turned and fled, disappearing into the night.

"You're under arrest, Earl Jones," he growled, his eyes blazing with righteous anger. "I could burn the whole town down with the heat I've got on you."

Suddenly, Jess's voice cut through the tension, a desperate cry filled with relief and concern. "Jonny!"

Jess, with Uncle Larry close behind, raced towards Jonny, who was staggering, his vision blurring, his body on the verge of collapse. Larry, his face etched with worry, shouted, "Can we get an ambulance over here!" His voice cracked with emotion.

Jonny, his voice raspy and weak, tried to reassure them, "I'm okay…"

Dave, his face beaming with pride, clapped Jonny on the shoulder. "You did it, Jonny! You really did it!"

Sally rushed to hug Jonny, her voice filled with relief. "You saved our town! You saved us all!" Her eyes were shining with pride and gratitude.

Jonny, leaning heavily on Jess for support, managed a weak smile. "We all did it," he said, his gaze sweeping across the crowd of townspeople who had come to their aid.

As the adrenaline began to fade, Jonny's gaze drifted towards the edge of the crowd. He could see Bronko, lurking in the shadows, trying to blend into the darkness. A flicker of recognition sparked in Jonny's eyes. "Bronko!" he called out, his voice still hoarse.

Bronko stepped out of the shadows, a wry smile on his face. "You look like shit, brother," he said, his voice laced with affection.

Despite the pain and exhaustion, Jonny couldn't help but laugh, the sound weak and shaky.

Jonny, with a surge of curiosity, asked, "Did you do all this?"

Bronko, with a hint of pride in his voice, admitted, "I put my connections to good use for once."

Jonny, filled with gratitude, shook his hand firmly, a silent acknowledgment of the triumphant battle they had won together. Bronko nodded, a rare display of emotion on his usually stoic face.

Under the soft glow of the streetlights, a sense of collective triumph washed over the bridge. The townspeople stood shoulder to shoulder, their faces etched with pride and relief. They had faced down the Night Hounds, not as individuals, but as a united community, reclaiming their town and their peace. And though his role was understated, everyone knew that Bronko's connections had been instrumental in turning the tide. As Bronko looked around at the faces of the townspeople, a flicker of hope ignited within him. Maybe, just maybe, he could finally begin to redeem himself for what he did. They had faced the darkness together, and in doing so, Bronko felt a glimmer of hope that he, too, could find his way back to the light.

Chapter 13 A Goodbye That Never Came

The final weeks in Cedar Bluff passed in a haze of healing and quiet contentment. Jonny's cracked ribs were mending well, aided by Jess's unwavering presence and Aunt Glenda's relentless fussing. Jess was always there, whether it was bringing him his favourite snacks, helping him with his exercises, or just sitting by his side. Aunt Glenda, on the other hand, was determined to nurse him back to health with her concoctions. The Night Hounds didn't bother coming back to Cedar Bluff, and the town breathed a collective sigh of relief, basking in the newfound sense of freedom.

With the immediate danger gone, Jonny and Jess found themselves spending hours dreaming of their future together. They'd sit on an old blanket down by Lake Weiss, watching the sunset, mapping out their lives as if they were drawing a treasure map. Jonny was determined to make his arborist business a success, pouring all his energy into learning everything he could about trees and landscaping. He spoke with unwavering conviction about how, as soon as he had enough money saved, he was going to return to Cedar Bluff. He envisioned buying a small, cozy home, a place where they could build their lives together, surrounded by the familiar comforts of the town and the love of their friends and family.

They made promises to stay connected, to write letters, to call each other every week, to visit whenever possible. Each promise was a lifeline, a tangible reminder that their connection transcended the physical distance that would soon separate them. Despite the bittersweet knowledge that their time together in Cedar Bluff was coming to an end, they clung to the hope that their love would endure, a beacon guiding them back to each other, back to the place where their story had begun.

The night before Jonny's last day in Cedar Bluff hung heavy with unspoken emotions. Jess had been working at the diner all day, and a dull ache settled in Jonny's heart knowing he hadn't gotten to see her much. He spent the day packing his meagre belongings and cleaning out his room at Larry and Glenda's, sad that his time here was coming to an end. The familiar scent of Glenda's beef stew simmering on the stove usually brought him comfort, but tonight it only amplified the bittersweet ache in his chest.

He picked Jess up on his bike after she finished her shift, but it was already nine at night, and the weariness etched on her face was unmistakable. He longed to pull her close, to lose himself in her embrace, but he could tell she was running on fumes. He wanted to savour every moment with her, to etch her image into his memory, because he knew that in just two days, he'd be back in Kentucky, a world away from her.

They made their way to Lake Weiss. As they sat there, the water lapping gently against the shore, they talked in hushed tones, their voices barely audible above the crickets chirping in the nearby woods. They had planned to spend the whole of tomorrow together, down by the lake, their favourite thing to do. Summer was fading away, and a cool breeze swept across the water, a reminder that the carefree days of the summer of '79 were also drawing to a close. He knew that tomorrow would be filled with laughter, tears, and a silent promise to keep their love alive, no matter the distance.

"I don't want tomorrow to come, Jonny," Jess said softly.

Jonny pulled her closer, wrapping his arm around her shoulders. "Neither do I, baby," he replied, his voice heavy with the same reluctance.

Jess rested her head against Jonny's shoulder, her body slumping with exhaustion. He could feel how tired she was, the weight of the day pressing down on her, and he felt a pang of guilt for keeping her up, even though he desperately wanted to savour every last moment they had together.

"Let's get you back to Sally's," Jonny said gently, stroking her hair. "I'll meet you down here tomorrow."

"One o'clock?" she mumbled, her eyes already half-closed.

"On the dot," he promised, leaning down to kiss her forehead.

He took her back to Sally's on his bike, the ride a silent journey filled with a mixture of tenderness and sorrow. She rested her head on his back, holding on tight as if she were afraid to let go. When they arrived, she swung her leg off the bike and gave him a lingering kiss, her eyes filled with a love that both warmed and broke his heart.

"I'll see you tomorrow," Jonny said, trying to sound more confident than he felt.

"See you tomorrow," Jess echoed.

Jess walked slowly up to Sally's house, turning back once more to look at him, her expression a mixture of love, longing, and a heavy tiredness. "Jonny… I love you," she said, her voice carrying on the cool night air.

"I love you," Jonny replied, his voice thick with emotion.

As he rode back to Glenda and Larry's on his motorbike, a lump formed in Jonny's throat, and he felt an overwhelming urge to cry. The night air was cool against his skin, but he felt a coldness deep inside, a sense of foreboding that he couldn't shake. He had a strong, unsettling feeling that he wasn't going to see her tomorrow, a premonition that clung to him like a shroud. He couldn't place where the feeling came from, but it was there, a heavy weight in his chest.

That night, his final night in Alabama, Jonny tossed and turned in bed, the unsettling feeling refusing to dissipate. The premonition that he wouldn't see Jess tomorrow clung to him like a persistent shadow, growing stronger with each passing hour. He found himself caught in a strange paradox, desperately wanting tomorrow to hurry up and arrive, just to prove himself wrong, to banish the darkness that had settled over him. Yet, at the same time, he dreaded the dawn, fearing that his worst nightmare would come true.

Sleep offered no escape, only a restless cycle of half-formed dreams and anxious awakenings. He'd drift off for a few minutes, only to be jolted awake by a sudden start, his heart pounding in his chest. Images of Jess filled his mind, her smile, her laugh, the way she looked at him with such unwavering love. He clung to those memories, desperate to hold onto the hope that their connection was strong enough to overcome whatever obstacle lay ahead.

But the bad feeling persisted, whispering doubts and fears in his ear. He tried to rationalise it, telling himself it was just the stress of leaving, the uncertainty of the future. But deep down, he knew it was more than that, a sense of inevitable heartbreak that he couldn't ignore.

The hours leading up to one o'clock crawled by with agonising slowness, each minute stretching out like an eternity. Jonny found himself caught in a torturous limbo, desperately wanting the time to hurry up so he could see Jess and hopefully dispel the darkness that had settled over him, yet simultaneously dreading the passing of time, knowing that each moment brought him closer to his departure. The sun climbed higher in the sky, mirroring the unease in his heart.

He tried to distract himself, helping Glenda with breakfast, attempting to engage in conversation with Larry, but his mind kept drifting back to Jess, to the promise of meeting her at the lake. The thought that he would get to spend one last day with her, that he would get to see her smile, hear her laugh, feel her touch, was a bittersweet comfort. It was a treasure he knew he wouldn't have for a long time, a memory he would have to cling to in the lonely days ahead. And so, he waited, suspended between hope and dread, as the clock ticked relentlessly towards one o'clock.

The ride down to the lake felt both familiar and alien. Every twist and turn of the road, every rustle of leaves in the wind, every ray of sunlight filtering through the trees, was etched in his memory, a reminder of countless happy journeys he'd made with Jess. But today, the joy was replaced by a gnawing anxiety, a sense of foreboding that grew stronger with each passing mile.

He arrived at their spot by the lake, the place where they had shared whispered confessions of love, their dreams for the future. He parked the bike, the kickstand echoing in the stillness, and scanned the horizon, his eyes searching for any sign of Jess. One o'clock came and went, and the minutes began to tick by with agonising slowness. Ten past one, and still no sign of her. But he refused to give up hope, clinging to the belief that there was a reasonable explanation, a simple reason for her delay.

He waited, pacing back and forth along the shoreline, his gaze fixed on the path leading to their spot. Half an hour went by, and the bad feeling that had haunted him all night began to solidify, morphing from a vague premonition into a chilling certainty. Was she really not going to meet him on their last day? Was she really going to let him leave without saying goodbye? An hour passed, and the reality of the situation crashed down on him with full force. He knew, deep down, that she wasn't coming.

But he couldn't bring himself to admit it, not yet. He stayed there, rooted to the spot, trying to figure out why. He worried, for a fleeting moment, that something terrible had happened, that the Night Hounds had somehow found their way to Cedar Bluff and taken her. But he quickly dismissed the thought, reminding himself that they hadn't set foot in town since they were driven out, that this felt different, more personal.

As he sat there, staring out at the tranquil water, a realisation began to dawn on him. She was avoiding him. She was trying to avoid saying goodbye. He recognised the pattern, the same pattern she displayed whenever she spoke about her mother, or her late father. She blocked out uncomfortable feelings; she ran from difficult situations. It was a defence mechanism, a way of protecting herself from the pain of loss.

He tried to reason with her in his mind, imagining what he would say if she were here, pleading with her to face him, to say goodbye. But even in his imagination, she remained elusive, a ghost just out of reach. The thought of not seeing her before he left, of not being able to hold her one last time, was heartbreaking. He had never felt so low, so utterly alone. He lingered at the lake for another hour and a half, the minutes stretching into an unbearable eternity. Two and a half hours. It was a ridiculous amount of time to wait, a measure of his desperation, his refusal to accept the truth.

But finally, with a heavy heart, he knew he couldn't stay any longer. Going back would make it real, would solidify the fact that he hadn't seen her on his last day, that she had chosen to avoid him rather than face the pain of goodbye. The thought was like a knife twisting in his gut, but he knew he couldn't escape it. He turned the motorbike around, the sound of the engine a mournful lament as he retraced his steps.

As he rode back to Glenda and Larry's, a sliver of hope flickered within him. Maybe, just maybe, she had changed her mind. Maybe she was waiting for him at the house, ready to explain, to apologise, to say goodbye. The thought spurred him on, giving him a renewed sense of purpose. He sped down the road, his heart pounding with anticipation, his eyes fixed on the familiar silhouette of the house in the distance.

But as he pulled into the driveway and cut the engine, the silence that greeted him was deafening from the outside. He scanned the porch, the yard, the windows, searching for any sign of her. But she wasn't there. A confirmation of his worst fears. She really wasn't coming.

Driven by a desperate, last-ditch hope, Jonny gunned the motorbike towards Sally's house. Maybe Jess hadn't gone to the lake because she was needed at home. Maybe something had happened, and she couldn't get away. The thought was a flimsy thread, but he clung to it nonetheless. He sped down the familiar road, the wind whipping through his hair, his heart pounding with a mixture of hope and dread. But as he rounded the corner and saw Sally's house in the distance, his heart sank. The house stood empty, the windows dark and lifeless. The car that usually sat in the driveway was gone. No one was there.

He sat there for a moment, the motorbike idling beneath him, the silence broken only by the gentle hum of the engine. The scene was surreal, like a still life painting, frozen in time. Then, just as he was about to turn away, Stu walked out of the darkened house, the door closing softly behind him.

"Jonny!" Stu's voice cut through the air, a note of surprise in his tone. He jogged over to the bike "That you!? What are you doing here?".

"I'm looking for Jess," Jonny said, his voice strained. "Is she in there?"

Stu shook his head. "No man. Sally and her folks are visiting family down in Montgomery. I was just feeding the cat. Pretty sure I heard them say Jess was staying out of town while they're away. She not tell you that?"

A cold wave of disbelief washed over Jonny. Why hadn't she told him? Maybe it didn't matter, he reasoned, because he wasn't going to be here anymore. But the thought gnawed at him, a seed of doubt taking root in his mind. Masking his confusion and hurt, he forced a casual tone.

"Oh yeah, must have slipped my mind," he said, trying to mask his disappointment.

"Hey, it’s your last day ain’t it?" Stu asked.

"Sure is," Jonny replied, the words feeling hollow on his tongue.

He found the small talk with Stu unbearable at this point, itching to escape the suffocating weight of his heartache.

"You’ve become a good friend Jonny," Stu continued. "I’ve enjoyed the summer. And damn, you kicked those Night Hounds asses’ all the way back to Antioch!"

Stu extended his hand, and Jonny shook it, the gesture feeling strangely formal, a final farewell.

"Don't be a stranger man!" Stu said with a genuine smile.

"I'll be back, take care, Stu!" Jonny replied, forcing a smile of his own.

He revved the engine and sped away, the wind carrying his words back to Stu. But the pain in his heart was like nothing he had ever experienced before, a gaping wound that threatened to swallow him whole.

He returned to Glenda and Larry's, the house feeling smaller, more confining than ever before. He quickly gathered his belongings. Glenda and Larry walked him out onto the porch; their faces etched with a mixture of sadness and understanding. He knew they cared, but their words of comfort felt inadequate, unable to penetrate the wall of despair that had built up around him.

As he stepped off the porch and onto the sidewalk, he noticed a small group gathered a short distance away. Dave, Bronko, and Pete stood there, their expressions sombre, their presence a silent show of support. He scanned the street, his eyes searching, hoping against hope to catch a glimpse of Jess. But she wasn't there. The street was empty, save for his friends and the heavy weight of his unsaid goodbyes.

Glenda squeezed his hand, her eyes glistening with unshed tears. "You ride home safe, Jonny. Call us as soon as you get there."

"I will do, Aunt Glenda," he replied. "Thank you for everything these past few months."

Larry clapped him on the shoulder, his grip firm and reassuring. "It's been a pleasure having you, boy. You come back whenever you want to. That bed will always be here for you."

He wanted to. He wanted to stay, or come back next week. He knew Glenda and Larry wouldn't mind at all. But a sense of obligation, of propriety, held him back. He couldn't impose on their generosity forever. He knew the family divide that would cause, the unspoken tensions that would eventually surface. Yet, casting a shadow over even saying goodbye to Glenda and Larry was the fact he had not seen Jess.

"Thanks for teaching me everything about cutting and fixing trees," Jonny said, offering Larry a grateful smile.

"You're gonna be the best in the business, kid," Larry replied, his eyes twinkling with pride.

With one final pat on the back, Jonny moved towards his bike, where his friends stood waiting.

"Man, it really aint gonna be the same without you here," Pete said, his voice laced with genuine sadness.

"I'm gonna miss you guys," Jonny replied, his own voice tinged with melancholy.

"We'll miss you," Dave echoed, his gaze steady and sincere.

Bronko stepped forward and enveloped Jonny in a bear hug, his frame engulfing him in a warm embrace. "You saved my life, brother," he murmured emotionally. "I love you."

"I love you, brother," Jonny replied, squeezing Bronko tightly before stepping back.

Pete and Dave followed suit, offering him brief, manly hugs, their affection unspoken but palpable.

"Make sure you two patch things up by the next time I come on down here, you hear me," Jonny said, gesturing between Bronko and Dave. "I can't be doing with this awkward shit."

Bronko and Dave exchanged a sheepish glance, acknowledging the truth in Jonny's words.

"We're gonna be fine," Dave said, a hint of a smile playing on his lips. "Take a lot more than that to stop this friendship."

"Ain't that the truth," Bronko agreed.

Jonny scanned the street one more time, a hopeful gaze. But there was no sign of her. His heart sank with a final, crushing wave of disappointment. He turned back to Bronko.

"Hey, if you see Jess, tell her…"

He paused, searching for the right words. There was so much he wanted her to hear, so much he wanted to say. But in the end, he kept it simple, distilling his feelings into a single, heartfelt message.

"Tell her I love her, and tell her to call me. She has the number."

Bronko nodded solemnly, his eyes conveying a depth of understanding that transcended words. Jonny climbed onto the bike and started the engine, the roar of the motor a final punctuation mark on his departure.

Jonny revved the engine, the powerful machine rumbling beneath him, a sound that did little to fill the silence in his heart. With a final nod to his friends, he released the clutch and the bike surged forward, carrying him away from Glenda and Larry's, away from Cedar Bluff, away from everything he had come to know and love over the past few months. As he rode, the familiar streets blurred into a watercolour of fading memories. He passed the diner where he'd shared countless meals with Jess, the park where they'd spent lazy afternoons, the old dirt road where they'd explore together. Each place was a painful reminder of what he was leaving behind, a stark illustration of the joy and connection he had found in this small town. Soon, he approached the bridge that marked the boundary between Cedar Bluff and the outside world, a bridge he had always loved riding over, the wind in his hair, the sun on his face, the promise of home ahead. But this time, it was different. This time, he wasn't riding into Cedar Bluff, he was riding out, and the weight of that realisation settled heavily upon him. A single tear escaped his eye, tracing a lonely path down his cheek before being swept away by the wind, a fleeting symbol of the profound sadness that consumed him. He was leaving; it was all over, and the most painful part was that he was leaving without seeing Jess, without saying goodbye, without knowing why. The thought echoed in his mind, a relentless refrain that amplified the ache in his chest, the sense of incompleteness that would forever be associated with Cedar Bluff.

Jonny rode on, leaving behind a chapter of his life that had been filled with both immense joy and profound heartbreak, unsure of what the future held, but knowing that a part of him would forever remain in that small town, in the summer of 1979.

Chapter 14 After Everything

2009

Now September the 18th, 2009. Jonny sat with his daughter, Charley, the lines on his face etched with the passage of time, his eyes holding a depth of experience that she was only beginning to understand. He had just finished recounting the entire story of that summer in Cedar Bluff, a tale he had never shared with her before. Charley listened intently, her expression a mixture of fascination and shock. She couldn't believe that her father had kept this part of his life hidden for so long. And more than that, she was stunned by the revelation of Jess, a name she had never heard him utter, a ghost from his past that had clearly left an indelible mark on his soul. Unbeknownst to them both, Amanda stood on the other side of the door, listening through a narrow crack. A wave of conflicting emotions washed over her–a pang of jealousy for a love she hadn't known existed, a flicker of resentment for the secrets he had kept.

"Oh dad, you never mentioned her before." she asked gently.

Jonny sighed, a faraway look in his eyes as he leaned back on the bed. "Had no reason to, honey," he said quietly. "I had your mother and you and your brother."

Charley leaned forward, her expression earnest. "Did she ever call? Did you see her after that?"

Jonny shook his head slowly, his gaze distant, lost in the corridors of his memory. "Never," he replied. "No calls, no letters. I rang Sally's about five weeks later. She said that Jess was gone by the time they got back from Montgomery; she never heard from her again. I thought I knew her well," he continued, his voice laced with a hint of self-deprecation. "I don't know if I ever did or not, how much was real to her, or was I just a summer fling until she got bored and moved on."

A wave of sympathy washed over Charley as she reached out to take her father's hand. "You still think about her?" she asked softly, her eyes filled with compassion.

Jonny hesitated for a moment, a flicker of vulnerability in his gaze. "I did for many years, Charley," he admitted, his voice tinged with a hint of regret. "Nowadays, not so much. Maybe once, twice a year."

Suddenly, the door burst open, and Amanda stormed into the room, her face contorted with anger, her eyes blazing with resentment.

"This is all very touching and all," she snapped, her voice dripping with sarcasm, "but I'd like to get back to the real world, not some fantasy from thirty years ago!"

Jonny's jaw tightened. "I'm going back. I'm going to find her."

Amanda scoffed, her lips curling into a sneer. "Do you hear yourself, Jonny? She's probably married with kids by now, you're pathetic."

Charley's eyes flashed with anger as she turned towards her mother, her voice firm but pleading. "Okay, Mom, go and wait in the car… please."

Amanda shot Jonny one last venomous look before turning on her heel and storming out of the room, slamming the door behind her, the sound echoing through the house like a thunderclap.

Charley turned back to her father; her expression filled with concern. "Dad, she could be anywhere," she said softly, her voice laced with a plea for reason. "I can see she meant a lot to you. I just… I don't want you to get your hopes up, just to get hurt by this all over again."

Jonny's shoulders slumped; his eyes filled with a mixture of pain and determination. "I have to do this, Charley, I have to," he said. "I've waited so many years to get closure."

Charley's heart ached for her father, knowing the depth of his longing, the weight of his unspoken regrets. "What if you don't find her?" she asked gently, her voice filled with trepidation. "Or what if you do and she's happy, with a family? What if she doesn't remember you?"

Jonny's gaze flickered with uncertainty, his voice cracking with emotion. "I don't know, Charley, I just… I don't have much purpose in life right now. All I know is I need to do this."

Charley could see the desperation in her father's eyes, the profound sense of emptiness that gnawed at his soul. She knew that she couldn't talk him out of it, that this was a journey he had to undertake, regardless of the potential for heartbreak. A silent understanding passed between them, a shared acknowledgment of the unyielding force that drove him forward, towards a past he could no longer ignore.

"How are you even going to start?" Charley asked, her voice both a mixture of concern and curiosity.

Jonny paused, his gaze drifting towards the window, his mind already picturing the familiar landscape of his past. "I need to go back to where it all began… Cedar Bluff," he replied, his voice firm.

As he spoke, a wave of memories washed over him, a bittersweet mix of joy and sorrow. He knew he had only a few friends left in Cedar Bluff; the passage of time having taken its toll on the bonds he had forged so long ago. Pete had passed away, young, back in 1999, succumbing to prostate cancer. A sad loss, a genuine and kind soul taken far before his time. He would have been Jonny's best bet; he was always around from what Jonny remembered in 1979. A stable, grounded pilar of friendship. Aunt Glenda had also passed away in 2003 after a nasty stroke; her funeral was the last time Jonny had been back to Alabama. Uncle Larry had been consumed by dementia and resided in a nursing home in Gadsden. Bit by bit he was fading away and now was a shell of the man he used to be. Dave was still in Cedar Bluff, and now a deputy in the police department. Jess was right, he thought, a pang of sadness tugging at his heart. She had clocked his friends so well it was almost as if she had seen the future herself. He was married with four children, girls at all ages and his wife Miranda was a good woman, they were happy together and that's all that mattered.

And of course, there was Bronko. Jonny knew little about Bronko, what he was up to. All he had was a number that he exchanged brief texts with over the years. He never knew if Bronko was going to reply or not. All he knew was Bronko had struggled multiple times with addiction over the years. He had been in and out of rehabs and psychiatric units. He never married, never had kids, or managed to hold down a stable job. Jonny couldn't remember the last time he saw Bronko. But he needed to try and get hold of him if he was to find Jess. He hadn't kept in touch with Sally and Stu since the summer of '79 and wouldn't know where to begin to find either of them, or if they had even stayed together.

Jonny finished packing his small bag, a modest collection of essentials that seemed woefully inadequate for the journey ahead. The worn leather of the bag felt familiar beneath his fingertips, a tangible link to a past he was now determined to reclaim. He and Charley walked downstairs together, the silence between them thick with unspoken emotions, a delicate tapestry woven with threads of love, concern, and a shared sense of uncertainty.

"You're really doing this, aren't you?" Charley asked, as if afraid to shatter the fragile atmosphere that enveloped them.

"Yeah baby," Jonny replied, his tone firm yet laced with a gentle reassurance, a silent promise that he would be careful, that he would not let his quest consume him.

"You said upstairs you don't have much of a purpose at the minute," Charley continued, her eyes searching his, her voice trembling with a mixture of vulnerability and strength. "That's not true, you're my dad and the best dad in the world. I really hope you get the answers you're looking for."

"I love you Charley," Jonny said, his voice thick with emotion, his heart swelling with a profound sense of gratitude for the unwavering love and support of his daughter.

"I love you," Charley replied, her words a balm to his weary soul, a reminder that even in the face of uncertainty, he was not alone.

Charley embraced him tightly, her arms wrapping around him in a lingering hug that spoke volumes of the love and concern she felt for her father. It was a silent promise to be there for him, no matter what the future held. She then turned and left, leaving Jonny alone with his thoughts and the daunting task that lay ahead.

Jonny walked out to the garage. He could hear Amanda and Charley driving away outside. His gaze fell upon his bike, a gleaming machine that had once been a symbol of freedom and adventure, but now lay dormant, gathering dust in the shadows. But now, all he had was the clothes in his bag, and his bike. With no idea what the future would hold, he got on his bike and rolled out onto the front drive. He checked his phone. Dave had already replied to his text and was looking forward to seeing Jonny. He had no idea if Bronko had even read his or if he was even going to see him. But he set off the engine roaring loud as he sped into the early evening, an unstoppable smile growing on his face, just like he did in

1979, back to where it all began, back to the small town that held a big place in his heart. Back… to Cedar Bluff.

Chapter 15 Return to Cedar Bluff

The asphalt blurred beneath Jonny's tyres as he merged onto Highway 68, the twilight deepening with each passing minute. The bike responded to his touch, a faithful steed carrying him away from the wreckage of his old life and towards the uncertain promise of a new beginning. With each mile marker that whizzed by, the weight on his shoulders seemed to lighten, replaced by a growing sense of exhilaration. He was leaving behind the bitterness of a failing marriage, the suffocating routine of a life half-lived, and embracing the unknown with open arms. The wind, a constant companion, carried whispers of the past, fragments of memories that stirred within him like long-dormant embers. Then, in the distance, he saw it – the bridge that arced gracefully across the landscape, a gateway to Cedar Bluff, with Lake Weiss underneath. A wave of anticipation washed over him, so intense it almost took his breath away. He twisted the throttle, the engine responding with a guttural growl, and the bike surged forward, devouring the miles with a newfound urgency. He was free, finally free, and he was ready. Ready to face whatever awaited him in Cedar Bluff, ready to confront the ghosts of his past, and most importantly, ready to find Jess, no matter the obstacles, no matter the cost. The thought echoed in his mind, a mantra that fuelled his determination: Find Jess. At all costs.

As Jonny crossed the bridge and the first familiar landmarks of Cedar Bluff began to appear, a pang of disappointment settled in his stomach. The town he remembered, the vibrant, carefree haven of his youth, was fading into a distant memory. Gone were the wild parties that spilled out from lake houses, the bonfires that lit up the night sky, the sense of endless possibility that had permeated the air. In their place were manicured lawns, gated communities, and an eerie silence that spoke of a town that had lost its soul. The once-bustling main street was now lined with empty storefronts, evidence of the economic forces that had slowly strangled the life out of Cedar Bluff. Caravan parks, filled with the transient hopes of those seeking a temporary escape, stood in stark contrast to the sprawling homes of the wealthy, perched on the hills overlooking the lake, their opulent facades a symbol of the growing divide between the haves and have-nots. It was no longer the Cedar Bluff he remembered, the Cedar Bluff that held the key to his past. It was just a small, forgotten town, a shadow of its former self, a place where the dreams of youth had been replaced by the cold reality of time and change.

The 360 Bar and Grill loomed into view, a beacon of light and noise amidst the encroaching darkness. Jonny pulled up, the rumble of his bike momentarily disrupting the manufactured tranquillity of the parking lot, filled with SUVs and rental cars. It was a tourist trap, he could tell at a glance – a far cry from the dimly lit, slightly seedy establishments he remembered from his youth. He dismounted, the scent of fried food and cheap beer assaulting his nostrils as he walked towards the entrance. The interior was a cacophony of clinking glasses, boisterous laughter, and the generic twang of country music. He scanned the room, his eyes searching for a familiar face amidst the sea of unfamiliar ones. And then he saw him. Dave was perched on a stool at the bar, nursing a beer, his back to the entrance. Jonny approached cautiously, a sense of disbelief washing over him. It had been years, six even, but still, the transformation was jarring. The long, flowing hair that Jonny remembered had vanished, replaced by a receding hairline and a shiny bald patch on top. A noticeable beer belly strained against the buttons of his police uniform, a contrast to the lean, athletic frame of his youth. The years had been unkind, etching lines of weariness around his mouth and puffiness beneath his eyes. It was only his eyes that resembled the man Jonny remembered.

Jonny's voice cut through the late afternoon air, carrying a familiar echo: "Dave Lannister!"

Dave turned, a flicker of recognition instantly lighting up his face. "Jonny Phillips, good to see you, old friend." A genuine smile spread across Dave's face.

They clasped hands, a firm grip. Time might have woven its way between their visits, but the bond remained, a silent testament to enduring friendship.

Dave greeted him warmly, clearly glad to see him back in town, and mentioned that Miranda had sent her regards. Jonny asked after her, and Dave, with a mix of affection and mild exasperation, explained that she was busy preparing outfits for the girls' upcoming literacy day. Jonny reacted with surprise at the thought of four outfits, only for Dave to correct him with a touch of pride, reminding him that Carly was in college now. The realisation caught Jonny off guard, and Dave matched his astonishment, adding that little Daisy was already ten.

Jonny pictured the chaos of their household, jokingly acknowledging how much it must keep Dave on his toes. Dave laughed, the sound carrying both fatigue and fondness, admitting that Jonny's text had given him a welcome escape from the constant noise at home. After a moment, Dave's thoughts shifted toward Jonny's own family, his tone softening with concern. Jonny's expression darkened as he told him the truth: he and Amanda were getting a divorce.

As if drawn by some unseen force, both Jonny and Dave's gazes drifted towards the front door. A figure had just entered, immediately commanding attention. He was a black man, tall and imposing, his face obscured by darkened sunglasses that seemed to absorb the light around him. A black leather coat, worn and creased, hung loosely on his frame, adding to the air of mystery and danger that clung to him like a shroud. There was something about his demeanour, a certain swagger in his step, that made people instinctively recoil. Conversations hushed, and eyes darted away as he moved through the crowded bar, an invisible force field pushing people aside. A thick golden chain, gleaming against the dark leather of his coat, was the only flash of ostentation, a subtle hint of the wealth, or perhaps the danger, that lay beneath the surface.

"Well, ain't this one big happy family reunion," a voice drawled, thick with sardonic amusement.

Jonny's head snapped up. "Bronko!?"

He might never have recognised him. Bronko was a shadow of his former self, heavier, his face etched with the harsh map of years fuelled by drugs and alcohol. Yet, despite the wear, he carried himself with a surprising stability.

"What's happening, my brothers! The years have been kind!" Bronko's voice boomed with forced joviality.

"Is that so?" Dave replied, his tone measured.

"Not you, Dave. You look like a middle-aged tub of butter!" Bronko roared with laughter at his own joke. It had been too long for Jonny to gauge whether Bronko was truly joking or not.

"I'm just playing with you!" Bronko insisted, slapping Dave on the back with surprising force.

"Good to see you again, man," Jonny said, a touch cautiously. "I didn't know if you were coming or not."

"Man, as soon as I saw your text, I hopped on the next bus back to this shithole!"

"You're not around town anymore, then?" Dave asked.

"Hell no! It's your sorry ass stuck in this bitch, haha. If only Pete was here now, god rest his soul."

Dave raised his beer in a silent toast. "Here in spirit. So, Jonny, what do we owe this visit? You moving back here now you and Amanda are over?"

"Well, I'm looking for someone, actually. I thought you guys might be able to help me."

"I'll try," Dave offered. "Who are you looking for?"

"A girl."

"A girl!" Bronko exclaimed, throwing his hands up. "Man, you need to be more specific!"

"Do y'all remember the summer of 1979?"

Dave's brow furrowed. "Oh, Jonny, my memory ain't what it used to be. How long ago was that? Like twenty, thirty years?"

"When I came back to Alabama for the summer. You know, Uncle Larry taught me to cut and fix trees."

"Oh yeah, I remember that happening," Bronko said, a glimmer of recognition in his eyes.

"Great!" Jonny thought, a surge of hope coursing through him. He was onto something already.

"Kinda," Dave said, still hesitant. "That was a long time ago."

"Do you guys remember the girl I was seeing? She was from out of town." Jonny watched them closely, seeing the gears turning in their minds.

Dave shook his head. "Sorry, man, ain't ringing any bells."

"Me either, dude," Bronko echoed.

"She was staying with Sally for the summer," Jonny said, trying to remind them.

"Sally who?" Dave asked, confusion clouding his face.

"Sally Strooker, she was a few years below us... Blonde." Frustration now slowly creeping into Jonny's mind.

"Yeah, that name sounds familiar. What was the name of your girl again?" Dave strained.

"Jess... Jess Judy," Jonny said, a little too quickly.

Dave and Bronko exchanged puzzled glances.

"I don't' remember a Jess Judy," Dave said in confusion."

"Me either, man. Are you sure you're not getting confused? A different summer maybe? In Kentucky?"

"No, it was here! Come on, guys, it was like the best summer of my life. We kicked the Night Hounds' ass!"

"Night Hounds!" Bronko exclaimed, as if the phrase had unlocked a hidden memory. "Yeah, I remember that summer, shit."

"You remember her?" Jonny pressed, his voice tight with anticipation.

"I remember the Night Hounds," Bronko said, his eyes distant.

"Was that the year I was dating Laurie?" Dave asked, grasping for something familiar.

"Yes! That's it! Come on, how can you not remember Jess? She hung out with us all summer!" Jonny continued.

"Sorry, man," Dave said, his voice softening. "Look, I can see how much that summer meant to you. She must have made a real impression if you're thinking about her all this time later. But for me, all I can remember is heartache that year. It wasn't as good a summer for me as it was for you." Dave said.

"Me too, man," Bronko said, his voice subdued. "I was fighting my own demons that summer. Sorry I can't remember much else other than those goddamn Night Hounds. I hope you find her, though."

"Wait! You guys are the only lead I have, think again. Please!" Desperation laced Jonny's voice.

"I've got to get back to the girls. I'll give it some thought, I promise I will. I'll call you tomorrow." Dave turned and walked away, leaving Jonny facing Bronko.

Bronko recognized the raw desperation in Jonny's eyes. "I was off my face for most of the summer. Jonny, I really don't remember a Jess, man. Are you sure..."

"Yes! I'm sure! I remember her. Her face is kind of faded, but I remember."

"Sometimes the years make it hard to remember reality, brother," Bronko said, his voice gentle. "Are you sure this isn't some fantasy in your head?"

Jonny paused, the seed of doubt planted. He saw Bronko's reasoning, knew how easily time could fabricate memories, how missing gaps could be filled with imagined details. But it felt so real. He was confused as to why his remaining two friends from that summer couldn't remember her when he could so vividly.

The bar's dim light stretched across the room as Jonny and Bronko remained, the air heavy with unspoken anxieties. Jonny felt the weight of helplessness pressing down on him. This first hurdle, his friends' inability to recall Jess, loomed like an insurmountable wall. He chased the frustration away with whiskey, each glass disappearing quickly as he signalled for another. The amber liquid burned a path down his throat, a temporary distraction from the growing despair.

Bronko watched, a strange unease settling in his gut. He saw the familiar signs of Jonny slipping away, drowning his sorrows in the bottle. It was usually Bronko who was falling off the wagon, but this time it was Jonny. The years had etched their own stories onto Bronko's face, marking battles fought and demons wrestled. He knew the path Jonny was treading, perhaps better than Jonny himself. For the first time, the tables had turned. It was Bronko, the one often lost in his own haze, who was now the sober observer, the worried friend looking out for Jonny.

Time blurred, marked only by the clinking of glasses and the slurred murmur of conversations around them. The barman, a burly man with a weary gaze, finally cut Jonny off. Bronko stepped in, his voice calm but firm, defusing the situation before it escalated. He guided Jonny out of the bar. Jonny stumbled, his steps unsteady, and Bronko wrapped an arm around him, supporting his weight.

Bronko hailed a cab, directing the driver to a nearby motel. At the motel, Bronko checked Jonny in. He helped Jonny into the room, the cheap motel furnishings a far cry from the life Jonny once knew.

Jonny pitched forward, collapsing onto the bed, and Bronko's back twinged in protest as he went down with him. "Steady, Jonny, man, it's me that's supposed to be the unstable one," Bronko muttered, more to himself than to his friend. A sharp clink echoed as a bottle tumbled from Jonny's jacket pocket, landing on the floor. Bronko picked it up, his eyes narrowing as he read the label. Prescription medication. A wave of worry washed over him as he looked at Jonny, now sprawled on the bed, mumbling incoherently, teetering on the edge of oblivion. Bronko suddenly feared Jonny's mental state was far more fragile than he'd initially realised. Maybe this divorce hadn't been the clean break Jonny claimed, but the final, shattering blow to a mind already stretched to its limit. Soon, Jonny's mumbles faded into the heavy, ragged breathing of a passed-out drunk.

The following day, Bronko walked into the hushed atmosphere of the police station. The air hummed with the low thrum of computers and the muffled murmur of conversations. He asked to see Dave, and after a five-minute wait that felt like an eternity, Dave emerged, his face a mask of professional neutrality. They exchanged a brief, awkward greeting before Bronko followed Dave outside, the fresh air a welcome change from the stale, institutional scent of the station.

"Have you heard anything from Jonny today?" Bronko asked, his voice low, a thread of concern woven into the question.

"Nope, you?" Dave replied, his gaze steady.

Bronko shook his head, a gesture of unease. "Something ain't right, man. He got crazy drunk last night, even by my standards. I had to carry his ass to a motel. In his pocket he had these pills I ain't never heard of before."

Dave exhaled slowly, rubbing his chin as the weight of Bronko's words settled upon him. A realisation dawned in his eyes, a dawning understanding of Jonny's vulnerability. "Jesus, you think he's losing it?"

"I can't remember a girl, can you?" Bronko pressed, his voice laced with a desperate plea for reassurance.

"No, but it seems so real to him," Dave admitted, a hint of helplessness creeping into his tone.

"I hate to say it, man, but I've been in those institutes," Bronko said, his voice grim, the words carrying the weight of personal experience. "Those real sick people believe the stuff that goes on in their heads."

Dave's brow furrowed, a flicker of memory sparking in his eyes. "I did remember something from that summer," he said, his voice thoughtful. "I'm almost certain he had a bike crash, spent days in hospital?"

"Sounds familiar," Bronko replied, searching his own memories, "I don't think I went in to see him, though."

"Me either, Pete and I spent days fixing up his bike. My point is… the man hit his head, hard," Dave said, eyes wide hoping Bronko would catch on.

"I see what you're saying," Bronko said, a dawning understanding in his eyes. "I'm worried about him, man."

"Me too." Dave's voice was heavy with concern. "How do we tell our oldest friend the best summer of his life didn't exactly happen how he thought it did?"

Bronko shrugged, a gesture of helplessness. Just then, Dave's phone rang, shattering the heavy silence. He glanced down and saw Jonny's name flashing on the screen. A wave of apprehension washed over him as he answered. "Jonny… Yeah, I'm with Bronko now. Meet us at the diner in an hour."

A wave of guilt washed over Dave, a cold knot forming in his stomach. He dreaded the upcoming meeting with Jonny, the thought of letting his friend down, of shattering his cherished memories, weighing heavily on him. When the time came, they sat in the window booth at the diner, both men silent, their gazes fixed on the street outside. Dave watched as Jonny's bike pulled up, the familiar rumble of the engine sending a fresh wave of anxiety through him. He saw Jonny dismount; his face etched with a hopeful anticipation that twisted the knot in Dave's stomach even tighter. As Jonny walked towards the diner, Dave steeled himself, preparing for the difficult conversation ahead. Jonny walked in and sat with them.

"How you feeling, man?" Bronko asked, his voice gentle, carefully probing.

"I'm fine," Jonny insisted, the word snapping out of him with such force that it only deepened their concern.

Dave leaned forward, his expression earnest. "Look, Jonny. I'll be real honest with you. I've been awake most of the night thinking about that summer. So much of it has washed away in my head. I remember the Night Hounds, I remember you fighting one of them—I can't remember his name. I remember Bronko falling off the wagon. And I remember the break-up with Laurie. Not much else."

Jonny's gaze darted to Bronko, a silent plea for confirmation. Bronko met his eyes, shaking his head slowly, a mirror of Dave's inability to recall Jess.

Dave continued, his voice softening with empathy. "I say this because we care about you, man. We're kinda worried about you. I think the summer didn't quite go how you remember it, man."

"SHE WAS REAL!" Jonny insisted, his voice rising in desperation.

"Okay, okay," Dave soothed, holding up his hands in a placating gesture. "Maybe there was a Jess, maybe you slept with her at a party or two…"

Jonny slammed his fist on the table, the force of the blow rattling the cutlery and silencing the surrounding conversations. Frustration and anger flared in his eyes.

Dave winced, but pressed on, his voice firm but gentle. "I know my memory isn't great at the best of times, but if Bronko can't remember her, either… surely that must mean something. You had a nasty knock to the head that summer…"

"Don't… Don't you dare go down that road," Jonny warned, his voice a low growl.

Bronko spoke up, his voice laced with reluctant concern. "I saw the pills, Jonny. They fell out your pocket last night."

"I'm not crazy!" Jonny retorted, his voice strained. "I just… I just take them for sleep. I'm going through a divorce!"

"You're going through more than that, by the sounds of it," Bronko muttered under his breath, his eyes filled with a mixture of pity and worry. Jonny stared at him, his face a mask of raw frustration.

Dave sighed, trying to steer the conversation back to calmer waters. "Okay, let's just take this back a few steps. Jonny, do you want me to call anyone? Amanda? Charley?"

"No… I do not!" Jonny snapped, recoiling at the suggestion.

Jonny slumped back in the booth, the fight seemingly draining out of him. He was beginning to question his own sanity, knowing his friends wouldn't be purposefully unhelpful. Maybe he was fantasising, distorting reality to fit a more appealing narrative. Then, a new memory surfaced, a dark and unsettling image that cut through the fog of confusion: the body they'd found down at the lake.

"We made statements!" Jonny exclaimed, his voice filled with sudden urgency. "Big Rick… we found the body! Something must be on record!"

Bronko's stomach churned, a wave of nausea washing over him. The blood ran cold in his veins. He had managed to keep it buried all these years, the secret that had haunted him since that fateful summer. He was the one who had killed Big Rick, acting on the orders of the Night Hounds. It was a horrible act, but he'd done it to protect Jonny and the others, a twisted act of love for his friends. It was the beginning of his downward spiral, the act that had tainted his soul and set him on the path of self-destruction. The thought of it resurfacing, of the truth being exposed after all this time, filled him with a desperate, primal fear. This was a secret he would take to his grave; a darkness he couldn't allow to see the light of day.

"The bar owner?" Dave asked.

"Jonny, why are you poking around in stuff like that?" Bronko interjected, his voice sharp, laced with a hint of desperation. "That was a dark time for all of us."

"Jess and I, we made statements to the police!" Jonny exclaimed, his voice rising with renewed urgency. "You're in the police, Dave, you could look back!"

"That's probably archived in storage," Dave replied, his tone dismissive.

"The case is closed, man, we can't just go poking around," Bronko insisted, his voice pleading.

"Please, Dave," Jonny begged, his voice cracking with emotion. "It'll confirm she was real. Please, do this one thing for me, and I promise I won't ask anything else of you. Please, brother."

Dave looked into Jonny's eyes and saw a raw, desperate plea, a vulnerability that tugged at his heart. Bronko's mind raced, a silent scream echoing in his head for Dave to refuse. A wave of panic washed over him at the thought of the past being unearthed, of secrets long buried finally seeing the light. He knew the potential consequences were catastrophic, that some things were better left forgotten, no matter the cost. Dave wrestled with his conscience, torn between his loyalty to his friends and his desire to help Jonny find peace. He knew that accessing those archived records could provide solid evidence, a definitive answer that would either validate Jonny's memories or shatter them completely. But the thought of potentially crushing Jonny, of further fuelling his descent into delusion, made his stomach churn. He wanted to help, but he also didn't want to be the one to break him.

"Fine," Dave said, the word hanging in the air like a sentence.

Bronko's heart sank, a lead weight settling in his chest. Beside him, Jonny visibly brightened, relief and gratitude flooding his features.

"I don't know if I'll find anything," Dave cautioned, his voice firm. "But I want you to promise me that if it comes to a dead end… you drop this. Focus on yourself and getting through this divorce."

"It ain't gonna be a dead end, man," Jonny insisted, a surge of unwavering belief in his voice. "That statement will be there."

Jonny visibly brightened, relief and gratitude flooding his features as he sat back in his chair. Bronko mumbled something about needing to get going, a flimsy excuse that barely masked his desperate need to escape. He practically bolted from the diner, leaving Dave and Jonny staring after him.

With a promise to call as soon as he had any news, Dave watched Jonny leave the diner, get on his bike and ride off. With time to kill and a restless energy buzzing beneath his skin, Jonny found himself drawn to the familiar streets of Cedar Bluff. He rode aimlessly, the town eerily quiet and lifeless. It was completely different from the vibrant, bustling place he remembered, more like a ghost of its former self. A wave of melancholy washed over him as he cruised through the streets, each corner, each building, a faded echo of a brighter past. The town felt hollow, the laughter and life that once filled it now replaced by an unsettling silence. Eventually, almost without realising it, he found himself parked outside Uncle Larry and Aunt Glenda's old house. It looked so different now, almost unrecognizable. A sleek, modern facade had replaced the cozy, familiar porch, and the sprawling, overgrown garden had been transformed into a manicured lawn. It was a stranger's home now; a symbol of how much things had changed. He lingered there for a long time, lost in thought, the weight of the past settling over him. All the while, he eagerly awaited the phone call from Dave.

The heavy metal door of the archive room groaned in protest as Dave wrestled it open with his keys, the lock clicking with a loud, echoing thud. He flicked the light switch, and fluorescent bulbs sputtered to life, casting a harsh, sterile glow over the cavernous space. Dust motes danced in the air, illuminated like tiny stars in the artificial light. The room was a labyrinth of towering stacks of cardboard boxes, each one labelled with dates and case numbers, a physical manifestation of the town's history, both good and bad. Dave sighed, steeling himself for the task ahead. He began his search, running his fingers along the dusty boxes, scanning the faded labels. Hours seemed to melt away as he navigated the maze, the silence broken only by the rustling of cardboard and the occasional creak of the floorboards. Finally, after what felt like an eternity, he spotted the box he was looking for: "1979 - Cases A-L." He carefully pulled it from the stack, the cardboard groaning under the strain. He carried it to a small, rickety table in the corner of the room and began to sift through the contents. Files upon files, reports and witness statements, filled the box, each one a piece of someone's story. With painstaking care, he began to read, his eyes scanning each word, each sentence, searching for any mention of Jonny, of Big Rick, of anything that might shed light on the mystery. He checked and double-checked every detail, cross-referencing names and dates, determined to leave no stone unturned. The weight of the past settled heavily on his shoulders as he delved deeper into the dusty files, the truth, whatever it may be, lurking somewhere within those yellowed pages.

The late afternoon sun bathed Tall Oaks as Jonny sat perched on his bike, the familiar view stretching out before him. This was where he thought he and Jess had shared their first kiss, a stolen moment beneath the towering trees, the air thick with summer heat and unspoken desire. But now, even that memory felt tainted, uncertain. Was it real, or just a fabrication of his mind? He squeezed his eyes shut, trying to recapture the feeling, the sensation of her lips on his, but the image remained elusive, flickering like a faulty lightbulb. Just as doubt began to creep in, his phone buzzed in his pocket. Dave. His heart leaped into his throat as he fumbled to answer it.

"Jonny, it's Dave. I have updates. Come on over to the house." There was a weight in Dave's tone, an undercurrent that Jonny couldn't quite decipher, leaving him both hopeful and apprehensive.

Adrenaline surged through Jonny's veins as he kicked his bike into gear, and sped toward Dave's house, his mind racing with anticipation. He needed to know, needed to hear what Dave had found. He pulled up to the curb, hopped off the bike, and practically sprinted to the front door. Dave opened it almost immediately, a weary smile on his face. The house was a whirlwind of activity, the sounds of Dave's young daughters echoing through the hallway, their laughter mingling with the clatter of pots and pans from the kitchen, where Miranda was clearly in the midst of making dinner.

"Hey, sorry about the noise," Dave said, gesturing towards the commotion with a wry smile. "Let's go out back."

Just then, Miranda appeared from the kitchen, wiping her hands on her apron. Her face, framed by soft, auburn hair pulled back in a loose ponytail, held a gentle beauty that spoke of a life well-lived. Her eyes, the colour of warm honey, were kind and intelligent, crinkling at the corners when she smiled. The subtle lines etched around her eyes and mouth hinted at both laughter and the occasional worry, adding a depth and warmth to her presence.

"Hey, Jonny. It's been so long!" Miranda said, her voice warm and welcoming, a genuine smile lighting up her face. He tilted his head and briefly caught up with her. Itching to get answers, Jonny followed Dave outside and they sat on the worn garden furniture.

"Did you find it?!" Jonny asked, his voice tight with anticipation, barely able to contain the hope that had been building within him all day.

"Took me a while, I think my senior's pissed off with me," Dave said, a hint of amusement in his voice, though his eyes held a serious glint. "But yeah, I found the investigation into Big Rick's death. The case was never actually closed. They couldn't pin the killer on anyone. Just speculation that it was one of the Night Hogs."

"Hounds, Night Hounds," Jonny corrected. "What about the statements?"

Dave hesitated, his expression turning sombre. He leaned forward, his gaze fixed on the ground. "It was all there, Jonny, the paperwork for the case," he said. "But there was only one statement… From you."

"No, no, that can't be," Jonny stammered, the summer he thought he knew so well dissolving underneath him.

"There was no statement from a Jess Judy," Dave stated, his voice gentle but firm, his eyes filled with concern.

Jonny was wrapped in utter confusion, a whirlwind of conflicting memories and emotions swirling within him. He distinctly remembered Jess telling him, with unwavering conviction, that she had made a statement to the police.

"Are you sure you checked it right?" Jonny asked, desperation creeping into his voice, his grip tightening on the arms of the chair.

"I read through the whole box, even looked through others, just in case it was somehow misplaced," Dave said, shaking his head, his voice filled with regret. "I'm telling you, man, there was only one statement. I'm sorry, Jonny, I really wanted to find something for you." He placed a hand on Jonny's shoulder; his expression filled with genuine concern and a deep sense of helplessness. "Please, Jonny, go back to your family. Get some therapy or something. I'm here for you; I'll call you from time to time just to make sure you're okay."

Jonny's sense of reality shattered. He'd braced himself for a tough fight, expecting resistance and obfuscation, but not this utter blank where Jess's story should have been etched. The chilling absence of her statement. But more importantly, the lack of any confirmation that she had ever existed, sent a jolt of fear through him. It was as if she'd been deliberately scrubbed from existence, leaving him with only the unreliable echoes of his own memory.

A familiar, heavy despair settled in his gut, the same desolate feeling that had consumed him when he left Cedar Bluff all those years ago, feeling untethered and directionless. A disheartening pattern was solidifying: a return to Cedar Bluff, a spark of anticipation, freedom and excitement. This invariably leading to disillusionment and a profound sense of isolation when he'd leave. The weight of this realisation pressed down on him, suffocating him with the knowledge that the answers he sought might be forever out of reach. The vibrant memories he clung to, the shared experiences that defined a significant part of his life, were now lost in a shadow of doubt, leaving him questioning his sanity and her existence at all.

Chapter 16 Between Memory and Madness

Weeks later, Jonny found himself back in Kentucky, disappointment booming within him. He had given Amanda their house, the one they had built together, filled with shared memories that now felt like shards of glass. Now, he was staying in his parents' house, a sprawling five-bedroom place behind a gated driveway. It felt like a gilded cage. He loathed being back under their roof, suffocating under their thinly veiled judgment and constant questioning. Explaining the divorce had been humiliating enough, but then trying to articulate the Jess situation, the years of anticipation and speculation about her, culminating in a recent search that had proved a devastating failure, felt like confessing to a madness that he, and perhaps others, were now starting to suspect lurked within him.

The worst part was the trip back to Charley. Seeing the pity in her eyes as he recounted Dave's findings, the way she carefully chose her words, as if he were a fragile object about to shatter, was almost unbearable. He could see the doubt creeping in, the unspoken question of whether Jess had ever truly existed outside of his own mind. Back in Kentucky, the days blurred together in a haze of Clyde May's whiskey. He'd start with a small glass in the late afternoon, just to take the edge off, and then another to get him through dinner with his parents, their polite conversation feeling like a barbed-wire fence. By nightfall, he'd be pouring a generous measure to numb the memories and finally drift off to sleep, only to have the same haunting questions chase him through his dreams. Dave would check in with a friendly text every few days, a simple "You okay, man?" that was both comforting and a painful reminder of his isolation.

Driven by a desperate need to find some tangible proof, Jonny became consumed by the search. He remembered the lighter Jess had given him when they first met, a small, silver thing he had cherished. He recalled her mentioning she was from Michigan. He spent hours scouring social media, searching for Jess Judys from Michigan, even extending his search to Alabama, clinging to the faintest of possibilities. He'd pore over countless profiles, searching for a familiar face, a spark of recognition, but finding nothing. Then, a new, even more terrifying thought would creep in: what if one of these faces was her, but so altered by time and circumstance as to be utterly unrecognisable after all these years? His days became an obsessive cycle of searching, questioning, and doubting, fuelled by whiskey and desperation. He was trying to prove her existence, to validate his own sanity, but everything and everyone seemed to be conspiring to convince him that he was chasing a ghost, a figment of his imagination, a phantom born of grief and regret.

Why hadn't he stayed in Alabama, just a few more days, to uncover the reason she hadn't shown up on their last day together? Why hadn't he returned a week later, a month later, to demand answers? Why had he even left at all? Now, the most agonising part was the fading of her memory. He desperately wished he could conjure her face with perfect clarity, hear the precise timbre of her voice, recall the unique scent that clung to her skin. He clung to the small, insignificant details, the things that made her her: the way her face would scrunch up when she laughed, the distinctive rhythm of her walk, the way she'd mispronounce certain words, or simply the image of her sitting lost in thought, idly flicking open and shut a lighter, a nervous habit that now seemed like a precious, irreplaceable piece of the past.

Jonny lay sprawled on his parents' pristine white sofa, the plush cushions doing little to ease the ache in his bones. The front door swung open, and his mother, Jane, swept in, a whirlwind of expensive perfume and tightly controlled energy.

Jane carried herself with the effortless grace of a woman accustomed to the finer things in life; every movement radiating an air of well-to-do confidence. Her dark brown hair was pulled back in a stylish clip, accentuating her sharp cheekbones and the carefully applied makeup that couldn't quite mask the worry lines around her eyes. She wore high heels and an elegant dress, a muted floral print that flared out slightly at the arms, giving her a sense of poised fragility.

She carried the bag of groceries and placed them on the granite island in the kitchen with a muted thud. Jonny sat up, the ice clinking softly in his glass as he drained the last of his whiskey. He was already in that hazy, tipsy state that had become his default setting. Jane walked in, her expression tight, having seen him toss back the final drops.

"Whiskey for breakfast, huh?" she said, her voice laced with disapproval.

"Hello, mother," Jonny mumbled, avoiding her gaze.

Jane sat down next to him, a subtle grimace crossing her face as she caught the sharp scent of liquor on his breath. "This isn't healthy, Jonny. I know more than most that alcohol isn't the answer to your problems. If you went back to work, gave yourself some goddamn structure, you wouldn't be feeling like this."

"That's what you did, was it, Mom? Just go back to work and it fixed all your problems?" Jonny said sarcastically.

"I am fifteen years sober, Jonny. I made something of myself. I built those little shops into a chain of successful businesses. I didn't sit at home and get drunk while obsessing over someone that doesn't even exist!"

"She did exist!" Jonny's voice rose, a raw edge of desperation creeping in.

"Then where is she, Jonny? Where is she?" Jane's voice was sharp. "Why couldn't you just have made things work with Amanda? She's a lovely woman. You had a family, a home. Me and your father don't know what to do with you anymore, Jonny, but you can't stay here getting drunk all day. I had to fight with your father the other night not to throw you out on the street. If he had it his way, you would be. I want to help you, Jonny, but you need to help yourself."

Jane stood up, her face a mask of weary disappointment, her shoulders slumping slightly as if carrying a heavy burden. She turned and walked away, her expensive high heels clicking sharply on the shiny marble floor, the sound echoing in the cavernous kitchen.

"And have a shower, for Christ's sake. You stink," she added, her voice softer now, tinged with a hint of pity.

The day stretched before Jonny, vast and empty, mirroring the hollowness he felt inside. Motivation was a distant country he couldn't find on any map. He drifted through the hours, the silence of the house amplifying his sense of failure. Then, a text message from Charley, his daughter, flashed on his phone, the screen illuminating his face with a brief, unwelcome light. It was a reminder of her younger brother, Dylan, and Dylan's band performance in town that night. A wave of guilt washed over him. Being a dad was the only thing he had left, the one role, the one connection to a life that still felt worth fighting for. He couldn't let Dylan down, not again. He pushed the half-empty bottle of whiskey further away, the amber liquid sloshing ominously. A flicker of resolve, fragile but present, ignited in his eyes. As sharp as his mother's words were, they had cut through the fog. She was right; he couldn't keep living like this.

That evening, a nervous energy thrummed through the house. Jonny found himself getting ready, the simple act of showering and changing clothes feeling like a monumental achievement. He chose a clean shirt, a dark blue that made his eyes seem a little brighter. He stayed away from the whiskey, the craving a constant hum beneath his skin, a phantom itch he desperately tried to ignore. Meanwhile, in another part of the house, Jonny's mum was carefully adjusting her pearl necklace, her face carefully composed. In the living room, Jonny's father, Ray, stood impeccably dressed in a tuxedo. His face was cold and expressionless, his posture ramrod straight. He was a well-put-together gentleman, known for his stern and harsh demeanour, his voice a low, deep rumble that commanded attention.

Jonny walked downstairs to the kitchen, his dad already there, his presence ever dominant, even without meaning to.

“Are you drunk, Jonathon?” Ray asked, his voice a low, deep rumble that seemed to fill the room.

"No, Dad, I’m not," Jonny replied, trying to keep his annoyance steady.

"Don’t answer me as if what I am asking is out of the ordinary," Ray said, his tone sharp and unwavering. "Tonight is about family, and I won’t have you ruin it for your son. Or your mother."

"I bet you’re loving this," Jonny blurted out, the words tumbling out before he could stop them.

Ray turned back, a flicker of confusion momentarily disrupting his usual stoicism. This was something Jonny had wanted to get off his chest for years.

"Excuse me?" Ray asked, his voice laced with a dangerous calm.

"You’ve never thought highly of me, Dad," Jonny said, his voice rising slightly, fuelled by years of unspoken resentment.

"Now you have a real excuse to express your disappointment. Failed marriage, life falling apart, no home..."

Ray shook his head, his expression hardening.

"What do you want me to do?" Ray asked, his voice laced with disdain. "Get the violin out? Pat you on the back and say poor Jonny? You dug this hole yourself, son, and the bottom of a bottle won't get you out. Take some responsibility for goodness sake and man up!"

His tone was harsh, almost like an insult. Jane walked down the stairs before Jonny could snap back at his father.

"Are we ready to go?" Jane asked, her voice smooth and even.

"Of course," Ray replied, his voice softening slightly as he turned to his wife.

The drive into town was a blur of passing streetlights. The building loomed in the distance, a monolithic structure of steel and glass that seemed to pierce the night sky. The elevator hummed as it ascended to the 12th floor, the doors opening to reveal a surprisingly vibrant concert space. The air buzzed with energy, a mix of anticipation and excitement. As they stepped out, Jonny immediately spotted Amanda, his ex-wife, standing near the entrance with Charley. A knot of anxiety tightened in his stomach, but he forced himself to walk forward. Jane greeted Amanda warmly, the two women engaging in easy conversation, highlighting their enduring friendship despite the circumstances. Charley rushed forward, throwing her arms around Jonny in a tight hug. "Dad! I'm so glad you made it!" she exclaimed, her genuine enthusiasm a balm to his wounded spirit. It seemed, in that moment, that while the rest of his family might be enduring his presence, Charley was truly happy he was there.

The lights dimmed, and the band took the stage, Dylan front and centre with his guitar. From the first chord, it was clear that Jonny's influence had taken root. They launched into a set of classic rock and roll anthems, songs that Jonny had played for Dylan countless times over the years. A wave of pride washed over him as he watched his son command the stage, his fingers flying across the fretboard with skill and passion. Dylan's voice, though still developing, had a raw energy that captivated the crowd. He caught brief glimpses of Dylan on stage, moments where their eyes met, and Dylan would flash a quick, genuine smile, a silent acknowledgment of their shared love for the music. The crowd cheered wildly, their energy infectious. Dylan, while playing the guitar, would look back at the drummer and the bassist, who was also doing backing vocals, with a smile, showing how much he loved playing with his friends.

As the band transitioned into "Sweet Home Alabama," a familiar pang resonated within Jonny. It was their song, his and Jess's, forever etched in his memory from the summer of '79. A specific memory surfaced: the two of them, young and carefree, on stage at the Tall Oaks party overlooking Lake Weiss, singing their hearts out as the crowd roared with approval. The warm summer air, the twinkling lights reflecting off the water, Jess's radiant smile – it had felt like the pinnacle of their shared joy, a moment of pure, unadulterated bliss. But now, as he stood there, watching his son perform, a seed of doubt began to sprout. Had it really been that magical? Or had time and loss distorted the memory, painting it with a false brilliance? He questioned if that was even real, his smile now lost from his face.

The lead singer stepped forward, a grin spreading across his face. "Thank you all!" he shouted, his voice slightly hoarse from the performance. "That one was a personal favourite that refuses to stay buried!"

The words "stay buried" struck Jonny like a physical blow, a memory snapping into sharp focus. The box! The box he and Jess had buried all those years ago! It was a time capsule of their love. If he could find it, unearth it, it would be certified proof, a tangible validation of the reality he was beginning to doubt. A desperate need to scratch that itch, to silence the gnawing uncertainty, consumed him. He wanted nothing more than to bolt out of the concert, to race back to Cedar Bluff and reclaim that piece of his past. The noise around him seemed to fade, the music blurring into a dull hum, the crowd dissolving into a faceless mass. The lead singer's voice, the opening chords of a new song – all of it became a distant, irrelevant drone.

"Dad, are you alright?"

Charley's voice cut through the fog, grounding him in the present. He looked down at her, her eyes searching his. A genuine smile, the first real one he'd felt in a long time, crept onto Jonny's face. A new lead on Jess!

"I'm fine, baby," Jonny said, his voice filled with a newfound energy.

The rest of the concert stretched out before him, an unbearable eternity. He tried to focus on Dylan, on his son's performance, but the image of that buried box kept intruding, a siren call he couldn't resist. He fidgeted, his leg bouncing nervously, his eyes darting towards the exit. Each song felt like a delay, each cheer of the crowd a mocking reminder of his own internal chaos.

Finally, the last chord faded, the lights came up, and the crowd erupted in applause. Jonny didn't wait for the encore, didn't offer congratulations, didn't even say goodbye. He mumbled a hasty excuse to Charley, something about needing to take care of something urgent, and then he was gone, pushing his way through the throng of concertgoers, his movements bordering on frantic. Soon, he found himself back on the road, the city lights fading behind him as he sped towards Cedar Bluff, once again succumbing to the impulsive nature that had defined so much of his life.

Under the oppressive darkness of the early morning, Jonny cruised into Cedar Bluff. The air was bitingly cold, a clear reminder of the season's relentless march towards winter, and it seeped into his bones as he drove through the deserted streets. Each familiar landmark seemed to whisper forgotten stories, echoes of a life that felt both intimately close and impossibly distant. Those memories settled uncomfortably upon him, a burden he carried willingly, driven by the desperate hope that the buried box held the key to unlocking a truth he so desperately needed to reclaim.

The journey back had been a frantic race against time and fading recollections. He had wrestled with the images of that day, the summer of '79, trying to reconstruct the landscape of his youth with the unreliable tools of memory. Different locations flashed through his mind, each one vying for prominence, each holding a piece of the puzzle. He had strained, pushing himself to recall every detail, every nuance, every sensory impression of that moment. He clung to those impressions, desperate to anchor himself to the reality of the past. After what felt like an eternity of mental wrestling, he had finally narrowed it down to the spot where they had planned to build a house, a place that held the promise of a future that never came to be. It was a gamble, a desperate shot in the dark, but it was the best he had, the only thread he could grasp in the labyrinth of his own mind.

Each step Jonny took was heavy with anticipation, his heart pounding in his chest like a frantic drum. The darkness pressed in around him, the silence amplifying the sound of his own ragged breathing. He rounded the final bend in the road, his eyes fixed on the horizon, searching for the familiar landmarks that would guide him to their spot. But what greeted him was not the open field he remembered, not the promise of a future waiting to be built. Instead, a looming silhouette dominated the landscape – a house. A sprawling, imposing structure. The air seemed to thicken, to suffocate him, as the realisation crashed down upon him: the box, their link to the past, was now buried somewhere beneath the foundations of this house, or worse, unearthed and discarded by some oblivious construction worker.

Jonny slumped onto his bike, the cold metal a jolt against his skin. He sat there for a long moment, the engine idling softly, his gaze sweeping across the fenced-off property. The trees behind the house loomed as dark shadows against the night sky, their branches swaying gently in the night breeze. He focused, trying to superimpose the landscape of his memory onto the reality before him. If he was remembering correctly, if his memory hadn't completely failed him after all these years, maybe... just maybe... the house didn't cover the entire area. The property stretched further back, towards the lake, a dark expanse he couldn't quite make out in the gloom. Maybe the box wasn't directly under the foundation. Maybe it was further down, closer to the water, in a part of the land that remained untouched by the construction. A flicker of hope, fragile but persistent, ignited within him, a tiny spark in the overwhelming darkness.

A battle raged within Jonny. The lure of the box, the desperate need to find it, warred with the ingrained sense of right and wrong. Climbing the fence, trespassing on private property, digging a hole in someone's garden – it was all illegal, a blatant violation of the law. He had the cover of night on his side, the darkness offering a cloak of anonymity. But would he really do it? Could he bring himself to cross that line? The risk was immense, the potential consequences dire. Yet, the thought of leaving without knowing, of abandoning his last chance to find the truth, was unbearable. He was caught between desperation and morality, teetering on the edge of a decision that could change everything.

The internal struggle reached its breaking point. Jonny made his decision. He couldn't leave, not without knowing. With a surge of adrenaline, he grabbed his shovel and torch from the back of the bike. He approached the fence, and with a grunt, he hauled himself over, landing silently on the freshly cut lawn. The darkness felt different now, no longer a cloak of anonymity, but a shroud of complicity. He walked slowly, deliberately, across the yard, trying to align the landscape of his memory with the reality around him. He measured his steps, trying to recall the exact spot where he and Jess had buried the box so many years ago. Here, he thought, it must have been here. He took a deep breath, switched on the torch, and plunged the shovel into the earth. The soil was surprisingly firm, resisting his initial efforts. He dug and dug, the hole growing deeper and wider, each shovelful of earth a demonstration of his growing desperation. He began to doubt himself. Maybe he was wrong. Maybe the house was built directly on top of it. Maybe he was just wasting his time, making a fool of himself. Just as he was about to give up, to succumb to the crushing weight of disappointment, the shovel struck something hard. A metallic thunk reverberated through the night. Metal on metal. Could it be? His heart leaped into his throat, a mixture of hope and terror flooding his senses.

Jonny dropped to his knees, frantically clawing at the earth around the object his shovel had struck. The soil was loose now, easily giving way to his desperate hands. Finally, he unearthed it – a rusted metal box, its surface pitted and scarred by time. Faint traces of red paint clung stubbornly to its edges, a ghost of its former vibrancy. It was the box. He knew it. His hands trembled as he pried at the rusted padlock, but with a gentle snap it broke free, the aged metal giving way without resistance. Inside, the contents were a jumbled mess of mud and debris. He carefully pulled out the items one by one. First, a lighter, its once-shiny chrome now dulled and corroded. He squinted, just able to make out the inscription: "Michigan 1977." Next, a green poker chip, its edges worn smooth with age. Then, a folded piece of paper, a note, but it was too far gone, the ink bled and faded, the paper disintegrating at his touch. Was this the note from her gifting him his first chainsaw? He carefully set it aside. Next, an old cassette tape, its plastic casing cracked and brittle. Finally, he saw it – the Polaroid picture. It was face down, buried beneath a layer of grime. This was it. This was the moment of truth. His heart hammered against his ribs. He reached down, his hands shaking so violently he could barely grasp the edge of the photo. Slowly, painstakingly, he turned it over, bracing himself for what he might find. He brushed away the dirt, revealing the image beneath. There he was, younger, carefree, his arm slung around someone. And next to him... Jess. Her face swam into focus, her smile as radiant as he remembered. Thirty years vanished in an instant. Her eyes, her nose, the curve of her cheek – it was all there, undeniable. She was real.

A wave of relief washed over Jonny, so profound it almost brought him to his knees. She was real. All that doubt, the whispers of disbelief, the gnawing uncertainty – all of it was washed away in the simple, irrefutable truth of that photograph. Seeing her face for the first time in thirty years was like a dam bursting within him, a flood of memories and emotions he thought long dead. The proof was right there in his hands, a tangible piece of the past brought back to life. He was so consumed by the moment, so lost in the rediscovery of her face, that he was oblivious to the sounds around him. He didn't hear the crunch of footsteps on the grass, didn't sense the presence of another person until it was too late. A shadow fell across the hole, and a glint of metal caught his eye. He looked up, his heart seizing in his chest. Standing behind him, silhouetted against the night sky, was a figure holding a shovel raised high above their head.

It was Bronko. His face, usually etched with a jovial grin, was now set in a grim, serious mask. He held the shovel, its blade raised high above Jonny's head, a dark and menacing shape against the stars.

"Sorry brother…" Bronko's voice rumbled, the words laced with a chilling finality, "but she don't wanna be found."

Before Jonny could react, before he could even register the betrayal in Bronko's eyes, the shovel came crashing down. The world exploded in a blinding flash of white-hot pain. He felt the sickening thud of metal against his skull, the force of the blow sending him sprawling backwards into the muddy pit. Then, everything went black. The image of Jess, her radiant smile, was the last thing he saw before the darkness consumed him.

Chapter 17 The Judas Mile

The first sensation was cold. A biting cold that seeped into Jonny's bones, dragging him from the depths of unconsciousness. He groaned, his head throbbing with a dull, persistent ache. His eyelids fluttered open, struggling to adjust to the pale light of dawn. He was lying on his side, the rough sidewalk scraping against his cheek. Disoriented, he pushed himself up, his muscles protesting with every movement. He was at the side of the road, his bike lying a few feet away, propped precariously against the railing of the bridge that marked the way out of Cedar Bluff.

The memories came flooding back, a torrent of betrayal and disbelief. Bronko. It had been Bronko, his supposed friend, standing over him with that shovel. Bronko, who had dismissed Jess as a figment of Jonny's imagination. But Bronko knew. He had to have known. The chilling words echoed in Jonny's mind: "…she don't wanna be found." What did that even mean? He scrambled to his feet, his head swimming. He reached for the side of his head, his fingers encountering a sticky, matted mess. Dried blood. It was crusty and stiff beneath his fingers, a grim reminder of the night's events.

His gaze fell upon the box, lying next to his bike. The rusted metal, the faint traces of red paint. He knelt down, his heart pounding with a mixture of anger and fear. He opened the box, his fingers trembling as he sifted through the contents. The lighter, the poker chip, the ruined note, the cassette tape – all present and accounted for. But the Polaroid was gone. The picture of him and Jess, the irrefutable proof of her existence, had been taken. In its place was a single, folded piece of paper. He unfolded it, his eyes scanning the terse message scrawled across the page: "Don't come looking." He knew it was from

Bronko. A wave of fury washed over him, eclipsing the pain in his head. He pulled out his phone, his hands shaking so violently he could barely dial. He called Bronko, the phone ringing unanswered. He tried again, and again, each unanswered ring a fresh wave of frustration. He sent a text, his fingers stabbing at the screen: "Answer me!" The message remained unread. Bronko wasn't answering. Bronko wasn't talking. And Jonny was alone, bleeding, and more determined than ever to find out the truth.

The morning sun streamed through the kitchen window of the Lannister's house. Dave sat at the kitchen table, a steaming mug of coffee warming his hands. The quiet hum of the refrigerator and the gentle chirping of birds outside were the only sounds breaking the morning stillness. Three of his daughters had just caught the school bus, their laughter still echoing faintly in his memory. Miranda, his wife, was busy clearing the breakfast dishes. It was a peaceful, ordinary morning, the kind Dave cherished.

Suddenly, the front door burst open with a jarring crash. The peaceful morning shattered as Jonny stormed into the kitchen, his face contorted with rage. He hadn't bothered to knock, hadn't even slowed down.

"Dave!" Jonny roared, his voice raw with fury.

Dave stood up, a knot of fear tightening in his stomach as Jonny charged into the kitchen. His eyes were wild and unfocused, radiating a frantic energy that scared Dave. He had never seen Jonny like this before.

"Jonny! What are you doing!?" Miranda's voice was sharp with alarm, cutting through the tense atmosphere.

"DID YOU KNOW!" Jonny's voice was a raw, guttural roar, barely recognisable.

"Jonny, what are you talking about!?" Dave tried to reason with him, but his words seemed to fall on deaf ears.

Jonny grabbed Dave, his grip surprisingly strong, and slammed him against the wall. The impact knocked the wind out of Dave, the breath catching in his throat. He could feel the rough plaster digging into his back, the sudden pain momentarily eclipsing his fear.

"JONNY STOP!" Miranda screamed, her voice laced with panic.

"Jonny! What's going on man? Your head's bleeding," Dave managed to gasp out, trying to appeal to some semblance of reason within his friend.

"I found proof!" Jonny shouted, his voice cracking with emotion. "Bronko, he knows about her! She's real. TELL ME IF YOU KNOW TOO!!"

"I don't know anything Jonny. I'm not lying to you brother," Dave said calmly, his voice measured and even, trying to defuse the volatile situation. He kept his gaze steady, hoping to convey sincerity and earn Jonny's trust.

Jonny released him, the anger seeming to drain out of him as quickly as it had appeared. Regret flickered across his face, a brief glimpse of the man Dave knew beneath the surface of this frantic stranger. But his eyes still held a desperate, confused plea, a silent cry for help.

"Tell me what happened. You said Bronko knew?" Dave asked gently, trying to steer the conversation towards a more rational ground.

"I dug up the box we buried years ago, there was a picture of us in there. I saw her face," Jonny's voice dropped to a near whisper, filled with a mixture of awe and disbelief. "Bronko came out of nowhere and hit me with the shovel, said something about her not wanting to be found."

Dave's face creased with concern. He reached for his phone, his fingers fumbling slightly as he pulled it from his pocket and dialled Bronko's number. He held the phone to his ear, listening to the rhythmic ringing in the empty space. No answer.

"He’s not answering," Dave said, a growing unease settling in his stomach.

"He’s not answering me either," Jonny replied, his voice flat and defeated.

"None of this makes sense. Why would Bronko lie?" Dave muttered, more to himself than to Jonny. The situation was spiralling into a bizarre and unsettling territory.

"I don’t know. Where does he live?" Jonny asked, his voice laced with urgency.

"I don’t know Jonny. We haven’t really kept in touch. I think he’s over the bridge, around Centre," Dave replied, racking his brain for any detail that might help them locate Bronko.

"Will you help me find him?" Jonny's eyes locked onto Dave's, pleading for assistance.

Dave looked into Jonny's eyes, seeing the raw desperation that burned within them. He knew he couldn't turn his back on his friend, not now. He nodded, a silent agreement to help him find Bronko and uncover the truth, no matter how strange or unsettling it might be. He knew, with a growing sense of dread, that whatever was happening was far bigger and more complicated than he could have ever imagined.

The journey to Centre was tense, the silence only broken by the hum of Dave's car engine and the roar of Jonny's motorcycle as they sped down the highway. Jonny, his jaw tight, stared ahead, replaying the events of the previous night in his mind. Dave, glancing in his rear-view mirror, could see Jonny's determined silhouette behind him, the bike cutting a dark figure against the morning sky.

Arriving in Centre, they were immediately met with a different atmosphere than the familiar streets of Cedar Bluff. They knew Bronko had always been a bit of a shady character, skirting the edges of the law, so they decided to look beyond the main streets, venturing into the back alleys and rundown areas where he might be more likely to be found. Dave pulled out his phone, displaying a photo of the three of them from about ten years ago – a rare occasion where they had all been together, a snapshot frozen in time. They approached people on the street, showing them the photo, asking, "Do you know this man?" Most shook their heads, offering a curt "No" before hurrying away. Others simply ignored them, their eyes cold and wary, as if they were unwelcome intruders in their world.

As the hours passed, frustration began to mount. The search was proving fruitless, each dead end adding to the growing sense of despair. They decided to split up, covering more ground in the hopes of increasing their chances of finding Bronko. "Keep your phone on," Dave instructed, his voice serious, "and be careful. We don't know what we're walking into." With a nod, Jonny revved his engine and sped off down the street.

Jonny's search was fuelled by a desperate urgency. He rode down every street, peered into every doorway, his eyes scanning the faces in the crowd with a feverish intensity. He even ventured into the homeless encampments, the makeshift shelters offering little protection from the harsh realities of the streets. He showed the photo to the men and women huddled there, their faces etched with hardship and distrust, but no one recognised Bronko. The rejection stung, each denial adding to the growing weight of his fear.

Jonny's relentless search continued, the hours blurring into a monotonous cycle of hope and disappointment. Just as his resolve began to waver, a flicker of movement caught his eye. Across the street, emerging from the dimly lit doorway of a rundown betting shop, was Bronko. He was trying to blend in, sporting a done-up black leather jacket and shades, but the attempt only made him more conspicuous. A smug look was plastered across his face as if he'd just won big. But the moment Bronko's eyes met Jonny's, the smugness vanished, replaced by a flash of terror. Recognition dawned on his face, and without a second's hesitation, he bolted, disappearing into the maze of narrow alleyways that crisscrossed the area.

Jonny didn't hesitate. Adrenaline surged through his veins. He lunged forward, legs pumping, determined not to lose Bronko. Bronko sprinted, weaving through the crowd. Jonny pushed through, focused on the fleeing figure.

The chase was on. Bronko darted down a narrow alleyway. Jonny followed, boots pounding. The alley twisted and turned. They vaulted trash cans, ducked under pipes. The alley opened onto a street. Bronko darted into traffic. Jonny followed, narrowly avoiding cars. He stumbled, losing sight of Bronko.

He scrambled up, eyes darting. He spotted Bronko disappearing down a side street, a narrow lane between buildings. Jonny sprinted after him, the buildings closing in. Bronko turned into a smaller alley; a dark passage filled with overflowing dumpsters and discarded junk. Jonny followed, the stench overwhelming. They scrambled over debris, the alley growing narrower. It opened into a larger back alley; a wide space lined with loading docks and warehouses.

Bronko sprinted across the back alley, dodging forklifts, and stacks of crates. Jonny followed, his lungs burning. Bronko leaped over a pile of tyres, disappearing behind a warehouse. Jonny followed, jumping over the tyres, his legs aching. He rounded the corner of the warehouse, scanning the area. Bronko was sprinting towards the back of the warehouse.

Jonny sprinted after him, gaining ground. Bronko reached the back of the warehouse and disappeared around another corner. Jonny followed, his heart pounding. He rounded the corner and found himself in a narrow passage between two warehouses, the walls towering above him. Bronko was frantically trying to pry open a heavy metal door, attempting to get inside one of the warehouses.

Jonny was closing in. Seeing he wouldn't get the door open, Bronko abruptly changed direction, darting down another narrow alley that ran perpendicular to the passage between the warehouses. This alley was even darker and more cluttered than the others, filled with rusting barrels and piles of discarded lumber. Jonny followed, his movements becoming more desperate, knowing that Bronko was running out of options. The alley twisted and turned, leading them back to the street. Bronko, without pausing, darted into the flow of traffic, dodging cars, and pedestrians with reckless abandon. Jonny followed, weaving through the chaos, narrowly avoiding a collision with a delivery cart. He scanned the street, his eyes searching for any sign of Bronko, the fear that he might have lost him clawing at his throat. Then, he spotted him, scrambling across the main road, dodging a bus and a delivery truck, his face a mask of desperation.

Jonny knew he needed to cut him off. He sprinted back the way he came, his eyes scanning the street for his bike. He spotted it parked haphazardly near the entrance to the alley. He vaulted onto the seat, kicked the engine to life, and roared back onto the street, weaving through the traffic with a newfound ferocity. He spotted Bronko disappearing down another alleyway, a narrow passage barely wide enough for the bike to fit. He didn't hesitate, gunning the engine and plunging into the darkness. The alley was a gauntlet of obstacles – overflowing dumpsters, stacks of crates, and discarded furniture. He navigated the hazards with a skill born of desperation, the bike bouncing and rattling, the engine screaming in protest. He caught a glimpse of Bronko ahead, his legs pumping furiously, his face contorted with fear. Jonny twisted the throttle, the bike surging forward, closing the distance between them. He was almost within reach when Bronko suddenly veered to the right, disappearing behind a building. Jonny slammed on the brakes, the bike skidding to a halt just inches from the wall. He jumped off, his boots hitting the pavement with a thud, and rounded the corner, his eyes scanning the area.

Bronko was nowhere to be seen. Then, Jonny looked up. A rickety wooden ladder led to the roof of the building, and silhouetted against the skyline, he saw Bronko scrambling upwards. A surge of adrenaline coursed through Jonny's veins. The chase wasn't over; it was just going vertical. He grabbed the ladder, his hands gripping the worn rungs, and began to climb, his muscles burning with exertion. He reached the roof, pulling himself over the edge, and found himself in a surreal landscape of tar and gravel, a maze of interconnected rooftops stretching out before him. Bronko was already leaping across the gaps between the buildings, his black jacket flapping in the wind, his movements desperate and erratic. Jonny followed, his heart pounding in his chest, his senses heightened, the city spread out beneath him like a concrete jungle. He jumped across the chasms, the wind whipping at his face, the ground a dizzying distance below. The chase was a dangerous dance on the edge, a desperate struggle between two men driven by secrets and lies.

Bronko's breath came in ragged gasps. He glanced around frantically, his eyes darting from one building to the next, searching for an escape route. But he had run himself into a corner, literally. He had sprinted to the very edge of the building, to the point where the rooftop ended abruptly, offering no further passage. Beyond its edge was only empty air and a long, unforgiving drop to the alleyway below. He was trapped, cornered. The wind whipped around him, a cold reminder of his exposed position. Then, he heard the sound of Jonny's heavy footsteps behind him, closing in, relentless and unforgiving. Bronko turned to face his pursuer, his face a mask of desperation and fear. He had nowhere left to run.

"Be cool brother, don't do anything stupid," Bronko stammered.

Jonny surged forward, his hand a vise around Bronko's throat. Bronko, weakened and terrified, couldn't summon the strength to resist. Jonny relentlessly pushed him back, closer, closer to the precipice. Bronko clawed at Jonny's arms, a desperate, futile attempt to break free, but Jonny held him implacably, his body a wall of unyielding rage. Bronko's heels scrabbled against the loose gravel at the edge, the drop a dizzying invitation to his doom.

"Where is she!" Jonny's voice was a guttural roar.

"Please brother..." Bronko choked out, his eyes wide with terror.

Jonny shoved him forward, the alleyway a dizzying abyss. A single misstep, a moment's loss of grip, and Bronko would plummet to his death.

"YOU DON'T GET TO CALL ME BROTHER!" Jonny spat, his face inches from Bronko's.

A desperate cry pierced the air from below. Dave, having witnessed the terrifying scene from the alley, his face etched with horror. He was coming to know Jonny's rage, relentless and fierce.

"Oh Jesus Christ!!" Dave's voice was laced with panic.

He raced down the narrow passage between the buildings, frantically seeking a way to intervene before Jonny crossed a point of no return.

"TELL ME WHERE SHE IS!" Jonny's demand was a raw, desperate plea.

"I CAN'T!" Bronko gasped, his face contorted with fear.

Jonny, a war raging within him, knew he couldn't kill Bronko. The answers he craved would die with him. With a surge of strength, he hauled Bronko back from the edge, throwing him to the ground with brutal force. The air whooshed from Bronko's lungs as he landed heavily. Jonny, his rage a living thing, kicked him twice in the ribs, the sickening thud echoing in the confined space.

"Tell me where she is, Bronko!" Jonny's voice was a low, menacing growl.

"Jonny, I really can't!" Bronko whimpered, clutching his side.

Jonny unleashed a torrent of blows, his fists connecting with Bronko's face, each punch fuelled by desperation and despair. Blood blossomed around Bronko's teeth, a gruesome display of Jonny's fury.

"JONNY PLEASE!" Bronko's plea was a broken sob.

"WHERE IS JESS!!!" Jonny roared, his voice cracking with anguish.

Jonny rained down hit after hit, a relentless assault fuelled by grief and rage. Each punch was a hammer blow, fuelled by the burning question that consumed him: Where is Jess? Bronko's body, once tense with resistance, gradually went limp, his struggles weakening with each blow. He was barely conscious, a broken mess of blood and bruises, his pleas for Jonny to stop a pathetic, slurred whimper that was barely audible above the pounding in Jonny's ears. Jonny barely registered the pain in his own knuckles; the world reduced to the rhythm of his fists and the sickening thud of flesh on flesh. He was dimly aware that he was crossing a line, that the rage was consuming him, but he couldn't stop, wouldn't stop, not until Bronko gave him the answer he desperately needed. Each punch was a desperate attempt to break through Bronko's silence, to unearth the truth that was buried somewhere within the broken man.

"Where is she!" Jonny's voice was a raw, guttural demand that tore through the night.

A strangled sob escaped Bronko's lips. "Jonny stop!!"

Jonny's fist tightened, poised for another blow. "WHERE IS SHE!"

"PLEASE!" Bronko's plea was desperate.

Jonny leaned in close, his face inches from Bronko's ruined features, his voice a low, menacing growl. "WHERE IS SHE BRONKO!"

A final, shuddering breath rattled in Bronko's chest, and then the words spilled out, a confession ripped from the depths of his despair. "SHE'S DEAD!"

The words struck Jonny like a physical blow, the force stopping his fist in mid-air. Bronko lay broken and bleeding, a ruined heap of humanity, the devastating truth hanging in the air like a shroud. A tremor ran through Jonny's body, a violent rejection of the unbearable reality.

Dave stumbled onto the rooftop, his face a canvas of shock and horror. The scene that greeted him was a nightmare made real: Jonny, a storm of fury unleashed, and Bronko, battered and broken in its wake. The air thrummed with unspoken dread.

"I'm sorry man..." Bronko's voice was a faint, pain-laced whisper, filled with regret.

"No…" The denial was a ragged breath, a desperate attempt to rewrite the past. Jonny's mind recoiled from the truth, seeking any escape from the crushing weight of it.

"She's dead..." Bronko repeated, the words a final, irreversible pronouncement.

The rooftop seemed to tilt, the city pressing in on him from all sides, a suffocating weight. Jonny reeled back, as if pushed by an unseen force, and collapsed onto the gritty surface, the fight draining out of him, leaving him hollow and empty. Disbelief clawed at his sanity, a desperate refusal to accept the gaping hole that had just been ripped in his world. Bronko lay on his back, each shallow breath a victory against the crushing weight of his injuries.

"Where?" Jonny's voice was a mere rasp, a ghost of a question lost in the wind.

Bronko flinched. "What?"

Jonny pushed himself up, his movements stiff and uncoordinated, his eyes burning with a desperate need to know. "Where is she buried?" His voice was stripped of all pretence.

Bronko hesitated; his face contorted with pain and remorse. "West Virginia… a small town called Bancroft. I didn't want to tell you man; I didn't want you to feel this way." His voice was a choked sob.

Dave stepped forward tentatively, his hand outstretched in a gesture of comfort, unsure of how to bridge the chasm of grief and violence that separated them. "Jonny… I'm sorry."

Jonny ignored him, his gaze fixed on some distant point, his mind already racing towards the next step, the next desperate attempt to make sense of the senseless. "I need to see her grave." The words were a hollow echo, devoid of hope, yet filled with a desperate need for closure.

He rose to his feet, a marionette with severed strings, and moved towards Bronko's broken form. His movements were mechanical, devoid of purpose. He rifled through Bronko's pockets, his fingers clumsy and unfeeling, until he found the Polaroid. He held it out to Dave, the image a faded memory of a life that was now irrevocably gone, a cruel reminder of what had been lost.

Dave stared at the picture; his face a mixture of guilt and sorrow. "Holy crap… yeah, I do remember her… Jonny, I'm sorry man, my stupid memory…" His voice was thick with remorse, but the words felt hollow, inadequate in the face of such profound loss.

Jonny barely acknowledged him; his eyes fixed on the faded image in his hand. "It's a bit late now, Dave." The words were flat and final.

He turned and walked away, leaving Dave paralysed by guilt and Bronko broken and bleeding on the rooftop, the weight of their collective sins a crushing burden in the cold night air. The silence that followed was more terrifying than any scream, a silence that spoke of broken promises and shattered dreams.

Chapter 18 From Bluff to Bancroft

Bancroft, West Virginia, was the kind of town you could easily miss if you blinked while driving through. Nestled deep within a valley carved by the Kanawha River, it was a place where the surrounding Appalachian hills seemed to press in on all sides, dwarfing the modest collection of buildings that made up its downtown. A single main street, lined with faded brick storefronts and punctuated by the occasional gas station or diner, served as the town's artery. The pace of life was unhurried, dictated more by the changing seasons than the demands of the outside world. The air hung thick with the scent of woodsmoke and decaying leaves, a pre-winter chill already settling in. A few houses still had remnants of Halloween decorations – a deflated pumpkin here, a faded ghost there – as if the residents were reluctant to let go of the festive spirit. The houses, mostly modest clapboard structures with peeling paint and sagging porches, huddled together as if seeking warmth and companionship against the approaching winter. A weathered church steeple, its paint chipped and faded, stood as the town's tallest landmark, a silent sentinel watching over the lives of its inhabitants. A faded banner welcoming visitors to the annual "Fall Festival" still hung crookedly above the town's only intersection. Beyond the town's small commercial centre, the houses thinned out, giving way to overgrown fields and dense forests, a reminder of the untamed wilderness that lay just beyond the edges of civilisation. The quiet, unassuming cemetery, perched on a hillside overlooking the town, was a reminder of the generations who had lived and died within Bancroft's embrace, their stories etched into the worn headstones that dotted the landscape. The whole place exuded a similar sense of quiet isolation and understated resilience that Jonny remembered so well from Cedar Bluff – the same feeling of being a world apart, where time moved at a different pace and the past clung to the present like the lingering scent of woodsmoke. It was a place of quiet beauty and understated hardship, a place that held its secrets close, a place where Jess was buried, now forever a part of its silent history, and Jonny couldn't shake the unsettling question of what brought her to this forgotten corner of the world.

Jonny sat in the cab of his truck, parked just off the narrow road that led to the Bancroft cemetery, the engine idling to keep the chill at bay. A light November rain misted the windshield, softening the already bleak landscape into a watercolour of grey and brown. He stared out at the cemetery gates, a wrought-iron archway visible through the gentle drizzle, a knot of something akin to dread tightening in his stomach with each passing minute. It hadn't been years of mourning Jess, but rather years of wondering, years of fleeting thoughts about what she might be doing, where she might be. Now, sitting on the precipice of confronting her final resting place, the reality of her death felt strangely distant, almost unreal. He was dreading going in there, not so much out of grief, but out of a fear of the unknown, a fear of seeing her name etched on a cold, unforgiving stone, a fear of the finality of it all, the undeniable proof that his wondering was over, that she was truly gone, lost to him forever in this forgotten corner of West Virginia.

Jonny finally killed the engine, the sudden silence amplifying the drumming of the rain on the truck's roof. He took a deep breath, steeled himself, and stepped out into the drizzle. The cemetery was eerily quiet, the only sound the gentle patter of rain on the fallen leaves and the frantic hammering of his own heart. He walked slowly through the rows of headstones, his boots sinking slightly into the soft earth, each step a heavy, reluctant advance. His eyes scanned the names and dates etched into the stone, a blur of unfamiliar names and long-ago lives.

The cemetery sloped gently uphill, and as he neared the crest, a flicker of white caught his eye. He moved towards it, drawn by an invisible force, his breath catching in his throat. It was a weathered, eroded headstone, half-hidden beneath a tangle of ivy, almost swallowed by the earth itself. He stopped a few feet away, his gaze fixed on the marker, unable to bring himself any closer.

And then he saw it, the name he had carried in his heart, unspoken, for so long: Jess Judy. A jolt ran through him, a physical shock that left him momentarily breathless. A wave of emotion crashed over him, a tsunami of grief, regret, and a sudden, overwhelming sense of loss. His breath hitched in his chest, a strangled sob escaping his lips. The stone was so old, so worn, the details almost lost to time, but he could make out the date of her death: 1984. She was only twenty-two. The numbers swam before his eyes, blurring into meaningless shapes.

He loved her, he realised with a sudden, crushing certainty that stole the air from his lungs, and he wished he had been there, with her, holding her hand, in her final moments. A raw, primal scream welled up inside him, a silent cry of anguish that echoed through the empty graveyard. Questions swirled in his mind, a chaotic vortex of unanswered whys. How had she died so young? What had happened to her? Had she been scared? Had she been alone? She hadn't deserved this, this cold, lonely end in a forgotten graveyard in a forgotten town. He sank to the ground a few feet away from the grave, his body wracked with sobs, the rain mingling with his tears as he mourned a love lost too soon, a life that had been stolen away before it had even truly begun. Yet relatively fresh lilies were by her grave. Who was visiting her, he thought to himself?

Jonny remained by Jess's grave for hours, lost in a silent communion with the past. The light November rain continued to fall, soaking him to the bone, but he barely noticed. He sat there, unmoving, his gaze fixed on the weathered headstone, his mind a whirlwind of memories, regrets, and unanswered questions. The graveyard grew darker as the afternoon wore on, the shadows lengthening and the air growing colder, but he couldn't bring himself to leave. He was trapped in a loop of grief, replaying moments from the past, wondering what might have been, mourning a future that would never come.

Eventually, as dusk began to settle over the valley, a figure emerged from the trees at the edge of the cemetery. It was a woman in her late forties; her face etched with the lines of a life lived under the West Virginia sun. Her hair, once probably a vibrant auburn, was now faded and streaked with grey, pulled back into a practical ponytail. She wore a simple, worn flannel shirt over a pair of faded jeans, and her boots were scuffed and muddy. Her eyes, though tired, held a spark of warmth and curiosity as she approached Jonny, her expression a mixture of concern and gentle understanding. She was the kind of woman you'd expect to see in rural West Virginia, a woman who knew hardship but also possessed a quiet strength and resilience, a woman who had likely seen her fair share of both joy and sorrow.

She approached him slowly, her footsteps barely disturbing the quiet of the graveyard. "Haven't seen you around town before, stranger," she said softly, seeing his genuine sadness.

Jonny cleared his throat, the sound raw and choked, and wiped away the tears that tracked paths down his weathered cheeks. "I've not been here." He avoided her gaze, focusing instead on the rain-streaked surface of Jess's headstone.

"She was a lovely woman, Jess," the woman replied, her voice gentle.

"Yeah," Jonny said, his voice barely audible above the whisper of the wind through the trees. "I only knew her back in 1979." He remembered her then, a vibrant, laughing girl, full of life and dreams. It was a far cry from the silent stone before him.

The woman's gaze lingered on Jonny's face, a knowing look in her eyes. "She must have made quite the impression."

"Yeah… she did." He finally met her gaze, a flicker of pain in his own.

"It's been a long time since I've seen anyone else visit her," she added, her voice tinged with a hint of sadness. The rain continued to fall, washing away the years, but not the memories.

Jonny found the woman's presence strangely comforting, a warm ember in the cold, desolate landscape of his grief. There was a quiet empathy in her eyes, a sense of shared understanding that eased the sharp edges of his sorrow. He figured she must have been a friend of Jess's, someone who had known her, laughed with her, shared secrets with her. The thought brought a flicker of warmth to his heart, a sense of connection to the girl he had lost so long ago. Perhaps this woman could offer him some answers, some insight into the life Jess had lived after he had left, the life that had led her to this forgotten corner of West Virginia. He felt a sudden surge of hope, a fragile belief that he might finally piece together the fragments of her story and understand the mystery of her untimely death.

"So, how'd you know her?" the woman asked, breaking the silence.

"Back in Alabama, we... we had a thing," Jonny replied, his voice still thick with emotion. "It was only brief, but I thought about her for a long time after. I just recently found out about her death."

The woman's expression shifted to confusion, a puzzled crinkle forming around her eyes. "Alabama? Back in seventy-nine? You must have been a young man."

"Twenty," Jonny confirmed.

"Forgive me, stranger, but I don't think my mother went to Alabama in nineteen seventy-nine."

Jonny stood up, a wave of dizziness washing over him. He looked back at the woman, his mind racing. Mother! Jess had a child, he thought to himself. The interaction was getting stranger by the second.

"Jess was your mother?" he asked, his voice laced with disbelief.

"My name's Lorraine Judy. Are you sure you have the right person here, sir?" she replied, her eyes searching his face.

"I met Jess in Cedar Bluff in Alabama, we had a summer thing and she never called after that," Jonny insisted, his voice rising slightly. "She knew a friend of mine, Bronko! Bronko Jackson!"

"My mother never left Bancroft," Lorraine stated firmly, shaking her head.

The woman pulled the ivy back from the headstone, revealing Jess's date of birth. 1910! More shock and confusion hit Jonny. This Jess Judy wasn't twenty-two when she died; she was seventy-four. It was too much to comprehend, a sense of disorientation that left him reeling.

The woman turned back to Jonny, her expression a mixture of pity and suspicion. "Let me ask you again, stranger… are you sure you have the right person?"

A little while later, the warmth of the Main Street Diner was a welcome contrast to the chill of the cemetery. Jonny and Lorraine sat across from each other in a worn vinyl booth, the Formica tabletop sticky beneath their elbows. The air was thick with the aroma of frying bacon and stale coffee, a comforting scent that spoke of small-town life and simple pleasures. They both sipped on steaming mugs of black coffee, the bitter liquid a welcome jolt to their frayed nerves. The initial awkwardness of their encounter had begun to dissipate, replaced by a cautious sense of friendliness.

Jonny stared at Lorraine, his mind reeling. "None of this makes sense," he said, the words hanging in the air of the bustling diner. "Why would Bronko think your mother was the same woman?"

Lorraine leaned back slightly, a thoughtful expression on her face. "That's a question for Bronko, Jonny. I have to say, hearing your story, it's pretty wild. Someone just disappearing from existence." She paused, tapping a finger against the table. "Did Bronko use a pen-pal service by any chance?"

Jonny shook his head, a wry smile tugging at his lips. Writing letters across the country wasn't exactly Bronko's style.

Lorraine continued, her voice taking on a nostalgic tone. "My mother's mission was to 'unite America.' She ran a pen-pal business from our home. She wanted people from different states to connect, even took in those that needed it—young men and women, mostly troubled. Gave them a place to stay when they needed it."

"She sounds like a generous woman," Jonny remarked, a flicker of admiration in his eyes.

Lorraine's smile faded slightly, replaced by a hint of cynicism. "Yeah, she was a real Mother Teresa, alright."

Suddenly, a memory sparked in Jonny's mind, pieces of a puzzle clicking into place. A pen-pal service… He was making connections. "My Jess," he began, his voice tinged with hope, "she met a friend, Sally. She stayed with her for the whole summer, and they were going to study at the same college together. Maybe that was through your mother's service?"

"That sounds possible," Lorraine conceded, her eyes narrowing in thought.

Jonny reached for his wallet. He retrieved the worn photograph of Jess. He slid it across the table to Lorraine, a nervous twinge inside, hoping she might recognise her.

Lorraine's eyes widened as she looked at the picture, immediate recognition flashing across her face. "That's your girl?!"

"That's her. You know her?" Jonny asked eagerly.

"Yeah, I remember that face," Lorraine replied, her gaze fixed on the photograph. "She came to stay at the house, twice."

Jonny sat forward, his body tense with anticipation. He was getting somewhere, finally.

"She was a few years older than me," Lorraine continued, her voice laced with concentration. "I don't really remember much. Except she just disappeared—twice. Come to think of it, might have even been seventy-nine."

"Anything you can remember will help," Jonny urged.

"Honestly, I just remember her face, but she sure as hell wasn't called Jess." Lorraine said, with confidence.

The words hit Jonny hard. If she wasn't called Jess, how much of her had he truly known at all? A wave of doubt washed over him, threatening to drown his newfound hope.

Lorraine, sensing his distress, offered a glimmer of hope. "My mother kept everything—visitors' logs, archived paperwork on her guests, files…"

"Do you still have it?" Jonny asked, his voice filled with urgency.

"It's all in storage. There's a lot to go through," Lorraine replied, a hint of reluctance in her voice.

"I'll pay you! How does two grand sound?" Jonny blurted out, his eyes pleading.

Lorraine's eyes lit up, a sly grin spreading across her face. "Well, shit, I was gonna do it for free—I'm invested now—but I'll take that two grand."

Jonny sat forward, a new sense of motivation surging through him. New leads and a new ally, found in the most unlikely of places.

"If you can speak to this Sally, you think she met through the pen-pal service, that'll speed things up a bit," Lorraine suggested. "Help me find what I'm looking for. I'll see what I know on this woman and where she ended up going."

"Thank you! Thank you!" Jonny exclaimed, his gratitude overflowing.

He lunged forward, impulsively kissing Lorraine on the forehead, startling her slightly. Jonny turned and strode out of the diner, his phone already pressed to his ear, ready for the chase. He was going to follow her footsteps, wherever they might lead.

Dave answered the phone. "Jonny?"

"It wasn't her, Dave!" Jonny declared, his voice filled with a mixture of relief and determination. "She's not dead!"

"Bronko got it wrong?" Dave asked, his voice laced with disbelief.

"I have no idea. I can't trust Bronko, but I've found someone who can help. The search is back on, brother… You in?"

Dave stood up from his desk, his eyes blazing with renewed resolve. He had doubted Jonny for too long, but now they would stand united and retrace Jess's steps from thirty years ago.

"Hell yeah, I'm in," Dave replied, his voice firm and unwavering. "Anything you need, Jonny, I'll help in any way I can."

"Do you remember Sally Strooker? And Stu… uh, Bronko's friend, what was it Pete used to always call him… Beef Stu?" Jonny asked, racking his brain.

"Yeah, they married, I think," Dave replied, pausing as he tried to recall details.

"I need an address," Jonny pressed, his voice urgent.

"Shit, they moved out of Cedar Bluff twenty years ago," Dave said, a hint of frustration in his voice. "Alright, leave it with me, man. Get back here, and I'll try and have the address for you."

"Thank you, brother!" Jonny exclaimed, his heart soaring with renewed hope.

As Jonny ended the call, a surge of optimism coursed through him. Jess wasn't just a ghost from the past; she was a real person with a history, a life that could be pieced back together.

With Dave and Lorraine on side, trying to find her, Jonny felt an unshakeable belief that he was finally on the right path, closer than ever to bringing Jess out of the shadows and back into the light.

Chapter 19 Where Loyalty Still Breathes

A few days had passed since the revelations at the diner. The nursing home was comfortably warm, the air filled with gentle activity and the faint, pleasant scent of lavender. Sunlight streamed through the large windows, illuminating the spotless room and casting a warm glow on the residents. There was a sense of quiet dignity here, a feeling that the staff truly cared for the people in their charge. In a cozy armchair by the window, an old man sat, his frame painfully thin beneath a soft, knitted blanket. His eyes were wide but vacant, reflecting nothing of the world around him. Dementia had stolen much of his essence, leaving him a shell of his former self, though his face still held a certain peacefulness. At the entrance to the living space stood Jonny, his hand resting on the doorframe, a wave of conflicting emotions washing over him. He remembered him as a vibrant, powerful figure, for who he once was.

Jonny crossed the room and settled into the chair beside him. "Hey, Uncle Larry. It's been a few years," he said, his voice soft.

Larry didn't react, his gaze drifting from Jonny to the window, lost in the fog of dementia. Jonny knew the words were falling on deaf ears. "It's good to see you again."

"I've come back for her, Uncle Larry," he murmured, almost to himself. "Jess. Remember her? The girl from '79. I bet if you still had your memory, you would."

Even though it was a one-way conversation, Jonny found a strange comfort in simply being near Larry. It was a connection to the past, a reminder of a time when things were simpler, when Larry had been a guiding force in his life. He was another person who had experienced that summer, who had known Jess.

"That was a good summer, wasn't it?" Jonny continued, filled with nothing but nostalgia. "You teaching me how to cut and fix trees... The parties... Jess. You two really got on like a house on fire, always teasing each other, trading those quick comebacks. And Aunt Glenda's beef brisket... Everything seemed so simple back then."

It was nice to sit there, to let the memories wash over him, to feel a connection to that simpler time with Larry beside him. But the comfort was laced with a sharp, bitter sadness. This wasn't the Larry he remembered, the vibrant, quick-witted uncle who had been such a force in his life. This was a shadow, a shell, and the reality of his absence was a heavy weight in Jonny's heart. And it wasn't just about Larry. It was about everything that had been lost, everything that had changed.

Jonny pushed himself up from the chair, the movement feeling heavier than it should. "I've got to go now, Uncle Larry," he said, forcing a lightness into his voice that he didn't feel. "It won't be so long next time. I promise."

He doubted Larry even registered the words, but he said them anyway, a hollow offering to the silent figure by the window. Turning, Jonny walked back towards the entrance, each step feeling like a retreat. At the doorway, he paused, his hand resting on the cool metal of the frame. He couldn't leave without one last look.

Turning back, he saw Larry still sitting there, bathed in the afternoon light, utterly lost in his own world. The vacant expression in his eyes was heartbreaking. Jonny wanted to say something, anything, to bridge the gap that dementia had created, but the words caught in his throat. He simply stood there for a moment, etching the image into his memory, a bittersweet reminder of what was and what would never be again. Then, with a sigh, he turned and walked away.

The air outside was crisp and cool against Jonny's skin. He walked slowly toward his truck, the gravel crunching beneath his boots a lonely sound in the quiet afternoon. The weight of the visit settled heavily on his shoulders, a mix of sadness and unresolved questions. As he reached the truck, his phone buzzed in his pocket. He pulled it out and saw Dave's name flashing on the screen. Taking a deep breath, he answered.

"Dave!" Jonny said, a hint of anticipation in his voice.

"Hey man, I got something for you!" Dave's voice crackled through the speaker, infused with a clear sense of satisfaction. There was a subtle energy in his tone, a hint of the enjoyment he derived from solving a good puzzle. This kind of investigation was a far cry from the usual small-town police work, and Jonny knew Dave was relishing the chance to play detective, piecing together a mystery, thirty years in the making. More than that, Dave was a fiercely loyal friend, the kind who would move heaven and earth for someone he cared about. He was a strong ally, and Jonny was grateful to have him on his side.

"Turns out Stu and Sally moved out of Bama twenty years ago," Dave continued, his voice losing some of its playful edge. "They're over in Georgia, Atlanta. I'll text you the address."

"You're a goddamn saint, Dave!" Jonny exclaimed, a surge of hope coursing through him. "Helps having a friend in the force."

"I didn't even need to use my job for this," Dave chuckled. "Turns out I have Sally on social media. My daughter helped me do something called 'stalking.' In the end, I just messaged her."

"How did she take it?" Jonny asked, a hint of reluctance flowing through his words.

"I didn't tell her what it was about, but she's happy to meet with you," Dave replied. "I'm gonna head into work and see what I can find on the system. I have to say, Jonny, whatever she was up to back then... it doesn't sound good. Using fake names, small towns off the grid, disappearing without a trace. It's all starting to form a pattern. Did you say she was from Michigan?"

"That's what she told me. I don't know if it was true or not," Jonny admitted, a knot of unease tightening in his stomach.

"Either way, I'll take a look," Dave said, his voice turning serious. "You best head on over to Georgia and see what ole Sally Strooker has to say."

The drive to Atlanta was a blur of highway miles and anxious thoughts. Jonny kept replaying the conversation with Dave, the pieces of the puzzle slowly starting to take shape, but the picture was still far from clear. He arrived in a quiet, suburban neighbourhood, a world away from the small towns and dusty roads he was used to. The address Dave had given him led to a modest, single-story home, nothing fancy, but well-kept and undeniably homely. A swing set stood in the backyard, and flowerpots lined the front porch, adding a touch of warmth and normalcy. Jonny parked the truck at the curb, took a deep breath, and looked at the house. Hope and nerves warred within him. This could be the key, the answer he had been searching for. But it could also be a dead end, or worse, a Pandora's Box he was not prepared to open. With a mix of trepidation and determination, he got out of the truck and walked up to the front door. He raised his hand and knocked. The door opened, and there she was. Sally. Thirty years had etched their mark, but the resemblance was undeniable. Her long hair, once a vibrant blonde, was now streaked with grey, pulled back loosely from her face. Her eyes, though, were the same – a bright, curious blue that Jonny remembered well. There were lines around them now, etched by time and experience, but they still held a spark of the girl he once knew.

"You must be Jonny," Sally said, her voice a little hesitant.

Of course. After all this time, they weren't friends, not really. Acquaintances from a lifetime ago, bound by a single, sweltering summer. Why would she think of him as anything more? As she turned to lead him inside, Jonny's gaze drifted to a gallery of family photos adorning a nearby wall. Two daughters, beaming with youthful energy, and a son, his arm slung casually around his father's shoulders. They looked like a happy family, a life carefully constructed, brick by brick.

"Sally Strooker," Jonny said, stating the obvious, the name feeling foreign on his tongue after all these years.

Sally laughed faintly, a delicate sound tinged with a palpable awkwardness. "I've not been Sally Strooker for twenty years or so."

"Of course," Jonny replied, feeling a little foolish, a trespasser in this carefully curated domestic scene. "My heads still stuck in the seventies. It's nice that you both stayed together this whole time. You have a lovely family."

"Thank you," Sally said, the word polite but distant, a carefully measured response that revealed nothing.

The air felt thick with unspoken words, heavy with the weight of the past. Jonny's sudden appearance was undeniably strange, an intrusion into their quiet suburban life, and he felt acutely out of place, like a ghost from a forgotten chapter. Sally led him into the kitchen.

"Jonny! Man, you haven't changed a bit!" A booming voice shattered the tense silence, and Stu appeared, his face splitting into a wide, welcoming grin. He clapped Jonny on the shoulder, the force of the blow almost knocking him off balance. Stu, on the other hand, was almost unrecognisable. Time had been far less kind to him. The lanky, clean-shaven youth Jonny remembered had vanished, replaced by a man with a thick, salt-and-pepper beard that obscured most of his face and a receding hairline that emphasized the years. There wasn't a single feature that Jonny could readily connect to the Stu he once knew. It was as if he were looking at a completely different person, a stranger wearing the mask of an old acquaintance.

"Stu, nice to see you again," Jonny said, offering a polite smile.

"You too." Stu chuckled, his voice a low rumble. "I had to remind Sally who you were when we got Dave's message. I told him it was from when we were kids back in Cedar Bluff. Hey, have you ever gone back there?"

"From time to time," Jonny replied, his gaze drifting around the room.

"Have a seat. Would you like a drink?" Sally asked, her tone polite but lacking warmth.

The hospitality seemed forced, the smile not quite reaching her eyes. Jonny knew the elephant in the room was his unexpected arrival after all these years. What was he doing here? What did he want? The questions hung in the air, unspoken but palpable.

"Thank you, coffee would be great," Jonny said, breaking the strained silence.

"I'll do it, honey," Stu offered, squeezing past them with surprising agility for a man of his size. He moved to the counter, the clatter of mugs and the whir of the coffee maker filling the awkward void. Jonny and Sally sat down at the table together, the distance between them feeling vast and unbridgeable.

"So, what brings you to Atlanta, Jonny?" Sally asked, her voice carefully neutral. Her eyes, though still bright, held a guarded curiosity, as if she were trying to decipher his motives.

"I'm looking for someone," Jonny replied, his voice low and steady. "Someone we used to know back in seventy-nine."

Sally's face was a cross between confusion, a visible effort to dredge up long-buried memories, and a dawning curiosity. The lines around her eyes deepened as she concentrated.

"We knew her as Jess Judy," Jonny continued, watching her closely. "She stayed with you that summer."

Jonny could see the wheels turning in Sally's mind, the cogs of memory slowly grinding into motion. The name seemed to stir something within her, a faint echo of a forgotten melody.

"Her name rings a bell..." Sally said slowly, her voice hesitant.

"She was going to college with you, to become a nurse?" Jonny prompted, offering a gentle nudge to her memory.

"Oh! The one that you used to write to you a lot?" Stu chimed in.

"Yeah, that sounds familiar," Sally said, her gaze distant. "Sorry, Jonny. That was a long time ago."

"Didn't you and her sleep together or something? Or like, have a thing?" Stu asked, his tone surprisingly blunt, cutting through the carefully constructed politeness.

"Yeah, we did, for the whole summer," Jonny replied, a faint smile playing on his lips. "We used to do all sorts, you two, me and her and Pete."

"Those parties were fun!" Stu exclaimed, the memory seeming to spark something in him, a flicker of the carefree youth they once shared, a brief escape from the responsibilities of adulthood.

Jonny could tell Sally was relaxing more, the more they spoke about that summer, as if the floodgates had opened and a whirlwind of forgotten memories were coming back to the surface. Jonny slid the Polaroid picture of he and Jess across the table to Sally.

"Yeah, I do remember her," Sally said, her voice soft. She paused. "My parents weren't keen, a stranger coming to stay but she was insistent. Strange when I think back."

Jonny leaned forward, his expression earnest. "How did you meet?"

Sally's eyes took on a faraway look. "We'd both signed up to a pen-pal service in West Virginia. It was this old-fashioned thing, where they tried to match people based on compatibility. I got Jess. We wrote letters back and forth for a while before she came to stay."

Jonny's interest deepened. "Did she mention anything that might help me find her?"

Sally shook her head, a shadow of regret clouding her features. "I can't remember, sorry. I remember thinking she was quite private. Never really spoke about home. In all honesty she didn't seem right in the head. She just vanished, had my parents going crazy trying to make sure she was okay. But I never heard from her after that. I remember waking up in our bedroom sometimes just listening to her sobbing. She'd cry a lot when she thought no one was around."

A heavy silence filled the room. Jonny was really starting to hear another side to her; a side she had kept private from him. A sadder side, one that was more vulnerable than she ever let on. He was already questioning if he meant as much to her as she did to him back then, but maybe he did? Maybe he was her one bit of light in a darkness.

Stu leaned forward, his gaze narrowed with a mixture of curiosity and scepticism, his eyes boring into Jonny. "I gotta ask, man, why now, after all this time? She was just a summer fling, right?"

Sally watched Jonny, her expression thoughtful and a little sad. She was trying to gauge the depth of his feelings, the sincerity behind his quest. She knew—Sally could see just how much she meant to Jonny.

"She felt more than a summer fling, didn't she?" Sally said, her voice soft, a gentle question hanging in the air.

Jonny offered a small, almost imperceptible nod, his gaze fixed on some distant point beyond the confines of the room. He was lovestruck and desperate, but beneath the surface lay a core of unwavering determination. Sally's heart ached for him, recognising the ache of longing and the relentless pursuit of a lost connection.

"So how far are you into your search?" Stu asked.

"Not very. All I know is she was in West Virginia at some point, and it's likely her name wasn't Jess Judy," Jonny admitted, a weary sigh escaping his lips.

Stu let out a low whistle, scratching his beard. "Damn, that's a real mystery you're caught up in. Who the hell was she really?"

"I wondered that for a long time after," Sally confessed, a wistful smile playing on her lips. "If you find out, let me know."

Jonny nodded, a spark of renewed resolve flickering in his eyes. The confirmation that Jess and Sally had corresponded for a year through the pen-pal service provided a fragile thread of hope, a new avenue for Lorraine to explore. A sudden glint of recognition sparked in Sally's eyes as she rose and ambled toward the liquor shelf, her movements betraying a hint of playful mischief.

"If my very terrible memory serves me, didn't you like a Clyde May's?" Sally inquired, her voice laced with amusement.

She retrieved a dusty bottle from the shelf, noting with a wry smile that only a quarter remained. Jonny grinned, touched by her thoughtfulness. It was a small, simple gesture, but it spoke volumes about her enduring kindness and her ability to offer comfort in unexpected ways.

"Yeah! Yeah, you remember," Jonny exclaimed, his face lighting up with genuine pleasure.

"Well, it would be silly to waste a visit!" Sally declared with a wink.

The afternoon dissolved into a haze of shared laughter and half-empty whiskey glasses. As the Clyde May's flowed, so did the stories, each one nudging aside the initial awkwardness of a reunion thirty years in the making. They reminisced about the summer of '79, a time when anything felt possible and the world stretched out before them like an endless highway. The initial stilted conversation began to loosen, replaced by the easy connection of old friends. It was as if the years began to fade, the decades shrinking with each shared memory. They remembered driving the Night Hounds out of town. The parties, the rock and roll music. And of course, there was the pot, smoked almost every day, the memory of which now brought forth peals of laughter, something none of them would dream of indulging in now.

The years had changed them, softened the edges of their youthful recklessness, but beneath the surface, the bond forged in those long, hot summer days remained. They were no longer the carefree teenagers, but they were rediscovering the easy connection that had defined their youth. It had been genuinely nice to spend the afternoon with Sally and Stu, a welcome break from the intensity of his search. But as the hours passed, it became clear that Sally couldn't recall much more about Jess, the details stubbornly refusing to surface. When the time came to leave, a pang of sadness tugged at his heart. Saying goodbye felt heavier than it should, a feeling that they likely wouldn't keep in touch. Life had a way of pulling people in different directions, and the effort required to maintain connections across the years often proved too great. It would have been nice, he thought, a small part of him wishing they could recapture the ease and joy of their youth. They always had fun when they were together, a spark of something special igniting whenever their paths converged. As he drove away, he couldn't help but wonder if this was the last time he would see Sally and Stu, a poignant reminder of the fleeting nature of time and the bittersweet beauty of shared memories.

The day was winding down, the fluorescent lights of the police department casting a sterile glow over the emptying hallways. But Dave, fuelled by a restless energy and a deep-seated desire to help Jonny, found himself wandering aimlessly into the archive storage room once again, the silence broken only by the hum of the ancient ventilation system. He ran his fingers along the dusty shelves, his gaze scanning the rows of labelled boxes, each one a repository of untold stories. Just as he was about to give up, his eyes landed on a battered cardboard box tucked away in a dark corner. Scrawled across its side in faded marker was the single word: "Michigan." A flicker of hope ignited within him. He pulled the box from the shelf, and began to sift through the files. Most were mundane, routine reports and long-forgotten cases. But then, as he reached the bottom, his fingers brushed against a folded piece of paper. He carefully unfolded it. The dim light seemed to intensify, focusing on the paper in his hands. He scanned the contents, his eyes widening in disbelief, a wave of shock washing over him. He stared at the paper, his mind racing, the implications of what he held in his hands sending a jolt of adrenaline through his veins. Without a moment's hesitation, he grabbed his phone and dialled Jonny's number, his voice trembling with shock.

"Jonny, it's me," Dave said, his voice tight with urgency, almost a gasp. "I've found something, something big. Let's meet." He stared down at the paper, a knot forming in his stomach. The information was unsettling, a disturbingly large piece to this complicated puzzle that changed the game. This was not something they could ignore.

Chapter 20 In the Wake of Revelation

With December encroaching like an unwelcome guest, the living room of Dave's house had become a casualty of forced festivity. Half-opened boxes vomited forth a chaotic jumble of tinsel, ornaments, and stubbornly tangled lights. Miranda, her smile strained, was attempting to quell a rebellion between the kids, who were engaged in a fierce power struggle over the placement of the star on the Christmas tree. A discordant chorus of carols, punctuated by whining and the occasional burst of manic laughter, filled the air. Dave was retreating to the supposed sanctuary of the kitchen when a sharp knock echoed through the house, momentarily silencing the miniature war zone. He wiped his hands on his jeans, a knot of apprehension tightening in his gut. Leaving the dubious safety of the kitchen, he headed towards the door. It was Jonny, his face a mask of grim determination that sent a fresh wave of anxiety washing over Dave.

Dave gestured to Jonny inside, offering a strained, "Come in, excuse the mess." Jonny offered a polite smile to Miranda and the kids, though Dave noticed Miranda's expression was tight, a clear residue of the previous, explosive encounter in their home. Dave led Jonny through to the relative quiet of the kitchen, immediately sensing the cloud of unease clinging to his friend. Jonny had always been able to read him like an open book.

"How were Sally and Stu?" Dave asked, stalling.

"They're good, really good actually," Jonny replied, his tone patient but firm. Dave's attempt at deflection was transparent.

Jonny cut through the pleasantries. "What did you find?"

Dave sighed, gesturing towards the table. "Sit down, man."

They settled into chairs, the familiar wood suddenly feeling cold beneath Dave's hands. He slid a folded piece of paper across the table, his expression troubled. "It doesn't solve this, but it confirms a few things."

Jonny unfolded the paper, his expression conflicted. He'd braced himself for something, but seeing it made it all the more real. It was a grainy, black-and-white police booking photograph. Jess. A side profile and a frontal shot, capturing a face Jonny barely recognised. Gone was the gentle smile, the playful glint in her eyes. This Jess wore an expression of hard-edged defiance, a coldness that settled like a stone in Jonny's stomach. It wasn't the face of someone who'd committed a petty crime. This was something bigger, something darker. There were no other clues, no booking number, no name – just the raw, unsettling image of her. The chilling thing was she looked the same age as when Jonny had known her, hair the same length. There was no denying that these photos had been taken the same year, 1979.

"She looks pretty hardcore, man," Dave murmured, breaking the silence.

Jonny stared at the photograph, a whirlwind of emotions churning within him. "What the hell did you do, Jess…" he whispered.

Dave leaned forward, his gaze intense. "I gotta ask, Jonny. Are you sure you want to find this woman?"

Jonny's jaw tightened. He could not stop now. This photograph only ignited more questions, deepened the mystery. But a chilling realisation was dawning: he barely knew her at all. Had any of it been real? Or had he only seen a carefully constructed facade, a version of Jess she had chosen to project?

"I'm not giving up now," Jonny stated, his voice firm.

Dave nodded slowly. "I can try putting it through the database, see if she was ever caught. But without a name, it might be difficult."

Jonny stared at the grainy image of Jess, the woman he thought he knew, and a maelstrom of thoughts erupted in his mind. A fugitive at large. It was a jarring revelation, yet it also clicked into place with a disturbing sense of inevitability. It explained so much: her sudden disappearance, her nomadic existence in remote towns, her carefully cultivated anonymity. She had always stayed under the radar, a quiet presence in the background. In their group, she had not wanted to draw attention to herself, had not wanted anyone to become particularly interested in her. But he, drawn to her enigmatic aura, captivated by her beauty and the undeniable spark of connection between them, had fallen deeply in love all those years ago. Her role as an observer, rather than a participant, now seemed less like a personality quirk and more like a calculated strategy to remain detached, to avoid revealing too much.

But the burning question, the one that threatened to consume him, was: what had she done? Was she a truly bad person, capable of inflicting real harm? Or was she driven by something else entirely? Had she ever been caught, brought to justice for whatever crime she had committed? Was she currently serving her time, languishing in some forgotten prison cell? Or had she already paid her debt to society, only to vanish once more into the shadows? The questions swirled around him, relentless and unanswered.

A wave of gratitude washed over him for Dave's unwavering support. Dave was clearly relishing the mystery. Yet, a part of Jonny, a small, frightened voice in the back of his mind, wished he had never started this search. The idyllic fantasy of that long-ago summer of '79, the sun-drenched days and carefree nights, was now irrevocably shattered, replaced by a harsh, unsettling reality. But the further he delved into this rabbit hole, the more determined he became to see it through to the end. He could not turn back now, not when he was so close to uncovering the truth, no matter how painful it might be. He owed it to himself, and perhaps, in some strange way, he owed it to Jess.

For hours, the two friends sat at the kitchen table, drinking lukewarm coffee and a shared obsession, dissecting the scant information they possessed. They tossed around theories, each more outlandish than the last, grasping at straws in the desperate hope of making sense of the fragmented puzzle. Jonny, clinging to the fading embers of his idealised memory of Jess, vehemently resisted any suggestion that she might be inherently bad, that the woman he'd loved could be capable of genuine malice. But the photograph, that stark and unforgiving image, haunted him. It was all speculation, of course, a desperate attempt to fill in the vast blanks in Jess's history. They were building castles in the air, constructing elaborate narratives based on nothing more than a grainy photograph and a handful of half-forgotten memories.

The weight of the unknown pressed down on Jonny, a suffocating blanket of uncertainty. He longed for a definitive answer, a clear path forward, but all he had were questions, doubts, and a growing sense of unease. He found himself oscillating between a desperate desire to uncover the truth and a gnawing fear of what that truth might reveal. Was he prepared to confront the possibility that the woman he'd carried in his heart for so long was not who he thought she was?

Just as the conversation began to circle back on itself, a familiar buzz vibrated in Jonny's pocket. He pulled out his phone, his heart leaping with a surge of hope as he saw Lorraine's name flashing across the screen. A text message, simple and direct: "Call me when you get a chance." Perhaps, just perhaps, Lorraine held a piece of the puzzle that had eluded him and Dave. Perhaps she could shed some light on the darkness that now shrouded Jess. He glanced at Dave, who also had a flicker of anticipation in his eyes.

Jonny, without hesitation, tapped Lorraine's number on his phone. He put the call on speaker, eager for Dave to hear whatever information she had unearthed. Lorraine answered, and the sounds that filtered through the speaker immediately painted a picture: the echoey resonance of a large, metal-walled space, punctuated by the distinct clatter of shifting objects. She was in her lock-up garage, a place Jonny imagined as a chaotic archive of forgotten lives and unsolved mysteries.

"Lorraine!" Jonny greeted her, his voice tight with anticipation.

"That was quick," Lorraine retorted, her tone laced with a mixture of amusement and exasperation. "You've got a real firework up your ass with all of this."

Dave couldn't help but chuckle, the tension momentarily easing.

"What your friend Sally said was really helpful," Lorraine continued, her voice turning serious. "I've narrowed it down with as much as I could find. It gets weird and confusing, Jonny. I hope you're ready for this. Try to keep up."

"What have you got?" Jonny pressed, his heart pounding in his chest.

"Remember I told you she stayed at the house twice?" Lorraine began, her voice measured. "If my intuition is right on this, then I think it was with two separate names. And she sure as hell didn't call herself by my mother's name. But there was a young woman here, a runaway from home at the age of eighteen… from Michigan, in March nineteen seventy-nine. Tell me that ain't just coincidence."

"What was her name?" Jonny demanded, his mind racing.

"Peggy Smith," Lorraine revealed.

Dave, who had been listening intently, interjected, "Surely Sally would have known that was who she was writing to?"

"Not necessarily," Lorraine explained. "A lot of the pen-pal users had usernames. But get this: Reason for leaving in May the same year… Left with police. It doesn't say why. My mother must have kept that from me."

"That must have been when the mug shot was taken," Dave murmured, the pieces of the puzzle slowly falling into place. It was two months before Jonny had met her in July.

"You said she came back?" Jonny prompted, eager to keep the momentum going.

"In nineteen eighty-one, someone returned by the name of Ally Phillips," Lorraine stated.

The name hit Jonny like a jolt of electricity. Ally Phillips. She had used his last name! Ally, a play on "Miss Ally Bammy," the name they'd jokingly given her, a reference to her supposed transformation. First, the name Jess Judy, a tribute to the woman who had taken her in, and now Ally Phillips. Her names carefully chosen, each a connection to the people she cared about. A flicker of hope ignited within him. Maybe he had meant something to her, after all.

"I remember her as Ally Phillips," Lorraine continued. "In my mother's notes, it says this was because of witness protection type shit, but I don't buy it. She stayed for a while before disappearing again."

"So we're looking for an Ally Phillips?" Dave asked, trying to clarify the situation.

"I don't know if this will be relevant or not, but looking at the visitor logs, a previous inhabitant, who my mother also took in, came back to visit her, sometimes daily and overnight. His name was Julian Bertotti. He was also at the residence when she stayed the first time under the name Peggy."

The revelation struck Jonny like a blow to the gut. Jess, with someone else. He didn't need confirmation that she was seeing this guy. But in 1981, this was almost two years after their relationship had ended.

"Have you got anything on him?" Jonny asked, trying to keep his voice steady.

"Where he came from, was Omaha, and when his stay ended, it looked like he was heading back that way. I think he and your girl left together. I know it ain't a solid lead, but Omaha might be where to look. If not for your girl, this Julian Bertotti might know something on her."

"Appreciate it, thanks, Lorraine," Jonny said, his mind already racing with possibilities.

"Good luck," Lorraine replied, her voice softening. "I hope you find her."

Jonny hung up the phone, the weight of the new information settling heavily upon him. He sat in stunned silence, as he processed all the information. Peggy Smith and Ally Phillips were the names Jess had used, each one a mask she'd worn to conceal her true identity. Julian Bertotti, however, was a different piece of the puzzle altogether – a recurring figure in Jess's life, present during both her time as Peggy Smith and later as Ally Phillips. The runaway from Michigan, the potential arrest, the carefully chosen aliases, and now a man who seemed to keep reappearing in her life. He felt like he was trying to assemble a jigsaw puzzle with missing pieces, the image of Jess constantly shifting and incomplete. Dave, on the other hand, remained unusually quiet, his brow furrowed in concentration as he mentally connected the dots, piecing together the fragmented narrative that Lorraine had presented. He needed a moment to fully absorb the implications of what they had just learned before he could articulate his thoughts.

In essence, they had discovered that Jess had used the aliases Peggy Smith and Ally Phillips during her stays at Lorraine's mother's house. After her initial stay in Cedar Bluff, a whole year had vanished, erased from the timeline before she resurfaced in West Virginia in 1981. Julian Bertotti, it seemed, was more than just an acquaintance; he was a man who had been present during both of Jess's stays, and who may have left with her in 1981, potentially heading towards his hometown of Omaha. Whether their connection was purely platonic or something more remained to be seen, but his recurring presence in Jess's life added another layer of intrigue to the already complex situation. The idyllic summer of '79 was fading further into a distant memory, replaced by a tangled web of secrets, lies, and a growing sense of unease.

The silence hung heavy in the air, thick with unspoken questions and the lingering echo of Lorraine's unsettling revelations. It was Dave who finally broke the stillness, his voice laced with a mixture of concern and cautious optimism.

"That's a hell of a lot," he said, his gaze fixed on some distant point in the room. "But it's a new lead. If you still want to pursue it?"

Jonny simply nodded, his expression a mixture of determination and a growing sense of bewilderment. The layers of deception surrounding Jess seemed to multiply with each new discovery, leaving him feeling lost in a labyrinth of half-truths and hidden motives.

"I think it's safe to assume Peggy Smith wasn't her real name either," Dave added, stating the obvious, yet the words carried a weight of their own. Each discarded identity felt like a further erosion of the person Jonny thought he knew.

"Do you think Bronko knows about all this?" Jonny asked, the thought of their old friend being somehow involved adding another layer of complexity to the situation.

Dave shook his head dismissively. "Not unless they stayed in touch, which I highly doubt. Man's completely gone under the radar. I've been trying to find him while you were in West Virginia. He's hiding under a big rock."

"I don't trust him anyway," Jonny muttered, a wave of resentment washing over him. "We can cut him off as a lead." He sighed, running a hand through his hair, his mind racing to make sense of the fragmented pieces of Jess's past. "Jesus, let's piece this all together. She goes on the run, flees Michigan to West Virginia to that refuge. Gets arrested, somehow escapes and winds up in Cedar Bluff. After that, she vanishes into the world, and a year later winds up back in West Virginia, and leaves with some guy called Julian from Omaha. Do you think you could do a search?"

"I can try," Dave replied, his tone resolute. "I'll head on down to the station tomorrow and see what I can find. What are you thinking?"

Jonny's jaw tightened with unwavering resolve. "I'm thinking this search is heading to Nebraska."

He spoke the words with a quiet intensity, not giving up, not backing down. Despite the growing complexities and the unsettling revelations, he was still determined to get to the bottom of all this, to unravel the mystery of Jess, no matter where it led him.

The next day dawned with a nervous energy. Jonny waited in the car, the morning sun glinting off the windshield. He watched Dave disappear through the station's heavy doors. It was a Saturday, and the police station was unusually quiet, most of the desks unoccupied, the usual cacophony of ringing phones and hurried footsteps replaced by a muted stillness. Inside, Dave moved with practiced ease, navigating the familiar corridors until he found a quiet, unoccupied desk in a dimly lit office. He powered up the computer, the hum of the machine cutting through the silence as he logged in, his fingers dancing across the keyboard. He initiated a search, his eyes scanning the screen intently as he entered the names: Ally Phillips, Julian Bertotti, Omaha. The seconds ticked by, each one an agonising eternity as the system churned through its vast database. Then, a subtle shift in Dave's expression – a barely perceptible widening of his eyes, a slight upturn of his lips – betrayed the fact that he had found something. The glow of the monitor reflected in his face, illuminating a look of quiet triumph, as if a long-dormant piece of the puzzle had finally clicked into place.

In less time than Jonny had anticipated, Dave hurried out of the station, his face flushed with a mixture of excitement and disbelief. Jonny, his own anticipation reaching fever pitch, got out of the car to meet him on the sidewalk.

"That was quick," Jonny said, barely able to contain his eagerness. "Did you find a lead?"

Dave's expression was almost bewildered, as if he hadn't quite processed the enormity of what he'd uncovered. "A lead? No, man… I think I found her."

Jonny's heart leaped into his throat, a wave of disbelief washing over him. It seemed too good to be true. Dave held out a slip of paper, the address scrawled in hurried handwriting.

"She ain't Ally Phillips anymore, though, Jonny," Dave explained, his voice tinged with a hint of awe. "She's Ally Bertotti, and they have both lived in Omaha since the eighties. That's the address right there, right off Lake Street. Julian Bertotti has a big long list of offences, looks like he's a real thug."

Married, Jonny thought, the realisation hitting him with force. She had married this guy she met at the refuge. The thought sent a pang of jealousy through his chest, quickly followed by a wave of apprehension. This made it seem less like fate and more like he was disrupting someone's life. She could have children, a life, a family with someone else. He had the answer he'd waited thirty years for, an open goal, and all he needed to do was turn up at the address to see her again. But now that he had his answer, he was questioning whether he should, even if just briefly. There were still so many burning questions, overshadowed only by the burning desire to see her again, to hear her voice, to understand what had happened.

"This is it, Jonny," Dave continued, oblivious to the internal turmoil raging within his friend. "Even got you a landline contact number. It's on the back."

Jonny's heart pounded in his chest. He had placed so much hope on this moment, the moment of potentially speaking to her again. But before he could gather his thoughts, a voice came from behind them, cutting through the tension. "Jonny."

Jonny and Dave turned to see Bronko standing on the sidewalk, his shoulders slumped, his gaze averted. He seemed smaller somehow, diminished, like a man burdened by the guilt he could no longer bear. His face, etched with remorse, could not hide the torment that had been eating away at him.

"What do you want, Bronko?" Dave asked, his voice sharp with suspicion.

Bronko swallowed hard, his eyes darting between Jonny and Dave. "Man, I can barely look at myself in the mirror for keeping what I did from you. It's been eating away at me. You're my oldest friends, hell, I think my only friends. I can't die until I make it up to you, Jonny. I'm sorry, brother."

Jonny could see the sincerity in Bronko's face, the genuine remorse that shone through his bloodshot eyes. But the anger, the sense of betrayal, still lingered, a bitter taste on his tongue.

"I should have told you when I heard she passed away," Bronko continued, his voice barely a whisper.

"She ain't dead, Bronko," Jonny retorted. "She's in Nebraska."

Bronko's face registered genuine shock and confusion. "I don't get it. I had the phone call? A friend of hers… Uh, I can't think of his name…"

"Julian?" Dave offered, his eyes narrowing.

"Yeah, that might have been it!" Bronko exclaimed, snapping his fingers.

Maybe Bronko was telling the truth. Maybe he had also been lied to, manipulated by this woman who had woven such a tangled web of deceit.

"So, are you gonna try that number, Jonny?" Dave asked, breaking the tense silence.

Jonny's heart pounded against his chest, threatening to burst free. He nodded slowly, his hand shaking as he copied the numbers into his phone. He paused, looking at his friends, their faces etched with encouragement and support. Before he could talk himself out of it, he pressed dial, holding the phone to his ear. The ringing seemed to stretch into an eternity, each pulse sending a jolt of nervous energy through his body. Then, an answer. Someone picked up, but there was only silence on the other end. Jonny, unsure of what to do or say, paused for a moment, swallowing the lump in his throat.

"Jess? Is that you?" he asked. Hoping she would recognise his voice.

The phone line remained silent, the only sound the faint static of the connection. He tried a new tactic, desperate for any kind of response. "Ally? Ally Bertotti?"

The silence persisted, unbroken. Jonny waited, each second stretching into an eternity. Then, just as he was about to speak again, the connection was cut. The line went dead. Had that been her? Had the woman he had thought about for thirty years been on the other end of the phone? Had she heard his voice? He looked back at his friends and shook his head, his face a mask of disappointment and confusion.

Jonny hesitated, the disappointment filling his mind. He desperately wanted to see her, to finally put an end to the decades of wondering, but the silence on the other end of the line had planted a seed of doubt in his mind. The reunion he had always imagined, the joyous embrace, the flood of shared memories, suddenly seemed like a distant, unattainable dream. A knot of apprehension tightened in his gut, warning him that confronting the reality of this woman might shatter the idealised image he had carried in his heart for so long.

"If you want to, Jonny, we'll go with you," Bronko offered, his voice laced with a newfound sincerity that surprised Jonny. "This is what you've wanted, man. We'll be right by your side. If you want us, or me at least."

Dave, who had been silent until now, seemed to be wrestling with his own thoughts. He knew that Christmas was approaching, and he had a family to consider. But after a moment of internal conflict, Dave's expression softened, and he nodded resolutely. His oldest friend needed him, and that was all that mattered.

A whirlwind of emotions churned within Jonny, a potent cocktail of gratitude, hope, and a lingering unease he couldn't quite shake. He had been so consumed by the search for Jess that he hadn't fully grasped the magnitude of his friends' sacrifice. Their willingness to drop everything and accompany him to Omaha, despite the uncertainties and potential for disappointment, spoke volumes about the enduring bond they shared. He was willing to give Bronko a second chance, though a part of him still wrestled with the betrayal. Bronko, who had deceived him and carried the weight of that secret for years, was now desperately trying to make amends, his remorseful look pleading for forgiveness. The offer to accompany him to Omaha felt like a sincere attempt at redemption, a way to atone for the pain he had caused. He nodded slowly, his eyes meeting those of his friends, an acknowledgment of their loyalty and unwavering commitment, and a hesitant acceptance of Bronko's outstretched hand.

A wave of relief washed over Bronko, his face lighting up with a genuine smile. He knew that he was finally on the path to earning back Jonny's trust, and helping him find Jess – Ally – was the first step on that long road, a chance to show that he was still worthy of their friendship.

"Alright, man," Bronko exclaimed, clapping Jonny on the shoulder, the force of the gesture conveying both excitement and a silent promise of unwavering support. "Let's go find your girl!"

Chapter 21 Too Close to the Flame

Adrenaline surged through Jonny's veins as the tyres devoured the miles towards Omaha, Nebraska. This wasn't just a drive; it was a full-throttle chase after a ghost, a desperate attempt to finally understand a past that had haunted him for three decades. Dave, the loyal wingman, shadowed them in his car, a silent guardian as Jonny and Bronko embarked on their own personal odyssey. Alabama vanished in the rearview mirror, swallowed by the vast, unforgiving heartland of America, a landscape mirroring the turbulent emotions churning within the car. The road became an arena for rebuilding, a chance for Bronko to prove his remorse and earn back Jonny's trust. They had already confronted the lie, the air cleared of the immediate poison, but now came the delicate work of piecing together the shattered fragments of their friendship. His voice, thick with sincerity, filled the car as he bared his soul, confessing the guilt that had haunted him for years. Jonny listened, his heart a battleground of conflicting emotions, the sting of betrayal battling with a flicker of forgiveness. As the sun painted the sky in fiery hues, the tension in the car began to dissipate, replaced by a fragile sense of hope. The soundtrack was a defiant roar of classic rock, the anthems of their youth, transporting them back to the summer of '79 in Cedar Bluff. Yet, beneath the surface of the music and the tentative connection, Jonny felt a knot of anxiety tightening in his stomach. The impending reunion with Jess – or Ally – was a terrifying unknown, a leap of faith into a chasm of possibilities. Would she recognise him? Would she welcome him? Or would he be met with the cold reality of a life irrevocably changed? The weight of thirty years pressed down on him, the unanswered questions, the unspoken longing, the need to finally know the truth. It all felt surreal, a high-stakes gamble with his own heart, and he couldn't shake the feeling that the truth, when he finally found it, might shatter everything he thought he knew.

The journey stretched on for what felt like an eternity, a relentless blur of fleeting landscapes. They started out on I-20 West, leaving Alabama behind, the familiar red clay giving way to the green hills of Mississippi. Crossing into Tennessee, the road cutting through the heart of the state, past Nashville's distant skyline. Then north in Illinois, the landscape flattening out as they plunged deeper into the Midwest. The endless fields of corn and soybeans blurred past the windows, broken only by the occasional small town with its weathered storefronts and sleepy gas stations. They crossed into Iowa on I-80 West, the miles marked by towering wind turbines and the vast, open sky. The sun rose and fell countless times, painting the sky in a kaleidoscope of colours, each sunrise a reminder of the new day dawning, each sunset a symbol of the past they were desperately trying to reconcile.

After two gruelling days and nights, fuelled by caffeine and nervous energy, they finally reached Nebraska. The signs for Omaha began to appear, looming large on the horizon like a beacon of both hope and dread. The city skyline, a cluster of steel and glass against the vast prairie sky, marked the end of their long pilgrimage and the beginning of a new revelation.

After checking into a nondescript motel on the outskirts of Omaha, a place that smelled faintly of stale cigarettes and disinfectant, Dave, ever the reliable one, took the wheel. He navigated the city streets with a quiet competence that belied the tension simmering in the car. Using an address Dave had managed to dig up on the system, they were guided through a maze of residential neighbourhoods, each one subtly different from the last, until they finally arrived at the address. The house was a small, single-story bungalow, painted a faded shade of blue, with a neatly manicured lawn that seemed at odds with the overall vibe. It didn't look welcoming or friendly; instead, it had the air of a solitary dwelling, a place where someone sought refuge from the world, a haven of quiet solitude. The windows were dark, the curtains drawn, giving the house an almost secretive feel, as if it were guarding a hidden truth. A closed garage stood next to the house, set back at the end of the driveway, its door a blank, unyielding face. As they sat there, parked across the street, the silence in the car was deafening, each of them grappling with their own anxieties and uncertainties, the weight of the past pressing down on them.

Jonny couldn't believe it. He was potentially sitting outside her house, the culmination of three decades of wondering, of longing. Anxious prickles danced across his skin, and he felt a suffocating pressure in his chest. Unsure of what would meet him on the other side of the door, he was paralysed by a potent mix of hope and fear.

Dave, sensing his unease, reiterated, "This is it, Jonny."

Jonny nodded slowly, unable to find the words to express the maelstrom of emotions swirling within him. Part of him wanted to flee, to turn the car around and drive as far away as possible from this unsettling place. The other part, the part that had driven him all these months, yearned to bang the door down, to demand answers. His anxiety was a palpable thing, radiating outwards and easily picked up by Dave and Bronko, who exchanged worried glances.

"Do you want me to come with you?" Bronko asked, his voice gentle, his eyes filled with concern.

Jonny nodded, grateful for the offer of support, for the presence of someone who understood the magnitude of what he was about to face.

Bronko clapped him on the shoulder, his grip firm and reassuring. "You ready?"

Jonny took a deep breath, trying to steady his racing heart, to quell the tremor in his hands. "Let's do this."

The car doors slammed shut with a muffled thud, the sound echoing in the otherwise silent street, amplifying the tension that hung heavy in the air. Jonny and Bronko stepped out, their movements slow and deliberate, each step laden with unspoken anticipation. They crossed the street, the ground feeling strangely uneven beneath Jonny's feet, each step a monumental effort. Bronko hung back, positioning himself slightly to the side, a silent sentinel allowing Jonny his moment, yet close enough to offer a sense of security, a tangible reminder that he wasn't alone.

To any casual observer, the scene would have appeared deeply suspicious: two men approaching a seemingly deserted house with an air of furtive anticipation. Jonny reached the front door, his hand hovering hesitantly before him. He tried to peer through the narrow gaps in the curtains, but the house remained stubbornly dark, an impenetrable void that offered no clues. He shifted his gaze to the frosted glass panels in the front door, but again, his efforts were thwarted, the obscured view revealing nothing.

Finally, with a deep breath, he raised his hand and knocked, the sound sharp and insistent in the stillness. Bronko, meanwhile, had drifted down the side of the house, his eyes scanning the perimeter with a practiced alertness. Jonny stood frozen, listening intently, but he could hear nothing from within the house, no sound of movement, no sign of life. He hesitated for a moment, unsure how long to wait before trying again, the silence stretching out like an unbearable torment. He knocked once more, a little louder this time, and strained his eyes, trying to detect any flicker of movement behind the frosted glass. Still, there was no response, no indication that anyone was home, or that anyone had even heard him.

As Jonny remained focused on the front of the house, Bronko continued his reconnaissance, peering over the fence into the backyard. It was unkempt, overgrown with weeds, but not overtly messy, suggesting a lack of attention rather than outright neglect. He then noticed a CCTV camera mounted on the side of the house, its unblinking lens pointed directly at him, whoever was inside would have seen him. He knew, with a chilling certainty, that their presence had been recorded, their every move scrutinised. Jonny, growing increasingly frustrated, abandoned the front door and stepped into the front yard, looking from window to window. He cupped his hands around his eyes, pressing his face against the glass, desperately trying to penetrate the darkness within, but the curtains remained stubbornly closed, shielding the interior from his prying eyes. The sense of unease deepened, the silence of the house becoming more ominous, more unsettling with each passing moment.

Bronko's voice cut through the silence, laced with a hint of frustration. "Nothing back here, man."

Jonny, equally disheartened, replied, "Nothing here either."

"Do you think she's out?" Bronko asked, voicing the question that was weighing heavily on Jonny's mind.

Jonny sighed, rubbing the back of his neck. "Either that, or she doesn't want to answer the door to two strangers."

They walked back to the car, their disappointment palpable, the weight of their failed attempt pressing down on them. Dave had rolled down the window, his expression a mixture of concern and curiosity. "That's a bummer," he said, his voice low. "What do you want to do, Jonny?"

Jonny hesitated for a moment, his gaze fixed on the house, as if willing someone to appear. "I'll wait," he said finally, his voice resolute. "See if anyone goes in or out."

Bronko nodded in understanding. "I gotta eat," he said, his stomach rumbling audibly. "Do you want us to bring you some food?"

Jonny shook his head. "I'm good," he replied, his appetite having vanished completely.

Dave got out of the car, leaving the door open for Jonny. "I'll go with Bronko," he said, "let us know if you see anything."

Jonny nodded, his eyes still fixed on the house. He slid into the car, the silence amplifying the sense of isolation that was creeping over him. He watched as Dave and Bronko walked off down the street, their figures gradually receding into the distance, leaving him alone with his thoughts and his unwavering determination.

Hours crawled by with agonising slowness, each minute stretching into an eternity as Jonny kept vigil in the car, his gaze fixed on the house across the street. The sun, a pale and distant orb in the winter sky, began its slow descent, offering no warmth to the unsettling scene. The early dusk deepened the shadows within the house, making it even more difficult to discern any movement behind the drawn curtains. But still, nothing. No sign of life within the walls. The silence was broken only by the occasional passing car, its headlights momentarily illuminating the interior of the car Jonny sat in, before disappearing into the night. As the hours ticked by, Jonny's initial determination began to wane, replaced by a gnawing sense of frustration and a growing emptiness in his stomach. He tried to distract himself, replaying memories of Jess in his mind. But the longer he sat there, the more the doubts crept in, whispering insidious questions in his ear. Had he made a mistake? Was he chasing a ghost? Was this even the right house? Just as his resolve was about to crumble, just as the hunger pangs were becoming unbearable, he saw two familiar figures walking towards him down the street. Dave and Bronko, their faces etched with concern.

Dave approached the car, peering through the window. "Anything?" he asked.

Jonny shook his head, the gesture conveying his disappointment and frustration.

Bronko, ever the optimist, chimed in, "Maybe she's on vacation?"

Dave sighed, his breath misting in the cold air. "Come on," he said, "let's head back to the motel. We can try again tomorrow."

The drive back to the motel was silent, each of them lost in their own thoughts, the weight of the day's disappointment hanging heavy in the air. Jonny tossed and turned throughout the night, his mind a relentless carousel of images and anxieties. The house, with its drawn curtains and silent facade, haunted his dreams, morphing into a symbol of all his hopes and fears. He wrestled with the nagging doubts, the insidious whispers that questioned his every decision. Was it the right house? Was Jess even there? He knew it was the middle of the night, that she would surely be there, but the thought of barging in unannounced, in the middle of the night, held him back. This was the only lead they had, the only tangible connection to the past, and he could not afford to squander it. The next morning, after a depressing breakfast of stale cereal and lukewarm coffee, Jonny decided. He couldn't subject Dave and Bronko to another day of fruitless waiting, of sharing his torment. He needed to do this alone. He grabbed the keys to his truck and slipped out of the motel room, leaving his friends to sleep. As he pulled up across the street from the house, the scene was eerily familiar. No car in the driveway, the house looking exactly as it had the day before.

The morning sun, weak and watery, did little to dispel the gloom that had settled over Jonny. He sat in his truck, the engine idling to provide a meagre source of warmth, his gaze unwavering as he watched the house across the street. Hours bled into one another, marked only by the shifting angle of the sun. He sent a few brief updates to Dave and Bronko, not wanting to get their hopes up. He ignored a string of calls and texts from his mother and Charley; their messages filled with the usual holiday cheer and gentle prodding about whether he would be back for Christmas. He couldn't deal with that right now, couldn't face the prospect of forced merriment and empty traditions. Still, the house remained stubbornly silent. As the afternoon approached, a sense of resignation began to creep in.

Jonny decided he would try knocking one last time, a final, desperate attempt to break through the wall of silence. He crossed the road once more. As he reached the driveway, he noticed the garage door was open. Before he could react, a black Range Rover roared out, tyres squealing, accelerating with frightening speed. It veered towards him, a dark, menacing blur, and Jonny instinctively dived out of the way, narrowly avoiding being hit. The Range Rover sped off up the street as if in a desperate hurry, leaving Jonny shaken and breathless in its wake. He couldn't believe what had just happened. Someone was in there! He scrambled back to his truck, adrenaline coursing through his veins. He jammed the key into the ignition, started the engine, and peeled out of his parking spot. He fumbled for his phone, hitting Dave's number and putting him on speaker, his mind racing as he tried to explain the situation.

"Jonny?" Dave's voice crackled through the speaker.

"Someone was in the house! Damn near ran me over!" Jonny yelled, his voice tight with adrenaline. "A black Range Rover, plate NST 007, heading west on Lake Street, they're in a hurry!"

Meanwhile, Dave and Bronko were sitting in a booth at a diner, halfway through their sandwiches. Dave shot to his feet, knocking over his water glass. "We're coming!" he barked, grabbing his jacket. "Bronko, let's go!"

Bronko, mid-bite, crammed the rest of his sandwich into his mouth and hurried after Dave, a trail of crumbs marking his hasty exit.

Jonny gripped the steering wheel, his fingers digging into the worn leather, as he navigated the maze of Omaha streets, the black Range Rover a dark phantom in his sights. He wasn't trying to be a hero, wasn't trying to force a confrontation. He just needed to know where they were going, needed to understand what was happening. He maintained a safe distance, two or three cars back, careful not to spook them, but close enough to keep them in view. The city traffic was a chaotic dance, a frenetic ballet of metal and rubber, where every lane change was a gamble, every green light a fleeting opportunity. Cars swerved and merged with a disregard for safety, their drivers oblivious to the silent pursuit unfolding behind them.

A sudden red light was a potential disaster, forcing Jonny to slam on his brakes, his stomach lurching as he watched the Range Rover pull further and further away. Each merging car was a threat, a potential obstacle that could block his view, causing him to lose his quarry in the urban sprawl. The air was thick with the smell of exhaust and the cacophony of honking horns.

"Still heading west on Lake," Jonny said into the phone, his voice tight with concentration. "Just passed 72nd."

Dave's voice, strained with urgency, crackled back, "We're about ten minutes out. Keep us updated."

The Range Rover weaved through traffic with an unsettling confidence, exceeding the speed limit just enough to stay ahead, but not enough to attract unwanted attention. Jonny mirrored their movements, his heart pounding in his chest, his senses on high alert. A yellow light flashed ahead, and the Range Rover accelerated, squeezing through just as it turned red. Jonny slammed on his brakes, his tyres squealing in protest as he came to a stop, watching helplessly as the Range Rover disappeared into the cross-traffic.

"Damn it!" he muttered, pounding the steering wheel in frustration.

He scanned the intersection, his eyes darting from car to car, desperately searching for the familiar black silhouette. Then, he spotted it, turning right onto Dodge Street. Relief washed over him, quickly replaced by a renewed sense of determination.

"They're on Dodge now," he reported, his voice regaining its composure. "Heading east."

The chase continued, a tense ballet of pursuit and evasion, through the heart of the city. The Range Rover made a sudden, unexpected turn onto a side street, and Jonny, caught off guard, almost missed it. He swerved sharply, narrowly avoiding a collision with a parked car, and managed to stay on their tail.

"Turning north on 40th," he relayed, his voice breathless.

The Range Rover responded by accelerating, its powerful engine eating up the road. Jonny matched their speed, his truck straining to keep up. The speedometer climbed, blurring the numbers. The world outside became a tunnel of concrete and steel, the wind screaming past his open window.

A sudden lane change by the Range Rover forced Jonny to react, yanking the wheel hard to the left. His tyres screeched in protest, the truck fishtailing wildly before he regained control. He swore under his breath, his knuckles white as he tightened his grip.

The chase continued, a high-stakes game of cat and mouse played out on the crowded city streets. The Range Rover, realising they were being pursued, became more aggressive, cutting off other cars, running red lights, pushing the boundaries of the law. Jonny, driven by a desperate need to know who was driving, matched their recklessness, his truck a shadow dogging their every move.

A wall of brake lights had materialised in front of him, a sudden traffic jam swallowing the road whole. The Range Rover, now a distant black speck, slipped through the gap, disappearing into the urban labyrinth. He was stuck, helpless, watching his quarry escape.

"Damn it, damn it, damn it!" he muttered, his frustration boiling over. He leaned on the horn, an act of futile defiance against the gridlock.

Suddenly, Dave's voice crackled over the phone, sharp and urgent. "Jonny! We've got them! Black Range Rover, just entered the city centre, heading towards the Old Market!"

Relief washed over Jonny, quickly replaced by a surge of adrenaline. "I'm stuck in traffic!" he yelled into the phone. "Keep on them! I'll catch up as soon as I can!"

Dave and Bronko were hot on the tail of the Range Rover, their car a blur of motion as they navigated the narrow, crowded streets of the Old Market. The Range Rover, its driver clearly panicked, was driving erratically, narrowly avoiding pedestrians and parked cars.

The chase snaked through the heart of the city; a high-speed game of inches played on the crowded streets. Market Street, a wide avenue choked with midday traffic, where Dave, with Bronko calling out directions, weaved through a chaotic mix of yellow cabs, delivery vans, and lumbering buses. "I'm clear, where are you headed?" Jonny's voice crackled through the phone. "We're on Market," Bronko barked back. A sudden lane change forced a taxi to swerve, its horn blaring in protest, a near miss that sent a jolt of adrenaline through Dave's veins. They threaded the needle between a double-parked truck and a stream of pedestrians, the side mirror narrowly missing a woman carrying a bag of groceries. The chase then plunged onto Elm Street, a narrower thoroughfare lined with shops and cafes, where the traffic became even more congested. Dave accelerated, the engine roaring as he dodged a cyclist, narrowly avoiding a collision that would have sent them both sprawling. "Turning onto Elm now, traffic's tighter," Bronko reported. He slammed on the brakes, tyres squealing, as a jaywalker darted into the street, a heart-stopping moment that tested his reflexes to the limit. The chase continued onto Oak Avenue, a tree-lined street with slower-moving traffic, where Dave weaved in and out of lanes, narrowly avoiding a collision with a street sweeper. "Oak Avenue next, things opening up," Bronko said. He jumped the curb to bypass a traffic jam, sending pigeons scattering and pedestrians scrambling for safety, a daring manoeuvre that gained them valuable ground. The chase then veered onto a side street, a narrow alleyway with tight corners and blind intersections, where the risk of a collision was ever-present. "Cutting through the alley off Oak," Bronko finished. Dave navigated the treacherous route with skill and precision, his senses on high alert, his focus unwavering. The chase was a relentless dance of speed and skill, a desperate gamble with every turn of the wheel.

The chase screeched to a halt as they slammed into a wall of gridlocked traffic, horns blaring a discordant symphony of frustration. "We're jammed up, Jonny!" Bronko yelled into the phone. "They're heading towards the old buildings and warehouses near the docks!"

Jonny's response was immediate. The tyres of his vehicle squealed as he accelerated down the adjacent street, weaving through the sparse traffic with unrestrained fury. He spotted an alleyway, a narrow gash in the urban landscape, and without hesitation, he swerved, plunging into the darkness.

Meanwhile, Dave and Bronko finally managed to break free of the gridlock. "We're moving again!" Dave shouted. Bronko, eyes scanning every direction, spotted a narrow opening. "Take that alley!" he yelled, pointing. Dave didn't hesitate, darting down the back alley, the vehicle bouncing and rattling over the uneven surface.

At the end of the alley, they found it: the Range Rover, abandoned, its door hanging open like a broken wing. It was parked in a forgotten corner of the city, where shadows stretched and the air hung thick with the smell of decay. The building loomed, a skeletal structure of brick and broken windows, its secrets guarded by layers of grime and neglect. "We found the vehicle," Dave said into the phone, his voice tight with anticipation. "It's abandoned in a back alley behind the old warehouse. Doors open."

Across the street, on the far side of the sprawling warehouse complex, Jonny slammed on the brakes, his vehicle screeching a protest against the sudden stop. He parked haphazardly, half on the sidewalk, half in the street, completely oblivious to the angry symphony of horns that erupted around him. He leaped out of the vehicle, his eyes scanning the imposing structure before him, trying to assess the situation. He knew Dave and Bronko were somewhere on the other side, in that labyrinth of alleys and shadows, and every instinct screamed that time was running out.

Back in the alley with Dave and Bronko, the silence shattered. A black saloon, sleek and menacing, pulled up abruptly behind the Range Rover, its engine a low growl that echoed off the brick walls. Two men emerged, each radiating an aura of danger that was palpable. The first was wiry, with close-cropped brown hair and a network of tattoos snaking across his neck, disappearing beneath the collar of his dark jacket.

His eyes, sharp and cold, darted around the Range Rover like a cornered predator. The other was a towering figure, bald and built like a brick wall, his face a mask of impassivity. Dave and Bronko looked worried. The man with tattoos spoke, his voice a low, dangerous rumble that cut through the city's ambient noise. "Any reason why you've been sitting outside my house for the past two days?"

The realisation hit Dave. This had to be Julian. Dave held up his hands, trying to project an air of calm he certainly didn't feel. "Easy," he said, his voice steady despite the adrenaline coursing through his veins. "I'm a cop."

Julian's expression hardened, his eyes narrowing into slits. The man beside him, a hulking figure with a shaved head, shifted his weight, his fists clenching and unclenching.

"I don't care what you are," the man snarled, his voice laced with venom. "Me and my friend here are about to imprint a reminder into your brains. One to leave and never come back. Or we kill you."

The situation was spiralling out of control with terrifying speed. Faced with the man's menacing words, Bronko, a man of action, raised his fists, bracing himself for a fight. He knew he was in for a tough one. Dave braced himself, ready to defend against whatever was coming.

Meanwhile, Jonny, driven by a desperate hope, abandoned his truck and sprinted towards the dilapidated warehouse that loomed nearby. Its boarded-up windows and graffiti-scarred walls hinted at the darkness within. He could not afford to waste another second. He burst through a rickety side door, the hinges groaning a mournful protest, and plunged into the inky blackness. The air inside was thick with the cloying smell of dust and decay. He moved cautiously through the labyrinthine interior, his eyes straining to pierce the gloom. He searched multiple floors, each one as desolate and decaying as the last.

Empty offices, stripped bare, echoed with the ghosts of forgotten businesses. Dark, cavernous storage rooms yielded nothing but dust and debris. He stood three stories up with a gnawing fear that he was too late.

A sudden click echoed in the oppressive silence, followed by the chilling sensation of cold steel pressing against the back of his head. It was the unmistakable feel of a pistol barrel. The hand holding the weapon was petite, adorned with manicured nails, clearly belonging to a woman. Jonny froze, every muscle in his body locking in place. He couldn't turn, couldn't see his assailant. A wave of paralysing anxiety washed over him, a sickening realisation of the danger he had dragged his friends into. The situation had taken a sharp, ominous turn, plunging them all into deeper darkness.

A woman's voice, sharp and laced with menace, cut through the air. "That's the business end of my nine-millimetre pressed against the back of your skull… Move an inch and I blow it all over this room."

The voice… it sounded strikingly familiar to him. Could it be?

"Easy," Jonny said, his voice carefully neutral. "I ain't here to cause trouble."

Silence descended, thick and heavy. Jonny knew this was not a sign of hesitation. They wanted answers, and he had to tread carefully. Whoever held that gun could be capable of anything.

"I'm looking for an old friend," Jonny said, hoping his voice conveyed sincerity. "Nothing more."

The pressure against his head eased. He heard the soft scuff of footsteps as the person took a few steps back. Jonny interpreted this as an invitation, a cautious reprieve. He turned around slowly, deliberately, careful not to make any sudden movements that might reignite the threat. He looked back, past the glint of the gun still held loosely in the woman's hand… and there she was. It was unquestionably Jess. She looked almost exactly as she had all those years ago—so much so that, for a moment, his mind struggled to accept the decades between then and now. Time hadn't carved her up or dimmed her beauty; it had only brushed against her, lightly, respectfully, as though it had not quite dared to change her.

Her hair fell the same way he remembered—loose, natural waves with just the faintest hints of age-softened colour woven through. Her skin held that same calm, unpolished glow he remembered, untouched by heavy makeup, giving her an effortless warmth that had not faded with time.

And her eyes completely unchanged. There were tiny lines at the corners now—small markers of years lived, not years lost—but they only deepened the expression he remembered: gentle, thoughtful, observing everything without rushing to speak. She did not look old. She did not even look particularly worn. She looked like *herself.*

Jess's eyes burned into him, a silent inferno of suspicion and steel. It wasn't just a warning; it was a promise of pain. He'd foolishly imagined a flicker of warmth, a ghost of the bond they once shared. Instead, he found only a chilling blankness. The gun was steady in her grip, a silent question mark hanging in the air between them, daring him to answer wrong. The most terrifying part was the simple, brutal truth: she didn't know him, and in her world, that made him a threat. A disposable variable. The air crackled with unspoken threats, and Jonny knew, with sickening certainty, that one wrong move could shatter everything.

Jonny's voice barely rose above a whisper as he stepped closer. "Jess?"

Her eyes flickered with something unfamiliar yet deeply familiar—a hesitation, a hint of recognition, as if she were slowly piecing together a memory, she hadn't allowed herself to remember. Questions lingered behind her gaze, guarded and sharp.

"It's me… Jonny Phillips."

Shock washed over her features, softening only for a moment into something more complicated—something he dared to call emotion. Yet the gun in her hand never wavered.

"You remember me," he said, careful, deliberate. "I know you do."

Her response was measured, wary. "How did you find me?"

"It's been a long road, Jess." He admitted.

She shook her head, eyes narrowing, voice cold and precise. "That's not my name."

"Okay. Okay." He raised his hands slightly, each movement deliberate, mindful of the lethal distance between them. She was capable—he could see that—and he didn't want to tempt fate.

"I just wanted to find you," he said, stepping forward with cautious hope.

The moment his foot crossed that invisible line, her other hand gripped the gun tighter, a silent but unmistakable warning: don't take another step.

"Why!?" The word cracked like a whip, her fear and anger entwined.

"Because… because I never stopped thinking about you," he admitted, letting the truth hang in the cold air between them, aware of the deadly weight of her gaze and the gun in her hand.

"What do you know about me?" Her voice dropped, dangerous and low.

"Honestly… not much. I just tried to chase your footsteps," he admitted softly. He paused, swallowing the lump in his throat. "I know you were on the run for something."

Her eyes darkened, serious now, carrying a quiet, dangerous weight.

"It's okay," he said quickly, voice threading with urgency. "I'm not here to do anything other than see you again."

"Now you've seen me. Get out of here. Go… and never come back." She commanded. A subtle tremor ran through her voice, just as a shout echoed from below.

"ALLY!?"

She tensed, then shouted down the stairs. "I'm okay. I'm coming now!"

As she leaned her head to shout, her hair fell back, revealing the swelling bruise around her left eye.

"Are you okay? Are you in trouble?" he asked, stepping slightly closer, careful not to cross her invisible boundary.

"There's a fire escape behind you," she said, tone sharp, unwavering. "It leads to the street. Go back home… and never come looking for me again." Her face was resolute. She meant every word. Jonny hesitated for only a heartbeat, then slowly pulled a business card from his pocket, so as not to spook her. It was scribbled with his parents' address, and tossed it gently in front of her. “I can help you. If ever you need me, come to that address.”

Her eyes flicked to the card, and for a moment, the tension in her posture softened.

“Promise me you’ll never come back.” She said almost like a plea.

He nodded, swallowing the longing in his chest. If that was what she wanted, he would respect it. Then he bolted. Footsteps clanged behind her, from the stairs below, closer now. He scrambled down the fire escape. By the time he reached the street, the black Range Rover and the saloon car had already slipped out of the alley, darting away up the street. Jonny ran toward the back of the alley, where Dave and Bronko were struggling to their feet, battered, bruised, and bloodied from their own encounter with the men who had beaten them to a pulp.

Bronko stumbled, his breath coming in ragged gasps. He clutched his side, wincing with each shallow inhale. "Jonny," he rasped, "I gotta stop rolling with you, man. I always end up getting my ass kicked."

Jonny, his face etched with concern and a hint of guilt, helped Bronko to his feet. Dave, nursing a split lip and a rapidly swelling eye, chimed in, his voice strained. "I think we bumped into Julian Bertotti and a friend of his. Jonny, these people are dangerous." He glanced nervously towards the mouth of the alley, as if expecting reinforcements to arrive at any moment.

"I know," Jonny said, his voice tight with a suppressed fury. "I spoke to her."

Dave's eyes widened in disbelief, his good eye nearly popping out of his head. "What?!"

Bronko's jaw dropped, his usual bravado momentarily forgotten. "Your girl! Jess?" He looked from Jonny to Dave, confusion warring with apprehension on his battered face. Jonny nodded, the simple gesture a confirmation of the danger they faced.

"What did she say?" Dave pressed, eager to know more.

"She wasn't exactly thrilled I'd found her," Jonny replied, a bitter edge creeping into his voice. He could still feel the cold steel of the gun pressed against his skull. "She held a gun to my head."

"Oh hell no!" Bronko exclaimed, his face a mask of outrage and disbelief.

"She told me never to come back," Jonny continued, his gaze distant, lost in the memory of her hardened eyes. "I think she's in trouble."

Dave shook his head, his eyes darting around the alley, searching for any sign of movement. "I think we're in trouble if we don't get out of here. Now." He emphasised the last word, his voice sharp and insistent.

"I don't know," Jonny said, his voice laced with doubt and a stubborn refusal to give up. "It just seemed like there was a part of her that was screaming for help."

Bronko scoffed, a nervous edge to his voice. "That ain't our problem, dog. These people aren't playing around. We're lucky to be alive. If she's telling you to go, I say we listen to her. Let's not forget this son of a bitch is on the run for something; she could be capable of anything." He gestured jerkily with his good arm, nearly clipping Dave in the face, his movements more frantic than aggressive.

"Jonny, I'm sorry," Dave said, his voice filled with genuine regret. He placed a hand on Jonny's shoulder, his touch firm and reassuring. “I had hoped for more for you. But Bronko’s right. Let’s go home to our families."

He desperately wanted to go back, to ignore the danger, to convince himself that he could somehow save Jess from the darkness that he suspected had enveloped her. But the chilling image of her, weapon in hand, the coldness in her eyes, held him captive. He knew, with a sickening certainty, that he had to listen to his friends. They had to leave Nebraska. He had to walk away. The realisation was a punch to the gut, a fresh wound that ripped open the old scars and amplified the emptiness inside him, a void that had been there since the day he left Cedar Bluff in 1979. The weight of that absence, combined with the nagging doubt that he was abandoning Jess to something he didn't fully understand, threatened to crush him.

Chapter 22 Eyes That Don't Match the Past

The drive back to Kentucky was a blur of grey highway and gnawing disappointment. Jonny stared out the window, the endless fields of Nebraska in December mirroring the barren landscape of his soul. No more searching, no more chasing shadows, no more Jess. He was adrift, a ship without a sail, the purpose that had driven him for so long now extinguished, leaving behind a hollow ache. He replayed the conversation in the abandoned warehouse over and over in his head, each word, each glance, each chilling moment with Jess etched into his memory like a brand. He tried to imagine a future, a life beyond this obsession, a way to move forward, but it all felt hollow, a pale imitation of the vibrant, purposeful existence he'd envisioned.

Then Christmas arrived, a jarring, unwelcome intrusion into his despair. He felt anything but festive, wishing the holiday wasn't happening right now, taking with it the pressure to be joyful, to be present, to be normal. But he knew he had to put on a happy face, for his family, for the sake of tradition, for the illusion of normalcy that they so carefully cultivated.

Christmas at Jane and Ray's house was always a high-pressure affair, a carefully orchestrated performance of familial bliss. Charley and Dylan were there, their presence the main reason he was forcing a smile and trying to summon some semblance of holiday cheer. He didn't want to burden them with his despair, didn't want to cast a shadow over their Christmas. The search for Jess was a forbidden topic, a source of disapproval in Jane and Ray's eyes, a reminder of his perceived failures and unconventional choices. And then there was Amanda, her presence a constant source of awkwardness. This was their first Christmas divorced, and the forced civility was almost unbearable, a bizarre charade orchestrated by his parents, who seemed determined to pretend nothing had changed. They hadn't spoken beyond the occasional, daggering glance she sent his way, each look a silent accusation, a stinging rebuke.

The living room in his parents' big house, usually a haven of warmth and togetherness, felt suffocating, a gilded cage of expectations. A roaring fire crackled merrily in the hearth, casting a golden glow on the impeccably decorated tree, laden with ornaments that told the story of a well-to-do, picture-perfect family. The scent of pine and cinnamon was in the air, and the sound of carols played softly in the background, a carefully curated soundtrack to their manufactured happiness. But beneath the veneer of holiday cheer, Jonny felt a profound sense of alienation, a stranger in his own home, trapped in a role he could no longer play.

Throughout the day, Jonny felt the weight of his father's gaze, a silent pressure to conform, to be the son Ray expected him to be. It was in the way Ray watched him across the room, a subtle disapproval in his eyes, a constant reminder of Jonny's perceived failures. The unwrapping of presents was a carefully choreographed dance of forced enthusiasm. Charley and Dylan seemed genuinely happy with their gifts, their laughter a brief respite from the tension that permeated the room. Amanda and Jane were getting along famously, their easy laughter and shared stories adding another layer of surreal awkwardness to the day. Later, Bronko arrived, a welcome dose of genuine camaraderie in the midst of the forced cheer. Jonny knew Bronko would be alone on Christmas, so he'd extended an invitation, hoping to offer him some company. Bronko, surprisingly, hit it off with Charley and Dylan, his boisterous personality and goofy jokes bringing a genuine smile to their faces. Even more surprising, Jane and Ray seemed to take a liking to him, drawn to his easy-going nature and genuine warmth.

The clatter of dishes subsided as dinner drew to a close. As Bronko began tackling the washing up, Jonny walked into the kitchen, carrying a stack of plates. It was the first moment they'd had alone all day.

"Put them behind the others, man," Bronko said, his voice warm with genuine gratitude. "I really appreciate you letting me spend Christmas out here with you and your family. It's the first Christmas I haven't spent alone in the last ten years."

A wave of sadness washed over Jonny at Bronko's words. If this whole ill-fated search had achieved anything, it was reconnecting him with his old friends. They'd only spoken sporadically over the years, sometimes with five or more years between calls. Now, Bronko was here for Christmas, and Dave texted regularly, even sending a Christmas greeting that morning.

"We haven't really had a chance to catch up since Omaha," Bronko continued, wiping his hands on a dish towel. "How you holding up?"

Jonny sighed. "Conflicted, mostly. Something didn't seem right with her."

"You gotta stay away, man," Bronko said, his voice laced with concern. "She seems hardcore."

"Dave said the same," Jonny acknowledged, knowing his friends were right.

"But you achieved it, you found her," Bronko said, a hint of admiration in his voice. "You got to see her after all these years, even if she did…" He trailed off, stopping mid-sentence.

Jonny followed Bronko's gaze to the doorway, where Dylan stood, having innocently stumbled upon their conversation. Jonny could feel the unspoken tension in the air, the invisible boundaries Jane and Ray had erected around the topic of Jess and the search.

"Hey, bud," Jonny said, forcing a smile.

"I'm just getting a drink," Dylan replied, his eyes darting between Jonny and Bronko.

"Sure thing," Jonny said, trying to sound casual.

Dylan grabbed a beer from the fridge, then, with a hesitant glance at his father, decided to address the elephant in the room. "I don't really know much about what happened with this woman," he said, his voice low. "Nobody seems to ever want to talk about it. Did you find her?"

"Yeah, we found her," Jonny confirmed, keeping his tone neutral.

"What happened?" Dylan pressed, his curiosity evident.

"Well, she's married, kiddo," Jonny said, sparing Dylan the more disturbing details. "So that's it."

"What was she like? When you knew her hundreds of years ago," Dylan said, a playful glint in his eyes.

Jonny chuckled at Dylan's remark, appreciating his son's attempt to lighten the mood. He glanced at Bronko, whose face lit up with a nostalgic grin.

"She was a firecracker, haha," Bronko said, his voice filled with fond memories.

"She was exciting," Jonny added, his mind drifting back to 1979. "Adventurous, always kept me on my toes."

"She drunk us all under the table," Bronko chimed in, chuckling.

"Kicked our asses at poker," Jonny agreed, smiling.

"Man, she was always one step ahead," Bronko said, shaking his head in admiration.

"You'd have liked her," Jonny said to Dylan, a hint of wistfulness in his voice.

"She sounds awesome," Dylan said, his eyes wide with interest.

"You should have seen the performance of Sweet Home Alabama we did at one of the parties," Jonny said, a mischievous grin spreading across his face.

"You… singing?" Dylan said, his voice laced with humorous disbelief.

"Both of us," Jonny confirmed, laughing. "You should have seen it, the whole crowd cheering for us."

"No way!?" Dylan exclaimed, clearly impressed.

"Really! It was a good time," Jonny said, his voice filled with a nostalgic warmth.

The moment was shattered as Ray walked into the kitchen, his face a mask of disapproval. He'd clearly overheard their conversation. Turning his attention to his grandson, he said, his voice calm but laced with a sharp edge, "Dylan, can you go and help your mother, please?"

"Sure, Gramps," Dylan said, nodding innocently before quickly exiting the kitchen.

Jonny braced himself, knowing what was coming. His father's voice was calm, but his words stung nonetheless. "You know you have a real family back in that room, Jonny," Ray said, his eyes fixed on his son. "It's time you got your head out of fantasy land and spent some time with us, don't you think?"

With that, Ray turned and walked back out of the kitchen, leaving Jonny to grapple with his words. Bronko was visibly taken aback by Ray's harshness. "Damn, Gramps," he muttered, shaking his head in disbelief.

Jonny and Bronko walked back into the living room, the atmosphere immediately shifting as they crossed the threshold. Jane's voice dripped with sarcasm as she said, "Nice of you to join us, Jonny," her eyes narrowed with thinly veiled disapproval. Amanda, perched on the edge of the sofa, took obvious delight in the exchange, a smirk playing on her lips as she took a delicate sip of her wine. Ray, seated in his armchair by the fire, shot Jonny a dark look, his disapproval palpable. But before Jonny could respond, Bronko burst into character, a side of him that Jonny hadn't seen in years, a persona resurrected from the hazy memories of 1979. With a mischievous glint in his eyes, Bronko announced, "Alright, folks, time to liven things up!" He gestured towards the already-present array of games, clearly laid out and waiting for the family to engage. Before anyone could protest, he'd launched into a flurry of activity, grabbing the charades cards with infectious enthusiasm. Soon, the room was filled with laughter and playful banter, the forced civility momentarily forgotten as everyone, even Jane and Ray, found themselves drawn into Bronko's infectious energy.

The afternoon dissolved into a blur of chaotic games, Bronko orchestrating the merriment with the energy of a seasoned ringmaster. Jonny, however, remained on the periphery, a detached observer in his own life. He watched as his family laughed and teased each other, pushing Jess to the back of his mind with a forced determination. Each forced smile, each hollow chuckle, was an act of self-preservation, a desperate attempt to maintain the fragile illusion of normalcy. The next game involved Bronko sporting a ridiculous Velcro hat, while everyone else hurled soft, fuzzy balls at him, trying to get them to stick. Just as the laughter reached a fever pitch, the doorbell shattered the festive atmosphere, sending Trueman, the family dog, into a frenzy of barking. The game abruptly paused, the room falling silent save for Trueman's frantic yelps. Amanda, with a practiced sigh, wrestled with the dog, trying to restrain him. Charley, ever the peacemaker, stood up and announced, "I'll get it." As Charley walked towards the door, a sense of mild confusion filled the room. They weren't expecting anyone else. The muffled sound of Charley opening the door was followed by a voice, faint but unmistakable, drifting in from outside. "I'm looking for Jonny Phillips." Jonny froze, every nerve in his body tingling with surprise. He recognised the voice instantly, a voice he never expected to hear again. He moved silently, drawn by an invisible force, and positioned himself behind Charley, peering over her shoulder. His eyes widened in disbelief as he locked eyes with *her*. It was Jess. Her face, etched with a mixture of exhaustion and relief, broke into a hesitant smile as she saw him.

Charley, sensing the electric current that had suddenly arced between Jonny and the woman at the door, quietly retreated, leaving him standing there, and walked back into the living room. Jonny could hear her trying to keep her voice down, but the words still hung heavy in the air. "I think that was *her*," she said, her voice laced with a mixture of concern and curiosity. The room fell silent behind him.

"You came," Jonny said, a mixture of disbelief and elation flooding his senses.

"I need your help," Jess replied, her voice tight with suppressed urgency.

Jonny searched her eyes, seeing past the carefully constructed facade to the desperation that lurked beneath. She was scared, he sensed it, and his heart fluttered at the realisation. She had come!

In the living room, a tableau of awkward anticipation awaited Jonny's return. Slowly, the door opened, and he walked in, Jess following close behind. She visibly recoiled under the weight of so many eyes, offering a tight-lipped, awkward smile that didn't quite reach her eyes. Bronko was still kneeling on the floor, the silly Velcro hat perched on his head, two fuzzy balls clinging precariously to its surface, creating a comical, almost surreal image.

"Everyone, this is..." Jonny began, his voice trailing off, unsure of what name to use. The silence stretched, thick with unspoken questions.

Sensing his hesitation, Jess stepped forward, filling the void. "Jess," she said, her voice clear and steady.

The room remained suspended in stunned silence, the only sound the crackling of the fire in the hearth. Finally, Jane spoke, her voice laced with sarcasm, mostly to herself. "Oh, she is real then."

"Hi," Jess replied, her smile faltering slightly.

Amanda, perched on the sofa, took a deliberate sip of her wine, her anger radiating like a palpable heat.

"Hi! Nice to meet you," Charley said, a polite but cautious greeting.

"My daughter, Charley," Jonny said, a flicker of pride in his eyes.

"Nice to meet you," Jess replied. "Hey, Bronko."

"Jess," Bronko said, his voice hesitant, his eyes betraying a mixture of surprise and concern. He knew more about her than the others, knew the darkness that clung to her like a shadow.

"We'll be back," Jonny said, his voice firm, guiding Jess towards the kitchen.

As he led Jess through the doorway and closed the door behind them, Bronko watched them go, his brow furrowed with worry, a fierce protectiveness burning in his eyes.

"Are you okay?" Jonny asked, turning to Jess as soon as they were alone in the kitchen.

Jess shook her head, her eyes wide and haunted. "I haven't been able to stop thinking about you finding me in Nebraska," she said, her voice trembling. "I couldn't believe it was you after all these years."

The door creaked open, and Amanda slipped into the kitchen, her eyes darting around the room. "Sorry, just getting a drink," she said, her voice dripping with false innocence.

Jonny rolled his eyes, knowing full well that this was nothing more than a thinly veiled attempt at snooping. Amanda grabbed a soda and walked back out of the room, casting a furtive glance at Jess as she left.

"Is that your wife?" Jess asked, her voice barely audible.

"Ex-wife," Jonny corrected, his jaw tightening. "Why are you here, Jess? You told me never to come looking."

"I know, I know," Jess said, her voice laced with desperation. "I panicked, you're right. I am in trouble. I have been for most of my life. I don't know what to do."

Jonny reached out and gently held her shoulders, offering what comfort he could. "What mess are you in?" he asked, his voice soft with concern.

"The man I'm married to…" Jess began, her voice trembling.

"Julian?" Jonny asked, clarifying.

Jess nodded, her eyes filled with fear. "He's dangerous."

"Does he hurt you?" Jonny asked, his voice hardening.

Jess nodded again, her silence speaking volumes.

The door slowly creaked open, and Bronko walked in, his presence a silent promise of protection for his friend.

"Does he know this address?" Jonny asked, his eyes searching Jess's face.

Jess shook her head, her gaze fixed on the floor.

"It's okay," Jonny said, his voice firm and reassuring. "You can stay with me. He won't get to you, you're safe now."

"No, I'm not…" Jess said, fighting tears. "It's more complicated than that."

"What's he done to you, Jess?" Jonny pressed, his concern growing with each passing moment.

"Is Jess even your real name?" Bronko interjected, his voice laced with suspicion. "Because we've heard Jess Judy, Peggy Smith, or Ally Bertotti."

"None of them…" Jess said, her voice weary. "They've all been names to keep me going."

"To hide from the police, more like," Bronko muttered, his eyes narrowed.

"Changing my name to Jess was easier," she explained. "Jessica is my middle name… Pamela Jessica Carter."

The words rolled off her tongue as if they hadn't been spoken in years, as if even uttering them was a betrayal of the secrets she had guarded for so long.

"If I'm going to help you… I need to know everything," Jonny said, his voice firm but gentle.

She nodded, knowing that what she was about to reveal was a risk, a gamble with her life and his. Was he ready to hear the truth? If he was the same man she had known back in 1979, she knew she could trust him, and Bronko. She looked at Bronko, a silent plea in her eyes.

"I'll tell you everything, Jonny," Jess said, her voice filled with a mixture of fear and determination.

"Everything?" Bronko echoed, a hint of reluctance hanging in his voice.

"He deserves to know," Jess said, her gaze unwavering.

Bronko swallowed hard, a lump forming in his throat. He was just as nervous as she was, Jonny noticed, his eyes darting between Jess and his. Bronko nodded in agreement, a silent pact passing between them that pricked at Jonny's senses. What was that about? It was clear now: Jess had a mountain of secrets, and Bronko was somehow entangled in them. A knot of suspicion tightened in Jonny's stomach. The air crackled with unspoken tension, the mystery deepening with every passing moment, fuelling Jonny's desperate need to know the truth.

"What did you do?" Jonny asked anxiously, the nerves pressing heavy on him.

Jess, her voice trembling, ready to unleash the torrent of secrets she had held captive for so long. "I'll go back to the very start…"

Chapter 23 Before the World Shifted

Her earliest memories were bathed in a golden light, fragments of pure, unadulterated joy that she clung to like precious jewels. She remembered their family home, a small but cosy bungalow filled with the comforting aroma of her mother's baking and the warm, woody scent of her father's pipe tobacco. But her fondest recollections were of her dad, a towering figure in his crisp army uniform, swinging her around and around until she was dizzy with laughter. A vinyl record would be spinning on the turntable, the infectious melody of "Peggy Sue" filling the air, and he would pretend to dance with her, lifting her high above his head as he stumbled and twirled. Her mum would be watching from the doorway, a soft smile gracing her lips as she laughed until her sides ached, her father's off-key singing only adding to the hilarity.

"There she is, my little Peggy herself!" Jack exclaimed, his voice booming with affection.

She beamed; her father was her idol, her hero. No matter how much life had gotten to him, how weary he was from his duties, he always made time to make his daughter happy, truly happy. She was the apple of his eye, and he made sure she knew it. Her mother, Joyce, walked in from the doorway after letting them finish.

"Jack, can I have your help with the pantry door? It's stuck again," Joyce said, her voice soft and even.

"Sure, honey," Jack replied, his gaze softening as he turned to his wife. "Hey, Pammy, I'll be right back! Why don't you go find a place to hide! I feel a game of hide and seek coming on!"

Her father pulled an overly dramatic, playful face, his eyes widening and his eyebrows arching in mock surprise, making her giggle uncontrollably.

"Okay, Daddy!" Pamela squealed, her eyes sparkling with excitement.

Jack followed Joyce into the kitchen, his footsteps heavy but light-hearted. Pamela, her heart pounding with anticipation, scurried behind the door, peeping through the crack, watching her father prise open the stubborn pantry door for her mother.

"Thank you, my love," Joyce said, her voice filled with gratitude.

Joyce kissed him lovingly on the cheek as he held his arm up in a humorous pose, flexing his non-existent muscles, making her laugh.

"*Right*," he said with a purposeful, raised voice so Pamela could hear, his eyes twinkling mischievously. "I BETTER SEE IF I CAN FIND PAMELA JESSICA CARTER SOMEWHERE!"

Joyce smiled, shaking her head at her husband's antics, kissing him once more, this time lingering slightly longer.

"I think it's about time we gave Pammy a little brother or sister?" Joyce said, her voice wistful, her eyes filled with a longing that mirrored his own.

Jack's smile faltered slightly, a shadow passing over his face. "We talked about this, baby," he said, his voice softening. "Let's get this war out of the way first. I don't even know if I'll be drafted. Then we focus on our family. I don't want to miss a part of our future kid's life." Joyce smiled faintly, her eyes filled with a mixture of love and sadness, knowing she wanted the same too, but wishing the circumstances were different.

Pamela's childhood was a tapestry woven with threads of laughter, adventure, and boundless affection. Even when her dad was away, serving his country, the house never felt truly empty. She missed him fiercely, her small heart aching with a longing that only his warm embrace could soothe. But she and her mum would channel that longing into elaborate plans for his return, crafting handmade cards, baking his favourite cookies, and decorating the house with colourful streamers. The anticipation would build with each passing day, culminating in a joyful reunion filled with hugs, kisses, and whispered promises of forever. Their home was a sanctuary, a haven of love and support where dreams were nurtured, and every day felt like a celebration of family.

It was 1967, and Pamela was six years old. Her dad's absence stretched on, each day an echo of the one before, and she sensed a growing unease in her mother. It was the worry, a silent companion that shadowed Joyce's every move. Sometimes, the strain would manifest as a fleeting sharpness, a momentary lapse in patience, quickly followed by a deluge of apologies and extra cuddles. But the underlying tension remained, a subtle tremor that shook the foundations of their once-unshakeable home. One cold, starless night, Pamela was tucked into her pyjamas, cocooned in the warmth of her favourite blanket, when a sharp rap at the door shattered the fragile peace. Her mother answered, her face a canvas of hope warring with dread. Pamela strained to hear, her small body rigid with anticipation. The man on the porch spoke, his voice carefully measured, laced with a deep compassion that sent a shiver down Pamela's spine. "Mrs. Carter," he began, his tone gentle but firm. "I'm afraid I have some very difficult news regarding your husband, Jack." He paused, taking a deep breath as if bracing himself for her reaction. "I'm so sorry to inform you that he was killed in action." The words hung in the air, heavy and suffocating, delivered with a tenderness that did little to soften the blow. Then, a sound erupted from her mother, a primal scream of grief that tore through the night, a sound that would forever be etched into Pamela's memory.

Joyce crumpled in the doorway, her body collapsing under the weight of the unbearable news. In that instant, Pamela's world shattered. The vibrant colours of her childhood faded to grey, replaced by a chilling understanding that her father was gone, never to return. The laughter, the dancing, the warm embrace – all vanished, leaving her adrift in a sea of sorrow.

Life after that night was a stark contrast to the warmth and security Pamela had once known. Her childhood faded into nothing more than heartache. Her mum, Joyce, was never quite the same. The light in her eyes had dimmed, replaced by a haunted emptiness that Pamela couldn't penetrate. Joyce struggled, desperately, with the weight of her grief, but instead of confronting it, she seemed determined to outrun it, to bury it beneath layers of denial and self-destruction. Pamela, in her innocent naiveté, wasn't allowed to grieve, wasn't allowed to express the profound sadness that threatened to consume her. Her mother, lost in her own pain, couldn't bear to witness it, couldn't cope with the raw, unfiltered emotions that mirrored her own.

As the years passed, Joyce's coping mechanisms grew increasingly destructive. She turned to alcohol, seeking solace in the numbing embrace of liquor, and then, inevitably, to drugs, chasing a fleeting escape from the unbearable reality of her loss. Many a time, Pamela would come home from school to find her mother slumped on the couch, lost in a heroin-induced slumber, her face pale and lifeless. Pamela, barely old enough to understand the full extent of her mother's addiction, knew instinctively to just leave her, to let her sleep. She learned to care for her from a young age, anticipating the inevitable withdrawals, knowing how to soothe her fevered brow, how to coax her to drink water, how to hold her hair back as she wretched into the toilet, her body convulsing with pain.

Pamela learned to fend for herself, to navigate the treacherous waters of her broken home. She taught herself to cook simple meals, to clean the squalor that accumulated around them, to get herself ready for school each morning, her small hands fumbling with buttons and zippers. But the most terrifying aspect of her new reality was the parade of strange men her mother would bring home, men with vacant eyes and predatory smiles. Pamela would often hear muffled sounds coming from her mother's room, sounds that filled her with a nameless dread. She would lock herself in her own room, barricading the door with whatever furniture she could move, her heart pounding in her chest, terrified that one of those men would try to come in, would try to touch her. The innocence of her childhood had been stolen, replaced by a chilling awareness of the dangers that lurked just beyond her door. All she wanted was her father.

It was 1971, and Pamela was ten years old when Floyd slithered into their lives, a venomous serpent disguised as a saviour. Her mum, Joyce, desperate for connection and a semblance of normalcy, latched onto him with a fervour that bordered on obsession. Pamela, however, felt a deep, visceral unease in his presence, a primal instinct screaming at her to run, to hide. Floyd had a gaunt, hollow-eyed look about him, his skin stretched tight over sharp cheekbones, his movements jerky and unpredictable. He always seemed to be on edge, his hands twitching, his eyes darting around as if searching for something he couldn't find. He reeked of stale cigarettes and a cloying, sickly-sweet scent that Pamela couldn't quite place, but knew was somehow connected to the little glassine bags he always seemed to have tucked away in his pockets.

Floyd quickly established a pattern of dominance, manipulating Joyce and isolating her further from the outside world. He would always conveniently want to do drugs when Pamela was in the house, he would make her cook elaborate meals, keeping her occupied while he and Joyce retreated to the bedroom, the air thick with smoke and hushed whispers. He was stealing her mum away, dragging her further and further into a black hole of addiction and despair, and Pamela resented him with every fibre of her being. He was always horrible to her; his words a venomous cruelty that belied his saccharine smile. He would leer at her, his eyes cold and empty, and say things like, "I'm your new daddy now, Pammy," but there was no warmth, no affection in his voice, only a chilling emptiness that made her skin crawl.

He used threats and intimidation to keep Pamela silent, to ensure that she wouldn't reveal the truth about his abuse to anyone. He would say mean things, whisper insidious lies in her ear, planting seeds of doubt and fear. He would lash out at Joyce, sometimes physically, leaving her bruised and battered, her body a roadmap of his cruelty. Sometimes, after a particularly brutal beating, Pamela and her mum would huddle together in Pamela's room, their bodies trembling, their voices hushed with fear, and they would make plans to leave Floyd, to escape to a small, secluded place where they could start over, a sanctuary far away from the horrors of their current reality. They would dream of a life of peace and tranquillity, a life where they could finally be happy. But that day never came.

When Pamela was fourteen, Floyd uprooted them, dragging them kicking and screaming to a dilapidated shack in rural northern Michigan, near the desolate town of Moorstown. He claimed it was a fresh start, a chance to escape their troubles, but Pamela knew the truth: it was simply another way to isolate them, to tighten his grip on their lives. Moorstown was a forgotten corner of the world, a place where secrets festered and hope withered. They were trapped, prisoners in their own lives, with no escape in sight.

It wasn't long after their arrival in Moorstown that Joyce realised, with a chilling certainty that settled deep in her bones, that there was no escape. The isolation, the constant fear, the insidious control Floyd exerted over every aspect of their lives – it had all coalesced into an inescapable prison. One evening, she sat with Pamela on the dilapidated porch of their shack, listening to the distant howl of coyotes. Floyd was out, as usual, drowning his demons in cheap whiskey at the local dive bar. They looked up at the sky, a vast expanse of black velvet studded with brilliant, shimmering stars.

"I'm sorry, baby," Joyce whispered. For the first time in a long time, she was clear-headed, the fog of drugs and alcohol momentarily lifted, allowing her to see the devastation she had wrought upon their lives.

"I've really screwed things up for us, haven't I?" she said, her voice a raw, self-deprecating honesty that pierced Pamela's heart.

"We need to leave, Mom," Pamela pleaded, her voice trembling with a mixture of fear and desperation.

"There's nowhere for us to go," Joyce replied, her voice flat, devoid of hope.

Tears welled up in Joyce's eyes, spilling down her cheeks, and Pamela, unable to bear her mother's pain, began to cry too. Pamela looked back up at the stars, searching for some kind of solace in their distant, unwavering light.

"Do you think Dad's up there?" she asked.

"Yeah, baby," Joyce replied, her voice softening, a flicker of warmth returning to her eyes. "He'd be looking down on us, watching over us."

Pamela looked at her mum, her heart aching with a mixture of love and sorrow. She tried to remember the vibrant, radiant woman from her childhood, the woman who had filled their home with laughter and warmth. Now, all that remained was a thin, gaunt shell, her body ravaged by years of addiction and abuse, her spirit crushed beneath the weight of her grief.

"Just remember I love you, my baby girl!" Joyce said, her voice filled with a desperate urgency. "You can be so many things, Pamela. Don't screw life up like I did. Go out and make something of yourself."

"I'm not leaving you behind, Mom," Pamela insisted, her voice firm, her eyes filled with a fierce determination.

More tears rolled down Joyce's face, blurring her vision. She reached out and kissed Pamela on the forehead, her touch lingering for a moment, as if trying to imprint her love onto her daughter's soul.

"Go on, get yourself to bed," she said, her voice weary. "I'll deal with Floyd when he gets home."

Pamela nodded, offering her mother a small, sympathetic smile, though her heart was heavy with dread. She couldn't help but feel that life would be so much different, so much better, if her dad was still alive. She loved her mum, she truly did, but she found it increasingly difficult to reconcile the woman she had become with the woman she remembered from her childhood. She tried to remember who her mum was under all of it, under the layers of addiction and pain, but it was like trying to grasp a fading dream. She kissed her mum on the cheek and went inside, crawling into bed and pulling the covers over her head, crying herself to sleep, her heart filled with a profound sense of loss and despair.

Pamela woke with a jolt, her heart pounding in her chest, to the loud, insistent shouting of Floyd calling her name. Panic-stricken, she scrambled out of bed, her bare feet hitting the cold, wooden floor, the urgency in his voice sending a shiver of dread down her spine. She ran into the living room, her breath catching in her throat at the sight that greeted her. Floyd was kneeling on the floor, cradling Joyce in his arms, his face contorted with a mixture of grief and something else, something darker, that Pamela couldn't quite decipher. Joyce's face was a pale, ghostly white, her eyes vacant and unseeing. A thin, red line encircled her neck, where she had tied a shoelace and twisted it tighter with a spoon, a desperate act of finality. A needle was still stuck in her arm, a cruel reminder of the demons that had driven her to this point. Her mother was dead, gone forever, and she had left Pamela in this world with the worst possible person, the monster who had haunted their lives for so long. Pamela was stuck, utterly and completely alone, with Floyd at fourteen, her world crumbling around her, leaving her with no hope of escape.

Floyd looked up at Pamela, his eyes bloodshot and wild with rage. "WHAT DID YOU DO!" he roared, his voice cracking with emotion. Pamela couldn't speak, couldn't move. She was frozen on the spot, paralysed by the horror of the scene before her.

"THIS IS YOUR FAULT!" Floyd screamed, his voice filled with a venomous accusation.

Pamela, finally snapping out of her stupor, turned and ran to her room, slamming the door shut and locking it tight. She could hear Floyd's sobs, a guttural, animalistic sound that made her skin crawl. He was insistently shouting, "This is your fault, Pamela! This is all your fault!" over and over, his words echoing through the thin walls of the shack. But Pamela knew better. She knew, with a chilling certainty, that this was Floyd's doing. He had systematically broken her mother down, isolating her, manipulating her, and driving her to the brink of despair. She had lost her father because of the war, a faceless, distant enemy that she had always blamed and hated. But now, her mother was gone too, this time at the hands of one person, one tangible, malevolent force. Floyd had driven her to it, leaving her with no option but to commit suicide, a final, desperate act of escape from the hell he had created.

After that day, life for Pamela became a living nightmare, a desolate landscape of fear, resentment, and unrelenting misery.

The hate between her and Floyd was a palpable force, a toxic cloud that hung heavy in the air, suffocating any glimmer of hope. She was trapped, utterly and completely, with the man she held responsible for her mother's death, a man who seemed determined to make her pay for something she didn't do. She grew up in those four years, her childhood ripped away, replaced by a grim determination to survive. All she could do was wait, clinging to the fragile hope that when she turned eighteen, she could finally escape, finally make a life of her own, a life free from Floyd's tyranny. She imagined that the world would take her more seriously as an adult, that she would be able to forge her own path, unburdened by the weight of her past.

In the meantime, she did everything, becoming Floyd's unwilling servant, her days a monotonous cycle of drudgery and abuse. She cooked every meal, scrubbing pots and pans until her hands were raw, cleaned the dilapidated shack from top to bottom, trying to create some semblance of order in the chaos that surrounded her. She waited for him to come home each night, bracing herself for the inevitable onslaught of drunken rage and venomous accusations. She listened to the abuse he would throw at her, the cruel, cutting words that were designed to tear her down, to break her spirit.

For the next four years, she heard it over and over again: how it was her fault her mum committed suicide, how she was a burden, a worthless piece of trash, how her mum had hated her, had resented her for ruining her life. Floyd seemed to take a perverse pleasure in tormenting her with these lies, twisting the knife in her already wounded heart. She tried her best to cling to the memory of her mother's love, to hold on to the belief that what Floyd was saying wasn't true, that her mum had loved her, had cherished her, had wanted a better life for her. But it was hard, so incredibly hard, to maintain that belief in the face of Floyd's relentless cruelty. Each day was a battle, a struggle to hold on to her sanity, to keep the darkness from consuming her completely.

Amidst the relentless drudgery and abuse, Pamela found an unlikely lifeline, a small spark of hope that flickered in the darkness. One day, while cleaning up Floyd's mess, she stumbled upon an advertisement in one of his discarded newspapers, a small, unassuming ad for a pen-pal service based in West Virginia. Intrigued, and desperate for any kind of connection to the outside world, she carefully cut out the ad and, under the cover of darkness, wrote a letter, pouring out her loneliness and longing for companionship.

Weeks later, a response arrived, a letter thanking her for using the service and informing her that she had been paired up with a woman whose username was BamaBird61 from Alabama. A wave of excitement washed over Pamela, a feeling she hadn't experienced in years. For the next year, writing back and forth to BamaBird61 became the only piece of comfort she had, a refuge from the horrors of her daily life. She eagerly anticipated the arrival of BamaBird61's letters, her heart pounding with anticipation as she tore open the envelopes, devouring every word with a desperate hunger.

Hearing about Alabama, about the warm sunshine and the sweet, Southern charm, filled Pamela with a longing to escape, to leave the desolate landscape of northern Michigan behind and start a new life in a place where hope still bloomed. She would listen to "Sweet Home Alabama" over and over on her cassette player, the music transporting her to a world of cotton fields and magnolia trees, a world where she could finally be free. As adulthood approached, she even found herself experimenting with Floyd's stash of Clyde Mays whiskey, finding the taste surprisingly nice, a small act of rebellion against the man who controlled her life. She loved hearing about BamaBird61's life in Alabama, admired her ambition to become a nurse, and envied her good relationship with a man named Stu. It made her dream of visiting Alabama someday, of experiencing the warmth and kindness that seemed to radiate from BamaBird61's letters.

Pamela's eighteenth birthday arrived, the 11th of January 1979, a day she had dreamed of for years, a beacon of hope in the darkness of her existence. She woke with a sliver of anticipation fluttering in her chest, a tiny spark of excitement that she had tried to suppress, but couldn't quite extinguish. But as she opened her eyes and looked around the dingy room, the reality of her situation crashed down on her with brutal force. There were no presents, no cards, no sign that anyone even remembered it was her birthday. Floyd had forgotten, or perhaps he simply didn't care. The realisation was a crushing blow, a reminder of her insignificance in his eyes.

Pamela carefully scooped Floyd's pancakes from the frying pan, the sizzle of the grease a discordant note to the tremor in her hands. She brought the plate and a steaming mug of coffee to the table.

"Do you know what day it is, Floyd?" she asked, her eyes fixed on his face, searching for a flicker of acknowledgment.

Floyd grunted, barely lifting his gaze from the newspaper spread before him. "Thursday," he said, his voice flat and dismissive as he dug into his pancakes.

"I'm eighteen today," Pamela said, her voice gaining a sliver of strength, her gaze unwavering despite the fear churning within her.

"So?" Floyd sneered, finally raising his head, his eyes like chips of ice. "No one cares about you, Pammy. You're nothing."

"I was thinking of getting a place of my own," Pamela ventured, the words trembling slightly on her lips, but her resolve hardening with each syllable.

The reaction was instantaneous and brutal. Floyd's hand lashed out, a lightning strike of violence that connected with her face, sending her staggering backward. The air left her lungs in a whoosh, her senses reeling from the unexpected blow. He had never struck her before, not physically. But the illusion of safety shattered with the force of his hand, replaced by the chilling realisation that adulthood offered no protection, only made her a more viable target.

"With what money?" Floyd roared, his face contorted into a mask of pure rage. He surged to his feet, looming over her, his finger jabbing at her chest. "You're a joke, Pam! You shine my shoes and make my goddamn meals because there ain't nothing else out there for you! You're worthless, a nobody!" His words were like shards of glass, cutting deep into her soul. "If you don't like it, then you can always do what your mother did! Kill yourself, Pammy! Do me a Favour, having to spend every second of my life with you is a god-damn chore!"

Tears welled in Pamela's eyes, blurring her vision, her body trembling with a mixture of fear and humiliation. The sight of her tears only seemed to ignite Floyd's fury further. He struck her twice more across the face with the back of his hand, each blow a hammer blow to her spirit, a crimson bruise blossoming beneath her eye.

"And stop crying, for Christ's sake, woman!" he snarled, his voice dripping with contempt.

He snatched up his plate, the uneaten pancakes a mocking reminder of her failed attempt to please him, and hurled it against the wall. The plate shattered into a thousand pieces, scattering across the floor like the broken fragments of her life.

"Your pancakes taste like ass!" he bellowed, his face contorted with fury. "You can't even get that right! You're a failure, a complete and utter disappointment! I truly wish it was you that died instead, at least your mother's pancakes were edible!"

With that, Floyd grabbed his jacket and stormed out the door, the slam of the door echoing through the small shack, leaving Pamela alone in the wreckage of her life. She sank to her knees amidst the broken pieces and splattered food, sobbing uncontrollably, the weight of her despair crushing her. She truly knew how her mother had felt now, the crushing hopelessness, the suffocating desperation, the overwhelming desire to escape. This stung, more than any physical blow ever could, a searing pain that went straight to her heart. But now she knew what she needed to do. A plan that had been in her head for a long time. It was time…

Chapter 24 What She Did

The night of her eighteenth birthday hung heavy with the familiar weight of despair. Pamela sat on the porch, the isolation of their rural home amplifying the darkness that clung to her like a shroud. She flicked a lighter open and shut, open and shut, the unlit lighter a nervous tic, a silent, repetitive motion. It wasn't the flame she sought, but the familiar click, the small, mechanical action that she often performed when she zoned out, a way to occupy her hands and quiet her mind, if only for a moment. Moths fluttered around the single, dim bulb illuminating the porch, drawn to the only source of light in the vast expanse of darkness. The house was surrounded by a sea of overgrown grass, a reflection of years of neglect, broken only by the muddy, rutted driveway that led to the distant road. She sat there, a black bruise blooming beneath her eye, a physical manifestation of the pain that gnawed at her soul, lost in a labyrinth of bitter thoughts. The click-click-click of the unlit lighter was her only companion. Then, headlights appeared, cutting through the darkness, the telltale rumble of Floyd's rusted pickup truck announcing his arrival. The truck lurched down the driveway, its tyres spitting mud and gravel, before finally coming to a stop on the overgrown grass next to his motorcycle, a machine that looked like it had been pulled from a junkyard, a relic of a life that never went anywhere. He cut the headlights, plunging the yard into near darkness, and Floyd emerged from the cab, his figure silhouetted against what little light remained from the porch, and Pamela felt the familiar surge of dread wash over her, a cold wave that tightened her chest and stole her breath. She closed the lighter one last time.

"What are you doing out here?" Floyd's voice was a thick, slurred mess, each word a struggle against the encroaching fog of alcohol. He swayed on his feet, a human pendulum threatening to topple with every gust of wind.

"Waiting for you, Floyd," Pamela replied, her tone betraying nothing of the turmoil churning within.

She moved to his side, offering a steadying arm. He lurched towards her, a dead weight threatening to drag them both down, and she braced herself against his bulk.

"Did you make my dinner, woman?" he demanded, the question laced with the expectation of a master addressing a servant.

"Yeah, I did," she said, her voice flat, devoid of inflection.

She strained to guide him up the porch steps, each upward inch a battle against gravity and his own drunken inertia.

"Best taste better than those pancakes. Your mother's cooking was much better," he grumbled, the well-worn complaint a familiar sting.

"I know, you tell me every single day," Pamela murmured.

She remained eerily composed, a deceptive stillness that hinted at something premeditated. It was as if she were detached, observing the scene, a puppet master about to set a carefully premeditated plan into motion. She steered him through the front door, her grip firm, her purpose now a dark promise hanging in the air.

"You're a dumb bitch Pammy, you hear me? A dumb bitch," he spat.

Floyd stumbled, his feet tangling in the rug, and Pamela caught him, preventing a disastrous fall. She helped him towards the living area.

"What's that smell?" he mumbled, his senses dulled by the alcohol.

"I don't know, Floyd, you're drunk," she replied, her voice a monotone.

"Better not be your cooking. Your mother was good for something, and that was cooking. She was a dumb bitch too, just like you," he slurred, the words a venomous cocktail of resentment and contempt.

Pamela shuffled him towards the sofa, her face a mask of impassivity, her eyes reflecting a cold, distant light.

"She was good for something else too," he leered, his gaze heavy with lust, his hand reaching out with a predatory intent. Floyd groped Pamela's breast, his touch rough and unwelcome. She recoiled, a flicker of disgust crossing her features, and struggled against him as he tried to force himself upon her, his drunken insistence a violation she fought against with surprising strength.

"Get off me!!" she exclaimed, her voice a sharp, defiant crack in the facade of calm.

Floyd, caught off guard and weakened by drink, lost his balance and tumbled backward onto the sofa, his body sinking into the soft cushions. Pamela wiped away the tears that welled in her eyes, fighting to suppress the emotions that threatened to overwhelm her. She walked back to the front of the house, her movements stiff, mechanical, her spirit numb. A bag sat by the door, packed and ready, a silent promise of escape. Floyd snored softly, already lost in a drunken slumber. She paused, casting one last, lingering glance at the man sprawled on the sofa, feeling nothing but hatred. She reached for the keys on the side table, her fingers trembling slightly.

"Goodbye, Floyd," she whispered, the words a final farewell.

She pushed the door open and walked away from the house. All the while, she played with the lighter in her hand, her thumb opening and shutting the lid in a hypnotic rhythm. Click, click, click. Then, with a deliberate act, she flicked it on, the flame dancing high, casting an eerie glow on her face. With a chilling absence of emotion, she tossed the lighter over her shoulder, back towards the house, a final, irreversible act. Her face was a blank slate, devoid of feeling, as she continued walking, never once looking back. The moment the lighter sailed through the open doorway, it met the invisible fumes that had been steadily filling the room from the gas leaking from the cooker she had deliberately left on for hours. The resulting explosion was instantaneous and deafening, the whole house erupting in a cataclysmic fireball, sending shards of wood and glass spiralling into the night sky. Yet, Pamela remained focused, fixed on the horizon, the inferno behind her a terrifying symbol of her liberation, a fiery phoenix rising from the ashes of her former life. She climbed onto Floyd's motorcycle. She twisted the key in the ignition, the engine roaring to life. She sped off into the darkness, the inferno burning in her mirrors, a distant echo of the destruction she had caused.

Pamela couldn't look back, not even for a second. The inferno she left behind was more than just a burning house; it was a pyre consuming her old life, and she knew the police would be looking for her, adrift in a sea of uncertainty. She was alone, utterly and completely. Trust was a luxury she could no longer afford; every stranger was a potential threat. The only person she could rely on was herself. Her plan, hatched in the darkest corners of her mind, was to reach West Virginia. She remembered reading about the pen-pal service that offered a refuge, a haven for young people in need. It was a long shot, but it was the only thread of hope she had left. Every passing car sent a jolt of paranoia through her, wondering if the occupants knew who she was, what she had done. Were they staring? Would they recognise her? Would they dial the police, reporting her location, sealing her fate? She dared not check the newspapers, terrified of seeing her picture splashed across the front page. Ignorance, in this case, was a shield, a fragile barrier against the crushing weight of reality. Instead, she focused on blending in, becoming a ghost in the crowd, a shadow flitting through the edges of society.

Floyd's beat-up motorcycle gave out on her way before the Michigan state line. With a frustrated snarl, she wrestled the heavy machine to the nearest riverbank and shoved it in. She couldn't risk leaving a trail for the police to find, so she abandoned it, leaving her with no choice but to walk. The next two months were a blur of hardship and desperation. She slept in barns, the hay scratching against her skin, the smell of animals a constant reminder of her isolation. Hitchhiking was out of the question; it would only draw unwanted attention. Instead, she stole food from gas stations, her heart pounding with each furtive grab, the guilt a bitter taste in her mouth. Her body ached with every step, every muscle screaming for rest. But she pressed on, driven by a primal instinct to survive, to reach that distant refuge in West Virginia. Slowly, her body adapted to the constant strain, the aches becoming a dull, familiar throb.

Finally, after what felt like an eternity, she arrived in Bancroft, West Virginia. The refuge was nothing fancy, just a simple, unassuming house nestled amongst the rolling hills. It wasn't a mansion or castle, but it was safe. It was a sanctuary. The owner met her at the door. She was an older woman; her face etched with the wisdom and weariness of a life well-lived. Her hair was the colour of spun silver, pulled back into a loose bun, and her eyes, though lined with wrinkles, sparkled with a gentle kindness. She was stout, her body rounded by years of nurturing others, and her hands, calloused and strong, offered a comforting warmth. She made Pamela feel welcome, not with grand gestures or empty promises, but with a quiet understanding, a silent acknowledgment of the pain she carried. In that moment, standing on the porch of that humble house, Pamela felt a flicker of hope ignite within her, a fragile ember in the ashes of her past.

After a warm shower—a luxury Pamela hadn't known for months—she found herself seated across from the old woman in a cluttered office. The woman shuffled through papers, her pen scratching across the forms as she began the check-in process. Pamela sensed a deep well of kindness in the woman's gaze, yet the unnerving feeling that she possessed some knowledge of Pamela's crimes, or that she would eventually hear of them kept her on edge, her defences tightly drawn.

"You ain't talked much since you been here, darlin'," the woman observed gently, her voice a soft drawl. Pamela managed a weak, awkward grin.

"Why don't we start with your name?" the woman suggested, her eyes patient and encouraging.

A jolt of panic shot through Pamela. She knew, with a sudden certainty, that she needed to bury her old identity so deep it would never be found. Memories swirled, and she clung to a fragment of happier times—her dad's off-key rendition of "Peggy Sue." The name was a shield, a disguise.

"Peggy… Peggy Smith," Pamela blurted, grasping for the most ordinary, forgettable surname she could summon. The sound of it, Peggy Smith, felt strange and new on her tongue.

"It's nice to meet you, Peggy. I'm Jess Judy," the woman replied, her smile radiating a warmth that Pamela hadn't felt in what seemed like a lifetime. Jess then led her through the unfamiliar corridors. With each step, Pamela felt the old her fading, replaced by this new persona. This was it, she was Peggy now. A clean slate, a chance to rewrite her story. The bedroom Jess showed her to was small and simple, but it offered a sanctuary, a place to rest her weary head and dream of a future where Pamela was just a ghost.

"Lights out at nine, and you'll be expected to contribute towards making meals," Jess explained, her tone matter-of-fact but not unkind.

Peggy settled into a routine of near isolation. She spent most of her days within the confines of her small room, the four walls becoming both a prison and a sanctuary. She ventured out only for the necessities: quick, almost furtive trips to the shared bathroom for showers, and silent appearances at mealtimes. Six other young people resided at the house, a mix of troubled souls and lost causes, but Peggy made no effort to connect with them. She was an enigma, a ghost flitting through their shared spaces. Knowing the refuge was temporary, she deliberately chose to sit out on the porch after lights out to avoid the others and plan her next move.

Weeks blurred into a monotonous cycle. Then, one night, Peggy found herself on the porch, the cool night air a welcome change from the stuffiness of her room. With a letter to BamaBird61 in her hand—a name she hadn't contacted in what felt like a lifetime—she sat quietly, rereading it in the dim light. A lighter was her only other companion. She began to flick it open and shut, the metallic click a new comfort she had found in the silence, a sound that reminded her of the inferno she had unleashed, an act of liberation. The lighter itself was a talisman, a symbol of the power she now possessed, a small, manageable flame that kept the darkness at bay. Something that made her feel safe.

As she reread her thoughts, she craved the life BamaBird61 possessed. The stability, the freedom, the normalcy. This house was only a stepping stone, a temporary haven. She needed a plan, something more permanent, something that would allow her to truly leave Pamela behind and fully embrace Peggy. Rereading the letter, she noted its insistent tone, a raw yearning that surprised even herself. She folded it carefully, a silent promise to herself to pursue this new direction. She wanted to go and stay in Alabama with her.

Lost in her thoughts, she didn't hear him approach. "Hey," a voice startled her. One of the other young residents stood a few feet away, a young man seemingly around her age, his expression unreadable in the dim light.

Peggy mumbled, "Hi," and immediately averted her gaze, a desperate prayer that the dim light would cloak her features, prevent recognition.

"Name's Julian," the young man said, his voice a low murmur that barely carried on the night air.

"Peggy," she replied, the name a fragile shield, a whispered falsehood.

Julian's next words cut through the darkness like a shard of glass. "No it ain't."

Her head snapped up, a surge of icy dread flooding her veins. He knew. How? The question clawed at her throat, choking off any response.

"Saw you in the papers back in Nebraska," Julian continued, his voice dangerously soft. "Police want to talk to you… and you're avoiding them. Says a lot."

Adrenaline exploded through Peggy's system, every instinct screaming for survival. Her eyes darted wildly, searching for an escape route, a weapon, anything to defend herself. The porch offered little: a rickety chair, a chipped flowerpot.

"Secrets safe with me," Julian said, a strange, unsettling smile playing on his lips. "You mustn't have many friends in the world. I've done some things I'm not proud of too."

Julian became a constant fixture in Peggy's life at the refuge. He seemed to materialise whenever she left her room, his presence a strange mix of unsettling and unavoidable. There was an oddness about him, a persistent intensity in his gaze that made her skin crawl. But he knew her secret, the truth she had fought so hard to bury, and that knowledge gave him a power over her. So, she was polite, offering small smiles and strained conversation, even when every fibre of her being screamed for her to retreat.

His attention grew increasingly obsessive. He would linger outside her door, waiting for her to emerge, his eyes following her every move during mealtimes. It was clear he wanted more than friendship, but his overbearingness was unnerving, a suffocating pressure that made her deeply uncomfortable. She dared not challenge him, dare not risk provoking him, for fear of what he might reveal. All the while, she continued her clandestine correspondence with BamaBird61, a lifeline to a future that seemed increasingly distant and unattainable.

Then, one day, a letter arrived that changed everything. BamaBird61 had written to say that her parents had agreed to let her come and stay with them in Alabama – or rather, to let Freckles14, the username BamaBird61 knew her by, come and stay. Relief washed over Peggy in a tidal wave, so potent it almost brought her to her knees. A way out. A chance to escape the refuge, and, perhaps most importantly, a way to leave Julian behind, to break free from his suffocating grip.

She told Julian she was moving, careful to keep the destination vague. She purposely omitted any details about Alabama, about BamaBird61, about the life that awaited her. He didn't seem to like the idea, his usual unsettling smile replaced by a flicker of something darker, possessive. He insisted on visiting, on staying in touch. She lied, telling him she was moving in with an aunt, a fabrication designed to appease him, to delay the inevitable confrontation. Freedom, she realised, always came at a price.

Then, one night, as she lay in bed, her mind racing with a mix of excitement and apprehension, there was a knock on her door. The sound was sharp, insistent, and utterly unexpected. In the refuge, privacy was a sacred, unspoken rule. Everyone respected the boundaries of their small bedrooms, treating them as individual sanctuaries in a sea of collective turmoil. A knock was an anomaly, a violation of that fragile peace.

A knot of unease tightened in Peggy's stomach. She hesitated for a moment, her hand hovering over the doorknob. Who could it be? And why now? She took a deep breath, steeling herself for whatever lay on the other side. Slowly, cautiously, she turned the knob and pulled the door open.

Standing in the dimly lit hallway was Jess Judy, her face pale and drawn. Behind her, two figures loomed, their silhouettes framed by the harsh glare of the overhead light. Police officers. The sight of their uniforms sent a jolt of icy terror through Peggy's veins. Her heart hammered against her ribs, threatening to burst from her chest.

The officers stepped forward, their expressions grim, their eyes fixed on Peggy. A wave of nausea washed over her. Her carefully constructed facade of calm shattered, replaced by a raw, primal fear. It was over. They had found her.

"Ma'am, we want to talk to you about the death of Floyd Rillstone," one of the officers stated, his voice devoid of emotion. This wasn't an arrest, Peggy thought, a fragile tendril of hope unfurling within her. Just questioning. Maybe, just maybe, she could talk her way out of this. So, she went with them willingly, but inside her anxiety was unbearable. Before the questioning began, however, she was photographed, the flash momentarily blinding, each click of the camera a chilling prelude to what was to come. Then, her fingerprints were taken; each swirl and ridge meticulously recorded, as if capturing the very essence of her guilt. With a deep breath, she forced herself to meet the officer's eyes, attempting to project an air of innocence she certainly didn't feel. She complied with their request, allowing herself to be escorted to the interrogation room, clinging to the desperate belief that she could somehow control the narrative, steer the conversation away from the damning truth.

The officer's words hung in the air. "Your stepfather, Floyd, was killed in your home back in Wisconsin."

Peggy gave the faintest of nods, a minimal acknowledgment.

"Yet you're all the way out here in West Virginia?" The officer's voice was deceptively calm, but his eyes held a sharp, assessing glint that made her skin crawl.

Peggy forced herself to meet his gaze, striving for an outward appearance of composure despite the turmoil within. "I heard about the refuge," she replied, carefully choosing her words. "Didn't have anywhere else to go." She offered the simple explanation, hoping it would sound believable, uncontrived.

"Before or after the explosion?"

The question was a carefully laid trap, and Peggy knew it. She hesitated, her heart pounding in her chest, knowing that her answer could very well seal her fate. The silence stretched between them, thick with unspoken accusations, amplifying the tension in the small room.

"So, you didn't really know what happened? Is that what you're saying?" The officer pressed, his gaze unwavering.

Peggy offered a hesitant nod, a silent plea for him to accept her version of events. She watched his face intently, searching for any flicker of acceptance, any hint that he believed her.

"It just seems like a strange thing to do, to immediately flee, coincidentally on the same night, don't you think?" The officer's voice remained calm and measured, but the question hung heavy in the air, laden with suspicion.

Desperation began to gnaw at Peggy's carefully constructed resolve, threatening to unravel her composure. "I was lost," she insisted, her voice trembling slightly despite her best efforts. "Both parents were dead, and then Floyd must have left the gas on and fallen asleep. He always did that." She rushed the explanation, hoping to overwhelm his doubts with a torrent of words.

The officer's eyes narrowed, his gaze intensifying as he leaned forward slightly. "I didn't say anything about gas…" He paused, allowing the implication to sink in, the unspoken accusation hanging heavy in the air. "You agreed you didn't know what happened?"

"Saw it in the papers," she stammered.

"Papers didn't release that information either. In fact, the papers advertised a search looking for you. Did you not see that?" The officer's voice was flat, devoid of emotion, but his words were like a hammer blow, shattering her carefully constructed defences.

Peggy's silence was her confession, the unspoken admission of her guilt. The weight of her deception crashed down on her, crushing her hopes of freedom. A freedom she so desperately wanted in Alabama. Leaving her gasping for air.

"I mean, you must have seen that if you were reading about it. Strange you didn't willingly report in to us." The officer continued, his voice relentless, unforgiving.

The room seemed to shrink, the walls closing in, the air growing thin and suffocating. Panic surged through her veins, threatening to consume her entirely, to strip away her carefully constructed facade and reveal the terrified girl beneath.

"Am I under arrest? Because I'd like to go now." The words burst from her in a desperate, uncontrolled rush, fuelled by a surge of adrenaline and a desperate need to regain control of the situation. She pushed back from the table with such force that the chair shot backward, scraping loudly against the linoleum floor, the jarring sound echoing in the tense silence.

The officer rose to his feet, his movements slow and deliberate, his eyes never leaving hers. His hand moved almost casually towards his belt, but Peggy saw the telltale glint of metal – the cold, hard steel of handcuffs. Her carefully constructed world shattered into a million pieces, and instinct took over, overriding reason and logic. In a desperate, split-second decision, she grabbed the officer's mug, the ceramic surprisingly heavy and hot in her hand. Without conscious thought, she hurled the contents at his face, the scalding coffee splashing across his skin. He yelled in pain, his hands flying up to shield his eyes, momentarily blinded and disoriented.

Seizing the opportunity, Peggy swung the heavy mug with all her might, connecting with the back of his head with a sickening thud. The ceramic shattered into jagged pieces, and the officer crumpled to the floor, unconscious.

A wave of shock and horror washed over Peggy as she stared at the unmoving officer, her mind struggling to comprehend the enormity of what she had just done. She knelt beside him, her fingers trembling uncontrollably as she searched for a pulse, desperate for any sign of life. Relief flooded her as she found it, weak but steady, a fragile thread connecting him to the world. He was alive.

Driven by a desperate need to escape the consequences of her actions, she snatched the keys from his belt, her hands shaking so violently she could barely fit the key into the lock. The door swung open, revealing the dimly lit hallway of the small-town police department. The oblivious figure of the front desk officer, his head slumped forward in apparent boredom, was the only other person there. Without a backward glance, Peggy casually walked out the front door and slipped into the night.

Peggy knew she had to disappear, and fast. The escape from the police station had been a desperate gamble, and she couldn't afford to linger in West Virginia any longer. She needed Julian's help, and she didn't care how she got it. He had become a strange, unsettling fixture in her life at the refuge, but now, his obsessive tendencies could actually be useful. She swallowed any lingering hesitation and, using a payphone, miles from the police station, called the refuge, disguising her voice as Julian's sister. She fabricated a story about a family emergency, easily convincing him that she needed him to bring her belongings to a pre-arranged meeting point under the cover of night.

Julian, predictably eager to please, readily agreed. Under the cloak of darkness, he slipped away from the refuge, carrying Peggy's meagre possessions to her. She offered him a false promise to call him when she arrived at her destination, a lie that rolled off her tongue with practiced ease. As she watched him disappear back into the night, she felt a surge of satisfaction, not guilt. He was a means to an end, nothing more. She was finally free, or at least, one step closer to it.

With Julian's unwitting assistance, Peggy began her journey to Alabama, clinging to the hope that this would be her first real chance at freedom. She walked out of West Virginia, hitching a ride with a weathered farmer on his way to a cattle auction. She sat in the back of his truck, perched on bales of hay, the scent of manure and sun-baked earth filling her nostrils. The incoming summer was making its presence known, the days growing hotter, the air thick with humidity. Finally, after what seemed like an eternity, she arrived in Cedar Bluff, Alabama, a town that felt a world away from the chaos and danger she had left behind. It was a small, unassuming place, nestled amidst rolling hills and sprawling farmlands, but to Peggy, it felt like a sanctuary. For the first time in what seemed like forever, she allowed herself to feel a flicker of hope, a fragile sense of freedom.

And then she met Sally. Otherwise known to her as BamaBird61. Sally, the woman whose letters had given her hope, whose kindness had pulled her through the darkest of times. Sally, who welcomed her with a warm smile and open arms, just as she had promised in her letters. Sally's family embraced her, making her feel like she belonged, something she hadn't experienced in years. In that moment, Peggy knew she couldn't continue to use her old name, a name that was now synonymous with lies and violence. Sally had only known her as Freckles14, giving her the chance to create a whole new identity, a fresh start. Jess Judy was the first thing that came to mind, a tribute to the woman who had saved her life, the woman who had given her a place to stay, the woman who was so kind to her when she needed it most. A new name for a new life, a life she would build. She enrolled into college, her confidence growing in the small world within Cedar Bluff.

Chapter 25 Meeting *Him*

Adjusting to being Jess Judy felt surprisingly easy, like slipping into a comfortable, well-worn pair of shoes. The weight of her past, the constant fear of discovery, seemed to lessen with each passing day in Cedar Bluff. She revelled in the simplicity of her new life, the absence of the constant tension that had plagued her for so long. She and Sally became fast friends, clicking almost immediately, their bond forged in shared laughter and whispered secrets under the vast Alabama sky. Jess also got on well with Sally's boyfriend, Stu, a laid-back, good-natured guy who welcomed her into their circle without hesitation. She settled into the rhythm of small-town life with surprising ease, finding a sense of peace in the familiar routines and the genuine warmth of the community.

She was finally free, living a life unburdened by the constant threat of abusers, a life where she could make her own choices and chart her own course. The question of whether she could truly get away with what she had done still lingered in the back of her mind, a nagging doubt that refused to be silenced. But for now, she pushed those thoughts aside, focusing on the present, on the joy of simply being alive and unconfined. Maybe, just maybe, she could outrun her past, disappear into the anonymity of this small Alabama town.

She enjoyed the parties, the bonfires under the starlit sky, the lazy afternoons spent sunbathing at Weiss Lake. She enjoyed everything Alabama had to offer, from the sweet tea and barbecue to the Southern hospitality and the slow, easy pace of life. She was able to have fun, to let her hair down and laugh without reservation, something she hadn't allowed herself to do in years. But even in her newfound freedom, she remained cautious, a habit ingrained from years of living in the shadows. She found it smart to blend into the crowds, to observe rather than be observed, to be the quiet listener rather than the centre of attention. She'd be the observer more than a talker, always aware of her surroundings, always prepared to disappear if necessary. Old habits died hard, but in this new life, those habits might just be what kept her safe.

The invitation to the bonfire down at Weiss Lake had been extended days ago, but she and Sally hadn't intended to go. They'd both been feeling a little tired. But Stu had insisted, saying he was meeting some friends, and Sally, ever the social butterfly, had convinced Jess to tag along. They promised each other they wouldn't drink too much, a pact easily made but just as easily broken.

As they pulled up to the sandy beach, the party roared to life around them. Trucks lined the edge of the woods, their headlights illuminating a chaotic scene of revelry spilling out onto the shore. Music blared from oversized speakers, a mix of rock and roll that vibrated through the sand. The air was thick with the aroma of grilled meat, cheap beer, and the sweet, unmistakable scent of marijuana. Laughter and shouts echoed across the water, punctuated by the occasional burst of fireworks that lit up the night sky. A bonfire blazed in the centre of the beach, casting long, dancing shadows that flickered across the faces of the partygoers and reflected in the dark expanse of Weiss Lake.

Stu disappeared into the crowd, eager to reconnect with his friends. Sally and Jess, feeling a bit overwhelmed by the sheer scale of the event, navigated through the crowd, sidestepping beer cans and boisterous groups. They found a relatively quiet spot on a log next to the bonfire, away from the main crush, where a lone guy sat on an overturned bucket, strumming a gentle melody on his acoustic guitar. It was a small oasis of calm amidst the surrounding chaos, a welcome respite from the deafening music and the drunken revelry.

Jess nursed her drink for most of the night, a watered-down beer that she wasn't really into. She found herself drifting into her thoughts, replaying scenes from her past, the events that had led her to this moment, to this new life in Alabama. The weight of it all threatened to pull her under, but she fought it back, clinging to the present, to the warmth of the fire, to the sound of Sally's laughter. She pulled out her lighter, idly opening and shutting the lid, the familiar click providing a small measure of comfort, a way to ground herself in the here and now. The repetitive motion was almost meditative, allowing her to zone out, to momentarily escape the memories that haunted her.

Then something brought her sharply out of her reverie. She looked up, seeing Sally and Stu greeting each other, their faces lighting up with easy smiles. She observed the interaction as some of Stu's friends also joined them, forming a small, boisterous group.

A small chap with a goofy grin stepped out of the crowd. "Sally Strooker? I didn't know you were Stu's girlfriend!... Mind you I didn't really know Stu till a couple hours ago."

Sally laughed. "Got any pot?"

"Smoked it all," the guy, apparently named Pete, replied with a shrug. "Bronko's getting more."

Jess was already figuring Pete out, harmless but simple, the kind of guy who was always looking for a good time.

Sally turned her attention to the other newcomer. "Groovy, who's your friend?"

Pete gestured towards the man standing beside him. "This is Jonny, our estranged brother. Back in town after five years," he said as if the president himself was standing there.

Jess watched the interaction, setting eyes on Jonny for the first time, and immediately sensing his good heart and kind nature, despite the blanket of muscles and undeniable good looks. Something about him captured her attention. Almost as if she wanted to know everything about him all at once. She watched as they walked over to where Jess and Sally were perched on the log. Jonny hadn't noticed her yet. He swayed slightly, suggesting he had already had a fun night drinking. He slouched down in the sand, resting his back against the log right next to Jess, his shoulder almost touching her legs. She couldn't help but smile, a small, involuntary curve of her lips, hoping an opportunity would open to talk to him. He placed a cigarette in his mouth and searched his pockets, realising he didn't have a light.

She flicked the lid off hers, the familiar click echoing in the relative quiet, and held it down to him, offering the flame. "Need a light?"

She noticed him stare up at her, his eyes locking with hers for a brief, intense moment that seemed to stretch on forever. Before he could even murmur a "Thanks," he paused, a flicker of something unreadable in his gaze – a spark of recognition, perhaps, or a shared sense of destiny. Maybe he felt the pull too, this invisible thread that seemed to connect them across the crowded beach. But she knew that look, that subtle widening of the eyes, that almost imperceptible intake of breath. He was interested, intrigued, drawn in by something he couldn't quite explain. This was her opening, her chance to step out of the darkness and into the light, to finally break free from the shadows of her past.

"Keep it," she said, offering him the lighter. A fragile offering of trust and hope. The last time she had used a lighter, its flame had been a harbinger of death, a tool of vengeance against the man who had tormented her. Offering it felt significant. Now, she was giving this lighter to Jonny, a man who radiated kindness and strength, a man who stirred something deep within her that she was experiencing for the first time. It was a small act, a seemingly insignificant gesture, but it felt like a symbolic severing of ties, a drawing of a line in the sand between her past and her future. Something was about to change, she could feel it in her bones, a seismic tremor deep within her soul, a sense of impending transformation that was both terrifying and exhilarating. And it was all because of this man, this Jonny, this stranger who held the potential to rewrite her story.

Jess found herself genuinely enjoying the rest of the party, thanks to Jonny. He seemed genuinely interested in her, in her thoughts and feelings, in the small details that made her who she was. She cautiously allowed him into her bubble, the invisible shield she had erected to protect herself from the world, her bubble away from the crowd, almost as if it was just them on a beach full of people. She liked that, the feeling of being seen, of being truly present with someone who seemed to care. He seemed to be the only one truly interested in getting to know her, not just the surface-level Jess Judy, but the woman beneath the carefully constructed facade. But she had to play it cool, she reminded herself, she couldn't reveal too much about herself, just enough to pique his interest, to keep him wanting more. She was surprised at the things they had in common, the shared tastes and perspectives that seemed to align with an almost uncanny precision. They both shared a deep appreciation for Clyde May's, a smooth, subtly sweet Alabama whiskey that felt like so much more than a mere coincidence, a secret handshake between kindred spirits. When Bronko finally arrived, he lived up to his reputation as the life and soul of the party, effortlessly drawing everyone's attention to him in a good way, his infectious energy and booming laughter creating a distraction that further helped Jonny and Jess carve out their own little space amidst the chaos. Their easy conversation flowed effortlessly, punctuated by shared smiles and comfortable silences. But the idyllic atmosphere was shattered when the Night Hounds crashed the party, their menacing presence instantly casting a darkness over the festivities. Jess admired Jonny's bravery, his unwavering willingness to stand up to them, to defend the people he cared about, a display of courage that only made him even more attractive in her eyes. She was undeniably sad when the party was effectively over after that, the carefree atmosphere replaced by a palpable tension. She could have stayed all night talking to him, exploring the connection that had sparked between them, but fate, it seemed, had other plans. As they drifted away from each other in the dispersing crowd, she took one last, lingering look at him, etching his image into her memory, hoping their paths would cross again soon, hoping that this chance encounter would blossom into something more.

Over the next few days, Jess found herself subtly orchestrating events to ensure her and Jonny's paths would cross again. It wasn't a conscious manipulation, or so she told herself, but rather a gentle nudge in the right direction, a way to see if the connection they had felt at the party was real, or just a fleeting moment fuelled by alcohol and bonfire smoke. She remembered that Jonny had mentioned helping his Uncle Larry cut trees. Knowing it was a perfect spot to go and hang out in the sun, she suggested it to their group of friends, knowing full well that they'd be easily persuaded. It wasn't just the sun she was interested in, of course; it was the chance to see Jonny again, to casually bump into him and gauge his reaction. When she bought the chainsaw with her poker winnings, she hoped it would make him happy. It was a small act of kindness, a way to show him that she was paying attention, that she cared about him. Yet most nights, after Sally had fallen asleep, Jess would lie in the darkness, tears silently streaming down her face as she thought about the past and the gaping hole her mum had left behind. She prayed Sally wouldn't wake up and hear her, wouldn't see the cracks in the carefully constructed facade of strength she tried so hard to maintain.

And then the invitation to the party at Tall Oaks came, a secluded spot deep in the forest overlooking the lake. She couldn't resist the opportunity to see Jonny again. She hoped, perhaps foolishly, that this night would bring them closer, that she could finally let her guard down, just a little, and allow herself to be happy, even if only for a few hours.

The party at Tall Oaks was surprisingly fun. The music was good, the company was even better, and for a few hours, Jess managed to forget about her worries and simply enjoy herself. But as the night wore on, she couldn't shake the feeling that something was off with Jonny. He seemed distant, preoccupied, not quite himself. Was it her? She worried, a familiar wave of insecurity washing over her. Was he losing interest? Had she misread the signals?

Their friends, fuelled by alcohol and high spirits, knew that "Sweet Home Alabama" was Jess and Jonny's favourite song, so they decided it would be hilarious to push them up on stage for karaoke. It wasn't the stage fright that scared Jess; she'd faced far more terrifying situations in her life. It was the thought of all those eyes on her, the potential for someone to recognise her, to connect her to her past.

Standing on the stage, microphone in hand, Jess felt a wave of nausea wash over her. She hesitated, her throat constricting with nerves. But then she glanced at Jonny, who gave her a reassuring smile, and she took a deep breath. It took her a while to warm up, her voice shaky and uncertain at first. But as she sang, she started to relax, the familiar lyrics and the energy of the crowd easing her anxiety. By the time they reached the chorus, she was belting it out with gusto, actually enjoying herself, the crowd cheering them on, their voices blending together in a joyful, chaotic chorus.

After, they navigated their way through the throng of revellers to the quieter outer edge of the party, finding a secluded spot by the dark, looming forest. Settling onto the cool earth, they passed the bottle back and forth, each taking a slow, contemplative sip. Jess felt a wave of relief wash over her as they escaped the crowded dance floor. The music was still thumping in her chest, a frantic rhythm that echoed the anxiety she constantly tried to suppress.

"That was pretty wild," Jonny said, breaking the comfortable silence.

"Never done anything like that before," Jess admitted, a nervous laugh escaping her lips. She hated being the target of so many eyes. It felt too much like being exposed, vulnerable. However, this she loved. "I hate all eyes on me."

"I kinda noticed that about you," Jonny said, a thoughtful expression on his face.

"Oh yeah?" Jess challenged, raising an eyebrow, trying to appear nonchalant, even though he was right. She liked that he noted the small details about her.

"Yeah, when the group gets big, you go quieter. I figured it's because of the observing. Studying everyone else."

Jess faintly nodded, a flicker of surprise in her eyes. He did see her. He saw more than she usually allowed anyone to see. It was unsettling, but also… strangely comforting. "Well, don't you just have me all figured out."

"Haha, I'm trying… But you're a hard girl to read. It's like you got this whole heart-on-your-sleeve thing… but I don't know, there also seems like a side you don't want anyone to see, what you're thinking, what you're feeling… Like a coin. Two sides"

Jess took another sip of the whiskey, the burn a welcome distraction from the intensity of his gaze. She kept her eyes fixed on the dark woods, the shadows mirroring the secrets she desperately tried to keep hidden. "I'm impressed." And terrified, she thought, but didn't say.

"You, on the other hand…" Jess paused, her eyes meeting his. "I can read you like a book. You're a good man, Jonny. Loyal. I'm glad I met you."

Unintentionally, their eyes locked, an undeniable chemistry sparking between them that neither could ignore. Jess found herself unable to look away, drawn to the warmth and sincerity in his gaze, a gaze that seemed to see past her defences, straight into her soul. That soaring guitar solo from "More Than a Feeling" by Boston suddenly filled the air, seeming to amplify the emotions swirling between them, turning up the volume on the unspoken desires that had been simmering beneath the surface for weeks. Seizing the moment, Jonny leaned in slowly, his gaze never leaving hers, and Jess felt a thrill of both anticipation and fear course through her veins. This was it. This was the moment she'd been both longing for and dreading. She mirrored his movement, her eyes reflecting a mixture of anticipation and desire, a silent invitation to cross the line, to break down the walls she'd so carefully constructed. Their lips met, a soft, tentative pressure that sent an electric current through Jess's entire being, a sensation so intense it almost made her forget her past, her secrets, her fears. For a fleeting moment, she was just Jess, a girl kissing a boy she liked, nothing more, nothing less. The first firework exploded in the sky behind them, painting the forest in a fleeting burst of vibrant colour, a dazzling display that mirrored the explosion of feeling within her, the shattering of her carefully controlled world.

Breaking the kiss, they gazed at each other, the intimacy palpable, and Jess felt exposed, as if Jonny could see straight through her, past all her carefully constructed defences.

"You've no idea how long I've been wanting to do that," Jonny confessed, his voice husky, and Jess felt her heart flutter in response, a giddy, almost childlike joy bubbling up inside her.

Jess's lips curved into a playful smile, a genuine smile that reached her eyes, chasing away the shadows that usually lurked there. "Then don't stop."

They kissed again, this time with more passion, their hands finding each other as the fireworks illuminated the night sky. Lost in her own private world, Jess was oblivious to the spectacle behind her, her entire focus consumed by the feeling of Jonny's lips on hers, the taste of whiskey and something else, something uniquely him, the promise of something new, something real… something utterly irresistible.

The weeks that followed were a blur of sunshine, laughter, and stolen moments. Jess and Jonny were inseparable, two halves of a whole. Every moment spent with him felt precious, fleeting, and Jess found herself wishing time would stand still, that she could hold onto these moments forever. The small gathering of friends they shared became a kind of makeshift family for her, a warm, supportive circle that embraced her without question. It was a feeling she'd longed for her entire life, a sense of belonging that eased the ache of her past, if only for a little while. Some days, when she was lost in Jonny's arms, or laughing at their friends' ridiculous jokes, she forgot, for a fleeting second, about all the things she'd left behind, about the secrets she kept buried deep inside.

She had freedom, something she had craved her whole life, a chance to be herself, to make her own choices, to live without fear. Even with the increasing presence of the Night Hounds looming over Cedar Bluff, she felt a sense of liberation she'd never known before. She knew Jonny wanted to stand up to them, to fight back against their bullying tactics and their growing control over the town. She knew men like the Night Hounds; she'd seen their kind before. They didn't intimidate her, not really. But for once, it wasn't her fight. This was

Jonny's town, his home, and she would stand by her man, supporting him in whatever way she could.

The night of the motorcycle crash was a nightmare she never wanted to relive. They'd been trying to evade Bullfrog, his pursuit relentless and terrifying. One moment, they were speeding through the darkness, the wind screaming in her ears, the adrenaline pumping through her veins. The next, everything was a violent, chaotic mess of screeching tyres and blinding pain. She woke not long after passing out, her head throbbing, her body wracked with pain, but her first thought was Jonny. Waving down a nearby driver to call an ambulance, she stayed by his side until he woke days later, her hand clasped tightly in his, whispering words of encouragement and love. Even as things in Cedar Bluff seemed to change for everyone else, as the tension with the Night Hounds escalated, Jess clung to her newfound freedom, to the love she'd found with Jonny. It was her anchor, her safe harbour in a storm.

The only time she truly struggled to contain herself, to maintain her carefully constructed facade, was when she and Jonny found Big Rick's body by the sand at the edge of the lake. The sight of his lifeless form, half-submerged in the shallow water, triggered a flood of memories, a visceral flashback to the night she found her mother dead in Floyd's arms. The grief, the horror, the overwhelming sense of loss threatened to consume her, to drag her back into the darkness she'd fought so hard to escape. She nearly broke down, nearly revealed the truth about her past, about the trauma that still haunted her dreams. But by the skin of her teeth, she managed to hold it together, playing it down as a simple lie, saying she had never seen a dead body before. A lie he bought easily.

Jess knew that Jonny would be returning to Kentucky in a few weeks, a fact she desperately tried to bury at the back of her mind, like anything uncomfortable or threatening to her fragile sense of peace. She had his parents' number tucked away in her wallet, the life he would inevitably return to. She didn't want to lose Jonny, not now, not ever. The promise that one day, after saving enough money, he would return to Cedar Bluff and they would have a house, a life together, was the only thing that kept her going, the only light in the encroaching darkness.

The war with the Night Hounds was escalating, particularly the personal feud between Earl and Jonny. Jess stood by him, her loyalty unwavering. She wasn't afraid to cross a line if she needed to, to get her hands dirty. She had done far worse before, and she wouldn't hesitate to protect Jonny, even if it meant risking everything. She helped him gather evidence against the Night Hounds, meticulously taking pictures of their illegal activities, keeping the Polaroids close, hidden away like a secret weapon. They were her insurance, her leverage, the proof that would incriminate all of the Night Hounds' high-ranking members, men like Earl and Bullfrog. If she needed them, she would use them, consequences be damned.

The night Jonny fought Earl was brutal, sickening. Each punch Jonny took was like a blow to her own gut, each drop of blood on his face an unbearable violation. She wanted to scream, to intervene, to protect him from the savagery of the fight, but she knew she couldn't. This was Jonny's battle, his way of defending his town, his honour. And he won. It was a hard-fought victory, a victory the whole town helped with, including the police, a collective act of defiance against the Night Hounds' reign of terror. But it was also a moment she needed to stay in the shadows for. She couldn't afford to have her part in this recognised by the townsfolk. The less attention she drew to herself, the better. This would only put her in the spotlight more, and the spotlight was the last place she wanted to be.

Jonny's last day in Cedar Bluff was imminent. Things were changing, shifting like the sands of the lake. Sally and her family were soon going to visit relatives, leaving Jess with an empty room and a hollow feeling in her chest. She had already booked a room in a motel, a temporary escape from the silence and the memories that would soon fill Sally's house. She worked all day in the diner the day before Jonny was leaving, the clatter of dishes and the endless orders a numbing distraction from the ache in her heart. She felt guilty, exhausted, but she couldn't stay awake that night, no matter how hard she tried. She knew she needed to make his last day extra special, to create a memory that would sustain them both through the long months apart. She had a day planned, a perfect day filled with sunshine and laughter and stolen kisses, but the day she had planned in her head, was far from what the universe had in store for her.

Chapter 26 Why She Didn't Come

Jess descended the stairs, the lingering droplets of her morning shower clinging to her hair. She was determined to make today special, pushing the ache of Jonny's impending departure to the back of her mind. The sounds of hurried footsteps and excited chatter drifted from the kitchen. Sally and her family were bustling about, preparing for a trip to visit relatives. "Goodbye!" she called to them, a forced cheerfulness in her voice as she stepped out into the thick, humid morning air.

The street was eerily quiet, save for a white Chevrolet van parked across the way. A short walk brought her to the town's general store. Inside, she gathered a few snacks, a mere pretext for her true purpose: a full bottle of Clyde May's, carefully concealed in her bag. She knew she was underage, but the thought of surprising Jonny with his favourite whiskey motivated her rebellious streak.

After paying for her meagre purchases, Jess emerged from the store. The same white Chevrolet van was parked nearby. This time, the sight sent a jolt of genuine fear through her. There was something ominous about it, a silent threat hanging in the air. Convinced she was being followed, she abruptly changed direction, quickening her pace. The van's tyres whined as it crept along the road, mirroring her movements. She risked a glance over her shoulder. The sun glinted off the windshield, obscuring the driver's face, but there was no mistaking it, they were following her.

Panic surged through her veins. She broke into a run, her heart pounding against her ribs like a trapped bird. The van roared to life, accelerating with terrifying speed. It swerved in front of her, tyres screeching as it blocked her path. The driver's side door swung open, and a man spilled out. He was older, his greying black hair clashed sharply with the black sleeveless shirt stretched taut over a prominent beer belly. A thick horseshoe moustache framed his mouth, and his eyes, magnified by thick, messy black eyebrows, pierced her with an unsettling intensity.

"There you are, you bitch," he snarled, his voice a low, guttural growl, as a rough hand clamped over Jess's mouth. Before she could scream, before she could even register the danger, she was lifted off her feet and thrown into the back of the van. He looked around to see if anyone had seen him do it before climbing back inside.

The van sped away abruptly. Each bump in the road sent a jolt of pain through Jess's body. The aggressive driving mirrored the rage she could feel radiating from her captor. Her thoughts raced, a desperate plea echoing in her mind. Jonny. He was so close, yet utterly oblivious to the nightmare unfolding.

The drive was short, suffocatingly so. The van lurched to a halt, the sudden silence amplifying Jess's fear. Was it the Night Hounds? Was Jonny hurt? She heard the man climb out, his heavy footsteps crunching on the ground. The door slid open, revealing the man silhouetted against the fading light, a switchblade glinting menacingly in his hand.

"Get out," he commanded, his voice a low, guttural growl.

She had no choice. Every muscle rebelled, but she forced herself to comply. They were in the forest, the air thick with the scent of pine and damp earth. Cedar Bluff couldn't be far. A dilapidated cabin stood before them, its darkened windows like vacant eyes. The man gestured with the knife, urging her forward. He stayed close, the blade a constant threat, his eyes scanning the surroundings for any sign of interruption. Inside, the cabin was a single, bare room. A chair sat in the centre, with a rope on the floor next to it. Jess's heart hammered against her ribs as the realisation dawned. She knew what was coming.

"Sit down," the man ordered.

Her legs trembled, but she obeyed. The rough rope bit into her skin as the man tied her to the chair, binding her arms tightly against her sides and the back of the chair. She was scared; all she wanted was Jonny.

The man stepped back, his eyes narrowed, assessing her. He circled her slowly, like a predator sizing up its prey. "Do you know who I am?" he asked, his voice gruff.

Jess shook her head, her throat constricted with fear. She tried to swallow, but her mouth was dry. "You don't look like you're capable of trouble. Scrawny little thing." He leaned in close, his breath hot and stale on her face.

"Who are you?" she managed to croak.

"You can call me Bud." A cruel smile twisted his lips. He pulled back, his eyes glinting in the dim light. "What do you go by nowadays?"

His words sent a chill down her spine. This wasn't the mindless violence of the Night Hounds. This was personal. This was someone who knew...

"Jess," she replied, her voice trembling. A desperate attempt at a way out of this.

Bud laughed, a harsh, grating sound that echoed in the small cabin. He knew she was lying.

"Pamela Jessica Carter," he spat, the words slow, like a taunt. Her breath hitched. The colour drained from her face. "You knew an old friend of mine... Floyd Rillstone."

Guilt, raw and undeniable, flickered across her face. "And you killed him, didn't you?" Bud's eyes burned with hatred. Jess swallowed hard, testing the ropes, searching for any give.

"DIDN'T YOU!" he roared, the knife flashing inches from her face.

"What do you want!?" she cried, her voice cracking.

"I want to hear you say it. I want you to acknowledge what you did."

"Why didn't you just call the police if you're so sure you got the right girl?" she shot back, desperate to buy time.

"I don't care for no police. I'm dealing with you myself. For Floyd, I'm doing what he'd be wanting me to do to you."

"How did you find me?" she asked bravely.

"I did a better job than the police," he sneered. "Followed your stupid little pen-pal trail. Luckily, I burned the letters so the police wouldn't have a lead, and I get you all to myself."

Bud walked back outside to his truck. Jess looked around, desperate to find anything she could use to escape, she tested the chair's strength, finding it firm, but not completely solid. A sliver of hope flickered within her. He returned; the sloshing of a jerry can preceding him. Gasoline. She knew what he was planning, and the thought of dying as Floyd had, consumed by flames, sent a fresh wave of terror and irony through her. Bud began pouring the petrol in a circle around her, the fumes stinging her nostrils. "Please, please don't do this," she pleaded.

Bud seemed unmoved, his face a mask of grim determination. Maybe… maybe if I play his game, she thought, confess, give him what he wants, he might see reason. Desperation clawed at her.

"Okay! I did it… I killed him… I turned on the gas and burned that house to the ground with him inside!" The words burst from her, raw and ragged.

Bud looked up, a flicker of surprise in his eyes, as if hearing the confirmation was a shock even to him. "Good," he said, his voice devoid of emotion. "It'll make doing this much easier."

He flicked his lighter, the flame dancing high, a mocking prelude to the inferno he intended to unleash. As his wrist snapped forward, sending the lighter arcing towards the petrol-soaked floor, Jess surged with adrenaline, used her legs to drive herself upward, slamming the chair against the wall with every ounce of strength she possessed. The lighter struck the ground, and the world erupted. A ring of fire blazed to life, consuming the room as the chair shattered against the wall, sending a jolt of agony through Jess's back. She crashed to the floor, the ropes finally broken, but the pain was a blinding wave. Bud was already gone, a fleeting shadow disappearing out the door, leaving her to face the flames.

The heat was a physical assault, the flames licking at her face, stealing her breath. She scrambled desperately, hugging the wall, the fire a ravenous beast devouring everything in its path. She sidestepped frantically towards the flimsy wooden door, her fingers fumbling for a handle that wasn't there. Locked. A fresh wave of panic, hotter and more consuming than the fire itself, threatened to drown her. She began to kick at the door with savage desperation, each blow fuelled by pure survival instinct, ignoring the white-hot pain searing through her leg. Finally, with a groan of protesting wood, the door splintered, cracking open just enough for her to squeeze through, and she stumbled out into the forest, coughing, choking, gasping for the blessed, smoke-tinged air, soot clinging to her skin like a shroud.

Unaware, she was taken by surprise as he lunged from the side, his strong hands gripping her neck. "You just don't die!" Bud snarled.

She fell back to the floor, the impact jarring her senses. Instinct took over, a primal surge of adrenaline overriding thought. Without conscious decision, her knee shot upward, connecting with brutal force against Bud's groin. He crumpled, a guttural cry escaping his lips as he fell to the side in the dirt, his body convulsing. His switchblade skittered from his pocket, landing within Jess's reach.

Adrenaline coursing through her veins, Jess rolled over, her fingers closing around the cold steel of the blade. Bud, his face contorted in agony and rage, turned back to grab her once more. This time, she was ready. With a desperate cry, she plunged the small blade into his leg, just above his knee, feeling the resistance of muscle and sinew before yanking it free. A crimson spray erupted, painting her hands in his blood as he fell onto his back, his screams echoing through the trees.

There was no room for hesitation, no time for remorse. Driven by a single, overriding instinct – survival – she scrambled to her feet, turned her back on the writhing figure, and ran. She plunged into the dense undergrowth, the trees swallowing her whole, leaving Bud's screams and the burning cabin behind.

The forest floor was a blur beneath her feet, a treacherous tapestry of roots and fallen branches. Jess plunged deeper into the woods, her lungs burning, her muscles burning with exhaustion. Every rustle of leaves, every snap of a twig, sent a jolt of fear through her. She wanted to run to Jonny, to bury herself in his arms and forget this nightmare, but she couldn't. Not with Bud out there, driven by vengeance and a twisted sense of justice. She couldn't risk her past, the secrets she had so carefully buried, coming to light. Not for Jonny, not for anyone. This was her problem, her mess, and she had to fix it, alone.

Behind her, she could hear him. The unmistakable sound of crashing undergrowth, punctuated by his ragged, pain-filled breaths. "Where are you?!" he roared, his voice a guttural echo that seemed to vibrate through the trees. "You can't hide, bitch! I'll never stop looking for you!" His words were a chilling promise, a dark cloud hanging over her desperate flight.

Jess pressed on, moving with a newfound stealth, a skill honed by years of running from her past. She darted behind the thick trunks of ancient pines, their rough bark scraping against her skin, a temporary shield against his relentless pursuit. She moved like a ghost, her footsteps light, her senses on high alert, every nerve ending screaming. Then, she heard it – the distinct crack of a branch, far too close for comfort. He was gaining on her. She risked a glance over her shoulder, and her blood ran cold. Through the trees, she caught a glimpse of him, his face contorted with rage, his eyes burning with a feverish intensity, his limping gait not slowing his pursuit. He was closer than she thought, close enough to reach out and grab her.

Panic threatened to overwhelm her, but she fought it down, forcing herself to think, to strategize. Ahead, she spotted a massive oak, its trunk wider than any she had seen before. It was a gamble, but it was her best chance. She sprinted towards the tree. Reaching the oak, she pressed herself against the far side of the trunk, flattening her body against the rough bark, holding her breath. She could hear Bud's heavy footsteps approaching, the sound growing louder with each passing second. He walked right past the tree, his laboured breathing filling the air, his eyes scanning the forest floor, missing her by mere inches. Jess remained frozen, every muscle tense, until the sound of his footsteps faded into the distance. Only then, when she was sure he was gone, did she allow herself to exhale, a shaky breath of relief that tasted like freedom. For now. She knew he wouldn't give up, but she had bought herself some time, a precious sliver of hope in the face of overwhelming despair.

A plan began to solidify in Jess's mind, a desperate gamble born of necessity. The Night Hounds. The very name sent a shiver of revulsion inside her, but they were her only option. Since Jonny had taken down their leader, they had retreated back to Antioch, licking their wounds and regrouping. She knew they wouldn't exactly roll out the welcome wagon for her, considering her role in their leader's downfall. But she had something they needed, something that could buy her safe passage and, more importantly, their help: blackmail.

The Polaroids. The incriminating evidence she had risked everything to obtain. They were a dangerous bargaining chip, a double-edged sword that could just as easily cut her as protect her. But she was desperate, and desperation bred a certain kind of courage. The risk was immense, but the potential reward – a solution to her Bud problem – was worth it.

Driven by a mix of fear and grim determination, she altered her course, her steps now firm and resolute. She was heading back to the lake house in Antioch, the Night Hounds' lair. She had been there before, with Jonny. Now, she was running, alone, towards the very heart of danger, towards the people she had wronged, hoping to strike a deal with the devil himself.

As Jess approached the lake house, the air grew thick with tension. The place was swarmed with Night Hounds, their menacing figures lurking in the shadows, their eyes glinting with suspicion. She needed to make a statement, to show them she wasn't afraid. With a surge of adrenaline, she made the brave decision to walk straight in, to face them head-on, purposefully getting noticed. Taking a deep breath, she steeled her resolve and started down the path, her footsteps echoing in the sudden silence, a deliberate challenge.

One of the Night Hounds, a hulking figure with a shaved head and a spiderweb tattoo on his neck, spotted her. His eyes narrowed, and he nodded curtly towards the house, signalling someone inside. A moment later, a figure emerged from the doorway – Bullfrog. His massive frame filled the entrance, his face a mask of disbelief. He was clearly shocked to see her, especially in her current state: soot smeared across her face, blood staining her hands, her clothes torn and dishevelled.

Jess met his gaze, her expression unreadable. She knew there was no turning back now. She had crossed the Rubicon, and her fate rested on the next few moments. Whatever happened next, she was ready. Or, at least, she hoped she was.

Bullfrog's eyes narrowed, his voice a gravelly tone. "Look who it is. What in the hell happened to you?"

Jess met his gaze, unflinching. "I need you to do something for me."

Bullfrog scoffed, his massive arms crossed over his chest. "You've got some big lady-balls, strolling in here like that. Do you have any idea what we all want to do to you? For Earl!"

"Yeah, I bet you do," Jess retorted, her voice laced with steel. "I'm not here to negotiate. You're doing this for me. I still have those pictures, Bullfrog. Do this, and you'll have your freedom. Or go ahead and kill me. I'll be dead, sure, but you'll be behind bars."

Bullfrog clenched his jaw, his anger building. How dare she? He could tell death didn’t scare her. "Don't think I'm bluffing, either," Jess added, her eyes glinting with defiance.

"Oh, I believe you," Bullfrog snarled. "That's why I want to rip your goddamn head off and feed you to the fish in Weiss Lake."

"One thing, Bullfrog… then it's over," Jess said, holding her ground.

"We already did what your boyfriend asked. We haven't been back into Cedar Bluff, and now you want more from us," Bullfrog said angrily.

"You made that deal with Jonny" Jess said. "Now you're dealing with me."

Bullfrog hesitated, his desire for freedom warring with his rage. "How do I know I can trust you?" he asked, the words grudgingly given. "How do I know that you won't keep hold of those Polaroids until you want something else from us?"

"Because I'm a woman of my word," Jess replied, her voice unwavering.

Bullfrog walked close to her, his massive frame looming over her. He looked down at the blood and soot staining her clothes. "What the hell did you do?" he muttered. "Shit, I don't even want to know. You're more than you look, figured that during our poker match."

"Do we have a deal?" Jess pressed, her eyes locked on his.

The other Night Hounds watched Bullfrog and Jess talk, their faces etched with curiosity and suspicion. They were unable to hear what they were saying, but they saw Bullfrog nod slowly before turning and walking back towards them, Jess walking away in the opposite direction.

Bullfrog addressed his men, his voice low and dangerous. "Alright boys, let's play her game. I don't trust her one bit. Get ready, we've got work to do… And find me Bronko. Me and him need a chat." Jess was, by all accounts, a small woman. Standing next to the hulking figures of the Night Hounds, she seemed almost fragile, easily crushed. They could overpower her in an instant, silence her threats with brutal efficiency. But there was something in her eyes, a spark of defiance, a hint of hidden strength, that gave Bullfrog pause. He knew she was dangerous, capable of far more than her petite frame suggested. He had seen it in her cool demeanour during their poker game; in the way she held her own against hardened criminals. He knew underestimating her would be a fatal mistake, and that was why, despite his burning rage, he was treading carefully.

As evening rolled in across Cedar Bluff, Jess felt a desperate longing to see Jonny, knowing she was going to miss his last day, but she suppressed that to focus on the task at hand. This had to be the priority, the only way to ensure their future. Walking back onto the main street of Cedar Bluff, she spotted it: the white Chevrolet van. It was exactly what she needed. As if summoned by her thoughts, the van roared towards her, its tyres churning. Jess didn't hesitate. She darted down an alleyway between two buildings, emerging moments later onto the back of a waiting motorbike. The driver revved the engine, and they sped away, leaving Cedar Bluff behind, heading towards Antioch. The van was hot on their tail, a relentless predator in pursuit. The motorbike finally stopped on a secluded road, one they knew no one would drive down, a place where secrets could be buried. As the engine died, Jess slid off the back, her eyes fixed on the approaching van. The doors swung open, and Bud emerged, his face a mask of fury, his limp more pronounced than ever.

Bud stomped toward her, fury tightening every line of his face. “There you are, bitch. You think this asshole is gonna stop me?”

Jess held her ground. Before she could reply, a low, growing rumble drifted up the empty road. The evening light—blue-grey and thinning—shivered as the sound swelled. Bud’s expression flickered.

Around the curve, headlights appeared one by one, the last of the daylight glinting off metal. A line of Night Hounds rolled into view, engines snarling as they fanned out across the secluded road. Another pair arrived from behind, hemming Bud in. The bikes slowed to a circle around him, tyres crunching over the gravelly edge of the tarmac. Bullfrog and several riders swung off their bikes and stepped forward. Bud swallowed. The last of his confidence drained from his face.

Jess tilted her head. "I thought I'd introduce you to some friends of mine, Bud… What's the matter? Don't feel like saying hello?"

"Karma's gonna catch you one day, you vile whore!" he spat, voice cracking. "You can't run forever!"

Jess's tone was firm and confident. "Watch me."

Bullfrog didn't glance her way. "Alright, boys… you know what to do."

The Night Hounds moved in. Jess gave Bullfrog a quick nod. "You know the deal. Don't kill him."

Bullfrog leaned in close enough for Jess to smell the oil and leather on him. "Get rid of those pictures. And make damn sure I never see you again."

Jess turned and walked away, heading down the quiet, half-lit road. Behind her, the evening air filled with the thud of boots and fists as the Hounds beat Bud to the ground. His shouting echoed off the trees lining the roadside.

Bullfrog crouched beside him. "Alright, old man. Here's the deal. You stay the hell away from her. You hear me?"

Bud coughed, curling in on himself. "Okay! Okay! I'll leave her alone! I'll leave her alone!"

Bullfrog straightened. “Good. Then let’s make sure that message sinks in.”

The Night Hounds fell on Bud with a savage hunger, their boots and fists hammering into him in a relentless storm that shook the quiet road. Blow after blow crashed into bone and muscle, splitting skin, breaking ribs, turning his breath into wet, choking gurgles. Gravel scraped layers from his face as they kicked him sideways, only to drag him back into the centre of their circle and continue the punishment with renewed fury. One rider stomped down on his wrist until it cracked; another drove a boot into his ribs so hard it lifted him off the ground for a moment before he collapsed in a heap of blood and spit. His cries turned thin, then desperate, then barely human as the Hounds kept pounding him without a flicker of mercy. And through it all, Jess walked away down the dimming road—steady, silent, unhurried—never once turning back to witness the carnage left behind her.

Jess hurried back toward Cedar Bluff, her lungs burning, her legs shaking from the run and from everything that had happened. By the time she reached the edge of town, night had fully settled—soft porch lights glowing, insects buzzing in the warm air, the familiar street looking impossibly calm compared to the storm tearing through her chest. She slowed, keeping to the shadows, the soot clinging to her clothes and the drying blood caked across her hands making her feel like she was drifting back into a life she no longer belonged to.

She stopped behind the thick trunk of an oak tree up the street, hidden in the gloom. From there she watched Jonny standing on Aunt Glenda and Uncle Larry’s porch, saying his goodbyes. Glenda hugged him tight, Larry clapped him on the shoulder, and Jonny offered that warm, easy smile—one that had lit up her entire summer. Her breath hitched. He turned and walked down to the sidewalk where his friends were waiting, laughing and nudging him, unaware of the girl trembling only yards away.

Jess pressed a shaking hand to her mouth to hold in the sob threatening to escape, her fingers leaving faint, rusty smudges on her skin. She couldn't go to him like this—soot-stained, blood-handed, shaking with adrenaline and fear. She couldn't step into that light and let him see the truth of what she'd done, couldn't face the questions or the look in his eyes. If she went to him now, everything would unravel. She knew it. But that knowledge didn't soften the ache tearing through her chest.

Before Jonny swung his leg over the bike, he paused and scanned the street. From her hidden spot up the road, she could read the expression on his face. His eyes flicked to every shadow, every corner, searching. The faint downturn of his mouth, the tension in his jaw—he was looking for her. He was sad he hadn't seen her and had no answer as to why she didn't show. He would never know she had been right there, hidden in the dark.

Tears streamed down her face as Jonny finally mounted the bike. His friends shouting their goodbyes and waving him off. Jess remained behind the tree, silent, shaking, unseen. The engine growled to life, echoing down the street. Jonny glanced around one last time—one final, searching look—before riding off into the night. She stayed in the shadows, watching the man she loved disappear, her heart shattering as the last traces of him vanished into the darkness.

Bronko, Dave, and Pete walked away from where Jonny had disappeared, the hum of his bike fading into the night. The three men drifted apart, each taking a different path down the quiet streets, the warmth of their farewell lingering in the cool evening air. Bronko made his way toward his trailer, the familiar outline of the small building growing clearer with each step.

When he reached it, something immediately set his nerves on edge—the door was wide open. A cold spike of unease ran down his spine. Bronko slowed, hand hovering near the handle, eyes scanning the interior. The trailer, usually quiet and empty at this hour, was now lit by a harsh overhead light that cast long, uneasy shapes across the floor and furniture.

He stepped cautiously inside, every instinct on high alert. Sitting at the small wooden table, calm and deliberate, was Bullfrog. Bronko froze for a moment, a chill creeping up his neck. The sight of him here—unexpected, alone—sent a knot of worry tightening in Bronko's chest. His gaze flicked around the trailer, searching for a sign of danger, a hidden trap, anything that might explain why Bullfrog was here.

"You ain't supposed to be in Cedar Bluff anymore," Bronko said, keeping his voice steady even as his pulse kicked.

Bullfrog leaned back in the chair like he owned the place. "Is that how you greet your old friends, Bronko?"

"We ain't friends neither." Bronko reached back and quietly closed the door.

"Sit down," Bullfrog said. "We've got business to discuss."

"Man, I ain't doing business with you." Bronko dismissed

Bullfrog's tone snapped like a trap. "I said sit down."

That look—sharp, feral, familiar—flashed in Bullfrog's eyes, and Bronko felt the fear crawl up his spine. He lowered himself into the chair, hands tight on his knees.

Bullfrog leaned forward. "I ought to kick your ass all around this room for what you and your little crew did to us. And let's not forget—you're not exactly innocent yourself, are you, Bronko?"

Bronko stiffened. He hated how quickly the memory rose—dark, ugly, unstoppable. The thing he tried to drown in drink and fists. The thing he could never undo.

Bullfrog didn't wait. "You killed a man."

Bronko's jaw clenched. "I did it because you were gonna hurt my friends!"

Bullfrog smirked, slow and venomous. "Well, now you're gonna do it again."

He slid a gun onto the table. It clicked against the wood like a coffin lid. Bronko's veins iced over.

"No way," he breathed.

"If you don't," Bullfrog said, tapping the gun with one finger, "I'll make sure you go down with Earl. I'll tell everyone—your boys, this town—that you killed Big Rick. You do this one last job, and it all disappears. You'll never see me again."

Bronko stared at the gun. At his own shaking reflection in the metal. He had no choice. Not really. The guilt he carried already felt like a chain around his neck, dragging him under. And now Bullfrog wanted to tighten it.

His voice cracked. "Who?"

Bullfrog's answer was cold as a grave. "Jess… Jonny's girl."

Bronko recoiled. "You're crazy!"

"I'm serious." Bullfrog sat forward, leaning in close. "I want her in the ground, Bronko. Tonight. You've got till morning, or your secret comes crawling into the light. She's staying in a motel outside town." Bullfrog stood, satisfied, and headed for the door.

When it shut behind him, Bronko sagged forward, breath shaking. For a moment—just a moment—he stared at the gun and thought about turning it on himself. A clean escape. Silence at last. But he wasn't ready to die. Not now. Not like that. The turmoil tore through him, raw and consuming, until he finally grabbed the gun with a trembling hand and stepped out of the trailer—heading into a night he didn't want to face.

The motel shower sputtered to a stop, and Jess stood still for a moment, letting the last beads of water slide down her skin. The steam curled around her like a blanket she didn't want to leave. For the first time in hours, she felt clean—no soot, no blood, no dirt clinging to her. But the relief was thin. Beneath it, the ache for Jonny pulsed hard and steady. She already missed him in a way that made her chest feel hollow, like something essential had been scooped out and carried off with him.

She wrapped a towel around herself and stared at the old motel phone on the nightstand. She could call him. Just to hear his voice. To know he made it home safe. To tell him she was sorry she didn't get to say goodbye. Her hand hovered for a long moment over the receiver, the longing sharp enough to hurt. But she pulled back. Calling him would only lead to questions she wasn't ready to answer yet—not with everything she was tangled in, not with the danger stomping at her heels. But with the intention of calling him in a few days. She was sure she wanted this relationship to work; she just needed to clean up this mess first.

With a sigh, she dressed in clean clothes, dragging a brush through her damp hair. The room felt too quiet now, the kind of quiet that made her thoughts too loud. She moved toward the window to close the thin curtain properly—and froze. A shadow moved across the glass. Not the motel sign flickering. Not a passing car. Someone. Standing just outside.

Her heart thudded once, hard. She backed away a step, breath catching. The switchblade she'd taken from Bud lay on the dresser. Her fingers snatched it up before she'd even fully decided to. Fear made her whole-body sharp with adrenaline. Every instinct screamed that she shouldn't go out there. But staying inside with whatever was lurking inches from her window felt worse.

Jaw tight, pulse racing, Jess pushed open the motel door and stepped into the night. The air was cool against her still-warm skin. She held the blade against her leg, hidden but ready, eyes scanning every corner. She was alone out there—or trying to believe she was—as she moved forward, heart pounding, listening for the slightest shift in the darkness.

A sharp metallic click shattered the stillness—the unmistakable sound of a slide being pulled back, a gun being readied. Jess whipped around, breath freezing in her throat. Bronko stood a few paces behind her, the gun raised and steady, its barrel aimed straight at her chest. His face was tight with conflict, but his hands did not shake.

"Bronko!" Jess's voice cracked, part shock, part fear. "What are you doing?"

He stood rigid in the moonlit clearing, the gun raised but his expression twisted with pain, like every part of him hated what his hands were doing. His jaw trembled, his eyes glassy.

"I've got a message," he muttered. "From Bullfrog."

Jess exhaled shakily. Of course. She should've known Bullfrog wouldn't let her slip away clean. But Bronko? That's what she couldn't understand. This didn't feel like him. Not even close.

He jerked the gun toward the tree line, toward the lake's dark shimmer beyond it. "Walk."

He hadn't spotted the switchblade yet. Jess slid it quietly into her pocket and moved where he directed, stepping into the cold darkness, tripping on sticks and roots she couldn't see. Bronko stayed behind her, his steps heavy, his breath uneven.

"I didn't have you pegged as one of them, Bronko," she said softly.

"I ain't," he snarled back.

"Yet here you are."

They reached the shoreline of Weiss Lake, water black and still, moonlight barely touching it. Jess turned. Bronko's face was tight with torment.

"I've got to do this," he said.

"Because Bullfrog told you to?" Jess stepped closer, voice trembling. "I can see you don't want this."

"Shut up! Stop talking!" His voice cracked, raw and desperate.

The gun wavered, his hand shaking violently as he fought something inside himself—fear, guilt, grief. Jess pressed on, sensing the break in the armour.

"If you do this, you can never go back. Bronko, think about Jonny… your best friend," she pleaded.

"STOP TALKING!" He shouted. She'd struck something in him. She could see it in the frantic way he swallowed, the way his eyes darted, the way his feet shifted like he wanted to run.

"You're a good man, Bronko," she whispered. "This isn't you."

"I DON'T HAVE A CHOICE!" His voice shattered. Tears streamed down his face. He slammed the gun against his own temple, as if beating back the thoughts tearing him apart.

Jess's heart twisted. "You do have a choice."

"No, I don't," he choked. "This is the only way out for me."

Jess stepped forward—slow, deliberate, taking a risk that made her whole body shake. She reached out gently, placing her hand over his, lowering the gun, offering him something he hadn't had in a long time: comfort.

"It's okay," she said, voice barely a breath. "What's he got on you, Bronko?"

Bronko shook his head, sobbing like a man finally breaking after carrying too much for too long.

"Whatever it is, I can help you." She said softly

"No, you can't," he said, voice torn. "Not this."

"I've done things I'm not proud of too," Jess whispered. "I've got people after me right now—not just the Night Hounds. Whatever you've done… you can tell me."

Bronko stared at her, bewildered, almost afraid. This girl—Jonny's girl—wasn't who he thought she was. He could feel it.

"Who the hell are you?" he whispered.

Jess swallowed hard. Her truth tasted like rust and regret. She knew that telling Bronko was the only way to save her life—and she also knew that speaking it out loud meant the last remnants of her life with Jonny would crumble for good.

“My name’s not Jess,” she said softly. “I’m hiding out in Alabama from the law. I killed someone. And trust me—what you’re feeling right now. It will haunt you for the rest of your life.”

Bronko let out a cracking sob, the confession ripping out of him. “I killed someone too.”

Jess closed her eyes. She didn’t expect him to say it, and hearing it broke something in both of them. “I killed Big Rick,” Bronko cried. “Earl said if I didn’t, he’d come after you… Jonny… Pete… everyone I care about. I didn’t have a choice.”

The pieces fell into place: the addiction, the anger, the spiralling, the weight he’d been carrying alone. Jess stepped closer and wrapped an arm around him as he collapsed into her, shaking.

“It’s okay,” she whispered, her voice trembling, thick with unshed tears. “You did it because you had no choice.”

He let out a broken, ragged sound, a raw cry that carried all the sharp, suffocating pain he had been burying. For the first time, he heard the words he had longed for—someone acknowledging the man behind the mistakes, the violence, the guilt. He clung to her voice like a lifeline, desperate for her to see beyond what he had done, to feel the weight it had placed on him, to understand the chaos and fear that had driven him here. Finally, someone was seeing the truth—the fear, the remorse, the helplessness—and not just the acts he had tried to forget. For the first time, Bronko didn’t feel alone in the darkness.

“I didn’t want to hurt anyone,” he cried.

“I know,” she murmured, her hand brushing lightly against his arm. “That’s not who you are.”

Bronko's shoulders shook violently, and he pressed a hand to his face, trying to wipe away the tears that betrayed him. "Now he's making me do it again," he whispered, almost to himself.

Jess steadied her own breath, swallowing the lump in her throat. "Let me go. I'll be out of town tonight. You can tell Bullfrog I'm dead… and you'll never see me again."

He hesitated, voice rough and uncertain. "Where will you go?"

She shook her head slightly, eyes glistening, but her voice remained calm, almost painfully resolute. "It doesn't matter. I'll figure it out. You… you'll finally be free of all this."

For a long moment, he just looked at her, torn, broken, and unwilling to fully accept the weight of her words. Then came the question that sliced straight through them both. "What about Jonny?"

Her chest tightened. She forced herself to keep her voice steady. "Jonny can never know. It would destroy him. I want him to remember me as the girl he knew this summer. Just that girl. One day, he'll forget me—and he'll move on. That's what he deserves."

Bronko lifted a trembling hand to wipe at his face. "He told me… he said, the next time I saw you… to tell you to call him. And that he loves you."

Her throat tightened painfully, tears threatening to spill. "I love him too. That's why he can never know."

For a heartbeat, the world narrowed to just the two of them—the truth of their actions, the shared guilt, the unbearable weight of knowing the innocent must remain blind. Jonny had to be spared, no matter the cost.

Bronko nodded slowly, a silent, sacred pact forming between them—an understanding that some truths were too heavy to bear, that some lives were meant to remain untouched by darkness. Together, they would shield Jonny, even if it meant carrying ghosts forever.

Jess pressed her hand to his shoulder, a small comfort, a silent farewell. Then she slipped into the night, leaving behind the life she had in Alabama. No belongings. No plan. Just the raw ache of heartbreak and the life she could never reclaim—Jonny, Sally, the fragments of the girl she had been here. Jess Judy was now a thing of the past. She vanished into the darkness, a shadow among shadows, carrying nothing but memory and grief. Her past was gone. Her future uncertain. And not a single goodbye would ever reach the one she loved.

Chapter 27 The Path That Became

The years after leaving Cedar Bluff had been brutally hard. Every day since 1979 had been a struggle—running, hiding, surviving, always looking over her shoulder, never able to stay in one place long enough to breathe. By 1981, Jess knew she couldn't go on like that forever. She needed stability, a home, a chance to reclaim some small measure of normalcy. West Virginia called her back, and Bancroft offered the best chance she had to start again.

By the time she arrived, she had become someone new: Ally. As she and Jonny had once joked, she was "Miss Ally Bamy," adopting his last name as a quiet tether to a past she could no longer indulge. She didn't allow herself to think about him—not really. Every memory carried too much ache, too much longing. Better to bury him entirely, suppressing the image of his face, the sound of his voice, keeping her heart safe from reckless hope that could undo her.

Returning to the refuge, Jess—now Ally—was immediately recognised by Jess Judy, the elderly woman who ran the place. Her sharp eyes lit up with recognition, though she said nothing of it aloud. Ally explained her story—witness protection, new identity, fresh start—and Jess Judy accepted it without hesitation. It wasn't a matter of believing or not believing; she had spent a lifetime providing sanctuary to troubled young people. Questions, she had learned, were a risk. Something about her could sense Ally's suffering.

In that quiet acceptance, Ally felt the first fragile threads of possibility. A chance, maybe, to exist without running, without fear, without the weight of a past she couldn't yet face. For now, this refuge would be her anchor, and she would learn to be Ally, the name that shielded her from everything—and everyone—she had lost.

Life at the refuge was slow, painfully slow, and for Ally, that was almost worse than the chaos she'd fled. Days stretched into long, quiet hours, and the routines that were meant to soothe her felt like chains instead. She kept herself to herself, lingering on the edges of the other residents, never allowing anyone too close. Conversations were short, polite, but never warm. She smiled when necessary, nodded when she needed to, but she never lingered.

Trust, she had learned, was dangerous. Every person she'd let in over the past two years had been a potential liability, a threat she could barely control. Friendships meant attachments, and attachments meant heartbreak. She couldn't allow herself to form bonds she would inevitably have to abandon, and so she remained on the outskirts, always watching, always calculating how much she could give without losing herself—or someone else—when the time came to leave again.

Even the boredom gnawed at her. There was no rush of fear, no pressing danger, no shadows chasing her through the night. Instead, there were endless quiet afternoons, the same faces she didn't allow herself to know, the same walls closing in. Sometimes she walked the grounds aimlessly, pretending to be absorbed in the scenery, while inside she wrestled with the ache of solitude. She was surrounded by people, yet utterly alone—protected, yes, but imprisoned in her own careful distance.

Ally had adapted to this, though. She filled her time with reading, small tasks, and routines that kept her mind busy, kept her hands from shaking, and kept her heart from wandering back to memories she could never confront. She existed in the margins, observing life without ever letting herself fully participate, a shadow of a girl who had once dreamed of love, laughter, and freedom, now reduced to survival in stillness.

And through it all, a small, stubborn piece of her heart kept whispering reminders of what she had lost—and what she had left behind. She would survive, as she always had. But she would do it alone.

Each night, when the refuge grew quiet and the halls settled into their usual uneasy stillness, Ally reached for the bottle of Clyde May's she kept tucked beneath her bed. It had become the only thing that softened the edges of her thoughts long enough to let her rest. She would take slow pulls from it, feeling the burn trace down her throat, chasing away the memories, the loneliness, the gnawing tension that never really left her. The whiskey wrapped her in a heavy, artificial warmth—just enough to dull the noise in her head, just enough to help her drift into a dreamless sleep. It wasn't comfort, not really. It was survival. And every night, it was the only way she knew how to quiet the world long enough to forget it.

Word travelled faster than she expected. Julian had caught wind that she was back at the refuge, and before long, he began showing up, unannounced, lingering just long enough to make his presence felt. His possessive nature returned with him, sharp and suffocating, but in a strange, twisted way, it was the only thing that cut through the crushing loneliness she felt. Julian was dangerous, no doubt about it, yet he was someone she could somewhat rely on—he knew the things she had done, including what she had done to Floyd, and he hadn't told a soul.

He thrived on chaos and didn't care who got hurt in the process. Petty crimes, lies, threats—it was all part of him, and Ally was never exempt. He wasn't careful around her; he was reckless, selfish, an ass through and through. But he knew her past, and for now, that gave her a strange, uneasy sense of shelter from the world she could never fully trust.

She started seeing him more and more, his visits growing longer, his gaze lingering, the air between them charged with a dangerous tension. And then one night, he kissed her. She didn't want to kiss him back, not really, but the overwhelming loneliness clawed at her, and before she knew it, she was giving in. That one impulsive moment spiralled quickly into a relationship she didn't know how she had fallen into. Julian wasn't loving; he was obsessive, controlling, and selfish. She knew he wasn't a good person, but he knew her past, and defying him could jeopardise the fragile safety she had carved out at the refuge. The one place she had left.

It was a dangerous compromise. She traded emotional freedom for the illusion of companionship, for someone who dominated her world and disregarded her well-being. Julian's obsession was suffocating, his recklessness constant, but it beat the crushing solitude she had spent years learning to endure. And so, reluctantly, she stayed—trapped between fear, need, and the quiet desperation that had become her life.

One sunny day, Ally had taken herself for a walk. Bancroft wasn't short of beautiful country paths, and she had spent the morning wandering through the hills, letting the quiet of nature settle her restless thoughts. As she made her way back toward the refuge through the town, she noticed the familiar calm of the streets—a rare kind of peace she had grown almost unused to.

Then something caught her eye. Across the road, a van was parked where it hadn't been before. The door swung open, and in an instant, the pieces clicked together. White Chevrolet. Bud. Her stomach dropped.

"YOU!" he roared.

Without thinking, Ally bolted, heart hammering in her chest, instinct taking over. She dove toward the edge of the forest. "Your biker friends aren't here to save you now!" Bud shouted, his voice carrying over the crunch of leaves and twigs beneath their feet. Ally's lungs burned as she pushed herself harder, dodging between trees and leaping over fallen roots.

Bud was relentless, crashing through underbrush, his footsteps heavy and menacing. He swung a wild glance over his shoulder and then roared in frustration as Ally gained a narrow lead. Her heart slammed against her ribs, each beat a countdown to either escape or capture. The open fields ahead promised speed, but they also left her exposed.

Breaking through the treeline, Ally sprinted across the tall grass, wind whipping at her face. Bud emerged moments later, and she froze for just an instant—he had pulled a revolver from his waistband, the steel glinting ominously in the sunlight.

"Stop!" he yelled, raising the weapon. Without hesitation, he fired. The shot rang out, echoing across the hills. Ally felt the heat and whistling crack of the bullet pass just inches from her, and adrenaline surged through her veins. She dove to the side, rolling down a shallow slope, barely keeping herself on her feet.

She scrambled to her feet and bolted again, zigzagging through the field, trying to make herself a harder target. Bud's shouts and the heavy clicks of his revolver followed her, relentless. Another shot rang out; this time a spray of dirt erupted where she had just been. Her chest heaved. Fear and survival pushed her onward.

By the time she reached the denser part of the forest, the canopy swallowed her in shadow. She slowed only slightly, listening for Bud's approach. His anger was like a storm behind her, but the trees gave her cover, and her lungs burned with determination.

Ally darted through the thick underbrush, pressing herself low and using every tree and bush as cover. Bud's shouts and the occasional crack of his revolver faded behind her as she twisted and turned, doubling back on herself through a maze of familiar forest trails. She leapt over fallen logs, scrambled up a small embankment, and slipped into a narrow creek bed, letting the sound of rushing water mask her movements. Every step was measured, every breath controlled—she couldn't afford a single miscalculation.

Minutes that felt like hours passed. The forest opened into a small clearing, and Ally risked a glance behind her. Bud was nowhere in sight. She kept moving, ducking into a line of trees that ran toward the outskirts of town. The relief that surged through her was fleeting; she knew he could still be out there, hunting, ruthless as ever.

By the time she broke through the last of the trees, the streets of Bancroft spread out before her. She ran without pause, eyes flicking back over her shoulder, scanning the quiet town for any sign of him. She made her way back to the refuge. Her heart thudded in her chest, and the ache in her legs was nothing compared to the terror clawing at her lungs. Then, through the blur of motion and adrenaline, she saw a familiar figure standing in her path. Lorraine Judy, the daughter of the refuge's matriarch, only a few years younger than Ally, appeared on the porch just ahead.

"What's the matter? Is that gunshots?" Lorraine asked, her eyes wide with concern.

Ally shook her head quickly, forcing a calm she didn't feel. "No… no, nothing's wrong. Just… people hunting, I think."

Lorraine frowned. "What's going on, Ally?"

"Nothing!" Ally cut her off, glancing toward the door. "Is your mom home?"

Lorraine shook her head, and Ally seized the moment, pulling her gently toward the house. Inside, Julian emerged from the living area as if he had been waiting, his eyes narrowing the instant he saw her.

"Where have you been?" he demanded, his tone sharp, impatient.

Ally froze. She couldn't say a word in front of Lorraine—couldn't let her see the truth of what was happening.

"Lorraine," she said quickly, voice firm, trying to mask the tremor in her hands. "Go upstairs. I promise… everything's fine."

Out of fear, Lorraine obeyed, disappearing quietly, leaving the room tense and still.

Ally swallowed hard, the lump in her throat refusing to pass. She had nowhere to run, no safe space to unload the fear and panic clawing at her chest. "I… I need your help," she admitted.

As she spoke, a cold weight settled over her. The more she ran, the more it seemed her past was catching up, inching closer no matter how far she fled. She had thought she could escape it, but now she realised it might never truly let her go.

Ally took a deep breath and explained everything about Bud to Julian—who he was, what had happened in Cedar Bluff, how he had tracked her down, but nothing more, her voice tight with fear and urgency. Julian's face twisted in anger the moment he realised she hadn't told him sooner. Ally swallowed, knowing the truth would make his jealousy flare. She hadn't wanted to tell him about Jonny—not the man she had once loved, not the memories that still haunted her.

Julian's expression softened for only a moment, then hardened again. "Come with me," he said, a low determination in his voice, as if he already had a plan. Ally hesitated, fear knotting her stomach, but she didn't have a choice. If she stayed, Bud would catch her. If she ran on her own, she had no chance. She nodded and followed Julian into the forest, her pulse hammering in her ears. The trees swallowed them as they moved. Julian led confidently, and Ally kept close, trusting the unspoken promise that he knew what he was doing. Soon, the sound of movement ahead made her stiffen.

There, partially hidden in a small clearing, was Bud. His head snapped up as they appeared, eyes locking on Ally. Recognition flashed across his face, twisted with fury and disbelief. Bud's stance stiffened, his hand hovering near his weapon. He wasn't expecting someone with her, but he wasn't surprised. And in that brief hesitation, Julian's presence became a shield, a warning that Ally was no longer alone.

Bud's eyes darted between them, his expression twisting with recognition and malice the moment he saw Ally behind Julian. He stepped forward with that same cruel swagger she remembered from Alabama.

"Who's this, another one of your friends?" he spat.

Julian didn't move. His jaw tightened as he positioned himself between them. "Her boyfriend actually."

Bud let out a harsh laugh, shaking his head. "Did she tell you what she did?"

Julian's voice stayed calm, unnervingly steady. "About your friend Floyd? Yeah, I know about him."

Something dark flickered behind Bud's eyes—old fury reigniting. "She has to pay for what she did."

Julian's stance hardened. "You'll have to go through me first."

Bud studied him a long moment, then scoffed. "You're not as scary as them biker folks in Bama. My fight isn't with you, stranger. Why don't you step aside and let me finish this. I'd hate to have to waste a bullet on you too."

Julian cast a glance back at Ally. She felt her pulse jump. Not because he looked afraid—because he didn't. He was calculating, weighing something she couldn't read. And then, with a slow, chilling nod, he stepped aside. Ally's stomach dropped. He was letting Bud reach her.
Letting him do whatever he came here to do.

Bud's grin stretched into something vile as he approached. "I been waiting a long time to do this."

He cocked the hammer back on his revolver—an awful, metallic sound—and pressed the barrel hard against her cheek. Ally froze. Every instinct screamed at her to run, but her body wouldn't move.

Behind Bud, Julian shifted—silent, deliberate. He drew a Swiss knife from his pocket and flicked it open without a sound. There was no hesitation in him now. No fear. Just purpose. Bud inhaled, ready to squeeze the trigger. Julian struck with violent precision. He drove the blade into the side of Bud's neck. Blood erupted instantly, spattering the leaves and dirt. Julian yanked the knife free.

Bud staggered forward, choking, gurgling, hands clutching at the ruin of his throat. He collapsed to the forest floor, drowning in his own blood, until finally the gurgles stopped and the woods fell silent.

Ally's breath came fast and uneven. She stumbled back, staring at the body in horror. "What did you do!"

Julian wiped the blade on his jeans, unfazed. "He was going to kill you, Ally. He was never going to give up."

She shook her head, voice cracking. "No! No! You just killed him!" Her hands covered her mouth as the realisation hit. This wasn't self-defence—it was execution.

Julian snapped back at her. "Don't act like you're the moral one. Let's not forget why you're in this mess. You're a murderer too."

The words hit her like poison. Yes, she'd taken a life—but in her mind she'd been freeing herself from an abuser, tearing loose from a man who had done nothing but rot the world around him. That had been survival, a desperate strike against cruelty. It wasn't the same as this—this cold, calculated murder bleeding out at her feet.

"He was angry, he lost a friend! He didn't deserve to die!" she cried, her voice trembling.

Julian's temper flared instantly. "A little gratitude for saving your ass, you ungrateful bitch!"

Ally's pulse hammered in her throat. Panic surged sharp and cold. "What do we do now?"

Julian grabbed her arm. "Go back to the refuge, get the shovels from the shed and don't let anyone see you, especially that nosy bitch Lorraine."

She couldn't believe what he was asking of her. A murder—and now she was entangled in covering it up. Julian held her past like a weapon, ready to expose her to the authorities if she dared defy him. She didn't have the strength to start over again, not after everything she'd already survived. So, she steadied herself. She would do this. There was no other choice.

Ally kept to the shadows as she approached the refuge, avoiding the windows and voices drifting from inside. She didn't dare go near the house—just slipped to the shed, eased the door open, grabbed the two shovels, and disappeared back into the trees before anyone could notice. Tears threatened, stinging her eyes, but she forced them back. Breaking down now would only make everything worse.

Julian waited where she'd left him, an orange leaf placed over Bud's face. Seeing him again—still, pale, stiffening—sent a shiver across her skin. Floyd had gone in an explosion, quick and distant, his death hidden behind smoke. But Bud… Bud she had to face. Bud she had to touch. She helped Julian move him, the coldness of his skin shocking her, his weight unsettling and wrong. When she tried to lift him, her stomach lurched; she nearly threw up, but swallowed it down hard and kept going. His arms didn't bend, his neck didn't turn, and every shift of his dead weight felt like handling something she had no right to touch.

They dug until sweat and dirt clung to them both, the forest growing darker and colder around them. It was slow, miserable work—each shovelful heavier than the last—but eventually the hole was deep enough, and Bud's body disappeared into it. Covering him felt endless. By the time they pressed the final layer of soil flat, night had swallowed everything.

The walk back was a blur of shadows and stumbling roots. They could barely see the path, barely see each other. At the edge of the clearing, Ally took the shovels on her own and slipped back to the shed, returning them exactly where they'd been.

Then she crept away again, unseen, her hands still shaking with soil in the creases of her skin—proof of everything she couldn't undo.

Julian wiped the dirt from his hands, breath sharp and irritated as he looked her over. “Take a shower and burn your clothes. Is there anyone else you’re not telling me about that knows what you did? Who might come after you?”

Ally shook her head, panic flaring hot in her chest because she wasn’t sure of anything anymore. Faces from her past blurred together—until one snapped into place. Bronko.

“Just one, I think!” she blurted, her voice thin.

Julian’s eyes widened with disbelief. “You *think!?* You’re the stupidest criminal in history. Who?”

“His name was Bronko, he’s back in Alabama, but he won’t come looking.” She stammered.

“How can you be so sure?” Julian asked. His insistency making Ally’s panic worse.

“He’s not the kind,” she said questioning herself.

Julian scoffed, shaking his head. “Okay, then we pretend you’re dead—send him a fake obituary or something. Leave it to me. And we need to get out of here, Ally.”

Panic tightened around her ribs. She didn’t want to leave Bancroft. She didn’t want to leave with Julian most of all. But she was already tangled too deep; every decision she made now felt like stepping into mud that only pulled her further down.

“We’ve got nowhere to go,” she whispered.

“I’ve still got some connections back home in Nebraska,” he said, already walking, already planning. “We’ve got no choice, Ally.”

That night, under the cloak of darkness and the quiet hum of the road, Ally and Julian packed what little they could carry and disappeared. Every movement was hurried, every glance over her shoulder a reminder that the world she had tried to find safety in no longer existed. They made their way west, leaving Bancroft behind like an open wound, moving state by state until Omaha, Nebraska, became their reluctant refuge. She tried to tell herself it was just another town, another chance at a clean slate, but the weight of her past, present, and future pressed down on her with every mile.

In Omaha, life settled into a grim rhythm, and Ally quickly learned that escape came at a cost. Julian was a man she could not leave—bound to him by secrets, by murders, by the things they had both done. He was controlling, abusive, and relentless in ways that made the walls of their house feel like a cage she couldn't climb out of. Days bled into nights under the constant shadow of fear, his temper a silent pulse in the room, and Ally learned to shrink, to disappear into corners, to bite back every instinct to argue, to scream, to fight. She was trapped, tethered to a man who could never love her, who could never see her as more than a part of his criminal world.

Chapter 28 Caught Off Guard

A few years later, news drifted to her that the refuge in Bancroft had closed. Jess Judy, the woman who had been one of the few safe points in her life, had passed away. Ally felt an old grief rise again, sharper this time because it reminded her that death followed her, always lurking just beyond the edges of her life. She thought of Floyd, of Bud, of the lives she'd touched and ended, and realised she couldn't do to Julian what she had done before. She didn't have the strength—or the heart—to kill him, though sometimes she imagined it in quiet, impossible moments. Instead, she endured, watching the years creep on, Julian's criminal enterprise slowly growing with him. He remained dangerous, violent, and cruel, and the irony wasn't lost on her. The universe, she thought bitterly, had a sense of humour: the girl who had killed to protect herself from abuse now found herself trapped in a marriage that mirrored it. Maybe this was her punishment. Maybe this was what she deserved.

Time passed in that quiet, tense monotony until one ordinary afternoon everything shifted. She had returned home from grocery shopping, hands full of bags and arms aching with the mundane weight of normal life. The phone rang, its shrill sound slicing through the quiet apartment. Ally's pulse spiked. She hurried to set the bags on the table, her mind already calculating, already bracing. The number on the screen was unknown, and in a life where every stranger could be a threat, every unfamiliar voice a risk, her defences went up immediately. She picked up the receiver, breathing shallow. She said nothing at all, holding the line and listening, waiting.

A voice cracked through, raw and unfamiliar. "Jess, is that you?" Ally's heart plummeted. For a moment she couldn't breathe. It had been thirty years—three whole decades—since anyone had called her Jess. The name felt like it belonged to another lifetime, another person entirely. She had buried Jess so deeply she sometimes forgot she'd ever lived as her. But hearing it now, spoken by a stranger's voice, sent cold panic racing through her veins. "Ally? Ally Bertotti?" Her knees nearly buckled. Whoever this was… they knew her then, and they knew her now. And if they could find her, after everything she'd done, after everything she'd run from… then maybe her past had finally clawed its way back. In this world, 2009—this age of records, databases, and digital trails—disappearing wasn't as easy as it had been in 1979. If someone was looking for her, they weren't guessing. They knew. Without thinking, she hung up the phone. She had to call Julian immediately.

He answered after a few rings, as if her call was inconvenient. "What do you want? I'm working."

"Someone's out to get me," she said, her voice trembling despite her effort to sound calm.

"What the hell are you talking about?" he snapped.

"Someone just rang the house asking for me," she continued. "I didn't recognise the voice… They called me Jess to begin with."

There was a pause. "You're being paranoid," Julian said dismissively.

"I'm being serious," she insisted, pacing the kitchen, her hand pressed to her forehead as if it could steady her racing thoughts. "What if it's someone who knows what I did? What we did?"

"That was a lifetime ago. Nobody's coming looking for us," he said finally, irritation still in his tone. "I've got to go. I'll see you tonight." The line went dead.

Ally stood in the quiet kitchen, the phone still trembling in her hand, groceries half-unpacked around her. Julian's indifference only made the fear worse. Because someone had said her name and she knew, deep down, that it wasn't a mistake. Someone was looking for her.

A few days later, the fear in her chest took shape. A car rolled to a stop outside her house—dark, unfamiliar, slow enough to make her blood freeze. Ally edged toward the front window, keeping the curtains drawn tight, and peered through the thin slivers of space between the fabric. Two men stepped out. One was Black, the other white. Neither looked like someone passing through. Both looked like men with a purpose. She backed away from the window until her spine pressed against the wall beside the door. The frosted glass didn't reveal details, but it showed enough—the silhouette of one man leaning in, trying to peer inside. Through the small reflection in the side window, she saw the other circling around to the back of the house.

Her heart hammered so loudly she feared they would hear it. A knock rattled the front door. She froze. Another knock, louder this time. She held her breath, refusing to move, refusing to make a sound. After what felt like minutes, she heard footsteps as the second man returned to the front.

"Nothing here," one of them said. Her stomach twisted—she recognised the voice instantly. The same one from the phone call. "Think she's out?" the other asked. The casualness in his tone only made the fear more suffocating. "Either that, or she doesn't want to answer the door to two strangers." Footsteps again. Then quiet. When she dared, she nudged the curtain just enough to look. Not with a full glance—just with a sliver of an eye. There weren't two men.
There were three. Two walked away up the street… but the third stayed inside, sitting behind the wheel, staring directly at her house. Waiting. Watching. He didn't leave until the sun went down.

That evening she told Julian everything—her voice trembling, her hands cold. He barely looked up from his beer. "If they come back tomorrow, let me know." That was it. No alarm. No strategy. Nothing to protect her. She didn't sleep a single minute that night.

And come morning—after Julian left for work—her nightmare returned. This time a different car, but the same silhouette. The same threat. This time she didn't wait for the knock.

She moved quickly, almost mechanically, as if fear had taken over her muscles. At the back of the living room, behind the framed picture of her and Julian at their wedding, she opened the safe. Her hands shook only slightly as she removed the 9mm pistol, checked the magazine, and clicked the safety off.

She didn't have a plan. She barely had coherent thoughts. Survival was the only thing she could hear in her head. In the garage, she slipped into the driver's seat of her black Range Rover. Her breaths came fast, fogging the windshield. She hit the garage door opener, and sunlight poured in—along with the sight of him. He stood at the end of the driveway. Waiting for her. Like he knew exactly what she'd do. Her pulse roared in her ears. No time to think. She slammed her foot on the accelerator. The SUV shot forward, as she aimed straight for him. He jumped aside at the last moment, but she didn't stop. She couldn't. She sped up the street with no destination, no plan—just raw instinct screaming at her to run. In her rearview mirror, she saw him sprinting back to the car. Seconds later, the pursuit began. He was catching up to her, chasing her.

She floored the accelerator, the engine roaring beneath her as the street blurred around her. One hand gripped the wheel; the other snatched up her phone with shaking fingers. She dialled Julian, her breath coming in short, ragged gasps.

"What is it now, Ally?" he asked, his voice sharp with irritation.

"He's back—he's chasing after me. I told you! I told you someone was coming for me!" Her voice cracked, raw with panic.

This time, something in her tone cut through his usual anger. His voice shifted, still sharp, but threaded with urgency. "Alright. You know the old sewing warehouse, the one we always meet the dealers in? Go there. Get inside. I'll deal with them."

The call ended, leaving only the roar of the engine and her own ragged breathing. Behind her, the car tailing her closed the distance.

They persisted, tyres squealing and engines snarling behind her, but Ally's fear sharpened her reflexes and she pressed the accelerator harder, weaving through the streets and finally putting distance between herself and the car, finally losing it. For a moment, she allowed herself the briefest relief—but it didn't last. Not long after, a second car appeared behind her, sliding onto the road as if it had been waiting. Who were these people, and why were they after her? Her mind raced as she pushed the Range Rover harder, desperation fuelling every turn.

Finally, the old sewing warehouse loomed ahead, its dark silhouette rising like a promise of temporary refuge. She skidded the SUV to a stop and bolted inside, sprinting up a few flights of rickety stairs until she reached the top floors. Panting, she pressed herself against the cold concrete, looking out a grimy window. Far below, Julian and his friend arrived in the black saloon. She couldn't hear what was happening over the pounding of her own heart, but she saw the scene unfold in stark clarity: Julian and his companion tore into the men who had pursued her, their blows unrelenting.

Ally's relief was short-lived. From somewhere inside the abandoned warehouse, she heard movement—another presence, someone else coming up the stairs. She ducked into a side room, hugging the wall, her body pressed tight, holding her breath as each step echoed closer. He moved methodically, checking every room.

Then, he stopped. She saw him pause, facing the other way, drawing in a frustrated breath. Her chance had come. Slowly, silently, she crept out of her hiding place, every nerve alert. She raised the gun, pressing the cold steel of the barrel against the back of his head.

"That's the business end of my nine-millimetre pressed against the back of your skull… Move an inch and I blow it all over this room," she said, her voice low, steady, and deadly.

"Easy," the man said. His tone was calm; hands lifted in a gesture of surrender. "I'm not here to cause trouble."

The voice—it hit her strangely. Familiar, but shadowed with something older. She tried to place it and failed. Did she know this man?

"I'm looking for an old friend," he went on gently. "Nothing more."

Old friend. The words felt dangerous. She tried to place him, tried to match the voice with the ghosts of her past. Who could possibly know her as Jess anymore? Who had survived long enough, remembered long enough, cared enough to track her down? Her pulse pounded. No… it couldn't be *him*. Not after all these years. She took a small step back, giving him space to turn around. She needed to see his face. Needed confirmation or relief or something she could use to anchor herself. Her heart hammered so fiercely.

He turned slowly. At first, all she saw was a stranger. But then recognition flickered across his face. His expression softened, painted with something painfully innocent, something like hope. "Jess?" he said quietly.

The name struck like a lightning bolt. Her stomach dropped. Her suspicions weren't just correct—they came crashing down with absolute certainty. After thirty years of burying her past, after thirty years of silence, Jonny Phillips was standing in front of her. She felt the world tilt. A lifetime of emotion surged at once—shock, fear, longing, grief—and she fought desperately not to crumble beneath it.

"It's me," he said, confirming it to her. "Jonny Phillips."

She stared at him, frozen. Time hadn't erased him. Older, yes—lines carved deeper around his eyes, shoulders a little heavier—but still him. Still the boy she once loved. But the years had shaped her into something else, something she didn't want him to see. Her mind snapped back into self-defence. How had he found her? What did he know? Was he here because he cared—or because he'd uncovered the truth she'd spent a lifetime hiding?

"You remember me," he said softly. "I know you do."

"How did you find me?" she asked, the words sharp, brittle.

"It's been a long road, Jess," he admitted.

"That's not my name," she retorted

The correction came out harsher than she intended. She hated that she had to shield herself from him, of all people. The bubble that was the summer of 1979 had just been burst.

"Okay," he murmured, hands still raised. "Okay. I just wanted to find you."

He stepped closer. She had to protect herself; she couldn't drop her guard just yet. Her other hand gripped the gun and he understood the message, clearly—not to come any closer.

"Why!?" she demanded, her voice trembling, the weight of thirty years pressing down on her.

"Because… because I never stopped thinking about you," Jonny said.

The words hit her. Her heart surged, butterflies bursting in her stomach so violently it almost knocked the breath from her. She had meant something to him—truly meant something. It hadn't just been a summer fling he would soon forget about. It had been as real to him as it was to her. And yet the question gnawed at her, sharp and deadly. She needed to ask.

"What do you know about me?" she asked, bracing herself.

"Honestly not much. I just tried to chase your footsteps. I know you were on the run for something." He knew. The one person she feared knowing her past—feared judging her—was standing right here. The man she had imagined a better life with. His knowledge felt like a spotlight on all the darkness she'd spent decades burying.

"It's okay," he said softly. "I'm not here to do anything other than to see you."

She wished with everything inside her that things were different. She hated that this was the life he'd found her in. Hated that he had come looking because she knew she would only disappoint him. And she hated herself for that truth most of all. There was no escape from Julian, no way out of the precarious hell she lived in. And now she had to get Jonny away from it—far, far away—before he became another casualty of her cursed life.

"Now you've seen me," she said, forcing herself to be cold. "Get out of here. Go… and never come back."

Before Jonny could reply, the warehouse downstairs exploded with the sound of a door slamming open. Heavy footsteps. A voice she knew too well. Julian. Her blood iced. Panic surged. If Julian saw Jonny, there would be no reasoning, no mercy. She couldn't let that happen.

"I'm okay! I'm coming now!" she yelled down, hoping to stall him—hoping to keep him from climbing a single step further. But she heard it anyway, the unmistakable tread of Julian and one of his men coming up the stairs.

Jonny's brow creased, concern sharpening his features. "Are you okay, are you in trouble?"

Of course he asked. That was who he was—fiercely protective, loyal to a fault. And that was exactly why she couldn't let him be a part of this.

"There's a fire escape behind you," she said urgently. "It leads to the street. Go back home… and never come looking for me again."

For a moment he hesitated, caught between instinct and obedience. Then he reached into his pocket, pulled something free, and tossed it onto the floor at her feet.

"I can help you. If you ever need me, come to that address." He said quietly, as to not alert the men below.

"Promise me you'll never come back," she said, all but begging.

He didn't argue. He climbed through the window, disappearing down the fire escape just as Julian's footsteps grew louder. She snatched the card off the floor, shoved it deep into her pocket, and forced her breathing steady. Julian and his friend walked in moments later.

"There you are," Julian said, scanning her face. "You okay?"

She nodded, trying to compose herself, trying to purge every trace of Jonny from her expression. The shock was still vibrating through her, but she buried it deep.

"We dealt with the guys outside," Julian said. "I don't think they'll be coming back. Come on, let's get out of here."

They hurried down the stairs and out into the fading daylight. Bronko and Dave were lying on the ground outside—broken, battered, barely conscious. The sight twisted her stomach. She recognised Bronko immediately. They had come all this way for her—and this was what greeted them. She wanted to help. Wanted to run to them. Wanted to call an ambulance, scream at Julian, stop this nightmare. She hated him for what he'd done. Hated herself for letting it happen. But she couldn't do anything. So she walked past them, forcing herself to look away. She climbed into the Range Rover with shaking hands and sped off into the darkening streets, the card in her pocket burning like a live coal against her skin.

She had kept the address folded tightly inside her pocket for weeks, hidden from Julian with the kind of caution that made her feel sick. In the days leading up to Christmas, she couldn't stop thinking about it. Every time Julian stepped out of the room, every time she lay awake beside him pretending to sleep, her mind spun through possibilities. She wanted to go to Jonny. She wanted to run, to leave this life, this fear, this constant edge she lived on. Maybe he could help her. Maybe he was the only person who ever truly would.

But the idea of leaving Julian felt too dangerous to entertain for long. Every time she allowed herself to imagine it, she'd force the thought away. He had eyes everywhere. He had people. He had a temper she'd learned to fear.

Then, on Christmas morning—before Julian so much as stirred beside her—something inside her snapped. She couldn't do it. She couldn't endure another hollow Christmas, another day pretending everything was fine while her life shrank smaller and smaller. She didn't plan it. She didn't think. She just left.

She slipped out quietly, taking only what she could hide on her person. She walked all the way into town so no one would see Julian's car missing, so none of his associates could report movement. When she finally reached the outskirts of the city, she called a cab with shaking hands and asked for the airport. Her pulse didn't slow until she was boarding a plane to Kentucky—some tiny last-minute flight that ended up empty except for her. The quiet should have been comforting, but it only magnified her thoughts.

By the time she landed, her phone was flooded—calls, texts, missed messages from Julian and numbers she didn't recognise. She turned it face-down in her lap and refused to answer any of them. Instead, she stepped outside, hailed another cab, and gave the driver the address she'd kept folded against her chest for weeks.

When she reached the house, she stood at the door with trembling hands. She didn't know what waited on the other side—anger, confusion, or something gentler—but she knocked anyway, her breath catching as she waited for it to open.

Chapter 29 Where All Roads Have Led To

Christmas 2009 unfolded in a way Jonny could never have prepared for. One moment he was standing in his parents' kitchen with Bronko—an unexpected reunion on its own—and the next, Jess stepped through the doorway as if pulled from another lifetime. Then came the truth—slowly at first, then in waves. Jonny listened as Jess and Bronko laid bare everything they had hidden back in 1979 —the fear she lived in. The man who hunted her. The pact she and Bronko formed out of sheer survival. The choices they made, the darkness they walked through together, the secrets they carried long after those summer nights ended. With every detail, Jonny felt the ground shifting under him. He hadn't known any of it—how could he have? Hearing it now, however, carved a sharp ache in his chest.

He didn't know what to feel—shock, grief, fury at the people who had hurt her, and disbelief that she had lived with all this alone. But stronger than any of it was the deep, steady pull he'd felt the moment he saw her again. After all these years, through all the missing pieces and unanswered questions, his feelings hadn't faded. Jess was standing in his parents' kitchen, carrying scars he never knew existed, and still—still—he loved her.

Jess's voice trembled as she broke the silence. "Jonny… say something."

Jonny's eyes scanned her face, taking in the years, the scars, the weight of everything she had carried. "I… I don't know what to say. You carried all of this on your shoulders the whole time."

Jess nodded, tears forming at the corners of her eyes, the past and present colliding in an ache she hadn't thought possible.

Jonny swallowed hard. His voice low and filled with awe. "Both of you… so many scars, for so long."

Bronko lowered his head, his tone quiet but firm. "We didn't want to pull you down with us, man. You were so happy that summer. We couldn't spoil that for you with the cold, hard truth."

Their actions were unforgivable, yes, but beneath it all was love and desperation—a truth that weighed heavier than any condemnation.

"All I ever wanted was the life we dreamed of, Jonny," Jess admitted, her voice trembling. "I can't expect you to fix this mess. But I had to see you again. You had to know"

"Nineteen-eighty. The year after Cedar Bluff. Where were you then?" Jonny asked, the final grey area over her lifetime.

Jess took a breath, looking out the window. "That's a story for another time." Sensing this was a different story altogether, and one that would only be just as difficult for her to tell as the one he had just heard, he decided not to press. He rubbed the back of his neck, thoughts tumbling fast. "I love you both. I'm not going to be the one to judge you. I can't even imagine what it must have been like for either of you."

Tears welled uncontrollably in Bronko's eyes, blurring the world around him. The weight of years—of secrets he had buried deep in darkness, of guilt that had gnawed at him day and night—was finally out, exposed to the light. And yet, in that moment of raw vulnerability, the one person he had feared would turn away, the one person whose judgment he had dreaded most, remained unwaveringly by his side. His closest friend, his brother in every sense that mattered, stood there, a steadfast anchor in the storm of his confessions, offering a quiet, unspoken forgiveness that made the crushing years of fear and isolation feel, if only for a moment, almost bearable. "I appreciate you, brother. More than you know," he whispered.

Jonny turned to Jess, resolve in his gaze. "We're going to fix this mess once and for all."

Jess shook her head, worry shadowing her features. "No, Jonny. He's dangerous. Julian isn't playing around."

Jonny's eyes hardened. "Neither was Earl, remember? You've suffered his torment for long enough. Let's do what we're best at… taking assholes down."

"I'm right there with you," Bronko said, quiet strength in his voice.

Jess allowed herself a small, admiring smile, though worry lingered. "I can't believe this is happening."

Jonny stepped closer. "I never stopped loving you."

Jess met his gaze, her own voice firm. "Neither did I."

She didn't hesitate—her arms wrapped around him as if trying to make up for the decades of longing, their bodies pressing together with a desperate intensity. Their lips met, and the kiss was everything they had both been denying themselves for thirty long years: raw, aching, and impossibly passionate, a collision of memory and desire, of loss and hope finally coming home. It carried the weight of all the stolen moments, all the whispered what-ifs, and all the heartache that had stretched between them for so long. Bronko stepped back quietly, a small, knowing chuckle escaping him, a smirk tugging at the corners of his lips as he moved toward the door, giving them this stolen, intimate moment, a brief reprieve in the chaos that had followed them for decades.

“Imma just give y’all a minute,” he said, leaving them a private moment amidst the chaos.

As Bronko quietly pushed the door open, Jonny’s family caught a fleeting, unmistakable glimpse of the embrace—the long-awaited reunion of two hearts separated by decades. Amanda’s cheeks flushed with fury, her eyes narrowing in disbelief, while Jonny’s parents’ faces tightened, etched with disapproval and shock. The air seemed to thrum with tension, heavy with unspoken questions and restrained emotions. Jonny’s plan was deceptively simple, but he knew better: Julian’s unpredictability loomed like a shadow over every decision, the margin for error impossibly thin, and a single misstep could have lethal consequences. Yet despite the danger, despite the precariousness of it all, Jess had to be free. They had no choice but to risk everything for her chance at life unchained.

The tangled road that had led them here—woven with lies, stitched together with love, marred by blood—was finally converging on its inevitable destination. Every betrayal, every heartbreak, every desperate act of survival had brought them to this moment. Jonny could feel it in his bones, in the rapid thrum of his heart. All roads were leading to this, the endgame, a final, decisive reckoning. To the place where it had all begun, and where, perhaps, it could finally end… Cedar Bluff.

Every road they had taken, every escape, every desperate choice, had led them here—to Cedar Bluff. Boxing day, The town rose before them like a phantom of the past, streets and buildings etched with memories, some bitter, some aching with longing. Jess felt her pulse spike, a storm of anticipation and fear coiling tight in her chest. Jonny’s plan had brought them here, a last desperate move to pull her free from the shadows that had clung to her for so long. The air seemed charged, alive with possibility, every corner of the town whispering of secrets and unfinished business. Jess could almost feel the weight of the past pressing down, yet beneath it, a thrill she hadn't felt in years: the chance to confront, to reclaim, to finally be free.

For Jonny, Cedar Bluff was a battlefield of memories, a place where every choice would matter, every move could change the outcome. The town was more than just the setting of their past—it was the stage for redemption, for justice, for love. As they stepped closer, the excitement and tension throbbed through them both.

It was dark that evening when they parked the bike on the sand beside Lake Weiss. The beach seemed smaller than Jess remembered, hemmed in by buildings, empty and silent, as if the fire that once drew laughter, music, and crowds had long since been snuffed out. This was the place they had first met, decades ago, where roaring bonfires had drawn more people than the town itself seemed to hold. Now, only shadows and memories lingered.

Bronko and Dave stood with them, the four of them together yet marked by everything they had endured. Silence stretched between them, a quiet acknowledgment they were the last ones standing. As well as the people they had lost along the way, heavy on their minds. Dave knew the plan inside and out—Jonny had left nothing to chance, every move calculated, every risk accounted for. Bronko, although question marks hung over him along the way, had been unpredictable, a wild card whose choices teetered between shadow and light. But now, in the weight of this moment, it was undeniable. He was loyal. Loyalty surged through him, raw and undeniable, anchoring him to the people who mattered most. Ready to right his wrongs. He would see this through to the end, standing by his friends no matter what came next.

Jess pressed the phone to her ear, the numbers already dialled, heart hammering. Julian's voice came through, sharp and venomous. "Where the hell are you, bitch! You think you can just walk away and leave me?"

Jess's lips curved with defiance. "You want to know where I am? I'm in Cedar Bluff… Alabama. Come and get me, you son of a bitch."

She hung up, letting the phone fall into her hand. Now came the waiting game—the stillness before the storm. The town around them felt different, as if Cedar Bluff itself had been holding its breath all these years, waiting for this moment. The streets were quiet, the bar dim and empty, shadows stretching where laughter and music had once filled the air. Every corner seemed smaller, every familiar landmark tinged with a strange weight, the place where love had once felt infinite now carrying a tension that made their hearts race.

Jonny felt it in every step, a pulse of something he hadn't realised he'd missed—the way the town smelled, the quiet creak of the streets, the way the light fell across familiar buildings. No matter how much Cedar Bluff had changed, being here with Jess made it feel right, like some fragment of the past had aligned perfectly with the present. Nerves coiled tightly in their chests, each step through the empty streets a reminder of what lay ahead.

The following evening, just days before 2010 began, Jonny and Jess sat in the quiet bar, each nursing a glass of Clyde May's. The dim light and low hum of the room mirrored the tension between them—too nervous to speak, both lost in their own thoughts, hearts hammering at the weight of what was to come. Then it happened: Jess's phone vibrated against the wood, making her jump. She answered quickly.

"I'm in this shithole," Julian barked. "Where do I find you?"

“Meet me on 75, just off the highway,” Jess said, her voice steady despite the adrenaline coursing through her. She hung up, already picturing the secluded stretch of road hidden beneath the trees, no one around at this hour to witness what was about to unfold.

Jonny set his glass down with a sharp clink, finishing his whiskey. “Let’s do this,” he said, his voice low but resolute.

They stepped outside together, the cold night air biting at their skin. Bronko leaned against a tree, cigarette smoke curling around his face, his eyes sharp and alert. The familiar curve of his jaw, the steady grip on his own nerves—this was the moment they had been waiting for. It was go time.

On the deserted stretch of road, Bronko melted into the shadows behind a gnarled tree, every muscle coiled and ready, his gaze locked on the unfolding scene. Jonny and Jess stood close to the bike, their bodies taut with anticipation, hearts hammering as if trying to outrun the danger creeping toward them. The road curved sharply behind them to the left, swallowing the darkened path in its bend, leaving only the narrow stretch ahead illuminated by the faint moonlight. From the direction they had come, headlights pierced the night, cutting through the shadows like knives. A black saloon rolled to a stop, its engine ticking in the silence, and Julian stepped out first, tall and imposing, flanked by three burly, scarred men whose mere presence seemed to press down on the air itself. Every instinct screamed at Jonny and Jess that the moment of reckoning had arrived, that the tension of years, the weight of secrets and danger, had finally culminated here in the darkness.

Julian’s eyes locked onto theirs. “There you are. I see you brought a friend.”

Jonny stepped forward, placing himself squarely between Jess and Julian. His muscles coiled, ready, unwavering. “Here’s what's going to happen." His voice cut through the tension like steel. "When you're talking, you talk to me. Not her, me."

Julian's face twisted with fury. "I don't know who you think you are, barking orders at me, when she's *my* wife."

Jonny's gaze didn't flinch. "Not anymore. She's not coming back with you."

A shadow of rage passed over Julian. "Is that so?"

Jess's voice trembled but carried a hard edge. "It's over, Julian."

Julian's jaw tightened. "It's never over. You're mine."

In a heartbeat, the dark threat became tangible—Julian pulled a pistol from behind his back, and the other three men mirrored him. The air thickened, heavy with anticipation, fear, and pure danger.

From the shadows, Bronko emerged. Small, black revolver in hand, he pulled the hammer back with a sickening click right beside Julian's temple.

"Just give me a reason to pull the trigger, asshole," Bronko growled, eyes ice-cold. "I've been waiting to get you back since Omaha."

Julian's lips curled in disgust, but he showed no fear. He still had them outnumbered.

"I will destroy you if you ever think about leaving me," Julian spat at Jess, hatred in every word. "You're never free. You belong to me."

Jonny stepped forward, a quiet storm. "She belongs to no one."

Julian's gaze flicked to him. "And who the hell might you be? The one that stalked her in her own home?"

Jonny's voice was calm, lethal. "I'm an old friend."

Julian's eyes widened—then narrowed as the pieces clicked together. Jess… or Ally, as he knew her. She was in love with him, the one she had known in Alabama years ago.

"Isn't this just one big happy reunion?" Julian said, a twisted smile spreading. "Well… I'm sorry, friend. But I think she's forgetting something. Something she can't run from."

Jonny's jaw clenched. "Oh, I know. I know everything. Every tiny little detail. I know what you did. I know everything you've done, Julian Bertotti, and it ends here."

Julian's smirk faltered slightly. "There's nothing you can do to stop me. Now Ally, it's time to go."

He stepped closer. Jonny didn't budge, a shield between them.

"Not another step!" Bronko barked.

Julian's eyes blackened with fury; gun levelled at Jonny's chest. "GET OUT OF THE WAY!" He shouted.

"You're gonna have to shoot me," Jonny said, steady, immovable.

Jess's heart hammered in her chest. She couldn't risk it. She leapt between them. "Enough, please. Julian, just let me go… I can't do this anymore."

"GET IN THE CAR!" Julian roared, veins standing out on his tattooed neck. She shook her head, nearly pleading, refusing to comply.

“I did everything for you, you selfish bitch! I KILLED A MAN FOR YOU! BURRIED HIS BODY IN THE GROUND SO YOUR SECRET KEPT HIDDEN!” He roared in anger, hoping to scare Jonny more.

The confession tore through the night like a jagged blade, sharp enough to split the air in two. For a moment, everything went silent—so still it felt unnatural. Then the darkness on the opposite side of the road erupted in pulses of blue light. Dave’s police truck, hidden just off the shoulder among the trees, flickered into view as the lights ignited, washing the entire road in a cold electric glare. Julian and his men froze as the lights cut across them. Dave and two officers stepped out with practiced precision, doors swinging open in near-perfect unison, their weapons already raised and trained on Julian. The atmosphere tightened instantly, the night holding its breath as the trap snapped shut around him.

Dave stepped forward, weapon raised, his voice steady but burning with authority. “Drop your weapon, Julian. And thanks for the confession… you’re under arrest.”

Julian’s face changed instantly — the confidence, the swagger, the sneer he always wore — gone. In its place was the hollow, stunned look of a man realising too late that he had been outplayed. He stood there in the middle of that quiet road, breathing hard. His world wasn’t just crumbling; it was folding in on him, crushing him from all sides.

“And what about her!?” Julian snapped, fury breaking through the cracks of his panic. He jerked his head toward Jess, eyes narrowing. “She killed someone too!”

“I said drop your weapons!” Dave shouted again, louder this time — not just a command, but a warning, a promise.

Jess felt Julian’s fury pulsing at her side, a heat that made her skin crawl. He turned and looked at her — not like a man seeing another human being, but like someone staring at the person he blamed for the hole he'd dug himself into. There was rage, betrayal, even a twisted kind of desperation.

"It's over," Jess whispered, breath trembling. "Just give up."

Julian's chest rose and fell faster. The noise around him muted, the night closing in like a tunnel, the sound of his own breathing pounding in his ears. For a split second, there was something almost human in his face — a man weighing his options, realising how close he was to losing everything. He *could* have ended it there. He could have surrendered. But then the anger surged back, vicious and blinding. "I'll never give up."

Julian raised his arm and pulled the trigger. The gun fired, the shot ripping through the night. It hit Dave, and he went down with a grunt, collapsing to the ground as blood began to soak through his clothes. The chaos exploded around them instantly.

"NO!" Jonny shouted, voice raw.

"SHIT!" Bronko exploded as the entire world detonated around them.

Gunfire burst wildly through the air — muzzle flashes strobing the trees, the smell of burnt gunpowder thickening instantly. Bronko dove behind the thick oak, firing blind bursts whenever he dared lean out. Jonny ducked low as bullets sliced past, splintering bark and whistling through the cold air.

He didn't see Julian move — not until Jess's startled gasp cut through the chaos. Julian lunged at her, fist tightening around her arm, yanking her backward. Jess didn't even have time to reach for Jonny before Julian shoved her through the open door of the saloon.

"Jess! Jess!" Jonny yelled, helpless as she disappeared inside.

Bronko got a clean shot and hit one of Julian's men in the leg. The man screamed and hit the ground. At the same moment, the saloon's tyres screeched, the engine revving high, ripping the car into motion as Julian sped away with Jess trapped inside.

The two remaining men froze — sandwiched between Bronko's fire and the officers closing in. Weapons dropped. Knees hit the road.

Jonny sprinted to Dave. Bronko was right behind him. Dave's shoulder was pouring blood, soaking through his shirt in thick, dark waves.

"Dave!" Jonny shouted, dropping to his knees.

Bronko grimaced. "Damn, Davey boy took a hit!"

"It went in and out," Dave groaned, voice tight with pain. "I can feel an exit wound."

Jonny tore off his jacket, hands shaking with adrenaline, pressing it hard against the wound. He glanced up — the road stretched empty into the blackness, taunting him. Jess was out there. Julian had her. Every second he wasted felt like losing her all over again.

"Jonny!" Bronko yelled. "Go after her!"

"Call an ambulance and keep pressure on it!" Jonny snapped, already pushing himself back to his feet.

He sprinted to his bike. Behind him, the last two men were being shoved to the ground, cuffed, wrists twisted behind their backs. Jonny didn't look at them. Didn't look at anything except the open road. He kicked up the stand so hard it clattered. His hand tightened around the throttle, knuckles white. For a heartbeat the back wheel spun uselessly, burning rubber against the asphalt — then it caught, violently, and the bike launched forward. Jonny ripped into the night after them, heart hammering, fear clawing at his ribs, determination burning hotter than the engine beneath him.

Julian's foot pressed hard against the accelerator, the saloon shuddering and groaning as it tore down the narrow backroads. His gun never left Jess, trained on her the entire time, a constant, terrifying presence in her peripheral vision. He had no plan—only instinct, only the raw need to get away.

"Julian! Slow down!" Jess cried, her voice cracking, hands gripping the edge of the door. Every turn came too fast, the lines of the road blurring into streaks under the headlights. Her stomach lurched with each sharp bend, each sudden jolt, and she could feel the sheer panic radiating off him.

"This is a mess you've made!" Julian raged, his voice cutting and cold. His eyes darted ahead, calculating angles, curves, and escape routes, all while speed clawed at his control. In the distance, a small flicker of light glimmered—the steady beam of a bike's headlight, closing fast, tracking them like a predator.

Without warning, Julian jerked the wheel hard and swung onto a narrow, overgrown backroad. The tyres thrashed over loose gravel, sending the car skidding for a heartbeat. The hill rose steep and sudden ahead of them, a jagged spine of earth forcing the saloon to climb aggressively. On their side, the cliff fell away like the world had been ripped open. Jess's stomach dropped at the sight, heart hammering. One wrong move, one slip of the wheel, and they would plummet hundreds of feet.

Julian slammed the accelerator, the engine roaring as they clawed up the incline. The cliff edge loomed ever closer, a constant, looming threat. Jess pressed herself as far into the seat as she could, praying that the car wouldn't fishtail or that Julian wouldn't lose control. The wind whipped through the open window, carrying with it the smell of earth and fear. Every second stretched impossibly long as the saloon danced along the jagged edge, a heartbeat away from disaster.

"Where are you going to run to?" Jess shouted, her voice trembling but defiant over the roar of the engine.

"Anywhere we end up!" Julian snapped, eyes wild, animalistic.

"You shot a deputy, Julian! There's no running from this!" she yelled, panic and anger lacing every word.

"If I'm going down, I'm dragging you with me! We're in this together, until the end!" he growled, voice low and dangerous.

Jess took a deep, shuddering breath, the fear clawing at her chest but her resolve harder than it had ever been. "I'm not doing this anymore, Julian! I've run my whole life, and now it's time to face it all. Even if I have to spend the rest of my life behind bars, I'm not running from this anymore! So do your worst!"

The words slammed into him, leaving a sudden, burning emptiness behind his eyes. Anger flared in his veins, uncontrollable and raw. She had him cornered at all angles, fearless and unyielding. She was ready to face whatever came, ready to take responsibility, ready to confront the consequences she had always ran from. And that realisation, that she had nothing left to lose, tore his control from him. If he couldn't have her… then no one would.

His hand went up, gun aimed at her head. Jess's eyes widened, heart hammering, but she didn't flinch. In a split second, she lunged, slamming her hands onto the wheel with every ounce of strength she had. The saloon jerked violently to the left.

Julian's control failed completely. The tyres tore through the loose dirt, kicking up rocks and dust in clouds as the car fishtailed violently down the narrow backroad. The cliff edge loomed next to them, jagged and merciless. The saloon slammed into the barrier, which cracked and gave way under the impact, and the car tumbled over the edge. Julian squeezed the trigger as the car hurtled over the cliff. The shot rang out, the passenger-side window shattering in a spray of glass. Trees and bushes tore past the windows in a blur, branches clawing at the bodywork as the vehicle plunged down the jagged slope. The world spun in a chaotic symphony of sound—metal crunching, glass shattering, wood snapping—until the saloon finally came to a stop, half-buried in undergrowth, branches and leaves covering it like a tomb.

Jonny sped down the empty road, the bike shaking beneath him as he fought to keep control, tyres skimming the surface. The night stretched out before him, dark and endless, with no other cars in sight, no clue where they had gone—only the void ahead and the echo of his own desperation. Then, with a curse tearing from his throat, he slammed the brakes and skidded to a stop in the middle of the road, chest heaving, hands trembling. She had slipped through his fingers, taken by that horrible man, and there was nothing he could do to reach her. Anguish tore through him, raw and suffocating. He threw his head back and screamed into the night, his voice ragged and hoarse: "JESS! JESS!" The sound ricocheted across the empty stretches of road, swallowed by the shadows. He collapsed to the ground, the weight of failure pressing down, his plan undone, his friend shot, and she nowhere to be found.

Jonny sat for a moment, gripping the handlebars, chest heaving as the adrenaline slowly ebbed into a tight, gnawing panic. The night was still around him, quiet except for the faint rustle of trees and the wind across the road. He took a deep, shuddering breath, forcing his thoughts to clear. Then, with grim determination, he swung his bike around and began retracing his path, scanning for any side roads, hidden turns, or tracks he might have missed—any clue that could lead him back to her. Every shadow, every flicker of movement made his heart jump, and every second wasted felt like another chance slipping through his fingers.

Jess lay with her head turned the other way, pressed against the bloodstained airbag, utterly still. Her hair clung to her face in dark, sticky strands, and her body slumped unnaturally, motionless. Appearing as though, heartbreakingly the bullet had struck true, leaving her silent, lifeless, with no breath. The twisted metal around her groaned softly, and the night outside the shattered windows pressed in around the car. Every second stretched unbearably, leaving her still never to move again.

Then, faintly, a shudder ran through her body. Her eyelids fluttered, and she stirred, a raw, painful groan slipping from her throat. The bullet had missed, but her face was a map of the crash: scratches cut across her cheeks, and a deep gash ran from the top of her head, blood soaking into her hair. Every nerve screamed, every muscle ached, and whiplash twisted her neck painfully, but she was coming to.

A weak, rasping voice broke the silence. "Ally…"

Her eyes shot sideways. Horror froze her in place. Julian was pinned in his seat, a branch driven through the windscreen and impaling him through the stomach, holding him against the leather. Blood poured from his mouth, his face pale and twisted with pain. Her jaw dropped, chin trembling as a cry ripped from her throat. "Oh God!"

He rasped, struggling to speak through the blood. "Call… call an ambulance…"

Instinct propelled her forward. She fumbled for her phone, cracked but still functional, fingers slick with blood and shaking. She took a deep, shuddering breath, forcing herself to focus. Then her gaze hardened, ice settling behind her eyes. Helping him would only keep her tied to him — stuck, controlled, dragged down with him all over again. She wasn't going back to that.

Her face hardened, cold and unyielding. Helping him now would only keep her trapped with him, bound to his chaos, his control, his rage. She wouldn't give him that power. Not this time.

"What are you doing? I'm dying here," he rasped, words spilling out instinctively, a plea he expected her to answer.

She didn't move. Not a flicker. Not a blink.

And then it hit him. The flicker in her eyes, the absolute stillness of her face. She wasn't shocked. She wasn't scared. She had made a choice. A slow, horrifying understanding crawled through him: she wanted him to die.

"Then hurry up," she said, sharp and precise, settling back against the torn seat as if she were already waiting for it to happen. Her eyes never left his. He stared, paralysed, and the realisation hollowed him out. She wasn't his to drag down anymore. She wasn't his at all.

Julian's breaths came shallow and uneven, each one a desperate struggle against the pain consuming him. Blood coated his hands and lips, warm and sticky, pooling around the branch that pinned him in place. His eyes, once full of fury and control, now glazed over, flicking toward her one last time. In those final moments, clarity pierced through the haze of agony: he could no longer control her. That truth burned hotter than the torment tearing through his body, and for the first time, fear and helplessness replaced the arrogance that had ruled him. His chest heaved once more, a wet, gasping sound that echoed against the wreckage, and then his head fell forward, resting limply against his chest. Jess's eyes never wavered, cold and unflinching at first — and then a wave of relief washed over her, sharp and undeniable, as the last flicker of life left him. Nothing—not rage, not violence—could bend her anymore.

Jonny tore down the backroad, tyres kicking up dust and gravel, the night air whipping against his face. Then, in the darkness ahead, he saw it — a break in the barrier, a sudden drop that made his stomach lurch. Panic surged through him, sharp and blinding. He skidded to a stop, threw the bike aside, and ran toward the edge, heart hammering so violently he thought it might burst from his chest. From the top of the cliff, he could see the black saloon below, tangled in the trees and brush, smoke and dust rising from the wreckage. His breath caught in his throat, and for a moment he froze, stomach twisting, unable to move. The world had narrowed to that single horrifying image.

"Oh god, no! JESS!" Jonny shouted into the night, his breath steaming in the cold air. Relief surged through her the moment she heard him.

"JONNY! JONNY, HELP!" she cried, voice raw and trembling, carrying through the darkness.

He heard her too, just barely, and panic surged through him. Heart hammering, he lunged toward the edge and began scrambling down the steep, loose dirt and rock, digging his hands into roots and jagged stones to steady himself. His boots slipped, sending sprays of soil tumbling over the cliff's edge, but he forced himself to move. Every scrape, every small cut from thorny branches, only drove him faster.

Finally, he reached the car, and horror hit him full force, stealing his breath. Julian lay pinned and lifeless against the seat, bloodied and impaled by the branch that had trapped him. Jonny froze, stomach twisting, breath catching in his throat, disbelief crashing over him. And then his eyes found her. Jess. Bloodied and battered, but alive. Relief surged through him, sharp and overwhelming, and it pushed him forward. Ignoring the terror coursing through his veins, he scrambled closer, desperate to reach her amidst the wreckage.

Jonny shifted carefully over the twisted wreckage, every movement measured to avoid loose metal and broken glass. The stench of smoke and blood filled his nostrils, and his hands were cut and scraped from gripping jagged edges, but he didn't stop. He reached her side, eyes scanning her battered form — bruised, bleeding, but alive. "I'm here, baby," he breathed, voice hoarse, and reached for the door, yanking it open against the stubborn push of the surrounding bushes. They clawed at it, snagging on the metal and slowing him, but he gritted his teeth and forced it wide enough to slip her arm through. She leaned into him, trembling from shock and pain, and together they inched her out of the seat. Finally, with a grunt and steadying her against his chest, he guided her free from the wreck, holding her close as the cold night pressed around them. She leaned against him, fragile and trembling. He didn't let go, holding her close, every instinct screaming to get them both to safety before anything else could happen. He had her, and this time he wasn't letting go.

A few hours later, they were in the hospital. Jess had been checked over thoroughly, and luck had been on her side — concussion and whiplash were the worst of her injuries. The cut on her head had been cleaned and carefully bandaged. The doctors kept her under observation for a while, monitoring her vitals. Once they gave her the all-clear, she made her way to the waiting room, and the moment she saw Jonny, a wave of relief washed over her. She was just glad he was here. He looked as worn as she felt, but the instant their eyes met, he swept her into a tight embrace, holding her like he would never let go. His lips pressed to her forehead, and she could feel the steady thrum of his heartbeat against her cheek.

Hand in hand, they walked down the sterile corridor toward another room. The door swung open, and Jess saw Dave sitting up in bed, his shoulder bandaged from the gunshot, the bullet having passed clean through. Miranda sat close on one side, offering quiet support, her hand resting lightly on his arm. The steady beeping of the machines, the scent of antiseptic, and the faint whir of ventilators filled the room, but it was almost comforting, a sign that the worst of the chaos was behind them. Jonny guided Jess closer, and for a moment they all simply breathed together, the tension of the night giving way to relief and the fragile sense of safety, a momentary pause in the storm that had consumed them.

Dave leaned back in his hospital bed, a faint grin breaking across his face. "There you two are. How are you feeling, Jess?"

Jess gave a weak smile, rubbing her temples. "I don't think there's a part of me that doesn't hurt."

Dave chuckled, nodding toward his bandaged shoulder. "Try having two holes in your shoulder," he said lightly, the humour a mask over the night's chaos.

Jonny grinned, teasing, "You're gonna be leaking like a sprinkler." Jess let out a small laugh. Her head rolling forward, just like it used to "I hope we can put this all behind us," Jonny added quietly, his voice steady but tinged with relief.

Dave's smile faded into seriousness. He glanced at his wife. "Honey, will you give us a minute?"

Miranda nodded, giving Jonny and Jess a warm, encouraging smile before stepping out, closing the door behind her. Silence settled over the room for a heartbeat before Dave spoke again.

"It's been quite the night," he said, his tone low.

Jonny's jaw tightened. "Dave… what you know, what she did—"

Jess raised a hand, cutting him off. "Don't, Jonny. Dave's already done too much for us. I'm ready to face whatever's ahead. I need to face justice for what I've done… I need to pay the price."

Dave shook his head slowly. "You've been paying for too long." His voice carried no judgment, only understanding. He knew the life Jess had lived, the torment she'd endured. Now, finally, she had a chance at freedom. He didn't want to stand in the way of that.

"Your secrets are safe with me," he said firmly. "Go. Be free."

Jonny opened his mouth, but Dave waved him off. "I mean it. Just make sure I get an invite to the wedding, okay?"

Jess couldn't help the small laugh that bubbled up, even in her pain. Jonny wrapped his arm around her, holding her close.

"I love you, brother!" he said, his voice full of gratitude and relief.

Dave smiled, seeing them finally together, the weight of the past lifted. It felt right. It was how it should be — soulmates, at last, allowed to be happy. After everything, after the chaos and the fear, seeing them safe, together, and whole filled him with a quiet, steady relief. For the first time in a long time, he could believe that the worst was behind them, and that somehow, finally, they had a chance to just be themselves.

A few days of rest had done its work. Dave had been discharged and returned home, his shoulder still sore but steadily healing, while Jess and Jonny had taken the time to recover from the bruises, aches, and relentless tension that had gripped them all. Now, the four of them — Jonny, Jess, Dave, and Miranda — stood outside Dave's house, gathered around Jonny's bike as he fastened the duffel bag to the back, making sure everything was secure for the journey ahead. The morning air was crisp, carrying the faint scent of pine and freshly cut grass, and for the first time in days, the quiet felt safe. The final day of 2009.

Miranda's hand rested lightly on Dave's arm, while he gave Jess and Jonny a nod that spoke volumes — pride, relief, and the unspoken permission to finally move forward. Jess leaned against Jonny, her energy renewed, her spirit lighter than it had been in years. Jonny squeezed her hand gently, and in that moment, neither of them doubted that this was the start of something new, something they could finally face together.

Bronko's cheerful voice cut through the calm, full of life and energy. Almost as if he was his old self again from thirty years ago. "Look at this! The old band back together again — the Cedar Bluff '79 gang."

Jonny grinned, the tension of the past days easing from his shoulders. "Hey, Bronko."

"Think you could leave without saying goodbye, huh?" Bronko said, stepping forward and wrapping Jonny in a firm, brotherly hug. "Be safe, brother. No more of this action-hero shit, you hear me?" Bronko joked.

Jonny laughed, shaking his head. "I've had my fair share of thrills, man. I'm not chasing anymore."

"That's what I'm talking about!" Bronko chuckled, turning to Jess. He pulled her into a brief hug, his grip warm and steady. "Take care of my brother, won't you?"

"I will," Jess said, her voice soft but sure. "You keep in touch, Bronko."

"You ain't getting rid of me that easy," he said. He placed his hands gently on Jess's shoulders and gave her a smile that spoke volumes — a smile that carried every danger, every fear, every secret they had survived, and the triumph of having come through it all. No more shadows. No more lies.

Dave stepped forward. "Hey, how about we all don't fall out of contact this time, huh?"

Jonny nodded firmly. "Not a chance."

They had been through too much together to let distance unravel the bond they had all built. Every shared danger, every secret kept, every narrow escape had woven them closer than ever, unbreakable even by time or miles. For the first time, the future felt safe, wide open, and theirs to shape — a canvas untouched, waiting for them to paint it.

"Go and be happy. You both deserve nothing less," Bronko said.

This time, his words weren't laced with his usual jokey tone — they were raw, sincere, coming straight from the depths of his heart. Jonny and Jess exchanged a glance, then swung onto the bike. The engine roared to life, a deep vibration beneath them, as Bronko, Dave, and Miranda waved them off.

For the first time, Jonny and Jess rode together without fear, without plans or destinations, carrying only each other and the promise of a future they could finally shape. The wind whipped around them, crisp and freeing, and the bridge out of Cedar Bluff stretched ahead like an open path. A strange, almost overwhelming feeling washed over him. He had crossed this bridge as he left Cedar Bluff countless times before, each time leaving with the same ache —

disappointment, heartbreak, the bitter taste of failure gnawing at his chest. But today was different. Today, the bridge stretched ahead like an invitation, not a reminder of sorrow. For the first time, he didn't feel the weight of loss. Instead, his heart swelled with hope, with love, with a sense of unshakable freedom he had never known leaving this town.

Jess pressed close behind him, gripping him with a quiet certainty, and Jonny could feel the warmth of her hold along his spine, steady and alive. For both of them, the road ahead was theirs to claim. Every mile carried them further from the shadows of the past, a step into a life they could finally build together. As they rode, Jess let her lighter slip from her fingers, tumbling onto the road behind them, a small, deliberate gesture that marked her freedom, and the feeling of being safe. At last, she was truly free — free from running, free from fear, free from the weight of a life spent looking over her shoulder. The road had been long and gruelling, the past unrelenting, but every hard mile, every danger faced, had led her here. And now, with the wind in her hair and Jonny guiding them forward, every step, every moment had been worth it.

The town shrank behind them as they sped forward, leaving old ghosts and broken memories in the dust. The wind rushed past, sharp and exhilarating, carrying with it the sense of everything they had left behind. For the first time in forever, leaving Cedar Bluff didn't sting with disappointment or heartbreak. For the first time, it felt like stepping into the life they had always dreamed of. With Jess holding on behind him, steady and real, Jonny knew — finally, truly — that they were free.

Together.

Printed in Dunstable, United Kingdom

78011629R00238